ABOUT THE AUTHOR

JANICE KULYK KEEFER is a bestselling Canadian author widely admired for her novels, short story collections, poetry, and nonfiction. She has been twice nominated for the Governor General's Award and is a recipient of the Marian Engel Award, the Canadian Authors Association Award for Poetry, two first prizes from the CBC Radio Literary Competition, and several National Magazine Awards. *The Ladies' Lending Library* is her fifth novel to date and the first to be published in the United States in more than fifteen years. She lives in Toronto.

THE LADIES' LENDING LIBRARY

A NOVEL

JANICE KULYK KEEFER

HARPER

NEW YORK · LONDON · TORONTO · SYDNEY

HARPER

First published in 2007 by HarperCollins Publishers Canada.

THE LADIES' LENDING LIBRARY. Copyright © 2007 by Janice Kulyk Keefer. All rights reserved. Printed in the United States of America. No part of this book may be used or reproduced in any manner whatsoever without written permission except in the case of brief quotations embodied in critical articles and reviews. For information address HarperCollins Publishers, 10 East 53rd Street, New York, NY 10022.

HarperCollins books may be purchased for educational, business, or sales promotional use. For information please write: Special Markets Department, HarperCollins Publishers, 10 East 53rd Street, New York, NY 10022.

FIRST U.S. EDITION

Designed by Joy O'Meara

Library of Congress Cataloging-in-Publication Data is available upon request.

ISBN 978-0-06-147907-6

09 10 11 12 13 OV/RRD 10 9 8 7 6 5 4 3 2 1

For Vera and Gus

THE LADIES' LENDING LIBRARY is not an institution; though communal, it certainly isn't public. It's just a group of women up at the cottage for the summer, alone with their children all week and needing something to amuse them, to get them through each long and repetitious day, and to look forward to at night, in the privacy of their rooms with their half-empty beds. Something to remind them that a few things in the world are designed for people over the age of twelve—something to give them a way of feeling sophisticated and daring: women of a wider world. And so, seven of the women spending the summer at Kalyna Beach decide to pass around the books they've chanced upon in drugstores in the little towns on the way up to the cottage, or that they've smuggled in from home. Not just *The Carpetbaggers* and *The World of Suzie Wong*, but books that Nadia Senchenko come across doing courses at the university: *Lady Chatterley's Lover* and *Portrait of the Artist as a Young Man*. But never mind the titles: the whole point is that it doesn't matter, the books aren't supposed to be that kind of "educational." That's why Sasha calls it the Ladies' Lending Library; that's why they meet for gin and gossip at Sasha's cottage every Friday afternoon, as their husbands are starting the long drive up from the city.

There are women who would never allow themselves to be part of the Lending Library, women whose blazing virtues are a scourge to the kind of fiction making the rounds of the cottages, slipped from hand to hand, wrapped up in a beach towel or a petaled bathing cap. Women like Lesia Baziuk and Nettie Shkurka, for example. They don't belong to anything; even their cottages are on the extreme edges of Kalyna Beach, one on the west side, one on the east. Lesia, for all her peddling of cosmetics, would go to the stake rather than read a dirty book; and as for Nettie, Sasha jokes that Nettie has vinegar in her veins and stuffs her bra with leftover Communion bread.

The Ladies' Lending Library is not wholly an affair of gin and gossip, though the group refrains from any discussion of the literary merits of the books they read. The women talk about certain characters as though they were their dearest, oldest friends or else their fiercest enemies; often they whisper questions to one another, lying on their blankets down at the beach while their children jump across the sand. *Valley of the Dolls* is a big hit, as is *Fanny Hill, Memoirs of a Woman of Pleasure*. Sonia makes them laugh with this one—at first she'd refused to read it, confusing it with the *Fannie Farmer Cookbook*. It's Sonia, too, who is most apprehensive about being a receiver of doubtful goods: she insists that they remove the shiny jackets from the hardbacks and make covers out of brown-paper grocery bags for the paperbacks. Though, except for Nadia, all the women hide the books at the bottom of laundry hampers or in the farthest reaches of their night-table drawers. They read them late at night, when the kids are not just in bed but asleep, and their husbands are back in the city. Not that Ivan would care if he caught his wife reading *Fanny Hill*—he'd be sitting beside her, turning the pages, Sasha jokes. But she likes the forbidden, hide-and-go-seek side of the Lending Library, which is far more exciting, at times, than the hot parts stashed between a book's covers. When she is recovering from sunburn one day, Sasha sends her kids over to Sonia's and stays in bed reading most of *Tropic of Cancer*, from which she derives sadly unfulfilled expectations regarding subway travel.

About sex, the Ladies already know everything. Almost all of them married young; they had their children right away—there's never been any time to wonder if things could have worked out differently. Sex and haste and exhaustion, sex and the fear of kids barging into the bedroom at any and all hours of the night. Never, ever, sex in the morning, sex in the afternoon. A kiss in the kitchen while you're mashing the potatoes for supper is the warning signal for what will happen later, after you've done the dishes and tucked the kids in for the night, and he's watched the hockey game or the news: not his hands, first, but the whole weight of his body sliding like a great warm seal on top of you. It takes forever, like being in a lineup at the checkout counter at the supermarket, but finally you feel the one sensation you are guaranteed: your husband's body crumpling in your arms, for all the world like a baby that's drunk its fill at your breast. Then he pulls away into a dead sleep, sometimes making room for you to lie close against his chest, sometimes turning his back to you, drum-rolling into a snore.

Oh, the women have read it all, at the doctor's or dentist's office, in articles in *Reader's Digest* and *Chatelaine*. How to save or add zip to their marriages—but who would go out and buy the expensive perfume, the sheer nighties (all needing to be hand-washed) like the ones they sometimes, somehow, see in cartoons from *Esquire*, not to mention the French wine and slow-burning candles the articles call for? It's all too much like work, another version of the sessions at the washing machine or kitchen sink, and besides, the magazines never tell you what to do with the children, who are likely coming down with chicken pox or getting their fingers stuck in doors, or waking with nightmares just as you're struggling out of your girdle into the negligee you'd have had to ask him to pay for, anyway, and of course he would have groused at the expense. And the awful, remarkable thing is this: the women aren't really resentful, most of them; they know they'd have much more trouble surviving if they had to make room, find the time—that's always it, the time—for any slower kind of sex than what they're used to.

Sometimes, serendipitously, they have known moments of feeling so intense that *pleasure* seems too mild a word for it.

In the pitch-black of the bedroom they bite their lips and close their eyes: if this is orgasm, they are wary of it. It happens far too rarely to be something they can count on, yet even if their husbands had the gift of pleasing them with the reliability you'd expect when switching on the burners of your kitchen stove, they would remain uneasy. The idea of physical passion—of becoming a prisoner, not to a lover so much as to your own body, its needs, its urgings—they are afraid of this. Though they're curious, of course, as to what happens to those who give way, as the saying goes, to passion. Bored, safely buttressed as they are, they are dying to know what happens, how, and why. Which may explain why, this summer of the Lending Library, the subject they discuss most often and with the most intensity isn't a book at all but the new film of *Cleopatra*: the film and its aftermath, the outrageous, irresistible love affair between Elizabeth Taylor and Richard Burton. A passion they read like the most forbidden, most enticing, and thus the dirtiest book of all.

Dirty books—this is, after all, the best, the only description that will do. Dirt is what they desire and dread in these books— no pleasure without shame, like a smudge, a soiled collar that must be scrubbed clean. For they are, above all else, respectable women: some of them may have had their lapses before marrying, but what you do in the cramped, guilty dark, you hide, and as long as nobody ever finds out, you can hold your head high. God forbid that you've been open, ignorant, unashamed: the way Olya had been, parading her belly for the whole world to see;

marrying when Darka was five months short of being born. The way Darka gives every sign of being and doing, parading around in her two-piece, like some teenage, tin-pot temptress of the Nile.

No one intends any harm to come of the Ladies' Lending Library—no one believes any book, never mind a Hollywood movie, could do any kind of damage to the families gathered at Kalyna Beach. You could argue that what happens this summer has nothing at all to do with Sasha's brainchild, except that the Library has added something to the atmosphere, a sense of possibility that breaks out like some contagious disease, something secret, underground, as distinct from what the women think of when they hear the word *dirty*. They are all pretty incorruptible, even after reading *Fanny Hill*; that is, they remain afraid. That's why what happens this summer appears to them a calamity, the social equivalent, Sasha thinks, of an earthquake or a hurricane. How it came to happen they can guess at from their reading— the step-by-step science of the thing. But that it should have happened in the first place, that it should have been allowed to happen by Whoever Is Supposed to Watch Over Us—this is the mystery, and it is terrible.

Because it will end up changing everything: they will lose their innocence by gaining imagination, understanding that it can happen to any of them. That you don't have to be Elizabeth Taylor to give way, to give yourself away. That it can happen in Hamilton as well as Hollywood. That you can make it happen.

PART ONE

LADYBUG

Olya moya,

*How I hate this place! I can't stand the sound of the waves
crashing, and the hevyness when the water is still. Water
and sky and sand—there's nothing else up here, nothing
to keep me from thinking. I wish, how I wish we were
girls again—things were hard then, but we could hope for
anything. But we went and got married, and now there's
nothing but the ever-after. Children keep coming, days
keep passing, but I'm not alive any more—my life has
stopped. Oh, why did we come here at all, Olya, was it
only for this? If I could wish myself back to the Old Place,
the way it used to be, I'd go in a minute. I swear it. I'd
leave it all behind, husband and house and even, God
help me, the children. Sometimes I catch myself looking
at them at the brekfast table, seeing them at the bottom
of the lake. All four of them in a row, holding hands and
sitting still, so still, the waves lifting their hair, ruffling the
frills of their bading suits . . .*

Sonia Martyn is staring at the empty place on the mantel, where a small plaster statue used to stand. She looks down at what she's just written; crumples it in her fist, but this isn't good enough. She takes the ball of paper to the fieldstone fireplace. In her thin pajamas measled with roses, she hunkers down and lights a match. The letter flares up, quick and bright as tears, then falls into ash. She stabs it with the poker till it breaks into small, bitter flakes. In the thriller Sasha's loaned her, a detective is able to piece together a letter that the murderer burned in a grate, picking up the charred pieces with tweezers. Sonia isn't taking any chances.

Dear Olya,

I hope things are going well for you and Walter in the city. Everything's fine here, no need to worry about anything. Darka's a big help with the children and she makes herself useful with cooking and cleening, too. You'll be happy to know she's settled down. Of course it's so quiet here—not much going on for a girl of her age, thank heven. Only two more weeks and the summer will be over, and we'll bring her back to you, safe and sound.

It's not yet six; she should go back to bed. Outside, the air is misty, as if someone's poured cream into the sky, though the sun's already scraping at the edges. Another fine, bright, endless day. Sonia opens the kitchen door, examining the shadfly skeletons still hooked into the screen, bleached ghosts of the insects that shed them. How, she wonders, do they crawl out so cleanly, leaving behind this perfect trace of their bodies, even the legs, thinner than eyelashes? Do they miss their old selves, do they ever mistake their cast-off bodies for some long-lost friend or forgotten twin? She doesn't dare step out onto the porch: she's afraid the hinge will squeak as it always does and waken Darka. A bad idea, giving her that poky room across from the kitchen. They would have put her in the sleep-house across the lawn, except that Sonia had promised Olya to keep both eyes on her daughter.

Olya, her best friend before their marriages: they hardly saw one another now, living as they did at opposite ends of the city, and in such different circumstances. For Olya had married Walter, a cutter at Canada Packers—had had to get married, while Sonia had bided her time until what they used to call "the right man" came along, a man with a profession, a future ahead of him. That future had turned out to contain, on his side, endless work at the office, and on hers, four children to raise. Walter Marchuk may have been as busy at the plant as Max Martyn was at his law office, but while Sonia was struggling with diapers and baby carriages and booster shots for her brood, Olya, who'd had only the one child, spent her time cleaning the houses of women who lived in suburbs similar to Sonia's, but who had names like Brenda and Patty and Joan. For Max and Sonia had moved from downtown to a big house in a development that had been farmland ten years ago. Whereupon Olya had found excuses to decline Sonia's invitations to visit and had stopped inviting the Martyns over for sloppy joes or lazy *holubtsi* at the duplex on Bathurst. It was Olya's pride, Sonia's mother had said; there was no forcing a friendship past the point of such pride. So now the Martyns and the Marchuks saw each other once a year, at the Martyns' shabby cottage at Kalyna Beach, where Olya and Sonia would cook together and reminisce about their immigrant girlhoods, pretending things were just as they'd been before husbands had barged into view, before addresses and oc-cupations had started to matter.

Sonia had promised to take Darka for the summer, see her through a difficult patch (she was driving Olya crazy) allow her to earn some pocket money, teach her some housekeeping skills—and keep her out of harm's way. This last part of the promise had been broken their very first night at the cottage. How could Sonia have known what Darka would get up to, dis-appearing into the bathroom once everyone else was in bed, experimenting with a jar of peroxide bleach she'd smuggled up in her suitcase? Max had grumbled about having to secure a box of Miss Clairol (Basic Brown) from the city so that Darka's hair could be dyed back at summer's end. Olya and Walter need never find out—but this turns Sonia into a traitor as well as a liar, as far as she can see. For this is the first summer that the Martyns have failed to invite the Marchuks up for a weekend. Darka has made it a condition of her staying on in this hole-in-the-wall at the edge of nowhere. She's promised not to hitch a ride into Midland and, from there, back to the city, on two conditions: that Sonia let her live this summer as a blonde and that Olya and Walter be kept in the dark.

Sonia puts her hands to her face, rubbing her eyes with her fingertips. Another half-hour's sleep might make all the difference between a good and a bad day, between drifting or dragging herself through the duties required of her, but it's so peaceful when she's the only one awake, the children cocooned, still, in their dreams. With the irresponsibility of a ghost she glides from room to room, watching her daughters sleep: Laura and Bonnie in the shady, sunken bedroom off the screened-in porch; Katia and Baby Alix in the sunny room across from her own. Opening the doors so softly, imagining herself all tenderness, beautifully good, like the Blue Fairy in the movie of *Pinocchio*. They are all of them so beautiful, so good when they are lying sleeping, whatever wounds they've got or given healing gently, as if without scars. She loves them so, she could be such a wonderful mother if only her children were always still like this, and lying sleeping.

On her night table, like a corpse waiting to be discovered, lies the paperback she should have finished by now: *Death by Desire*. Halia had passed it on to her, saying she'd stayed up till three one night to finish it. Sonia has been trying for a week, now, to get through it. Three people have been murdered so far, but she couldn't care less: she doesn't like any of them, she doesn't believe in them. They're all parties and yachts and sex,

sex, sex—nobody phones their mother or has a kid up all night with the croup . . . That's the point, Sasha would say—it's supposed to be an escape. But what good's an escape made of paper and ink, Sonia sighs. Instead of racing through the book to see what was going to happen next, she kept putting it aside; kept walking back into the warm rooms of her familiar worries.

Sonia shoves *Death by Desire* into the drawer, to the very back, where no one will find it unless he's looking for it. Now the night table's all innocence, showing the nicks in the dull-white paint, paint thick like her own skin, skin of a thirty-nine-year-old woman who's had too many children too quickly. Bare, dull-white paint with something marring the finish—a bead broken off a dress: if she were in the city right now, she'd say a small jet bead. Though it's not black at all, but dark red— she pushes at it with her finger, and legs spring out; it waddles off. *Sonechko.* The children have another name for it, an English name. They sing a nursery rhyme, too; she knows what the words are but not what they mean. She understands nothing of this childhood she's given them by this miracle she's never quite believed in—a new life in a new country. Their skipping games, the poems they learn at school, the cards they make for Christmas, birthdays—foreign territory in which she'll never be at home. The very idea of a card for a birthday, of wasting something as precious as paper!

Flat on her stomach, face pressed into the dough of the pillow, Sonia plays at suffocation. Tonight Max will arrive with his sister Marta and there'll be endless rearranging. She'll have to send Darka to the sleep-house for the week: Katia and Laura can't be trusted together, they are always at each other's throats. Why, oh why can't they get on? There's a hard little lump in Sonia's heart, like the pit of an apricot. If only she had had a sister, someone to talk with, confide in—how different her life might have been. All the things she could never tell, even to Olya; hurts and shocks from the village in the lost, the long-gone country. Or the most private things, secrets crawling up and down the inside of her skin. How tonight he'll walk in while she's sorting dirty laundry for the next day's wash, will plant a kiss on her neck, and she'll stiffen; before she says a word, he'll feel her body closing up against him, and it will start all over again. He'll tell her how exhausted he is, fighting traffic the whole way up, as if he were a frontline soldier. And she'll answer back, without meaning it to spurt out the way it always does: "Do you think it's any picnic for me up here, with four kids, and Darka too—I can't take my eyes off her for a second. And now you bring me your witch of a sister. What am I supposed to do with her? I'll go to the office and *you* stay here with her—*you* look after her and the kids all week, see how *you* like it."

And he will, yes, how could it ever be otherwise, he'll turn away from her in the hallway where she's getting out the sheets to make up Marta's bed. He'll kiss whichever of the children are still awake, take them out on the lawn to look at the stars, not even thinking to ask if she'll come out with them, because of course she can't, she has a million things to do before they can all go to sleep for the night. And the children will leap to him like fish, like sunfish to a scrap of bacon, even Laura who loves no one and wallows in her own misery; the children he almost never sees and who love him all the more because of it, more than they'll ever love her. And then, once she's got them all into bed—which they'll fight like little Tatars after the excitement of being out under the stars, laughing and shoving each other till Marta will call out, in her vulture's croak, "Can't you keep those children under control?"—then he'll come to bed at last, smelling of the city and the cigar he's smoked out on the porch. For the children and the stars are only an excuse to indulge himself. He knows how she hates the stink of cigars.

He'll undress in the dark, roll in like a driftwood log beside her, the sag in the mattress pushing their bodies together, no matter how hard she tries to keep to her side. Tonight he'll be too tired, highway-tired, much too tired. But tomorrow, after a day spent fixing the roof or tinkering with the septic system, or replacing the rotten wood on the porch steps; after getting too much sun and putting up with the kids quarreling over who is to hand him the nails, and who will hold the hammer when he doesn't need it—then he'll turn out the lights after they've undressed with their backs to one another; he'll turn to her and she'll lie there beneath him, good as gold. What else can she do, when you can hear through the skin-thin walls every sigh or cry anyone makes in their sleep?

Max wants a son. Ever since she was pregnant that first time with Laura, he's had the name picked out: his father's name, Roman. A boy called Roman had followed her home from school all one winter, a skinny, dwarfish boy she couldn't stand to have near her. Give him his son and he will never bother her again, that's what it means, his turning to her each Saturday night, his body so heavy it crushes the life from her. And yet no one is a better dancer—so light on his feet, whirling her across the floor as if she were swan's down chased by a summer breeze. She sees herself and her husband like those tiny dolls placed on the top tier of wedding cakes, gliding over the stiff white icing, while all around, people are watching, envying. *Law's such a respectable profession; he'll go far, all the way to QC.* Such a handsome man, so distinguished-looking in his tuxedo, the spotless white cummerbund, the deep red carnation in his lapel. He would always bring her a gardenia—roses were common, he used to say: she deserved something as rare as she was. A gardenia, a cummerbund—had she really married him for that? And has it really led her to this? A house in the suburbs, a tumbledown summer cottage, a body scarred with stretch marks, like silverfish crawling over her belly and across her thighs: an aging body stranded in the washed-out garden of her pajamas.

Never mind, she has one sure consolation: her dress for the Senchenkos' party. She has hidden it away, like the book in the night-table drawer. Sonia tiptoes to the closet, reaching into its soft depths, finding the dress—*the gown*—by the metallic feel of the fabric. She can hear her mother's tongue clucking at the clinging folds, the low-cut neck, but as she holds the dress up against her she is overcome by its sheer gorgeousness, the cloth dropping from her breasts like golden rain. Slippery and cool like rain, her skin drinking in the gold. If she were to step into the dress, study herself in the mirror, move in the clinging fabric as if she were on a runway and about to launch herself on a sea of unknown, admiring eyes . . . But she resists the lure: she makes herself shove the dress to the very back of the closet; she swears not to look at it again, to try it on, until the night of the Senchenkos' party, lest she damage its rareness with too much looking.

Sitting on the end of the bed, facing the stained satin headboard (too good to be thrown out, too soiled to use back home), Sonia counts the waves beating against the shore as if they were knocks at a door she'd double-bolted. She longs for the city—not the vast, empty-seeming suburb where she lives now, but downtown where she used to work: the streetcar sparks and honking of horns, the wholesale fabric sellers on Queen, the roar of sewing machines in the factories on Spadina. Her mother's house on Dovercourt Road: sitting out on the porch on summer nights, people walking by, calling hello, everyone breathing in the scent of melting chocolate from the Nielson factory nearby. And it doesn't matter how hot it gets on summer days, how steamy and drenching; in spite of the lake, in spite of Sunnyside pool, no one expects you to jump into the water.

Whereas here, if one of the children were drowning, she wouldn't be able to run in and rescue her. It's got so bad now that she can't go down to the water's edge without the hairs on her arms sticking into her like pins, her fear like a rag in her mouth. Even if all four of them were to plead with her from the bottom of the lake, their arms stretched out, their mouths wide open, she wouldn't be able to put a foot—not so much as a toe—into the lake to save them.

THE CHILDREN THINK it must be God's hand drawing ridges in the sand beneath the water every night. The God whose eye is painted on the dome of the cathedral back in the city: one huge, blue, unshuttable eye, trailing gold and locked in a triangle.

There is no church-going at Kalyna Beach: no onion-bulb cathedral, no bishop with a glass eye and thick black veil strung from a pillbox hat high on his terrible gray head. No cross to kiss, no thick, consecrated bread to force down to an empty stomach, no incense smoking from censers in front of the icon screen with its gold grape vines and glimmering lamps. Here there's just the bay, what they call "the lake," though it's a mere scallop on a gigantic body of water stretching farther north than any of them has ever dreamed of going. The lake and the cottages on the bluff above it, and the tree-tunneled roads behind them. And the beach, of course, a snaking shore of sand coasting up to dunes with spikes of grass like long, green needles stuck in a cushion.

Sometimes the lake's a pale blue, cloudy as shards of glass smoothed to pebbles by the waves. Sometimes the lake is orange, rose, peach, after one of the perfectly calm, bright days, when the children have camped out at the beach, except for the naps they're forced to take in the afternoon, lying in cedarscented rooms, watching leaf-shadows dart and flicker on the walls. After sunset, when darkness pools in the roofs of the cottages and the cars stranded beside them, the lake becomes the color of night itself, so that if you were to flout the rules and sneak down for a swim, the children think, you would emerge with skin blue-black, telltale as ink.

But their days are far too full of sun and sand and water for them to think of anything but sleep by the time dark falls. Under the covers of their narrow beds, the older ones may read with flashlights, but when they hear the grown-ups yawn and stumble off to sleep, the children finally give in. Letting their eyelids shut at last, they walk out the doors of their dreams to shores where it's impossible to tell where water ends and sky begins.

A GILDED BARGE with sails of purple silk and a hundred silvermounted oars beating through the oiled and snaky waters. Pyramids on either side of her; palm trees like huge green moths overhead. Charmian and Lotos kneeling with jeweled beakers of strawberry juice. Languid under a canopy of cloth of gold, her raven tresses fingered by the breeze raised by her slaves' ostrich-feather fans, her bosom rising like dough in a mixing bowl, she waits for Marc Antony. Together they will rule the world and found a dynasty of mighty kings and queens.

Sails billowing, oars beating through the waves—but the harder they beat, the clearer it becomes that the barge, far from moving, is stuck in water thick and stiff as week-old Jell-O. She is about to call to her oarsmen to go faster, faster, when the chief slave, who has the face of her younger sister Katia, turns to her with her hands on her hips, saying, "*You*—Cleopatra? Who do you think you're kidding? You've got no breasts, your hair's the color of dirty dishwater, and you wear glasses. Big, ugly, blind-girl glasses!" And then the voice alters: "What on earth do you think you're doing, spilling strawberry juice all over the clothes I've just washed!" For Katia's taunts have turned into their mother's exasperated scolding; the billowing cloth of gold is a ripped flap of screen, and waves, not oars, pound at her ears.

It's still dark when Laura wakes, though she can make out a streak of light at the window, feel it like a tongue against her open eyes, as if she's got specks in them that have to be licked away. She wants to close her eyes and turn herself back into Cleopatra on her way to Tarsus: if she only tries hard enough, she will be able to shove the light away. But it has woken Bonnie, too; here she is, shivering beside Laura, a corner of the bedsheet clutched in her hands.

"I'm scared, Laura. Please, can I come sleep with you?"

Laura sighs and shoves herself to the edge of the mattress. "All right. If you promise not to kick."

"I promise. But sometimes I kick and I can't help it. Tell me a story, Laura, please?"

Bonnie is nine, by which age Laura would never have dreamed of confessing night terrors or daytime fears. Laura is the only one who knows Bonnie's secret, and she marvels at her small sister's talents as an actress. Of all the sisters, it is Bonnie people describe as open, sunny, just like a little daisy. They know nothing of the monsters lurking in cupboards and drawers, waiting to jump out and grab her the moment it gets dark each night. It's become a ritual at the cottage for Bonnie to fall asleep next to Laura, who must then lug her back to her own bed and tuck her in as best she can. It's become a ritual, as well, for Bonnie to crawl back beside Laura as soon as she wakes up each morning. It's just as bad at home, where Bonnie has a room all to herself, a room Laura has to inspect each night, closing every drawer, shutting the closets, making sure the windows are locked tight.

That night last winter when they'd watched Boris Karloff in *Dracula*, Bonnie had taken a small pad of colored notepaper and drawn a cross on every sheet. Then she'd torn them all off and thumbtacked them to the headboard of her bed. Laura's face burns to remember how cruel she'd been—telling Bonnie that she, Laura, was really Dracula, and that just when Bonnie was drifting off to sleep she would steal to her room and bite her neck till the blood ran dry. What use, then, could paper crosses be? Bonnie had ended up in Laura's room, burrowing into her bed and pleading, "Even if you are Dracula, won't you let me sleep with you?" How stricken she had felt and how full of love for her sister, who'd so wholly forgiven and forgotten. As if Bonnie really were as carelessly bright as a daisy, and as incapable of resentment or revenge.

Bonnie snuggles as close as she can to Laura, hands clasped over her heart like the Praying Hands on the Easter card someone's stuck to the wall. Laura doesn't need her glasses to see the look on her sister's face, so warm and so golden. If she hates Katia for being quick and clever and pretty, then why doesn't she hate Bonnie even more, since, though she looks so little like their mother, she is still, as everyone says of Sonia, perfectly beautiful? Bonnie has never fought with their mother, nor has she staged the astounding tantrums Katia has—Laura is prone to sulks, instead—yet Laura loves Bonnie with that fierce, self-less love she'd have given to the dog she will never be allowed to have. *Because I have enough to do as it is; you can't even pick up after yourself, how are you going to take care of an animal? It isn't a toy, you know, I can't just throw it in a box when you're tired of playing!*

Feeling Laura's body stiffen beside her, Bonnie unlocks her hands, stroking her sister's cheek till Laura gives in.

"All right—but just one story, a short one, because I'm still sleepy. I'll tell you how Caesar arrived in Alexandria after—"

"Not a Cleopatra story, Laura. Tell me the one about Our Mother. When she worked at the sportswear factory, and Mr. Streatfield picked her out from all the sewing-machine girls."

Laura sighs; she is as tired of this story as Bonnie is of Cleopatra.

"One morning at Modern Sportswear, the owner, Mr. Streatfield, happened to be walking along when he saw a beautiful young girl behind a sewing machine, and he said to her, 'You ought to be modeling those shorts instead of sewing them. Come to my office this afternoon, and we'll see what we can do for you.' And so Our Mother went to his office with a hatpin hidden in her sleeve—"

"Because Baba Laryssa told her to watch out for men," Bonnie prompts.

Laura gives a sigh disguised as a yawn, knowing that this time, like all the others, she won't be allowed to leave anything out. "Because Baba Laryssa always told her, 'Men are like that,' and Our Mother would say, 'Like what?' and Baba just said, 'You'll find out.'"

Bonnie closes her eyes. Laura goes on with the story, wondering all the while how many weeks or months her mother had worked in the sportswear factory before Mr. Streatfield discovered her. Why was he in such a dingy place, if he was such a famous designer? What did the other girls think when he singled their mother out like that? Mr. Streatfield is an old, fat, bald man with yellow-stained fingers, so why would their mother have needed that hatpin? Her mother has never ever struck her, even when she gets so mad her lips go white. How would she have dared stick a hatpin into Mr. Streatfield—and where?

When Laura reaches the part of the story where the handsome lawyer notices Sonia Metelsky's picture in an ad for Beaver Bakery in the *Ukrainian Herald*, she waits for a whole minute, listening to Bonnie's soft breathing weave through the beating of waves on the shore. Gently, Laura disengages her arm, which is falling asleep under the weight of her sister's head. She lies back on the pillow, shutting her eyes as best she can against the sun that has risen higher and higher with each sentence of the story being told. *Crash, crash, crash* goes the water—there must be a wind, perhaps a storm's on its way, although the sun promises another hot, clear day. She loves the sound of the waves breaking; she can never hear it enough. It's the part of being at the cottage that she misses most when they're back in the suburbs, in the big, split-level house where no one else has lived before, with the trees chopped down, and all the grass in patches on the front lawn, sewn together like a quilt.

Laura stares up at the ceiling, void, now, of the cracks and stains that will leap into view when she puts on the glasses that sit on her nose like a fat blue butterfly, glasses she's tried and tried to outgrow. When Elizabeth Taylor auditioned for the lead in *National Velvet*, they told her they wanted someone taller; she went home, grew three inches, and got the part. That's what it says in the *Cleopatra* souvenir booklet: "How she accomplished the trick she doesn't reveal." Laura's parents wouldn't take her with them to see *Cleopatra*; they said she'd have to wait until she was older, it wasn't suitable for children. She'd done everything, crying, pleading, being helpful around the house; she'd even gone to her father as he sat in his den, watching the hockey game: "If you love me you'll let me see *Cleopatra*. It's educational, please Tatu, if you love me you'll take me with you. I bet you don't love me, I bet you wish I'd never been born." But it was the Maple Leafs against the Canadiens and she couldn't tell whether he hadn't heard or didn't want to answer her. She'd never asked him again, and so her parents had gone to *Cleopatra* without her. When they brought her the souvenir booklet, she'd thrown it into the wastepaper basket, snatching it out when they'd left her to mope; staying up half the night reading, learning it by heart.

In a low voice, Laura recites the final lines of the story Bonnie has asked her to tell: "And Mr. Streatfield was going to take Our Mother to California, she was going to model a new line of outdoor wear, when she met Our Father, and he proposed, and she got married and had us instead." She wonders, for a moment, if her mother had felt the same despair at giving up California as she herself had felt at not being able to see *Cleopatra*. And then she frowns, lines forming like staple marks between her eyebrows. She isn't going to make excuses for her mother: that's bad strategy, you must never feel sorry for the enemy. Listening to the waves slap against the shore, she turns toward her sister, to the small, warm body that smells so sweetly of soap and sun.

"DARKA, LEAVE THEM, it's better to let them drip-dry. It's more"—and here Sonia pauses for a moment—"*hygienic*"—a word she's learned from *Reader's Digest*.

The children have been fed, the soggy Rice Krispies scraped from cereal bowls into the garbage, and the bowls washed, dried, put away. Sonia's forever telling Darka not to bother with drying, but will Darka ever listen? She seems to enjoy making Sonia feel guilty—little flutings of guilt like burned pastry-edging on a pie—at how hard Darka's being forced to work. There are beds to be made, clothes to be scrubbed in the old tin tub down in the cellar, baskets of cotton sheets to wring out. Slaving at the wash while they traipse off to the beach, Darka grumbles to herself, hands reddening as she flaps each piece of . laundry before pegging it on the line.

At all of the cottages nearby, children are being sent to collect shovels and pails, beach balls and towels; mothers are gathering blankets and baby oil. Family by family, they begin the processions down from the log and board-and-batten and shingled structures cresting the small bluff over the lake, along the zigzag paths between scrub and saplings, to each day's brand-new, shimmering bay.

By ten in the morning the sun has sizzled you through—you have to wear flip-flops and goggle-eyed sunglasses, you have to don beach hats with wide brims and fading raffia flowers woven into the straw, remnants from distant honeymoons in Jamaica or the Bahamas. You have to cart coolers filled with lemonade and iced tea, picnic baskets with snacks for the children, calamine lotion for insect stings. And even though you've remembered everything you could possibly want or need, and have laden yourself and even the smaller children with bits of that everything to carry down to the water's edge, something will always be forgotten. Messengers will endlessly ascend and descend the zigzag paths of the hill to the abandoned cottages.

Once they reach the sand, the children run straight to the water, hair flying, arms churning. Their mothers snatch up the very youngest and call the oldest back to spread out the blankets, securing the edges with stones so the wind won't keep flapping them about, flinging sand into everyone's eyes. No one has beach umbrellas or folding chairs—only the Senchenkos and the Plotskys possess such luxuries, but Nadia never comes down to the beach, and Sasha's umbrella's been ripped by her children, who are rough and wild and allowed to get away with murder. Katia spends most of her time at the Plotskys' cabin, eating Cheez Whiz sandwiches, practicing cartwheels *inside* the living room, and plotting mischief. Not something Sonia encourages, of course, but she can't help relying on anything that keeps her two oldest daughters out of shooting range of each other. Why can't they get along—why can't they be friends, best friends, like Katia and Tania?

Katia Martyn and Tania Plotsky. They'd begun their conspiracy their first summer at Kalyna Beach, when they were seven-year-olds. Selecting a patch of smooth, packed sand at the edge of the lake, they'd seized their shovels and started to dig. They were on their way to China, they'd explained to their mothers, who were concerned that someone walking along the beach in the dark might trip into the hole and break an ankle. By then it had become quite a deep hole, and they'd agreed to set up a cairn of stones to alert passersby. The next day, when their fathers had come up for the weekend, Mr. Martyn had hunkered down beside them, asking to help with the digging. In the course of the afternoon he'd given them a lesson in elementary geology, explaining how, under the earth's crust, there was a fiery kind of liquid stone called magma. He'd even taken a stick and written the word *magma* in the sand for them, as if on a blackboard at school.

But the girls had gone on digging: geology was all very well, but it had nothing to do with their plans, which were far more important than magma. Once they got to China, they were never going to come back: they would wander the earth, getting jobs in circuses to pay their way. Katia was going to be a trapeze artist, Tania a bareback rider (she had been on the ponies at Centre Island lots of times). They would send postcards to their parents every now and again, but they knew even then that family and adventure do not go together. They did not plan to marry or have babies: they never once toyed with the idea of disguising themselves as boys. Katia had had a low opinion of boys, confirmed by what Tania had told her of her brother's anatomy: that he'd been born with a peanut between his legs, and a little sac like a change purse. For some time afterward, Katia had refused to eat the peanut butter sandwiches Baba Laryssa would make her for lunch, throwing them into the bushes behind the sleephouse, instead.

Finally, Mr. Martyn had come down one night and filled in the tunnel the girls had constructed. The next morning, they'd refused to believe such a disaster could have happened—they'd walked up and down the beach, thinking they must have been digging somewhere else, that so magnificent a tunnel couldn't just have vanished overnight. "Explain it to them," Sonia had pleaded with Max, who'd refused, saying, "Let them think the waves washed it in. They'll forget about it soon enough." And it was true that the girls, having finally accepted this first defeat, had given up on digging holes; they had started plotting a quicker, more reliable route to China. They would run away to sea. To save up for their passage, they had started filching nickels from drawers where their mothers kept their loose change, collecting coins in small glass jars that they would bury under the trees, marking each spot with an X of pebbles.

Katia and Tania have outgrown the digging of tunnels, but "China" has remained their code word for acts of risk and rebellion. It's to a suburb of China that they've agreed to run right now, disappearing down the beach, their long, dark ponytails streaming out behind them. Sonia knows they are off to the store; she also knows she should run after her daughter, scold her—she'll gorge herself on cream soda and Fudgsicles and have no appetite for lunch. Instead, Sonia calls out from the faded red blanket where she's settled herself; calls to the water's edge where Darka is hunkered, watching Baby Alix kick her little legs against waves splashing up to her waist. *Is it dangerous?* Sonia wonders. Are all the other mothers staring at her, whispering about how careless Sonia Martyn is, how she'll end up one day with a drowned child on her conscience? What if she asked Darka to bring her the baby and run after Katia? Alix could make sand pies with the plastic molds that lie forgotten near Sonia's blanket: gay, bright colors, nothing like the dreary aluminum in which real food is cooked. But Darka doesn't hear Sonia call, or pretends not to. It is just as well—if Katia's fetched back, she'll make a scene in front of everyone. The baby will lose interest in the sand pies and wriggle back to the lake, into the lake where her mother, a grown woman, will be terrified to follow her. And that, in truth, is the real reason Darka's spending the summer with the Martyns at Kalyna Beach.

Darka in her polka-dotted two-piece, from which breasts and buttocks brim, always threatening to spill. She's only sixteen but, as the mothers say, "fully developed," which is another way of saying "trouble." She alarms and irritates the women lying in groups of twos and threes on worn cotton blankets with the stitching coming loose at the edges, blankets no longer good enough even for the beds at the cottage. All of the women were once as pretty or at least as young as Darka is now, but they would never have flaunted themselves the way she does. *Flaunt*: they use it often that summer, talking of Darka Marchuk. It's a word that flew up from the pages of *Teahouse of the August Moon* or *The Casting Couch*, they can't remember, now, and it doesn't matter. What matters is the pleasure they feel at learning something they could never have picked up from their mothers or from their high school English books. What matters is the deep satisfaction they feel at using a word as showy and special as the porcelain teacups they keep locked up in glass cabinets, at home. How much more satisfying than their mothers' reproach: *Have you no shame?* The way Darka parades the softness and fullness of her body, the obvious pleasure she takes in the bounce of breasts and bum: *Has she no shame?* The shame that these mothers and wives were born with, an Old Country birthmark flaring in the shared bathrooms and bedrooms of their own teenage years in rooming houses on Manning Avenue and Shaw Street. How they'd cowered inside their drab, prim, good-girl clothes, bodies hunched, skins pitted with secrets.

They've known each other for years now, these women sitting on blankets, examining their legs for varicose veins or flapping their arms periodically in attempts to improve what their magazines call "muscle tone." They have attended each other's weddings, watched each other's bellies swelling with children, and those children growing up and up. They've shared church pews as well as beach blankets, served out *varenyky* and *holubtsi* at banquets in community halls, taken turns driving each other's children to Ukrainian school on Saturday mornings, gossiped about each other's marriages, ferried cakes and casseroles to each other's houses when a new baby or a death arrived. Mrs. Vesiuk, Mrs. Stechyshyn, Mrs. Bozhyk, Mrs. Plotsky, and Mrs. Metelsky. Annie, Stefka, Halia, Sasha, Zirka. And Sonia Martyn (once Martyniuk, but altered when her father-in-law developed political ambitions), born Sonia Metelsky. She'd modeled for five years before her marriage, under the name of Sunny Sloane.

It's good of Sonia to have Darka up to the cottage, the women agree; it will give poor Olya a rest. Nothing but worry that girl has been from the day she first put on a skirt. And who better than Sonia to take her away from the city, where the boys clustered around her like flies on a coil of sticky paper? They'd sewn side by side at the sportswear factory, Sonia and Olya; even when Sonia had stopped sewing and started modeling, they'd stayed closer than sisters. But when Olya married Walter Marchuk, the friendship had cracked, like a thin, dark line along a china cup out of which you must drink gingerly, never pressing too hard. There is no Ukrainian word for *snob*; these women, growing up as they had in rooming houses downtown, their parents working at foundries and meat plants and factories, have had little chance to practice snobbery. Sonia has pulled away from Olya, they believe, out of fear, as if her good luck in marrying Max could be put at risk were she to try to keep up old ties. Sonia's a bad one for fears and superstitions—she takes after her father that way, the women agree.

No, it isn't snobbery that's spoiled the friendship between Olya and Sonia, it's just—marriage, the women sigh, each of them shaking her head, patting a stomach that the control panel built into her bathing suit never flattens enough. The friendships you make after marriage are never as strong as the ones that come before: it's your girlfriends you lose on your wedding day, as surely as you lose something else on your wedding night. And who knows the arithmetic of it all, whether what you gain is worth what you have to give up? You married because you fell in love, or else because you were so afraid no one would have you that you grabbed onto the first boy who asked you out. In either case, you were stuck for life, for better or worse, only it was hardly ever for better—at least, any better than you had a right to expect it would be.

Unless you were Nadia, and who could have foretold her fortune? They'd all laughed at her for getting hooked by Jack Senchenko, who'd got off the train from Canora with wheat in his hair and a bellyful of ambition. Only Nadia had seen him through his own eyes, for what he was going to make of himself. A professor's daughter, was Nadia; a professor's daughter with an English accent and an education. No one had ever been good enough for her, certainly not Peter Metelsky, who'd have flown to the moon and back if she'd snapped her fingers. Who could blame her—think of that spectacle he'd made of himself last Saturday night, at the Plotskys' get-together! Of course she'd given poor Peter the shove—she had far bigger fish to fry, which was why Peter had ended up with Jack's sister Zirka as a consolation prize. That's why they're lying on the same blanket now, Sonia and Zirka, a husband and brother in common and nothing else.

Sonia's hair is the color of buckwheat honey with not a trace of gray; of course she doesn't dye it like Zirka does, she's never been a bottle blonde. Do you see how her hipbones jut out below a stomach flatter than a washboard, for all that she's had four kids, and lost one along the way? Just look at Zirka beside her: short, stocky like her brother Jack; the dumpling, Sasha calls her, and not just because of her figure. She has nothing upstairs but flour and water, Sasha explains—and a little native cunning. Poor Peter . . .

They all call him that, with a sigh built into the "poor," because he's such a charmer, Sonia's brother: handsome as any movie star, far handsomer even than that scar-faced Richard Burton. One thing you had to say about the Metelskys, they had looks on their side. Good looks and bad luck: Jack's had to bail Peter out more times than you can count. If it weren't for Jack's help, the Metelskys would have had to give up their house a long time ago. And Jack had given them the cottage as a present, hadn't he? Of course he could afford to—he'd made a killing, buying up the lakefront property years before anyone thought of spending their summers here, selling lots to all his friends in the Ukrainian community, telling them they'd have a beach that was *nash*, no snooty WASPs around, the kind that expect you to be a janitor or a garbageman if your name ends in *-ski* or *-chuk*.

They've had to work hard, the cottagers of Kalyna Beach, to become respectable in the eyes of what they call their "English" neighbors, even if those neighbors are Scots or Irish or Welsh; even if those neighbors' families have been settled in Ontario for a hundred years or more. "Tell me all about your tribe," a business associate of Jack Senchenko's had once asked Nadia at a dinner party. "I hear your people have some very colorful customs." "Ask him about his ancestors painting themselves blue with woad, for Chrissakes," Sasha had bristled when Nadia told her the story. "Tell him about the daggers our men slip into the waistbands of their *sharovary*." But one of "our men" was a senator now, and another a judge; one a member of Parliament and another a surgeon at Saint Joe's; the last thing the community needs is a spoiled, careless creature like Darka getting into trouble, bringing shame on them all. What are her parents up to, letting her run around the way she does?

Darka doesn't hear the women whispering together on their blankets, throwing her glances like poisoned darts. She picks up Baby Alix as if she were a book with especially hard covers,

tucks her under her arm, and bounces up to the dunes, where
the girls' encampment lies.

MRS. MAXIMOYNKO'S STORE is called Venus Variety but not on
account of its wares: beach towels, pails, shovels, licorice ropes,
jawbreakers, Black Cat, Player's and Export A cigarettes, Hostess Twinkies, corn flakes, bakery cakes wrapped in cellophane
that gives them a chemical smell, hot dog buns and Maple Leaf
Wieners, condiments, paper napkins, sanitary napkins (kept
behind the counter), baby oil, and odds and ends of hardware,
for emergency repairs. There is nothing remotely resembling an
erotic or contraceptive device for sale, and while the shelves
have a few issues of *Archie* and *Superman* comics, what Mrs.
Maximoynko calls *gerrrrlie* magazines are out of the question.
She keeps a clean shop, under the portrait of the Youthful
Queen in Coronation Robes beside the Canada Dry clock over
the counter.

The store was called Venus Variety when the Maximoynkos
bought it years ago. It's unlucky to change names, and besides,
Mrs. Maximoynko likes the sound of it, the Vs at the start of
each word, the ripple of vowels. Under that name is written her
own, M. MAXIMOYNKO, PROP., and beside it, taking up all the
leftover space, is a picture of the red-wrapped planet spinning
like a top, commissioned from an acquaintance of Mr. Maxi-

moynko, a man who was a portrait painter back in Ukraine and who now works at General Electric.

Tania Plotsky is wandering the center aisle of the store, sucking on a licorice rope that leaves stains like bruises on her lips. In front of her walks Katia Martyn, her head bobbing up and down. Mrs. Maximoynko knows what she'll find when she's finished ringing up the Durkowskis' groceries (a tin of alphabet soup, a jar of pickles, a pint of cottage cheese). All the cakes along that center aisle will have the maraschino cherries in their middles pushed down to the filling, the cellophane stretched tight, if not broken, so she'll have to put them on the Reduced for Quick Sale shelf. She'd have spoken to Sasha and Sonia about their daughters long ago, but Sasha is one of her best customers (she spends a fortune on cigarettes and hot dogs each week) and Sonia's been low since the death of her mother, whose health had started to suffer at Christmas, and whom they'd buried before Easter. Cancer they said it was; Sonia had nearly gone out of her mind with grief, was what they also said.

"Katrusiu, Taniu," Mrs. Maximoynko cries out from behind the cash register. *"Shcho vy tam robyteh?"* And then she switches to her broken, superbly theatrical English: "I aska Momma. You gonna get it, vunna dese days."

The girls rush out of the shop, slamming the screen door behind them; as soon as they reach the road, they collapse, writhing, kicking out their feet, helplessly abandoned to their laughter. "Did you see her *tsytsi* when she was yelling at us?"

Katia shrieks. "They were shaking like—" "Hostess cupcakes!" Tania supplies, which sets them off into fresh snorts of laughter. Finally they wind down, wiping their mouths with the backs of their hands. Propped against one another, they start singing a song they'd had to learn at Ukrainian school: *My chemnyi deetyh, ukrayeenski kveety.* Their high, sweet voices dart in with the flies through the worn screen door. *We obedient children, flowers of Ukraine.*

Mrs. Maximoynko shakes her head, and her massive bosom shakes in sympathy. Pan and Pani Durkowski nod. (They are always addressed by these Ukrainian equivalents of Mr. and Mrs.; they seem to demand that dignity, for all that they work as janitors at the Cathedral Hall.) When they'd first come to Kalyna Beach, they'd gone around to the various mothers, suggesting they could organize a morning program for the children right on the beach. Calisthenics and recitations from the national poets, followed by a round of Ukrainian folk songs. All the mothers had thanked them, saying what a wonderful idea such a program would be, but when it came to the first session, half of the children hadn't shown up, and the rest had wandered away before the stride jumps were finished. The mothers apologized, but there was nothing they could do. "They go to Ukrainian school all year," one had explained, "so they really want a holiday while they're up here." And as Sonia Martyn had ventured: "The children were born here, they don't feel the same way about the Old Country as we do, there's no point in forcing them." But then, Pan Durkowski had growled to his wife, look at those Martyns, changing their name, making it English-sounding. Their children had been the last ones of all to be enrolled at Ukrainian school. In vain had Sonia explained that Laura, who had spoken nothing but Ukrainian till she was five, had come home from English school one day with a note from the principal: *It would be better if your child stopped speaking Russian in the playground.*

"Russian!" Pan Durkowski had snorted. "The idiot principal thought that they were Russian?" Pani Durkowska had tried to explain it to her husband: "Max has to be careful, he has his practice to build, and Sonia has always been frightened"—adding, under her breath, "the way all of us who weren't born here are frightened—that we could be picked up and shipped back, without so much as a word of warning." Her husband had made no sign of having heard. "To let some stupid *Anhleek* believe there is no difference between speaking the noble, the ancient, the beautiful Ukrainian tongue and being communists!" he had roared. "That is a crime, I tell you—a crime as bad as murder in the first degree!"

He is fond of roaring, Pan Durkowski: here he is now, thundering on as his wife stares up at the portrait of the brown-haired, pudding-faced woman in diamanté armor, to whom she'd sworn allegiance at her citizenship hearing the year before. "Who is going to carry on the battle?" he exclaims, bringing his fist down hard on the counter, so that the jawbreakers rattle in their jar. "Who will hold their hands over their hearts and march off to free our poor Ukraine? The youth of today? Pah! They have no respect; all their parents teach them is to put out their hands for whatever they want. While in the Homeland, children are beaten for speaking Ukrainian instead of Russian in the schools! Beaten!"

He looks as if he would like to run out and perform that precise punishment on Tania and Katia. Instead, he takes off his glasses, breathes against them till the lenses steam, polishes them with a pale blue handkerchief in his shaking hands. His wife brings her gaze back from the portrait of the Youthful Queen to Mrs. Maximoynko's small, heart-shaped face, so incongruous against her steel-wool hair, the bulk of her breasts. Pani Durkowska is anxious to change the subject; thankfully, she remembers that they need a length of copper pipe to repair the bathroom sink: her husband is a real handyman, she tells Mrs. Maximoynko, using the English word, *hendy-men*. The proprietor of Venus Variety checks her supply of hardware, sells them the pipe, and bids the Durkowskis good day.

The old people walk out into the stinging light, shoes scraping over the asphalt as they make their way along Tunnel Road, back to their cottage. For it is far too hot for them to be on the beach at this hour: they have had their morning walk long before breakfast and will return when the families are all indoors eating their suppers and the beach is deserted. The Durkowskis prefer quiet pursuits: reading, gardening, playing solitaire.

Perhaps they are not so very disappointed, after all, that their Beachside Ukrainian School has come to nothing.

KATIA AND TANIA are far, far ahead of the elderly couple, on the part of Tunnel Road that goes to the Shkurkas' cottage—they still call it that, even though Mr. Shkurka's been gone for the past eight years—"probably married again and fathered a dozen sons." At least that's what they've heard Katia's aunt Zirka say on the Plotskys' veranda, talking with the other mothers. The girls are a little drunk with what Katia calls "being bad." It's their defining attribute; their mothers have had endless phone calls from their Ukrainian school teachers—Miss Marchenko, who wears her hair in a lofty coil, and whom the girls call Bagel Head in her hearing; Mr. Khriniuk, who does have a peculiar habit of tapping his front teeth with his forefinger, and whom they've christened Pan Pecker.

Pan Pecker had caught the girls drinking Cherry Cokes at the Sombrero Restaurant next to the funeral parlor when they were supposed to be in class, doing dictation; the week before that, they'd disrupted the rehearsal of the Harvest Dance by the most disgraceful jerking and shoving (by which Miss Marchenko meant the twist). The only way their mothers could get them to behave was by threatening to take them out of Ukrainian school altogether, which would have meant that, except for the summers, they'd never see one another at all. For Tania lives in the north and Katia in the west end of the city; and though Sonia and Sasha see a lot of each other at Kalyna Beach, once they're back in Toronto, they could be living in different provinces. Chastened, the girls would behave for a few Saturdays, and then come up with some new piece of *deviltry*—Pan Pecker's word for it—whereupon the long, complaining phone calls would begin again.

Dark hair, dark eyes, olive-colored skin over their toothpick bodies—they are so alike they could be twins, thinks Lesia Baziuk, catching sight of Tania and Katia from the front porch of Mrs. Shkurka's house. The women are sitting at a small table facing the road: Mrs. Baziuk has opened her little case of cosmetics and is showing Nettie Shkurka the five different shades of nail polish Avon is stocking this season. Mrs. Baziuk has one eye on Mrs. Shkurka's face, its show of superior suspicion at the names and colors of the products; Nettie is such a prude that she'll end by rejecting any hint of what even a bit of face powder and a natural-tint lipstick could do for her, settling instead on the invisibles: moisturizer, cleanser, and the inevitable cotton balls.

Lesia Baziuk's other eye is trained on her son Billy, who is sitting patiently on the porch steps below them, looking out at the road, his hands folded nicely in his lap. Every morning she gives him his medicine: one pill to ward off seizures; the other, as the doctor said, to settle him down and make her life a little easier. For Frank Kozak gives her no help at all with Billy. "Another guy has sown the seed and done the deed" had been his response to Lesia's first few pleas for assistance. Now, she wouldn't trust him to comb Billy's hair or shine his shoes. Frank Kozak, as everyone knows, thinks only of himself; besides, he's always tippling from that sleek silver flask he keeps in his pocket wherever he goes. He is also married, though not to Mrs. Baziuk, whose husband died in a hunting accident many years ago. When the children are nearby, Frank Kozak is referred to by the adults as Mrs. Baziuk's "special friend." Sasha has been heard to exclaim that she can't for the life of her understand why Lesia Baziuk has anything to do with him, and Sonia Martyn responds that it might have something to do with Frank's having a clean and decent job, working for the Insurance.

Lesia's made sure he's kept that job; at home, she ladles his booze out to him, glass by glass, calculating how much he can take and still do a reasonable day's work; she's arranged to get a portion of his paycheck deposited in her own account each month. His boss is a kind man with a son Billy's age; he is willing to overlook a lot to help Lesia out, as long as Frank's numbers keep adding up all right, as by some miracle they do. There's a trust account in Billy's name, and when the time comes he'll have to go into a Home, but not while there's a breath left in her body. He's an affectionate boy, obedient and thoughtful in his own way. Unlike those giggling show-offs. Cruel as if they had—Mrs. Baziuk thinks for a moment—knives instead of hearts in their chests. Jackknives! She can see the faces they're pulling as they look at her Billy; she tells herself that it's their mothers who should be pitied instead of her—better to have a sweet, slow boy like Billy than those two she-devils.

What his mother can't see, and what the girls are making faces at, is Billy's hand pumping at his crotch. This isn't a matter of peanut butter sandwiches: Billy is old enough to drink, and drive, and even get married. "Meat on a stick," Katia whispers to Tania, who snorts with laughter as Mrs. Baziuk shakes her fist and shouts down the road, "Have you no shame?"

ON A PINE-CROWNED bluff well beyond Venus Variety and as far away from the other cottages of Kalyna Beach as a lord's manor house would be from the huts of his serfs, rises the Senchenkos' cottage with its white-stuccoed walls, its long pine balconies, and giant windows bordered by undersized shutters with heart-shaped holes cookie-cuttered out of them. Though it's called The Senchenkos', Nadia has never believed it to belong to her—or her to it. She grew up with the word *cottage* meaning something entirely different. Not a magnified, mutant Swiss chalet, but a small, snug home in an English village with delphiniums and hollyhocks growing in the garden. Not that she'd ever lived in one, herself, or known anyone who had, but she'd grown up on books like *The Secret Garden* and *The Mill on the Floss*, books in which cottages had nothing at all to do with suntan oil and beach balls and poison ivy.

In the early days, when the cottage had still smelled of the pine it had been built from, she'd taken her sketchbook out to a clump of sumac and returned with welts on her feet and hands. Unlike the short-lived rash from stinging nettles, poison ivy led to sores that itched and burned and oozed for weeks. Jack had laughed; he'd called her a greenhorn. She hadn't minded the laughter as much as the fact that, for a good week, she'd been unable to draw or to even hold a book.

It's past eleven; she should make herself some breakfast. She should go down to the beach and join the other women, but she's as likely to do that as she is to plunge back into the poison ivy. She only feels safe with them when they're all gathered at Sasha's; otherwise, Nadia is afraid that the women will see right through her—read her like a book, as the saying goes. The only one here she can talk to is Sasha, and Sasha's as discreet as a fire alarm. Sonia—if there's any woman here she needs to speak to, it is Sonia, who would be able to tell her—but no, she could never ask, and even if she did, Sonia wouldn't say.

On the kitchen table Nadia finds the sketch she was working on last night. She is getting careless, leaving things around—if Jack should see . . . But Jack could look and look, and not see a thing—whereas to her it is as clear as lake water, this sketch of the back of a man's head, seen from the top, as if you were looking down at him kneeling before you. The nape of his neck, as tender and exposed as the fontanel on a baby's head—Nadia looks at the drawing she's made, looks at it as an artist would, sensing its shortcomings yet astonished at how some of the lines are good, are true to what she was thinking, feeling, as she drew them on the page. And then she gets herself a cup of the coffee that's been perking for the last half hour and returns to her armchair and a jumble of books lying on the seat. *The Story of Art, The Nude, Art and Illusion, The Complete Paintings of Delacroix.* On top of them all, a book of short stories, its pages lying open.

How could that writer understand so much about her characters? Not just the fact of their lying to themselves about what they really felt and wanted, but all the ways they hid the truth from themselves or brushed against it only to persuade themselves they were imagining things, things of no more consequence than tarnish on a teaspoon. She wants Sasha to talk with her about it, Sasha, to whom she'd loaned the book, and who'd gulped it down the way she did anything made of paper and ink. Suddenly, Nadia wants all of the other women at Kalyna Beach to read this book and tell her what they think. Have they ever felt like the woman in the story? Have they ever thought of getting up the courage one day to say to themselves, this is what I have, this is what I am—but *that* is what I hoped I could be and do, and perhaps might still—

The book lies where she left it, its covers hidden, its print a fine black blur. Nadia puts her hands to her head, as if her hair were on fire, then drops her arms to her sides, walks back to the kitchen, and rips out the drawing of the man's head, the nape of his neck, from her sketchbook. She folds the paper, first in quarters, then in eighths, and throws it into the garbage. And then she returns to the pile of books on the armchair. But instead of making room for herself to read, she sprawls on the floor, like a child. Taking up her pencil, she finds a fresh page in her sketchbook and begins to draw, from memory, a man's crumpled shirt, with a button hanging by a thread.

MORNINGS BELONG TO the beach. The children spend their time running back and forth between the water and the dunes: roasting, then plunging into the lake, running across the sandbars till the water rises up to their knees, and then their waists, and then their shoulders. They play tag, or practice dead man's float, or just bob up and down: on stormy days they dive right through the breakers, swallowing pints of water and spluttering onto shore only when their mothers force them out, hovering with faded beach towels, rubbing them dry till their skins feel as though they've been pushed through graters.

Mostly, the weather is cloudless: by the time the children have quit the lake and raced to their different fortresses behind the dunes, they're seared with sun. On the east end of the beach, the boys are sequestered; on the west, the girls. Even though two of those boys, Yuri and Andriy, are their cousins, the Martyn girls have agreed to their banishment, on the beach, at least, and in daylight. But in the evenings, when their mothers lie slumped on sofas, having cooked supper and swept the floors for the hundredth time, having rinsed out bathing suits and hung them on the line with the sodden, sand-clumped towels, some of the older boys and girls go off in groups of three or four, walking along Tunnel Road, playing tag at the edge of the woods; spying at the lighted windows of other people's cottages.

Right now the Martyn girls and their friends—Tania, Vlada, Lenka, Rocky-short-for-Roksolana—lie flopped on their towels for as long as they can stand the sun. Every so often, they spring up and sprint to the water, shrieking at how the sand is cooking their feet. Their mothers grumble as this same sand sprays into their faces while the brown bodies leap by, an exotic species of animal they've no idea how to name.

Between nine a.m., when the mothers march the children down to the beach, and noon, when it's time to gather them up and head back to make lunch, the women may get five minutes all to themselves, spread-eagled on their blankets, drinking the sun through their pores, the hot sand cradling their bodies like the most gentle of lovers. Sometimes it's so still they can hear flies crawling over the debris of potato chips or browned apple slices; sometimes a strong, warm wind plays over the women, fanning skin redolent of baby oil or the first-aid smell of Noxzema. Waves thump the shore and a few gulls screech lazily overhead while, neither far away nor too close by, children's voices bubble up like water from a spring. When the children are being good, making sandcastles or playing tag behind the dunes, their mothers can shut their eyes and let themselves drift, as if they were pieces of wood bobbing up and down in water so clear and shallow it couldn't drown a spider.

On her blanket, red bleached out to pink, Sonia stretches her body into the endless air and sun; she's a kite floating wherever the wind will take her. Max and Marta are still far, far away in the city, small red ants she could stretch out her finger and crush, one after the other. No one is drowning, no one is crying or shouting or grabbing at her; she could sleep here forever and ever. Except that a shadow's suddenly fallen across her, a cold, soaked towel of a shadow that knows her name, and sits down beside her, and begins to talk. Because the shadow is married to her brother, and Sonia will never hear the end of it if she pretends Zirka is merely a cloud passing overhead, she must stop being that kite sailing away and attend to what her sister-in-law is saying in that piercing voice of hers.

"She's growing up fast, your Laryssa."

"Laura. She only answers to Laura, now."

"Fourteen in November, isn't she? We'd like to buy her something special—it's an important birthday, she's getting to be a young lady."

"We're getting her contact lenses. There's a man at the Medical Arts Building who fits them."

"*Bozhe,* Soniu—it's dangerous, putting things in your eyes. You can go blind. I know I'd never forgive myself if—"

"Max has checked it out—it's perfectly safe. They've been wearing them for years in the States. And I know girls who've worn them without any trouble—models I used to work with."

"Oh. Models." Zirka's voice puckers with disapproval. She may have worked before she married, but at a respectable job at Beaver Bakery, making and decorating cakes for birthdays and weddings. Whereas Sonia had exposed herself to photographers (from outside the community, most of them); she'd even spent time in New York, staying in hotels, meeting heaven knows whom. Of course, the Metelskys had been as poor as fleas; whatever Sonia earned must have come in all too handy but still— "Models," Zirka repeats, nodding her head. "Like the one you named Bonnie after—what was her name?"

"Bon-nie Mac-Leod." Sonia produces the syllables as if they were weights from a pair of kitchen scales: years ago she'd been taught how to pronounce them correctly: *Not* clee-odd, *Sunny, but* clowd, *like those puffy white things up there in the sky.*

"What a time you had with Max's father over that name." Zirka's voice is like the reek of an opened bottle of nail polish. "What was it he said? I remember, I was visiting you in maternity, and Mr. Martyniuk came in and shouted—the whole ward could hear him—'Bony! What kind of name is that? You gonna starve her?'"

"I have a headache, Zirka," is all that Sonia says. Though she can't keep herself from remembering what had followed the "Bony" crack, what Zirka, mercifully, hadn't stayed on to hear.

He'd said it there in the hospital room, her father-in-law. He'd leaned right over her, to where Max was standing, as if he'd meant to grab his son by the shoulders; as if she weren't lying in the bed between them, her newborn in her arms. "You gonna let her get away with naming her that?" he'd roared. And then, "Three chances she's had now and she can't even give you one son?"

Max had knuckled under, pleading with her to change their child's name from Bonnie to anything Ukrainian: Oksana or Marusia or Motria, after his mother. But she'd stood her ground. Staring into her baby's face, the tight-shut lips and lids, all she'd been able to think of was Bonnie MacLeod. How forthright and free she'd always been, that friend of her lost life—how stunningly unburdened. That's what she'd wished for this new child; with her whole heart she'd wished for her the gifts she'd so envied in Bonnie MacLeod.

"Your poor Laryssa," Zirka was saying. "Of course, she'll look much prettier without glasses, and if she can manage to lose some weight . . . It's so important when you're at that age to look your best. And children can be so cruel," she adds smugly.

Sonia doesn't deign to reply. How dare Zirka say a word about Laura's size: doesn't she know that all girls on the verge of puberty put on puppy fat? And Zirka's one to talk: look at her—look at her youngest; now there's a fatty in the making! Laura's chubbiness will melt away, all in good time, isn't that what Sonia's told her, over and over? Yet she acts as if it's her mother's fault she's gaining weight, her mother's fault for making the Jell-O and lemon meringue pie that Laura loves, always first in line for second helpings, first in line for picking fights, taking offense, being *difficult*. Sonia's headache stabs in earnest now; she feels the first squirm of nausea. Stretched on her stomach, her cheek nuzzling the blanket, sun beating down on her bare back and long, long legs, Sonia tries to turn Zirka's words into horseflies buzzing around her, settling on places she can't reach to swat; letting them drink their fill before they leave her be. It's not her fault that Laura's the way she is.

Before she'd emerged from the womb, they were already fighting. A breech birth: "You look like a battlefield inside," the nurse had told her, after the anesthetic had worn off. Things had gone from bad to worse, Laura biting the nipple with her milk teeth when put to the breast or else refusing to nurse, so that there'd been endless fussing with a breast pump before Sonia had given up, at last. She'd felt such a failure, her breasts deflating like pricked balloons, Laura throwing up formula in her lap or into a pile of freshly washed diapers. After all the hopes she'd had, with that first pregnancy—this great lump of a Laura with glasses thick as a telephone book, and the fine, limp hair they can do nothing with, in spite of pin curls and home permanents. Perhaps if they dyed it, gave it some body . . . Maybe Laura would be happier that way—sunnier—with contact lenses and blond hair. Maybe she'd stop picking fights with Katia, who can't help being as clever, as pretty as she is, dark and thin and dancing almost before she could walk. While Laura still trips over her own two feet: bandages on her knees, a scowl on her face, and that huge, sharp chip on her shoulder. So much like Marta it's terrifying.

Max is bringing Marta with him tonight; she'll be here for a whole week, Sonia groans to herself. Every summer since they bought their cottage at Kalyna Beach, Max has brought his sister up to stay. Because it's so hot in the city, he always says. Though, as Sonia's told her husband once, ten, a hundred times, it's Marta's own fault she nearly boils herself alive: she won't open the windows for fear of burglars; she refuses to turn on the fan they bought her because it costs money, and besides, how can she complain about the heat if the fan's turned on? Max is also bringing Marta because he feels guilty, has been made to feel guilt all his life about his only sibling, who plays him like a virtuoso, pulling from him any tune she wants. She'll complain about the children being too loud, tracking sand into the cottage, which she'll then insist on sweeping up, though the doctor's told her it's bad for her to exert herself. She'll find fault with the cooking, and the poorness of the children's Ukrainian. Most of all, she'll shake her head and mutter darkly about how Sonia's failed to produce a son: *Girls are useless. It's the boy that counts.*

If she could only let it all go in one ear and out the other, the way her mother had counseled her. Her mother was the only one who could handle Marta—the only one whom Marta had respected or, perhaps, feared enough not to try to lord it over her. Why is it her mother who's dead and not Marta, Marta who's always off at somebody's funeral, then phoning to announce that she'll be the next to go? Why take a woman who loved life so, even the hard life given her; why take someone who was always singing or laughing, or helping out this or that neighbor, and leave that mean, sour rind of a woman instead?

Reluctantly, Sonia turns onto her back, opens her eyes, and stares through her dark glasses straight up into God's blue, blue eye. Zirka puts a hand like a stone on her sister-in-law's head:

"You really ought to have a hat on. No wonder you get those terrible headaches, lying in the sun like this."

Sonia sits up, raking her fingers through her hair. Her skin is the color of brown sugar, her eyes behind the dark glasses are almost turquoise, Zirka thinks. Her father was Polish, wasn't he, half Polish? She looks like a Pole, not a Ukrainian.

"It must be nice to have Darka to take the children off your hands," Zirka goes on. "Especially Alix—though I guess you couldn't ask for a better baby, so . . . quiet all the time. And thank heavens Annie Vesiuk is such a strong swimmer—it makes me nervous, all these children in the water and no life-guard around. My Yuri has his Junior badge, he can always pitch in if there's an emergency. And Annie's boys—it's incredible, isn't it—eight boys and all of them champion swimmers. Even the baby's started and he's only six months; she has him right in the water with the rest of them. Eight boys! You and Annie should trade recipes, Sonia."

This time Zirka's voice makes Sonia think of a sink full of cold, greasy water, the drain choked. "I'm going to check on the girls," she says, not caring if Zirka thinks her rude for walking off. But instead of struggling to the girls' encampment at the top of the dunes, Sonia stops halfway, turning her eyes in the direction of the lake, as if looking for a boat on the water or some distant sign of land: a place where she will feel, at last, guiltless, requited, *home*.

"MAKE SURE SHE keeps her hat on, and don't you dare let her out of your sight."

Darka drops the baby into Laura's lap and makes for the lake; Alix immediately scrambles to Katia. Nearly three, Alix is small for her age, small and thin and even darker than Katia, her eyes and hair black instead of brown. And she holds herself so rigid, it's like a bundle of sticks falling into your lap when she plunks herself down, sucking her two front fingers, her black eyes watching everything, everyone. Bonnie hands Alix a plastic shovel to dig with and a small blue sieve. The baby holds the shovel in her hand as if she's never seen anything like it before, and then, as if to reassure them, as if she were a grown-up joining in a child's game she only half remembers, pats the shovel against the hot, loose sand. Baby Alix has never said a single word, though all her sisters were chattering away by the time they were two. Language stays locked in her throat like a safety pin she's swallowed, but that's bound to show up, sooner or later, like in an X-ray on the cartoons. Or so their father reassures them. There's nothing wrong with her, she's perfectly capable of speaking, the doctor says so. If anyone asks about Alix, they are to say that she's perfectly normal, bright as a button, though it's never explained what buttons have to do with it. She's just taking her time, that's what they're supposed to say: good things are worth waiting for.

But none of the girls assembled in the little hollow behind the dunes says anything nasty about Alix. If the boys were here, it would be different—they would tease the legs off a spider. They are such babies, the girls agree. Any boy older than thirteen is off at the Ukrainian summer camp in Oakville, a camp run along military lines, whose discipline, the fathers argue, is good for boys of that age—"that age" meaning old enough to argue with their fathers and be rude to their mothers. At the camp, they learn to carry messages across enemy lines, to dig trenches, and communicate by semaphore—explained to their sisters as something involving flags and cunning. Any boy older than thirteen is at the camp, except, of course, for Billy Baziuk, who spends every second of every day and night with his mother. As for the boys at the beach this year, they occupy themselves by hanging around the service station across the road from Venus Variety, inhaling the sharp smell of gasoline from the pumps, or else diving from a raft anchored at a part of the lake where the sandbars stop and the water's cold and deep and dangerous.

Today the boys have decided to forgo the diving raft: overnight, a huge driftwood log has rolled up onto the beach. None of them has ever been in a canoe; some have never seen one, unlike their friends at English school who go to summer camps with names like Gitchigoumi and Oconto, learning to identify animal tracks and survive in the bush. So the boys decide to turn their find into a galley instead of a giant canoe; eight of them sit astride the log, paddling furiously out into open water. They're going to Australia, the huge rock thirty yards offshore, close enough that you can swim back easily if you've got your Junior badge. Even so, the mothers take turns pacing along the shore, and the girls take no chances, posting spies at the edge of the dunes where they spread their beach towels and sit rubbing baby oil onto their arms and legs, already brown as barbecued duck. The tall, rough grass makes a perfect screen, and the dunes themselves could be the high walls of a Cossack fortress, below which Turks and Tatars lie plotting.

The girls' talk jumps about like the sand fleas they bury in shallow graves at the edges of their towels. Bonnie is the youngest; Laura the oldest, and Katia and Tania have both turned twelve this summer. As for the others, they take up the slack between Laura and Bonnie. There's something insistent, authoritative, about this ranking according to birth date, something Laura's grateful for, knowing as she does that otherwise they'd never give her the time of day, not only Katia but all the other girls at the beach, except for Bonnie. If Anastasia Shkurka were here, she'd have a natural ally, but Nastia is delicate, prone to sunstroke and heat rash, and her mother keeps her inside in the mornings, when the sun is hottest.

Somehow the conversation turns to Nastia, to how sickly she is, how pale and nervous.

"I don't think she's delicate at all," Tania observes. "I think Nastia Shkurka's about as delicate as a rubber tire. She hasn't any guts, that's all."

A thrill goes through the group of girls on hearing the word *guts*—it's a boy's word, and there's something daring just in hearing Tania speak it.

"If Nastia woke up one morning with a pimple on her face, she'd get a heart attack," Katia crows. "Nasty Nastia."

"Shut up." Laura says this out of loyalty, not because it isn't true. If Nastia were to grow a pimple on her chin, she probably would walk around with her chin cupped in her hand, to hide it. She's always scared to do things her mother wouldn't like— things her mother would never find out about in a hundred years, like looking at the book Laura found in Sonia's bedside table and brought with her once to the Shkurkas' cottage. "You shut right up," Laura says, adding a word that's higher up on the forbidden list than *guts*: *"Dupo. Smerdiucha dupo."*

The girls shiver. Everyone knows that there's a war going on between Katia and Laura. Their last fight has acquired mythic status among the girls at Kalyna Beach; everyone's heard how, that one day it rained, that day of being cooped up indoors with already thumbed-through books and decks of cards with the queens or aces missing, Katia had started teasing Laura about her weight. Laura had thrown a book at her—a book that had hit not Katia but the statue their mother had brought up to the cottage and placed on the mantelpiece, a plaster statue in the shape of a boy and girl kissing under an umbrella. The Martyn children knew the story of that statue by heart: how it was the first luxury Baba Laryssa had ever owned, the first thing she'd ever possessed that couldn't be worn or eaten. Dyeedo had bought it for her just before he died; it was priceless, their mother claimed. Though if it were such a treasure, why was it up at the cottage? And why had the children heard their father refer to it, when their mother wasn't around, as "that monstrosity"?

The statue had fallen almost noiselessly; Katia had quickly swept up the pieces with dustpan and brush, but Sonia had known at once. She'd marched in from the screen porch directly to the garbage can, slipped the lid open, and, with her bare hands, pulled out the shards of the statue. And then she'd had *highsterics*, as Laura called them. When she'd finally got around to asking which of them was responsible, Katia had yelled "Laura," and Laura, "Katia." They had both been punished: made to stay indoors the whole of the next clear, sunny day, with Laura forbidden to visit Nastia, and Katia to run off to

Tania's. As for the statue, its pieces were put in a cardboard box, labeled in Sonia's uncertain script, BROKEN STATU, and placed on the shelf beside the screen door, so that every time they went in or out of the kitchen, the girls would see it and feel appropriately guilty.

But they didn't: they were preoccupied with other feelings. It hadn't been the punishment so much as the sense of injustice that had poisoned the aftermath, each of the sisters convinced that the other was to blame, both unwilling to bury their differences and unite against their mother. There'd been something else, as well, something ugly and invisible, like a terrible smell that seeps into a room. For the first time in all the years of their being sisters, Laura and Katia had understood that in spite of what people were always telling them, there *was* something thicker than blood. There was the possibility of something hard and persistent, something you couldn't un-feel: something they could only call hate. Instead of deflecting their shame at having broken their Baba's treasure, instead of whispering to each other, "stupid old statue" and "who cares if The Monstrosity got broken," they'd put an icy silence between them, broken only by jabs at each other whenever an audience cropped up.

Smerdiucha dupo. Laura's taunt hovers in the air, a party balloon that won't pop. Hearing it in Ukrainian is far more exciting for the girls than if Laura had used the English words—it's as if they've overheard their grandparents swearing. Everyone waits for Katia to hit back, knowing she's taking her time, waiting for effect, preparing an insult far more devastating than "smelly bum," when Bonnie pipes up in her sweet, clear voice. "Tell us a story, Laura," she pleads, picking up a fistful of sand and letting it dribble out her fingers, the white and black grains finer, even, than salt and pepper pouring from the shakers. "Tell us 'Ball Erectory.'"

Tania sniggers. When Laura pokes her with her elbow, she puts her hand to her lips, as if the snigger were a fly that had flown into her mouth and disappeared.

"It's called 'Ball *Rectory*,' Bonnie, and I told it yesterday, and last night, and I'm sick of it."

Laura's been elected storyteller this summer—from the girls at English school she's picked up dozens of ghost stories that they've learned at summer camp along with how to make pine-cone necklaces and miniature teepees out of birch bark. "Ball Rectory" is about Albania, whose lover is killed by an evil lord in a duel. She has a child out of wedlock in a convent, and both of them perish of hunger and cold at the hands of the Abbess, who is the sister of the evil lord, and who is tortured ever after by the wails of the perished Albania and her newborn child.

"I'm sick and tired of that story," Laura grumbles. "I'll tell you 'Cleopatra' instead." Bonnie exhales slowly, careful not to let her sisters see her relief; determined to keep the peace for as long, and as invisibly, as possible.

The girls lie spread out on their towels, sometimes spitting a few grains of sand from their mouths or twitching their bodies when flies crawl up their calves. Laura alone sits cross-legged, reciting from the souvenir booklet. Her voice takes on a deep, reverent tone, ringing out over the blankets and echoing between the dunes:

We, as we read of the deeds of the Queen of Egypt, must doff our modern conception of right and wrong; and, as we pace the courts of the Ptolemies, and breathe the atmosphere of the first century before Christ, we must not commit the anachronism of criticizing our surroundings from the standard of twenty centuries after Christ.

"Is that English?" Tania asks. Laura ignores her, but then Katia joins in.

"What does 'anachronism' mean?" Katia's only asking because she thinks Laura doesn't know—that she can trip her up in front of all the others.

"It's a kind of sin," Laura says loftily. They seem to expect something else, and so she blunders on. "It's something you commit. Like communism." She's thinking of the photograph that appears in the book above the words she's just recited, words picked out in huge black print. The picture shows a banquet hall with silk-draped walls under green and purple lights that remind her of the peels of cucumbers and eggplants. It's a small picture, but you can still see a man whose skin only goes as far down as his hips, and whose legs are covered with fur. Two other men are wearing skorts, like in gym class, and ladies in bikinis perch like budgies on swings, watching as the men in skorts leap between lighted torches.

Beautiful and seductive Cleopatra was, but she was also a hereditary ruler, a woman of rare spirit and courage, cosmopolitan and yet superstitious, ardent and, at times, lonely. And always proud. Her conversation was known to be scintillating, her mind keen.

This is the part Laura likes best, for though she knows she'll never be beautiful, a rare spirit and scintillating mind are things she can train herself to acquire, the way she was able to cure herself of flat arches by picking up marbles and pencils with her toes every night for a year. The word *ardent* especially enchants her: it makes her think of small golden arrows, thin as fish bones and with flames instead of feathers at their ends.

Cleopatra's father, Ptolemy XIII, had stated in his will that she was to share the throne of Egypt with her younger broth-er, Ptolemy XIV. But he plotted against her and threatened to kill her and she was forced to flee to Syria.

"Who's Syria?"

Impatient with the interruptions, Laura stops quoting from the souvenir booklet. She tells them how Julius Caesar, having defeated his rival in battle, travels to Alexandria to decide who should inherit the throne of Egypt, and how Cleopatra has herself wrapped up in a carpet and carried in to him, just like a hot dog in a bun, so that her brother won't find out and stab her in the back. Tania nods, hearing this; her brother is nine; he would stab her in a minute, she says, if she didn't watch out. Laura ignores her.

"Cleopatra's faithful retainer, Apollodorus, who is silently and hopelessly in love with the queen, carries her into Caesar's apartments as if he were trying to sell him the rug."

"Why would Julius Caesar need to buy a rug if he was Absolute Master of the Roman World? Why wouldn't Apple—whatever his name is—take the rug to Caesar's wife instead?" Katia's questions are imperious.

"She was in Rome," Laura shoots back. "The wife doesn't matter—Cleopatra does. When she stepped out of the rug—"

"Like a showgirl from a cake?"

"—he was charmed by her beauty and her cleverness, and fell in love with her forever after."

"But you said he had a wife."

"If all you're going to do is make stupid remarks, I won't tell you anything," Laura fumes.

At which point Darka returns, dripping water from her brassy hair and clutching a movie magazine with the words SYB-IL'S ANGUISH screaming from the cover. Darka bends down to wipe Alix's nose; the baby retaliates by grabbing the magazine, tearing off the back page, and crumpling it into a ball, which she proceeds to suck on. Darka retrieves the rest of the magazine; expertly, she spreads out her towel, flopping on her back, pulling her straps down from her shoulders. The girls nudge one another—even Laura's included—at the sight of Darka's big breasts bulging under the top of her two-piece. And then their heads dive down and they pretend to sleep; the noise they hear this time is a mother's flip-flops climbing up the dunes.

It's Sonia, all out of breath, her hand like a visor over her dark glasses. All she sees is the baby stuffing paper in its mouth while Darka soaks up sun like a great, soft starfish. "Darka," she shouts.

The edge in her voice makes Laura think of the strip of metal on a pack of waxed paper.

"I need you up at the cottage, it's time to start lunch. Bring the baby with you."

Darka slowly folds her arms and legs together, and, her eyes still closed, starts pulling up the straps of her bathing suit. For some reason, this irritates Sonia more than the baby's chewing on the page from Darka's magazine.

"For God's sake, don't take all day, Darka, I'm not paying you to sunbathe!"

"You're not paying me, period," the girls hear Darka grumble as she stands up and kicks her feet into her flip-flops. The baby bats at her with the plastic shovel as Darka stoops to pick her up.

When Sonia reaches the path up to the cottage, she turns and calls to her daughters: "Laura, Katia, Bonnie—shake out your towels and come up with us. Right now! Do you hear me? No dawdling. Laura!"

Laura just sits with her fine hair flapping into her eyes, listening to the howls of Baby Alix. She is saying her mother's name over and over to herself, as if calling her Sonia rather than Mama will diminish her power, shrink what Laura calls the World of the Mothers, a world apt to swell up over their children and press down on them at the same time. A world of *Because I Said So,* and *I Told You So,* of *What Is It Now?* and *That's Just the Way It Is.* It's this last refrain that troubles Laura most: the law, verging on commandment, that life—everyone's life, from Chucha Marta's to Baby Alix's—is fixed in a pattern rigid as the wool of Baba Motria's *kylym,* the black rug woven by Baba Motria herself, a treasure, a monstrosity like the statue of the boy and girl beneath the umbrella. Recalling the stiff heaviness of the *kylym,* Laura thinks of how different men's lives are from women's. In men's lives there's some give to the weave, there are holes you can slip through and escape from, as Nastia's father did; as Uncle Peter tries so hard to do with his jokes and his playacting. Whereas women are stitched fast to their lives: stitched and slammed and stuck-together like the wool of the *kylym,* with its clumsy, shrimp-colored roses, its moldy-basement smell.

Bonnie is running over to their mother, telling her not to

worry, that they'll all be right up, so that Sonia can turn to leave, her dignity intact. The girls follow her up the hillside, Laura lagging behind on the worn logs that serve as steps. When she reaches the top, she pauses, reluctant to cross the lawn to the cottage. Clutching the edges of her towel around her neck, she whispers, "Thus stood the great Marc Antony at the Battle of Philippi, when he faced Brutus on the desert sands!" She lets the towel drop; she is dragging it behind her as she walks across the crabgrass to the kitchen door when, halfway there, she stops. From the patch of tall weeds beside the sleep-house comes a rustling sound. As if someone is crouched in the shadows, someone who means no good, like Cleopatra's brother. Suddenly, Laura forgets about Cleopatra; suddenly, she knows that something dangerous is hiding in the weeds. It's not something out of a story or a souvenir book but something real over which she has no power, even of words.

Darka's started yelling at her out the kitchen window, ordering her inside to eat lunch. Shaking, Laura turns her back on the weeds and runs up the stairs, slamming the screen door in that savage way her mother can't stand.

AFTER LUNCH, EVERYONE'S happy to stay inside: if you were to go outdoors, your skin would turn lobster-red and all the next day you'd have to lie in a darkened room, your back and shoulders puffing, then peeling, while your mother says I-told-you-so and pours on calamine lotion that stains the sheets a cloudy pink. After lunch, you stay shut up at the cottage, digesting your meal; you nap, if you're too small to do anything else, or leaf through comics and old magazines on your bed. By three o'clock it's safe to go swimming again; everyone goes back down to the beach, the same procession as in the morning but quieter, calmer. The mothers scold less and hardly shout at all: they've had time to drink coffee or tea, to visit each other, or just to lie down with cold cloths on their heads while their children sleep and stay out of trouble. Spreading their blankets back over the sand, the mothers know that the most demanding part of the day is done. Later, when they stare out their picture windows or from lookout points to the sun setting over the lake, they will remind themselves how it's been another perfect day, and how lucky they are to be at the cottage instead of the city. How much simpler it is to cook and clean when they haven't got their husbands around checking up on things, asking them how much they paid for the roast, expecting their dirty shirts to be washed, ironed, and put away as soon as they've been tossed in the direction of the laundry hamper.

All the women, except for Nettie Shkurka and Lesia Baziuk, who have no husbands to worry about in the first place. And Nadia Senchenko, whose husband pays a housekeeper to do the things, Zirka always says, that any self-respecting woman wants to do for herself: grocery shopping, cooking, cleaning. But if

Nadia Senchenko has missed performing any of these tasks, she doesn't seem to be grieving, up in her cottage away from all the others—not a cottage but a House-Beautiful, with no one but herself to rattle around in it the whole week long. What she can possibly find to do with herself all alone there, none of the women can guess; they spend hours and hours speculating on the subject, all except Sasha Plotsky, who is Nadia's friend, and Sonia Martyn, who won't say a word one way or another about Jack Senchenko's wife.

A fly settles on Sonia as she lies sleeping in the hammock on the screened-in porch. Its feet move delicately over her collarbones and up the slope of her throat. It sits back and rubs its front legs together, preening itself, and then continues on its way. In her sleep, Sonia moves her hand to her neck—by the time the fly reaches her lips, she's awake, wide-awake, and she shoos it, her hand flapping in disgust. Startled, she looks at her wristwatch: it's late, everyone else will be at Sasha's already. But what on earth was she dreaming about when the fly woke her? If she holds tight to the edges of the hammock, she'll be able to pin it down, this dream that's made her heart race and her head hurt. Dinner—she was late getting dinner, there were guests waiting, a man and a woman sitting at the table. The woman had no head and no arms: she was just a burlap torso, like a dressmaker's dummy. The man had a pencil mustache and looked like Walter Pidgeon; he was plucking at the table-cloth as if he expected to find dirt underneath.

"Mr. Streatfield," Sonia says out loud. "It was Mr. Streat-field." Suddenly she's remembering, with abrupt clarity, the day she told her boss she'd got herself engaged to Max Mar-tyn. Mr. Streatfield had taken her out to lunch, not at the diner on Bathurst Street where he usually went, but to a restaurant with linen cloths and a rose in a skinny vase at every table. And he'd tried to talk her out of it. "What do you need a hus-band for, Sunny? You can have everything you need if you stick with me—I'll even name the line after you: Sunny Sportswear, how's that? Think of it, a house in California, an apartment in Manhattan—all the clothes, all the flowers and dinners out, all the money you could ever want. You'll be in all the glossies—*American Vogue*, I guarantee it! Hell, you could even get into the movies!"

Sonia's fingers loosen their hold on the hammock. Bees hum drowsily in the plants on either side of the porch steps; a bird calls out, making the sound of a door creaking on its hinges. She's so grateful for this part of the day, when the children are out of her hair and nothing is expected of her. It's too hot to do any work—leaves hang in the air outside as though suspended in syrup. If she were to lift her head and look directly out the screen, she would see the remnants of her mother's vegetable garden. Every summer she'd come up and plant carrots and beets and lettuce for them; runner beans, garlic, dill, onions. So they wouldn't always be running to the store, and because she couldn't stand the sight of all this good earth going to waste.

The year they bought the cottage she'd got down on her hands and knees, sixty-eight years old and yanking up weeds with her bare hands. The weeds had turned out to be poison ivy. Thank God Al Vesiuk had been there—he'd given her something to take care of the blisters.

Sonia's eyes swim with tears: sleek, useless tears. The doctor's given her prescription after prescription that she never fills: sleeping pills, Valium. Sometimes she thinks that the only real thing in her life, the only real thing about her, is this ragged, unquenchable grief at her mother's death. She gets up from the hammock and goes out to sit on the steps of the porch, a lean, tanned woman in faded blue shorts and a striped tube top exposing the delicate wing bones of her back. *American Vogue*. The movies . . . She wipes her eyes, makes a little grimace, frowns. The porch steps are rotting—Max has been promising for the past two years to replace them.

If her father were alive . . . He'd been a fine carpenter in his spare time; she still had a little cupboard, a sort of treasure chest he'd made for her as a welcome gift when she'd come to Canada, this father she'd barely known, who'd left the Old Place when she'd been a baby. Who'd been rushed to a hospital a week after he'd met them at Union Station, having been injured by some brutal, overefficient machine at the foundry that employed him: no safety gear, no workers' compensation, nothing. He'd recovered, somehow—even found work again because of the war, making shell casings to blow up the *Fasheesty*.

And then, after the war had ended, and life had become slower and easier, and his children had married, and he'd held his first grandchild in his arms, a blood vessel had burst in his brain and he'd died twelve hours later. Never coming back to consciousness, unable even to tell them good-bye.

Sonia sits on the rotting steps and holds her head in her hands, weeping for her father, who'd widowed her mother far too young, and for the mother who'd died before her time. A *baba*—meaning "old woman, granny"—but to Sonia she was still that lonely young woman who'd read out letters from their father, letters all about the distant country where they, too, would go one day, once he'd made a home for them. A country so magical that no one used naphtha lamps and you could flood a room with light just by pushing a button! How could any of them have known how long it would take for them all to be together again, with the Depression starting even as he was crossing the ocean to that place that had sounded like the name of a kind of candy: *Kanáda*.

Sonia wraps her arms across her stomach, as if there were a huge stone there, or as if a huge stone had been dug out of her and she has to push back the emptiness with her bare hands. It's still only afternoon, and she can't pretend away the eight endless hours till the children will be asleep for the night and she can climb into her bed as if it were a ship sailing away. From eternally damp bathing suits sagging on the line like flags from a conquered country; from the endless heaps of sand that get transferred from floor to dustpan to ground and then work their way back inside so there's always grit under your shoes or eating away the enamel of the tub. If only you could do all the things that have to be done each day just once; if only you could marry your husband and have your children, and then climb onboard a ship bound for nothing but the sea. There you'd stand, waving to the people gathered on the dock, waving once, twice, then making your way to the other side of the enormous ship, the side facing nothing but sky and water. Where the line between them dissolves, somehow, so that you're not afraid of the water so far below you. Because there's nothing, anymore, to fear; everything's turned to sky, the wind blowing past you, blowing right through you, as the ship moves off into a blue that isn't emptiness or nothingness but everything you've ever longed for . . .

Suddenly, more clearly than she's ever known them, clear as in life, Sonia sees her father and her mother. Where the vegetable garden used to be, there's the boat, or part of it; they are standing on the varnished deck, their arms wound tight around one another, staring in her direction but not waving, not calling—not seeing her at all. Sonia can't help herself; she throws out her arms and calls to them, heedless of who might walk by and hear her, "Take me with you, don't leave me here alone—oh, take me with you!"

Her words sail into the air like the planes her children make from folds of scrap paper. The bees hum and the fly that had crawled over her neck and up to her lips rubs its thick body against the screen. Sonia rubs her knuckles into her eyes, the way a small child does to try to staunch its tears.

THERE'S A LOOSE piece in the latticework covering the foundations of the Plotskys' log cabin. Katia pushes open the wobbly wood as if it were a door and crawls inside. It is beautifully cool and there are no insects here except for the fat, white grubs, which, as Tania points out, don't do any harm to them or to the cracked tools and broken furniture shoved here for temporary storage and long forgotten. It's Tania's favorite hiding place, though she's careful not to use it too often. It's the best place to be when she wants to eavesdrop on her mother's company.

This afternoon it's the ladies from what Tania's heard her mother call the Lending Library, though it's not as though they come to the Plotskys' cottage every Friday afternoon to read books. What the women do is talk around them, all the forbidden, unimproving tomes they've raced or stumbled through, talk from and beyond them into their own lives, binding themselves together through the secret act of reading. What they feel, dipping into the pages of the books they share, is something very different from what happens when they read the *Ladies' Home Journal* or, for heaven's sake, the recipe and homemaking books they received as brides. It's the difference between going for an afternoon splash in your swimsuit and bathing cap—and stealing down to the lake in the dead of night for a skinny-dip.

The ladies feel glamorous, slightly wicked speaking English together instead of the Ukrainian they always use when-the-kids-are-not-supposed-to-understand: for most of them, English is a second language and they feel not so much at home in it as away. Away from their mothers and the examples set by those mothers—brave, hardworking women, all of them, but all too accepting of the sag of their skin and the folds ironed into their faces; of the flesh padding their hips and bellies, and the dumpy floral prints they wear almost as uniforms. In the Old Country, a woman was old at forty; none of the tea-drinkers at Kalyna Beach will confess to thirty-nine, except for prematurely gray-haired Annie Vesiuk, who's more often to be seen in a swimsuit than anything like a housedress.

In a word, Sasha and the other members of the Lending Library are ladies—something their mothers would never care or want to be. Being a lady, however, is not inconsistent with gossiping or listening to Sasha's bawdy jokes, a fact for which the girls hidden beneath them are extremely thankful. Sometimes the talk is as dull as a casserole recipe, though last week someone had mentioned a scene in a book where a woman was having a baby. That got Mrs. Vesiuk going. *"I was about to clean up the mess, scrape it into a bedpan and flush it away, when I saw there was something else there in all the blood, something alive. It was just a scrap, its heart hardly beating—hardly worth saving, we thought. But the doctor started working on it, and we managed to pull it through, though the damage, Bozhe miy!"* Mrs. Vesiuk had been a nurse before she got married. She had said right out loud, once, that Dr. Vesiuk had proposed to her on account of her big feet and wide hips: your pelvic floor, she'd said, and your shoe size are correlated, and as for big hips, everyone knows it makes having babies as easy as squeezing toothpaste from a tube. And then Mrs. Stechyshyn had talked about her Caesarean, which Katia had always thought was a kind of salad dressing until Tania told her how they take a knife and slit your belly, whisking out the baby still in its plastic bag.

Tania's brought her Barbies along, in case there's nothing useful to be overheard today. The Barbies are dressed in strapless satin evening gowns, with marabou trim. On their permanently arched feet are high-heeled pumps, the heels thinner than toothpicks. The girls have no interest in dressing up the Barbies; instead, they strip off the dolls' clothes, making faces at the smooth, bare plastic, the lack of hair and nipples that they know, thanks to the magazines at the smoke shop near their Ukrainian school, belong to any woman Barbie's age. Above them, the ladies are going on about mumps and scarlatina, so the girls decide to play Marie Antoinette, marching the Barbies to the guillotine (a pair of scissors lifted from Sonia's sewing basket). Katia holds the scissors open; just as she sends the blades crashing down to the imagined cheers of an equally imagined multitude, Tania snaps off Barbie's head. It's a delicate maneuver, for which perfect timing is essential; the girls have become marvels of precision. Sometimes the blond Barbie is Marie Antoinette and the brunette merely watches; other times, it's she who's marched off to the guillotine, while blond Barbie plays Madame Lafarge, kicking away the popped-off head with a diminutive foot still in a powder-blue mule.

Over their heads comes the noise of a door slamming and the chink of ice in glasses: Sasha's brought out the gin and tonic. Most of the ladies come not just to talk books, or brace themselves for their husbands' arrivals from the city, but also to catch a glimpse of Nadia Senchenko, about whom they're fiercely curious as well as jealous. They want to be able to tell their friends who are sweating out the summer in town how they have tea every Friday afternoon with the reclusive, the fastidious, the mysterious Nadia, wife of the only millionaire they are ever likely to know. Nadia, the Queen of the Rock of Gibraltar, as the kids have named the bluff on which the Senchenkos' cottage stands, after the insurance-company commercials on TV.

Tania pokes her friend's shoulder. There's been a drastic shift in the conversation: Katia's aunt Zirka is speaking in her permanently shocked, girlish voice. "Is it any wonder, making *that* movie? Going off for a weekend together, leaving his wife and her husband behind. *Of course* they shared a bed, Annie— *of course* they spent their nights together, stark-naked for all we know!"

"You think Liz Taylor wears baby dolls when she goes to bed with that stallion?" Halia Bozhyk laughs.

"You think they only go to bed together at night?" Sasha's voice, cool as the ice cubes she's splashing into the glasses.

"Darka does. Wears baby dolls, I mean."

Katia's ears prick—it's her mother who's said this, ignoring or diverting Sasha's question.

"I told her it was the wrong thing for the cottage," Sonia sighs, adjusting the dark glasses she wears to hide the redness of her eyes. "It gets cold at night. She said she didn't have anything else to wear, but I know for a fact that Olya packed her some good flannelette nighties to bring up here."

"Oh, Sunny, what does it matter what she sleeps in? Give the kid a break. As long as there's no one dipsy-doodling in the sack with her, you don't need to worry."

The girls hear, or imagine, a little intake of breath, half-guilty, half-glad. Sasha says all the things no one else would dare to.

"But she lied to me, and God knows what she did with the nighties her mother made her. Olya's not made of money, you know. And what does it tell you—a girl who'd lie about a thing like that?"

"Give it a rest, Sunny. She's not your daughter, and you've done your best. Sometimes you just have to let nature take its course. If Darka wants to wear baby dolls and freeze her buns off, let her. The worst she'll come down with is a cold. Especially if we do our bit—keeping our husbands' hands away from her, I mean."

This time the silence is like fat forming over gravy. Sonia clears her throat, and Nadia Senchenko asks Sasha if she has any limes.

"Just ReaLemon, sweetheart. Down here we're peasants, remember?"

Zirka Metelsky makes a clucking sound, which the other women ignore. They'd all be happier if Zirka didn't belong to the Lending Library, but Sasha insisted she be let in. A sharp one, Sasha, with a tongue like a razor, and yet she has a weakness for underdogs and pariahs; she always finds a place at the table for even the worst-behaved of guests. And Zirka, with her eyes the color of boiled gooseberries, her plump little body and flappy lips, always makes a show of being scandalized by Sasha's talk, the liberties she takes with Nadia Senchenko, who, as Zirka never ceases to remind the women, is her brother's wife. Never, in Zirka's conversation, do you hear "Jack and Nadia" or "Jack this, Jack that," but always "My brother Jack."

The ladies are sitting in a semicircle of folding chairs across from Sasha's chaise longue, safe, snug, the gin making a warm fizz inside their heads. Their children are asleep, locked up in their cottages; their husbands are still miles and miles away, dinner a cloud of smoke on the horizon. Even the whine of mosquitoes in their ears, the slaps they administer to themselves or one another with a *"Got 'im!"* or *"Almost got 'im!"* add to their relish in the one hour of their week that can be given the name of Leisure. There are six of them: Sonia, who's come late; Zirka, wearing one of her husband's shirts over her pedal-pushers, to keep the sun off her, though everyone knows it's to hide the weight she's put on over the winter; Annie, her hair cut short as a boy's; Halia and Stefka, whom Sasha calls, right to their faces, the Siamese twins, because they think as well as talk and dress exactly alike, and are both married to men in the "medical business"—a pharmacist and a maker of dentures. Last of all, Nadia, her dark hair pulled into a French roll, and her black-rimmed glasses making her look like Nana Mouskouri, of whom even Zirka's heard tell.

Of course there's Sasha, too—Sasha the magician, who brings all the women together and keeps them in line, she says, by which she means holding on to the same rope, the one that gets them through each day and every night, the belief that they are all of them friends, neighbors, even sisters, through thick and thin—even distant Nadia, even loud-mouthed Zirka. It may be a short, thick rope, and it may be made out of hemp instead of silk, but it's strong enough and it's tied in a circle, tied and knotted by Sasha Plotsky's hands. Sasha with her thick, brown, wavy hair that makes up for the pockmarks on her face, a con-stellation of scars from teenage acne. Remembering that gawky girl with a face full of fiery lumps, Sonia wonders how she ever turned into this arch-sophisticate, lying back in her chaise longue with her cigarettes, the gin she serves up instead of tea, her extravagant cheekbones and wide, red, wicked mouth. Sonia knows she ought to disapprove of Sasha, if only for the mess pouring out onto the veranda from inside the cabin: beach toys and hardcover books, their spines split open, cereal bowls with the toasted Os crusted inside them, bathing suits lying in soggy pools instead of hanging neatly on the line.

The community has never quite known what to make of Sasha. Partly because her father wasn't Ukrainian, or even Polish, but Russian, and thus the worst kind of enemy by Old Country standards. Partly because Sasha's mother had suffered from some kind of wasting disease, which left her in no condition to rein in her wild and reckless daughter. But mostly because of Sasha's father's politics. Viktor Shcherbatsky was a Red; he'd marched with Tim Buck in the worst days of the Depression, and he'd got his daughter singing "The Internationale," hoisting a red banner, and marching all the way down University Avenue one fine Labor Day during the war. The Catholic priest had called at the Metelskys' house that very evening, warning them to keep away from Viktor Shcherbatsky and his family. If the Metelskys didn't watch out, he warned, if they kept associating with such dangerous people, they'd be shipped back, once the war had ended, to toil on the collective farm that had gobbled up those narrow strips of land they'd left behind and never sold. Laryssa Metelsky had heard the priest out, she'd bid him good day, and she had kept on bringing pots of soup over to the Shcherbatskys, as Sasha's mother became weaker and weaker, at last taking to her bed, and from there to the dark, narrow plot she'd managed to save up for, in Prospect Cemetery.

Sonia lifts a tumbler of gin and ginger ale to her nostrils: just the smell of the liquor makes her giddy. *"Ta deh!"* she can hear her mother say. It was the only thing she'd said after the priest had left them with the stale bread of his warnings about the Shcherbatskys. *"Ta deh"* was her mother's favorite expression, a cross between "no way" and "so what?" and a charm against that embrace of disaster that had scarred her husband's life. Stefan Metelsky had never stopped brooding over the insults he'd faced as an immigrant who couldn't speak decent English, and he'd never lost his belief that the police would arrest him for speaking his mind, would beat him up for going out on strike. Perhaps he'd fallen in love with Laryssa because of her flagrant optimism, the way she never let herself worry past *peevneech*— midnight—the start of a new day. If only, Sonia thinks, she'd inherited her mother's unshakable confidence, instead of her father's gloom and suspicion. *"Ta deh,"* Sonia whispers. Hadn't her mother been right, after all? Neither Sasha nor her father had brought any grief to the Metelskys; even "The Internationale" had done Sasha no harm. True, when she'd run off at nineteen with Ivan Plotsky, everyone had agreed it would be the end of her. But look where Ivan's ended up: in advertising, of all things, where the money's even better than in law or dentistry!

Sasha has English friends in the city, women who do volunteer work for the museum and the art gallery, in which most of the ladies on the veranda have never set foot. It's as if these places were on far-off planets, the cool, thin air of which they could never hope to breathe. Sasha never goes to church; her kids have practically brought themselves up. Tania does much of the cooking now; Nick shovels out the house when things get too bad. Yet Sasha's children adore her. Sonia would never want to be as slapdash and careless as Sasha, and yet she'd never be able to bear Kalyna Beach without her. What if Ivan decides he's bored with the cottage—not a proper one at all, but a dark log cabin built some sixty years ago by a pair of lunatic spinsters who'd actually wintered-over in it? What if Ivan finally persuades Sasha they should sell the cabin and buy a farm instead, somewhere near Guelph or Newmarket? Where will the rest of them be? Minus dirty books and fast talk and Sasha's hoarse, smoky laugh. Her splash and verve, which, time and again, Sonia takes in dumbstruck, like a kid at her first circus.

The ladies are back to talking about *Cleopatra*. A cigarette in her wildly waving hand, Sasha holds forth:

"Rex Harrison's all right—and some of the actors in bit parts, you know, Hume Cronyn and Roddy McDowall and, oh yes, *oh my*, Cesare Danova—now *there's* a man! But Liz Taylor? Her idea of acting is to heave her boobs up and down."

"No." Silence follows on the heels of this one word, for it has been spoken by Nadia Senchenko—Nadia, who almost never speaks at Sasha's tea parties, Nadia with her clear-as-crystal English from England.

"I disagree," Nadia continues. "I think Taylor is convincing, in the first half, at least—a woman who knows exactly what she wants and means to have it. She's in love, of course, but she also wants power, she's capable of wanting power not just over a kingdom but over her own life—"

"On your knees!" Sasha's mimicry is perfect, if a bit abrupt: it's as if she's trying to shut Nadia up rather than encourage her. "Don't we just wish we could tell our husbands that—and make them obey?"

"What about Burton?" Zirka pipes up. "What do you think about him, Nadia, about Dick and Sybil?" It's as though she's been waiting for a chance to spotlight her brother's wife, to fix her, center stage.

Nadia does look a little like she's on a film set, with her capri pants and silk shirt, and her hair twisted up on top of her head. She speaks as though Zirka's question is a fly to be brushed away. "I think I prefer Shaw's version of the story—and Shake-speare's, too, of course."

The names Shaw and Shakespeare blow a chill among the women. Theater for them is what happens in the church base-ment on Mother's Day and Shevchenko's birthday: poetry reci-tations, a little folk dancing, speeches. Except for Sasha and Nadia, of course, though Sasha's never been to London, En-gland, like Nadia. Ivan has taken her to New York and even to Los Angeles on business trips. Sonia's been to New York, but that was as a runway model—they'd worked her so hard she hadn't wanted to do anything but throw herself into bed at night, having pushed a chest of drawers against the door of her hotel room, as she'd promised her mother she'd do.

No one feels comfortable around Nadia except for Sasha. This is curious, considering that Nadia's father was a professor of religious studies, and Sasha's a communist. It's not that Sasha's always running off to Nadia's—Sasha doesn't go anywhere much except down to the beach and back up to the cabin, trailing the smoke of her Export As, her face buried in whatever book she's devouring at the moment. Nadia's famous for being a loner and a night owl: they say she stays up till three or four in the morning, and sleeps in till lunchtime. All kinds of impossible rumors float in Nadia's wake: that she walks around her house in the nude, that she lives off smoked oysters and sparkling wine, that she's writing a book, though no one can swallow this last one. But still, where Sasha's merely outrageous, Nadia's mysterious: not romantic mysterious but opaque, frightening. She isn't pretty at all, but there's something about her that makes you want to look at her again and again, hoping she won't look back. She used to draw a little, paint a little, before she got married, the Ladies seem to remember. And now she's enrolled for a degree at the University of Toronto, where her son's just started engineering. She's supposed to be studying for her courses while she's up here—there are reports of textbooks lying all over her cottage: books on the history of art, of all things, and expensive reproductions of work by the Old Masters. It makes Sonia nervous.

Nadia could tell you exactly what and who an Old Master was, without blinking an eye; Sonia, on the other hand, never had a chance to get past grade six, in either her old or her new country. Once Katia had caught her writing *waistpaper basket* on a shopping list and looked at her as if she were a beggar. Clever, pretty Katia, who'd rather spend her time in Sasha's sloppy home than helping her own mother; Katia, who worships her father and declares she wants to be a lawyer when she grows up, or even a judge.

"—better than *The Robe*," Stefka's saying. "He was in that, too, with Jean Simmons, remember?"

"I liked him best in *The Rains of Ranchipur*," Halia sighs. "With Lana Turner. They put some kind of brown dye on his skin—he plays an Indian prince, and it's so sad when—"

"He's a weakling," Zirka blurts out. "He's let that Taylor woman make a spectacle out of him. The way she flaunts herself—"

"We're supposed to be seen and not heard?" Sasha hits back, doling out the remains of the gin, a teaspoon each, into the ladies' glasses.

Annie Vesiuk wades in now. "But, Zirka, she's a movie star! It's her job to make things spectacular." It's just like Annie to want to smooth things over. Annie's the perfect sport, a blue-ribbon mother. She doesn't have a jealous bone in her body, Annie, though her husband must see a hundred nurses every day, and you know what men are like, even the best of them.

Annie who wears no makeup and makes no effort to hide the varicose veins snaking up her calves and thighs—such muscular legs, Sonia thinks, pitying her a little, but envious, too, of how strong Annie is, how tireless, cooking, cleaning, wiping noses, rinsing out endless diapers and bathing suits, never complaining. Eight boys, as well as a mother-in-law in permanent residence. *You and Annie should trade recipes.*

"Any woman," Zirka continues, her hands on her hips, her round face reflected in Nadia Senchenko's dark glasses, "any woman who could walk out on her husband, the father of her children, in order to chase after another woman's husband, is plain indecent. Even the pope's condemned her—'a woman of loose morals,' that's what he's called her. Don't take my word for it, read it for yourselves in the *Catholic Times*!"

"I can understand being married twice," Sonia ventures, "if you've been widowed. But four husbands, and now five, if he gets his divorce?"

"One died—don't forget that," Stefka volunteers. "Mike Todd, he was something in the movies, not an actor, a producer. It was tragic—he was the love of her life."

"Of course he was," Sasha jumps in. "He gave her a ninety-thousand-dollar diamond bracelet as a wedding present."

"I can't remember husband number one—he was somebody's son, somebody wealthy, maybe in real estate." This from Stefka, catching the ball from Sasha: instinctively, the women are trying to keep Zirka from getting back on her high horse.

"And then Mike Todd," Halia adds. "He died in a plane crash."

"No, no, Michael *Wilding*—the *Anhleeyetz*—the *gentleman*. She made mincemeat out of him all right." Sasha grins.

"And *then* Mike Todd, and after that Eddie Fisher. But she didn't have any children by Eddie Fisher." Stefka speaks with surprising authority. "There was that article in *Life*—do you remember the pictures of her little boys and the girl, asking who their daddy's going to be this time?"

"She can't have any more kids, did you know that?" Annie says sadly, as someone says "Shh," and there's a pause, during which Annie blushes, remembering that Zirka, too, has had her problems making babies.

Zirka dashes into the breach. "Eddie Fisher has kids of his own—and a wife in a million. Debbie Reynolds—she can out-act Elizabeth Taylor any day of the week!"

"Neither of them is exactly Sarah Bernhardt," Sasha observes.

"Debbie Reynolds is a *lady*," Zirka trumpets. "Taylor's nothing but a you-know-what!" And then, taking a step toward Nadia, sitting so straight in her chair, addressing her words to no one but Nadia, she pounces: "Any woman—any *decent* woman would be satisfied with one husband, especially if he'd given her children and enough money to get by on. More than enough. So what is she after? I'll tell you: she's only after—"

The ladies aren't listening to Zirka anymore. They are too

busy watching Nadia as she rises calmly from her chair and goes to lean against the railing, turning her back to them all.

"Sex!" Zirka cries, so shrilly that the girls under the veranda bite their lips, trying not to give themselves away in their delight. "It's nothing but sex. It's dirty and selfish and disgusting." And now, with Nadia turning her back on her, Zirka trains her volleys on her hostess. "Just like those books of yours, Sasha Plotsky—you ought to be ashamed of yourself, passing them around. What if the children get their hands on them?"

Sonia's face goes red as a bowl of borshch. Half of the things in those books make her squirm, and the other half go straight over her head. *Death by Desire*. She'd promised Annie she'd pass it on to her today. She can't imagine Annie reading dirty books—surely she doesn't need to, having been a nurse.

Sasha starts piling glasses on a scratched aluminum tray. "I don't notice *you* saying no to all those disgusting books, Zirka."

"You want me to bury my head in the sand? You want it so that I don't know what's going on under my very nose?"

"Shh, Zirka, it's crazy to make such a fuss, and over what? A movie star, a woman none of us even know!" Annie has stretched out her hand, is pressing Zirka's plump little knee.

Zirka shakes her off. And then, without taking another step, she crosses the line the ladies have drawn so carefully around their reading and gossip and the lives they lead from day to day in the confines of Kalyna Beach. "Ask Nadia," Zirka shrieks.

"Ask Nadia what she thinks about women who, who lust after other people's husbands!"

The ladies look down at their feet in their flip-flops and frayed sneakers. Zirka's last words, Sasha thinks, are like a line from *The Valley of the Dolls*. She's exaggerating, as she always does. Except that this time something in Zirka's sheer pigheadedness, her very use of those words—*flaunt* and *lust*—pulls Sasha up short. That party on this very veranda, last Saturday night . . . Everyone had been having a wonderful time, lots of laughing and teasing and more than a little tippling, when suddenly there'd been a noise like a gunshot: the unmistakable sound of a hand smacking a face. And there was Peter Metelsky, looking as startled as anyone; he'd been kneeling before Nadia Senchenko, his hand over his heart, his eyes staring down at his shoes. He'd been reciting something from *Cleopatra*, he'd been pretending he was Marc Antony, awestruck before Egypt's beauteous queen or some such nonsense. And then the slap, and Peter going through the motions of a rejected suitor, his forearm to his brow, his head all hangdog. Everyone had laughed, especially Jack, who'd slapped Peter on the back and told Nadia he'd never known she was of royal blood. The whole veranda had laughed, and shrugged, and relaxed again.

At the time, Sasha had thought it was nothing to worry about—it was only Peter, a little drunk as usual, hamming it up for old times' sake. And Nadia, bored with his attentions, maybe a little under the weather, or the least bit sozzled, had let him have it. Of course she'd felt ridiculed: Nadia was no Cleopatra, and she's hardly a look-alike for Elizabeth Taylor with her violet eyes and double row of eyelashes, and a bosom large and quivery as angel food cake. But what if something else was at play, Sasha starts to thinks, something complicated, like in a book. Sure, everything had seemed to settle down, no one had bothered to talk or fuss about it until now, but why was Zirka so determined to make a scene, bang her shoe on the table like Khrushchev, force a response of some kind from her brother's guiltless wife?

Nadia is still leaning out over the railing, staring at the lake. Slowly, she turns around so that she's facing them all. She takes off her glasses, and her dark, myopic eyes blink helplessly, unable to focus on any one of the faces before her.

"I was thinking," she says at last, "about our Labor Day party, our *zabava*. You'll all be coming, won't you?"

It is, of course, the perfect response—the only possible reply. And the ladies, who are staring at Nadia as though she were some master diplomat brokering a peace treaty among half a dozen warring states, fall into line. Of course, they tell her. Of course they're coming to Nadia's and Jack's *zabava*. Even Zirka nods, biting her lips as if she enjoyed the taste. Who could possibly miss a party—*the* party—at the Senchenkos' cottage? Nadia slips her glasses back on again and leaves her half-full tumbler on the tray before nodding good-bye to Sasha and the rest of them, and walking down to the shore.

The ladies watch her graceful progress until she's vanished from their sight. Sasha gets up from her chaise longue and throws her cigarette over the railing. From their vantage point under the latticework, Katia and Tania watch it burn down into the sand.

"Ladies," Sasha says in her throaty voice, "the gin's all gone and our husbands will be home before we know it. If anyone's got some books to swap, now's the time to do it. I've just finished *Wuthering Heights—again!*—I'm still waiting for someone to slip something else my way, something I haven't read a hundred times already."

"*Wuthering Heights?* Come on, Sasha, that's a *movie*. Merle Oberon and Laurence Olivier," Zirka blurts out, eager to show off.

Sasha looks at her almost kindly and gives a small shrug. "My mistake. But look, ladies, I haven't got a clue whether my kids are still playing Crazy Eights inside, or whether they've gone off and got themselves drowned, so—"

Halia and Stefka, Annie and Sonia, pertly smiling Zirka— they all unpeel themselves from their chairs, rising a little unsteadily. One by one they take their leave, Sonia last, about to hide the fact that she's still got a glass full of watery gin by spilling it into the bushes off the veranda. Before she can do so, Sasha's taken the incriminating object from her hands, and Sonia feels more than ever like the youngest in the group, the one who isn't fully clued in, the tagalong.

"Stay for a minute, will you, Sonechko?" It's not a request, nor yet an order, but a plea.

"I can't, Sasha, I've got to get the kids to the beach."

"It's important. We need to talk. Inside."

When the veranda stops shuddering over their heads, its planks holding nothing but the shadows of empty chairs, Katia and Tania creep out from underneath, their legs stiff as dresses ironed till they scorch.

"What do you think is going on?" Tania whispers. "Do you suppose old Maximoynko told on us?"

"So what if she did? We didn't steal anything from her stupid old store—not this time, at least."

Tania doesn't answer. She's thought of something else, now, some other trouble they could be blamed for. Billy Baziuk on the porch steps, playing with himself. She looks up at Katia, who's been thinking the same thing.

"It's not about him," Katia says. "Nobody saw that but us."

"How do you know? Maybe his mother did—she'll say it's our fault. And our mothers will think we're just as bad as he is, they always do."

The girls stare at one another and shrug. Then they spit into the palms of their right hands and clap those hands together, folding and interlacing their fingers. It's their ritual of friendship—more than friendship or even sisterhood. It's their sign that they'll remain loyal to each other *till death do us part*. Carefully, they make their separate ways home. Down in the dark beneath the porch, the Barbies are stuck like scissors in the earth, and the scissors lie forgotten, blades pressed primly together, trying to gleam.

THE COTTAGE IS as quiet as if Martians had landed and carried everyone away. Sonia's off at the Plotskys'; Bonnie and Alix are fast asleep; Darka's slumped on the sofa with a *Hollywood Romance* slipping out from a *Life* magazine. But she's not reading, and she's certainly not looking at the bright blue spill of lake through the picture window put in with such care and at such expense the year before. Perhaps she's asleep—yes, Laura decides, Darka's dozing, which is far better than she'd hoped for. As for Katia, who cares where she's off to as long as she's not here?

In her parents' room, on the makeshift vanity table with its faded cotton skirts and rough, plywood top, lies Sonia's paltry array of makeup. Three tubes of lipstick standing like soldiers in their shiny golden tubes: Pretty Pink, Koral Kiss, Ice Peach. A round container of face powder: *Madame DuBarry* under the picture of a lady with a pale satin dress and gray hair puffy as a mushroom. Inside, the powder puff smells the slightest bit sour, as if it should be left in the sun instead of shut up in a box, in the pale, pink dark. When Laura puts back the lid, a rim of powder sighs onto the table: she picks it up on her fingertips, rubbing it along her nose to make it look longer, finer, as the magazines advise. Her mother doesn't wear eye makeup—she says it's cheapening, and besides, her eyelashes are naturally dark and thick. No fingernail polish, either. Sonia's father had made her promise she would never paint her nails; it's one of the stories each of her daughters but the youngest knows by heart, and Alix will learn it soon enough. How, the morning that Dyeedo Metelsky noticed on the tips of his daughter's hands ten blood-red ovals, he'd brought over a basin of scalding, soapy water, demanding she wash that poison off *immediately* and never even think of painting herself again!

Laura frowns, wishing there was something here she could use to transform herself, something scarlet or gold or inky-black. She can't bring herself to put Sonia's lipstick on her mouth; it would be too much like having to kiss her mother in company, showing what an obedient, affectionate child she is. Even if there were any eye makeup she could put on, it would all be hidden by her glasses, and if she were to take off her glasses, she wouldn't be able to see what she looked like in the mirror. Why is she the only one of them all to be nearsighted? Baba Laryssa wore glasses, but that doesn't help: Sonia always looks at her daughter's eyes as if Laura had ruined them just to spite her. Why couldn't Katia have been the one needing to sit closer and closer to the television screen and to the blackboard at school?

Baba Laryssa's glasses had had small, thick, rimless lenses:

when she took them off, her eyes looked naked and so raw they made Laura think of an onion cut in half. When she'd first seen Laura in glasses, Baba had told her to take them off as much as she could, so her eyes wouldn't get lazy. But once the lenses had slid over her eyes and the world jumped into sharp, stinging focus, Laura could never be without them. She'd even tried to wear her glasses to sleep, in case there was a fire in the middle of the night and she needed to see to escape the flames. Now her eyes are so weak she can see next to nothing without her glasses, only blots by day and blurred circles of light by night. Her mother has perfect vision, and her father has eagle eyes— that's how he made it through the war, he says: he could see the snipers before they fixed their sights on him.

A fly bumbles against the screen, trying to get out through holes far too small; it's too stupid to notice the rip farther up, through which it flew in. Too stupid, or else its eyes are bad, like Laura's. She turns away from the mirror, running her hand over the curved iron footboard of the double bed. How can it be so cool against her palm when this room is so hot, the air so thick and stuffy? She tries to imagine her father lying sleeping here tonight, his body like the prince disguised as a bear in "Snow White and Rose Red." Once she'd come into her parents' room when she wasn't supposed to; had seen her father coming out of the bath, a tall, heavy body with pads of dark fur all over it. She couldn't imagine how her mother could fall asleep beside a man who looked like a bear. Brown hair on the backs of his hands and springing out of his open shirt; dark brown eyebrows and hair so thick on his head, he'd joke about taking the lawn mower to it. Not bald like Mr. Plotsky, who is always mopping his shiny scalp with a pocket handkerchief, but thick, dark hair combed straight back from his forehead.

When she was younger, Laura believed that her father unzipped his skin every night; that he stepped out of his pelt the way he'd step out of his car coat after shoveling snow. She believed that her mother had some special gown she wore at night, stiff as armor, thin as silk, to keep her from being eaten up by the bear. Laura was very, very stupid once; she knows that now. Sliding open the closet door, not to touch anything, only to look, she drinks in the good, dry smell of the lavender talc her father always buys her mother for Christmas. It's concentrated, this scent, in the clothes left hanging so sadly on their hangers, as if their only joy lay in hugging Sonia's skin. The closet, unlike the vanity table, is packed full: shorts, skirts, pedal-pushers, and blouses all in bright, cool colors, a garden of flowers hung by their metal stems. Without thinking, Laura pushes farther and farther into the deep, narrow closet, feeling the texture of the cloth: satiny, or nubbly, or gauzy. Until she comes to the very end, to something that feels like nothing else under her fingers. She pulls at it, tugging it past the other clothes till at last she holds it up to her eyes, a long shimmer of gold. The dress Cleopatra wore on her triumphal entry into Rome, bringing her son Caesarion to be crowned.

Gingerly, Laura holds up the dress, her legs in their customary knock-kneed lock. In the full-length mirror on the back of the bedroom door she confronts her body. It's an entirely different shape from her mother's. It's more, she knows, like a tub of lard than an hourglass, and the collarbones which, on Sonia, project like a pair of budding wings are swallowed up by fat— puppy fat, Laura's heard her mother call it. So—a dog in a tub of lard, that's what she looks like, but somehow it doesn't matter with this dress. There's no waist to it; the material expands to cover her, seems to melt the thickness of her stomach and thighs. If she were to put it on, she would become Cleopatra: everything about her would change, would turn clear and sharp, the way the world had done when she'd first put on her glasses. Outside, a squirrel starts chittering as she pulls the dress over her head, not even bothering to tug off her shorts and her top, fighting down the panic she always feels when she's getting dressed, as if the cloth is out to smother her.

It looks all wrong; it looks ridiculous. Because of the bra sewn into the material, foam cups like pointy balloons: if you press them, they collapse like those cakes at the store, the ones Katia and Tania spoil by pushing down the maraschino cherries. If she could take out the foam cups, it would fit, it would have to fit; it would be perfect. She tugs the dress back over her head, trying not to choke when the cloth sticks; she grabs the scissors from her mother's sewing basket under the vanity—the big, clumsy ones, since the smaller set are missing—and presses a steel tip against the tight, white stitching binding the foam to the gold lamé.

ONCE ALL THE other ladies have gone, and they are on their own inside the Plotskys' low-ceilinged log cabin, Sonia attempts to deflect the urgency of Sasha's summons. She preempts her with a question: Does Sasha think it's normal, this obsession their daughters have with their bodies? For Tania and Katia are always going on about breasts and bras, right in front of everyone.

"Of course it's harmless," Sasha sighs, lighting another cigarette, shaking the match out and exhaling in that actressy way of hers. "If they were boys they'd be comparing the size of their wienies, and seeing who could pee the farthest. I'd much rather have them discussing how big their boobs are going to be than worrying that they don't have a penis, wouldn't you?"

Sonia makes no reply—she's remembering the sight of Darka in a halter top: at sixteen, the girl has bigger breasts than Sonia's were when she was breast-feeding. And then she blushes, thinking of how, with all her movie magazines, sixteen-year-old Darka must know more about sex than *she* had known on her wedding day. *Men are like that. Like what? You'll find out.*

"Look," Sasha declares, "that's the least of our worries." She puts her cigarette down in one of the asbestos ashtrays Nick or Tania have made in arts and crafts at school.

Sonia watches the cigarette burn itself down: she disapproves of smoking, and she thinks it extravagant, letting all that good tobacco go to waste. Sasha laughs, and Sonia blushes: she's convinced Sasha can read her thoughts. Sasha the Gypsy, the one who knows everything about them all.

"You saw that performance Zirka just put on," Sasha begins. "Why was she on the attack like that—in public, in front of the whole damn Lending Library, for Christ's sake? She's had a whole week to ask Nadia what was going on between her and Peter—or vice versa. If there was anything going on, that is, other than Peter being even more of an idiot than he always is."

"Don't, Sasha. You don't know him, you don't under-stand—"

"All I understand is that Zirka's on to something that you and I have been too dumb or too lazy to notice. She may not be a rocket scientist, but she's nobody's fool. She's nosed something out between Nadia and Peter and she wants us to know about it—wants Nadia to know that we know. She's made that clear enough."

"He got a little drunk, that's all," Sonia says. "He got a little drunk last weekend, and he started acting, the way he always does. For God's sake, Sasha, it's been twenty years—"

"Eighteen, by my reckoning. But forget Peter for a moment. Let's focus on Nadia. For her to have acted out of character, to have shown her feelings like that—she might as well have blown a trumpet or shouted from the rooftops, as slap Peter's face."

"Doesn't that just go to show it was all a joke, just like Peter's ham-acting?"

Sasha puts her hands to her head. "I wish I could believe

that, Sonechko. I wish I had the least goddamn clue as to what is going on here. Nadia hasn't been herself all summer—since before the summer. She's always been so remote, so perfectly controlled. And Peter—if he'd just been drunk and full of himself, he would have thrown himself at me, or Annie, or even Zirka. But he went after Nadia. He went out of his way to make a fool of himself and a spectacle of Jack Senchenko's wife."

"You're starting to sound like Zirka," Sonia says.

"Don't I know it," Sasha moans. "But listen, Sonechko, you've got to help me with this: it's important."

Sonia nods, and Sasha speaks, but her words drift about Sonia's head like the furred parachutes of dandelion seeds. Sasha has given her a headache with her cigarettes and suggestions. The only way to keep her balance is to think of something else, which she manages to do, though it doesn't keep her head from hurting. A picture of the broken statue flashes into her mind, or, rather, the moment of the statue's breaking, the moment it started to fall from its place on the mantelpiece, the lines along which it would smash already shivering. And then, on its heels, comes an image of Baba Motria's *kylym*, woven back in the Old Country and transported, at such cost and trouble and for such small purpose, to the new. Sonia has always hated that *kylym*. Max's mother had given it to her just before she died, expecting it to be hung in the place of honor on the living-room wall. Instead, Sonia had laid it down in the rec room, where the children had worn holes in it, driving their tricycles over it. Max has never said a word about the banishment of the *kylym*: he, too, dislikes it. There is something so constricted about the weave, so dismal about the black background and the pink and orange roses—for all the world like two-day-old funeral flowers.

Sonia is holding the two things in her head: the shattered plaster statue, so frivolous in its fragility, and the rugged, worn *kylym*, shelved in the basement. It will outlive them all, she thinks, its weave as strong as her memory of the river in the Old Place, the urgency of its current.

"Do you get it now, Sonia? Do you understand why this is so important, and why you've got to talk to Peter?" Sasha is pleading once again, this time almost angrily.

Sonia nods her head, yes, wanting to placate Sasha. "I really have to go," she cries, seizing the latch of the door, rushing outside.

Once down the veranda steps and back on Tunnel Road, she stops to catch her breath. Doesn't Sasha understand that their only safety lies in keeping silence? Words are dangerous—speaking makes things happen, frightening, unpredictable things. As soon as she says a word to her brother, he'll be off, running—and where? To kidnap his brother-in-law's wife, that brother-in-law who has fished him out of one whirlpool after another. And if Peter goes and makes a fool of himself again in front of Nadia, what will Nadia do but twitch her lips into that frozen smile of hers, turn her back on him, and walk away? Nadia cares no more for Peter than she does for her own husband: she is all ice and stainless steel. Didn't she show that to Peter and to anyone who cared to see, all those years ago?

Peter, she thinks, with the shiver she always gives when she lets her thoughts rest on her brother. A small shiver of muddled love and guilt.

DARKA'S CURLERS ARE the hard kind, filled with stiff bristles and fastened with plastic pins like bayonets, for all they're such a pallid pink. She'd wanted foam rubber; it was too expensive, her mother said, but that wasn't the real reason—Darka holds out her hand, scrutinizing fingernails naked as earthworms— the real reason was that her mother had wanted to punish her. *Wait till you have a daughter and she goes wild and breaks your heart, after all you've dreamed for her, done for her.*

What's the point? Who is here to look at her fingernails except Sonia, who'd have a fit if Darka were to paint them up? She might as well have shaved her head as bleached her hair—who is there to care? Dead and buried, that's what she is; she might as well throw herself into the lake, walk out into the water with a ball and chain around her leg. At home they'll all be going to the Hot Spot for Cherry Cokes and cheeseburgers tonight: if she were home, Jamie would pick her up in his red convertible, his black-and-white dog in the back seat, the radio blasting. They'd drive all over town and she wouldn't get home till after one. She'd have to sneak into her room by climbing the fence and then jumping up into the Manitoba maple right outside her window. All the next day her mother would walk around with swollen eyeballs, showing off how she's been sobbing her heart out over her wayward daughter. Olya doesn't need to worry, make herself sick over nothing; if she had half a brain she'd know that. But how can Darka tell her? There's no language between them anymore, no shared hopes or plans, however much Darka wants to escape from the kind of life her mother's led, and however much Olya dreams of a future for her daughter, a life not dissimilar, in fact, to Sonia Martyn's.

Darka drums with her fists on her thighs, then pushes her palms over the cloth of her shorts, fingers outspread like powerboats, idling. She thinks of the city, how good she feels with the hardness of pavement under her feet and a thousand shop windows to pore over when she skips a day off school and walks around downtown for hours on end. She is thinking of the attention she gets, not just wolf whistles but looks of interest, admiration from men in costly suits and well-cut sports jackets. All of a sudden, Darka smiles; her pretty face burns with something like beauty. All because of this feeling she has, more than a hunch, a glow that starts in her toes and spreads itself through her whole body. Sometimes she feels it give off this golden hum as she's walking down the street or into a room, or when she just sits, as she's doing now, waiting. The golden hum tells her she is somebody special, that no harm can ever come to her, that wonderful things are about to happen. She won't end up in a dump on Bathurst, like her mother; she's headed for far-off places, she'll wear orchids and a snakeskin dress; men will leap to light her cigarette in its ebony holder. Lean, handsome men always at her elbow, lighters clicking, her face reflected in their eyes, in the satin trim of their dinner jackets.

Nonsense, her mother calls it, dime-novel romance, nothing but daydreaming. Sonia's word for it is *loafing*; she's always on at her for loafing on her bed with her movie magazines. Loafing! When all she wants, Darka assures herself, is to work: real work for real pay. She could have got that job at the Hot Spot; she could have made big money this summer instead of the pennies Sonia's doling out, not to her but to Olya to spend on school supplies and a new uniform for Darka's last year at Saint Demetrius. Why didn't they just slap her in reform school instead? Good as jail here—nothing to do except slave over a washtub or a sink and run after the kids, rude, mouthy, even the baby a handful. Alix hardly ever sleeps for more than an hour in the afternoon, and it spooks her sometimes, the kid never talking, never making a sound, hardly even laughing or crying—and they think *she's* dumb just because she failed her year!

When Darka had bleached her hair, Sonia lit into her as if she'd robbed a bank. *Beauty's only skin-deep; men look for more than glamour in a woman; sex isn't everything; you want to be looking out for a respectable man, the steady kind that talks marriage.* Well, she's not even thinking about getting married yet; she has a life—doesn't anyone here understand that? She'd rather die than marry a lawyer or accountant and be buried with a pack of kids at a cottage for eight weeks every summer. They think they're so smart with their advice, and their frowns, and the click-cluck of their tongues. They think they know everything, and they haven't a clue. She'll show them, won't she just? But how—marooned as she is among mothers and children? She could have been spending the summer with Jamie Ashford. She says his name aloud, loving the Englishness of it, the soft cadence of the normal-sounding name. He knows her as Darlene. She's never told him her last name: she's never had to. All he has to do is look at her and she can feel his eyes turn into the warm palms of his hands, sliding over her shoulders, down to her breasts.

Darka sinks back against the sofa, as deep as the curlers will allow. Closing her eyes, she puts both hands to her face, the bones of her cheeks and jaw, the roundness of her throat. She holds her breasts, stroking with her thumbs through the thin cotton, as if they were her only friends in all the world, the only ones who understand her and love her no matter what she does. *All golden, orchids,* his lighter so close that if she were to stick out her tongue instead of the cigarette, she would catch fire, burn, burn up altogether.

A CANDY ON the pillow beside her: a red candy, smaller than the nail on her baby finger. Alix touches it so gently she can hardly tell if it's smooth or sticky. Candy hearts her sisters give her— *stick out your tongue*—laying them on the very tip. She has to flick them into her mouth so they don't drop in the dirt. *Never, ever eat things that fall on the floor: they're poison.*

Poi-son. *Ot-ru-ta.* Heart. *Ser-tseh.* Red. *Cher-vo-na.* Alix watches the words fly in pairs, English and Ukrainian, across the sky inside her head. Where her mouth is, there's a window, *dangerous*; the birds think they can fly through it; they throw themselves so hard against the glass they break their wings and have to limp back to their roosting place. Pulling their heads in small, so small that no one can find them.

On her pillow a candy, like a cinnamon heart, the kind that burns on your tongue. A candy, but no sugar smell like the one her mother sprays on her neck; she pushes the pump, a cloud comes out and makes a smell like candy. This one has black spots so small she has to blink to see them, pushing with her finger. It stops being a candy: hairs shoot out its sides, black hairs like the ones around your eyes. Alix watches the red spot push itself up her finger, tickling her skin. Lets it crawl up one finger to the finger on her other hand, climbing up and over, like on the monkey bars at the school when they're waiting for Bonnie. Up to her arm, meeting the fence her finger makes, and down again, and up and down. Till she holds it to her mouth and blows gently. Two small, dark scarves shoot out from the red, a buzzing sound, and it's gone, her finger bare now, nothing.

If she knew its name, she could call it back. When her mother wants them, she calls and they have to come; even if they run away, their names catch up with them. Names can't catch you till you say them out loud; you must never, never let them go; you must keep them safe inside, heads tucked tight, blind, under their wings. But that small, red crawling thing—not a fly, flies buzz—she wants it back, she wants to keep it. Pushing down off the bed, her feet meeting the sand on the floor. Little lines up and down all over the windows, little squares where the flies crawl, they get trapped inside; Katia squishes them with her bare fingers. *Katia, that's dis-gus-ting.* Not *fly,* not *mukha,* that's not its name. When she finds it, she'll hold out her finger, whisper it back to her hand, carry her hand to her mouth, and the thing will step with its small, small feet onto her tongue; she'll close her mouth and keep it forever, flying inside her.

Darka and Laura hear it at the same time, through different walls: a crashing sound from the baby's room, smack of wood against wood. Darka jumps up from the sofa and runs to where Baby Alix has fallen from the chair she's dragged to the window. Darka holds her and lets her wail, a gush of sound you could almost mistake for words; maybe it's the way she speaks, thinks Darka, singing to her, taking the baby's hands and clapping them together: *toshi, toshi toshi, svynya v horoshi.* Till the child forgets what she's crying for, listening to the nursery rhyme, watching the face of the grown-up girl, the girl who talks and talks and talks, words flying out from her mouth, disappearing forever.

Laura stays frozen in her mother's room, sitting on the floor, her back against the bed, the scissors gleaming in her lap. At the sound of Alix screaming, the scissors forgot the small nick they were taking out of the tight, white stitch; they jabbed into the cloth, fine and slippery as her hair but golden, shining. Now there's a hole she can never patch up. Alix keeps wailing, sounds flooding out of the mouth that makes Laura think of the mail slot in the front door at home, not a mouth at all, not something that belongs to Alix's body, but something hard and metallic stamped down on her. Darka's heavy footsteps, the door to Alix's room banging shut, and then Darka singing nonsense rhymes, making baby-talk against the baby's silence, now that the shock is over.

So it wasn't Sonia coming home, the crash she's heard, but what does it matter? As soon as she does come home, she'll know. If Sonia went crazy about the breaking of a useless statue, then she will kill Laura over the dress, just for taking it off its hanger. Laura grips the scissors in her sweaty hands; now that she's started she's got to finish; maybe her mother won't notice the foam cups are gone, maybe she'll think it looks better this way. Laura stabs the blade into the tight, white stitches, breaking them one by one, breaking their little necks. Until at last the foam falls into her lap, and the dress stops being a dress, is just a pool of something bright, a loose skin that can hardly cling to its hanger as she shoves it to the back of the closet.

Now the screen door slams; now her mother's really back from Sasha's tea party, calling to them all to get ready to go back to the beach. Laura manages to steal out before anyone sees that she's been in her mother's room. And all the while, in the dark press of the closet, her mother's dress runs its hands up and down itself, learning the holes slashed into its skin.

"Didn't you hear her?" Darka shouts from the kitchen, as Laura runs out the door and across the lawn, disappearing behind the sleep-house, where she stoops and pushes a bundle of hacked sponge-rubber and short, ripped threads behind the foundation blocks.

FROM THE TOP of the dunes, where she's come to find her children, Sasha looks down to the beach, her shadow streaming away from her in the afternoon sun like a lightly fastened banner. She puts her hand to her eyes, counting heads, finding Tania and Katia at last at the very edge of the lake, letting the small waves roll in over their legs and splash up to their waists. The boys seem to have set up camp on Australia, where the driftwood log is pulled up like a delivery van—there's Nick's red head flaming among all the brown and black and blond heads of this summer's crop of boys. What are they plotting, far away from their sisters and mothers? Most likely they're chanting that silly song Nick brought back the other day, driving Tania crazy by singing it over and over in a whining, baby voice:

> *What's your name, little boy?*
> *My name is Lemmie.*
> *Lemmie what, little boy?*
> *Lemmie kiss you.*

No doubt it will be kissing parties next—did those come before or after playing doctor? Sasha decides it doesn't matter, not at this age.

She should call out to her kids, round them up, organize a massive cleanup of the cottage before Ivan gets in. A cleanup whose effects will last a few hours or so: a day, if they're lucky. Entropy, Sasha long ago decided, is her native element. Then why is she so determined to keep everyone together, everyone where they belong at Kalyna Beach? "Everyone" being the couples who are her friends and more—her family, she supposes. Family into which you are born and that you adore or worry over or put up with, as the case may be. Nadia, Peter, Zirka: triangle heaven. How can she have been so blind?

But maybe Sonia's right, Sasha thinks, stubbing her cigarette out in the sand and folding her arms in that defiant way she picked up from her father. Maybe the best thing is to be dumb, and blind, and deaf—to let things play out and get back to normal, as they always do. Maybe what had happened with Nadia slapping Peter and Zirka laying into Nadia was just the usual combination of liquor and hot weather and boneheadedness. Zirka's histrionics might just have been a way of showing how important she thinks she is, how much her feelings matter—have to be *made* to matter. How had Peter stood it all these years?

"Ah, but she can cook," Sasha says out loud, shaking her head. She starts wondering, as she always does at this time of day, how she is ever going to sling a meal together, and whether she can get away with serving Ivan hot dogs for dinner. The kids have eaten them four nights in a row, but that's fine with them, they won't even notice.

No one will notice, everything will be fine. Sasha decides she's too tired to think anything else right now, as she unfolds her arms and takes a last look over the lake. She wonders, again, what the boys could be getting up to, all of them clumped together like that. Maybe it's nothing so innocent as a song about kissing. After that episode at the service station last week— setting fire to a roll of tar paper. Thank God the owner had been working late, had seen what they'd got up to, though they'd all run away before he'd been able to put his hands on even one of them. Thank God again, Sasha thinks, for she's not at all sure that Nick hadn't had a hand in lighting the match. The fathers had read them the riot act, forbidden them to go anywhere near the service station, which meant that the boys now had to bribe their sisters or cousins to fetch them their contraband from Venus Variety: jawbreakers and Popsicles and wax shaped like a pair of teeth, with some kind of syrup inside.

What would Sonia ever have done with boys? Sasha wonders. Maybe they would have cured her, once and for all, of her fearfulness, her lack of confidence, her habit of always looking at the wrong side of the cloth. Although where Peter's concerned—but here Sasha stops in her tracks. She's talked to Sonia, made her promise to talk to Peter, and as for herself, she'll go up to Nadia's sometime this weekend, see what's cooking there. Although she can hardly believe that Nadia would allow herself—there are children to think of, after all, and besides, Peter's never had two spare nickels to rub together. *Kholyera yasna!* Sasha gives herself a shake and heads back to the cabin, thinking that before she starts supper, she'll reread that chapter in *Wuthering Heights* where Heathcliff rushes in to the dying Cathy, the one she'd been about to start just before the Ladies had dropped by for tea.

The Ladies, the Ladies—*oy Bozhe*, the Ladies. Sometimes, Sasha thinks, folding her arms across her chest, as if bracing for battle—sometimes she wants just to shut herself up with a book, a whole room full of books, and do nothing but read, read, read. Everything from "Rumpelstiltskin" to *On the Beach*, *The Nun's Story* to *Forever Amber*. She'll never bother going back to school, like Nadia. She doesn't want to sit in a classroom while some professor drones on and on about everything but what makes you fall for a book, fall as hard and fast as you could fall in love. Or about how, when you finish certain books, you feel as though you've been locked out of the house in which you grew up. And how you walk around as if you're blind or lame and can't get your bearings until you've found another book that will take you away to someplace you've never dreamed you wanted or needed to go.

Sometimes, when she's sitting up later than any late show over a book, and Ivan is pleading with her to come to bed, and she says, "Just let me finish this chapter—it's a short one, I promise"—Sasha tells herself that the only heaven she wants to get to is a heaven that's a library, with endless shelves of all the books she's never read but always meant to or never had the time or chance to discover. A library where all the chairs are filled with other people reading as intently as you are, all of them having a conversation together, talking through their eyes and the ink on the page and worlds spilling out of words, as many worlds as there are words in every language under the sun—and the stars, as well, for good measure.

ON THE ROCK they call Australia, Yuri Metelsky is launching the Cossack Brotherhood of Kalyna Beach. Australia, he announces, will henceforward be known as the *Seech*, after the island fortress established by the Zaporozhian Cossacks in the sixteenth century—or seventeenth, he can't remember which. It's not so much of a stretch to convert Georgian Bay into the mighty Dnipro, as none of the boys has ever seen Ukraine's principal river except in blurry photographs in which it looks to be made of cement instead of water. Yuri is almost Laura's age and a natural choice for leader, not that there'd been any pretense of choice; as the whole thing is his idea, he takes ownership of the risks and of the glory too.

If he could have his way, he'd dress up his band of brothers in baggy satin trousers and scalp locks. But the *sharovary* have been left behind in the city, and there's hardly time for anyone to try to grow a *choob*, the long, dangling lock of hair that identifies the warrior. They will have to make do with swimming trunks and crew cuts. For it's the spirit, he tells the boys, the spirit, not the clothes, that counts. It goes without saying that secrecy is paramount—all the boys are sworn to keep the broad, flat rock's new name to themselves: the *Seech* is not to become the laughingstock of mere girls and women, and as for the Brotherhood, it is sacred.

Teyko and Olek, the youngest boys, are shaky on their Ukrainian history, and so Yuri repeats, as well as he can, the lessons he's learned at Saturday school, or at least the only part of the curriculum that holds any interest for him. Cossacks—the *kozaky*—are free agents owing nothing to masters or mothers. They chose to throw off their chains as laborers for landlords (Rapacious Russians and Plundering Poles) who worked them like slaves. Striking out for the wild east, they lived as frontiersmen—sort of like the cowboys in *Gunsmoke*—in perfect equality, fraternity, and justice. When Pavlo Vesiuk interrupts to ask why, if they're all equal, there has to be a hetman, Yuri pulls a face as if sickened by the stupidity of the question. "I am your hetman because I'm the oldest and because it's all my idea, anyway. So if any of you wants to challenge me—"

He breaks off with his hand in the air, clutching an imaginary, spike-studded mace, symbol of the hetman's authority. His younger brother Andriy quickly intervenes: "Of course you'll be hetman—we can't have a *Seech* without one," and the other boys agree, all except Pavlo, who crosses his arms and sticks out his lips in that funny way he has of showing disdain more than displeasure.

No one remembers, afterward, that it was Andriy who stood up for Yuri's right to lead them. Andriychyk, or Little Andriy, they call him, though he's just as tall as his older brother and a good deal heavier, as well. Andriychyk or, as the boys prefer to call him, *Pampushok* or *Pampukh*, after the doughnuts filled with rose-petal jam or poppy seeds, which their *baba*s make. The cruelest nickname of all is provided by the girls, who've dubbed him Titty because of the way his chest and tummy wobble over his swimming trunks when he plays on the beach. Once Sonia caught Katia taunting her cousin in this way and sent her up to the cottage for a whole afternoon as punishment.

"The Cossacks were warriors," Yuri is insisting to the boys gathered around him; there is just enough room for them to sit at Yuri's feet and for Yuri to perch on a small jut of rock that Pavlo refers to, sarcastically, as "the throne."

"Meaning?" Olek inquires. It's a habit he's picked up from an older brother, who responds to almost any kind of speech, especially anything in the lecture department, with this one-word question.

"Meaning," says Yuri patiently, and a little triumphantly too, "that we have to prove ourselves as warriors. We can't just ride around on a log and talk big—we have to *do* something, something courageous and—"

"Warlike," Pavlo finishes for him. "And just what are we going to declare war on, Yuri? The lake? Our mothers? Your cousins and their stupid friends?"

There is a long silence, until finally, of all people, little Teyko pipes up: "We could kidnap Darka!"

"Girls aren't allowed into the *Seech*," Yuri says sternly. He stands up, arms folded and knees locked, pitching his voice as low as he can. "What we've got to do is something big and brave, something worthy of the *Zaporozhtsi*."

He will think up something appropriately warlike, he promises them all. They will meet at the *Seech* at exactly the same time on Monday and he will inform them of his plan. For the moment, all must be secrecy, on pain of—

He hesitates. Pavlo smirks, and Andriy offers, "the hetman's fury," after which Yuri nods sternly and springs onto the driftwood log and motions for the rest of them to follow him. They must paddle back to shore and return to the cottages, where their mothers are waiting dinner for them, before anyone suspects what they are plotting.

CANNED PEAS AND mashed potatoes are being transferred from their pots onto six plates of three different patterns, spread out on the counter. Never enough room on a counter, especially in this hole of a kitchen, Sonia thinks. For the past five years, Max has been promising to tear it out and put in a new one for her, twice the size. He hasn't ruled out a dishwasher, like the one at Nadia's place; he says he's waiting till they get all the bugs out of them and the price comes down to something he can afford. One for the cottage and one for the home, and then what will she have left to wish for?

When she was Bonnie's age, she'd fetched water from the pump they shared with five other families in the village. Her hands still carry the scars of blisters from the thin metal handles of the pails she carried; she tried always to hide them when she was modeling or else to wear gloves. They were ruined, her hands, when she was still a child; she had worked since the time she was old enough to close her hands around a hoe or a needle or the teat of a cow. And yet, compared to the other children in the village, she had been spoiled. Especially compared to Peter, who always earned beatings for daydreaming when he should have been working, beatings with a switch across his small legs or skinny back. Peter, *the man of the family*, expected to stand in for his absent father.

Six plates: for Sonia, Laura, Katia, Bonnie, Alix—and Darka. Darka's setting a bad example with her elbows on the table, chewing-gum stuck to the edge of her plate—but until Max gets here, Sonia needs Darka on her side, can't trust herself alone with the children. Baby Alix is staring out of those huge black eyes of hers. Laura and Katia are fighting again—Laura's face purple with rage; Katia's eyes bright, hard as pebbles. She must have been teasing Laura, jabbing at her weak spots, and God knows

. . . But Sonia stops herself from pitying her firstborn; two years older than Katia, she should be able to stick up for herself instead of snapping and sulking. No wonder Katia's always kicking her under the table, pinching her ribs: Laura, the perfect target. Sonia knows, she knows everything they get up to, but she's not God, it's not for her to stop them killing each other inch by inch.

The peas have boiled dry: she'd left them just for a minute to change into a skirt and blouse, for Max's return, but the peas are branded, each one of them, with a small black scar. They are the only green vegetable she has left; she'll put mint sauce on them, the children won't notice the burned taste. She bites her lips to distract herself from the pain zigging across her scalp, homing in behind her left eye. First Zirka this morning, twisting all those knives she keeps at the ready, and then Sasha in the afternoon, Sasha and her cigarettes, Sasha and the plots she's concocted from all those books she reads and passes around. Another spasm stabs through Sonia's body, up from her heel, along the length of her leg, across her breast to the top of her head. A spasm of irritation so pure, so lethal, she sees the tunnel scorched inside her, she can feel her body smoking.

"For God's *sake*, Laura, *stop* playing with your food and eat *up*. And stop smirking, Katia. It makes you look like a little jar of poison."

Katia mashes her peas with the back of her fork, lifts them to her mouth, and makes a great show of swallowing them. Laura sits staring at her plate, her spine rigid.

"I said, eat your peas, Laura."

"They're burned."

"They're not burned. If Katia can eat them, so can you. We don't waste food in this family, you know that. If you'd even once had to go hungry, you wouldn't put on this—this *ridiculous performance*." It's not her own voice speaking, it's something from a radio show, *Lux Theater*, from which she learned English at Sasha's house when she was a twelve-year-old. This has nothing to do with Laura or the peas on her plate, but by this point Sonia can't stop herself. She stands up from the table, her hands on her hips, the jut of her elbows pinning them all. "Don't think I don't know what you've been up to, all of you, sneaking money from the change drawer, buying candy at the store. No wonder you can't eat your dinner. Why do I waste my time cooking for you? Go on, be stubborn, you can sit there all night for all I care. But just you wait till your father comes home!"

"With Chucha Marta," Katia says, almost innocently.

Laura hasn't even shifted in her chair, her hands on either side of her plate, wrists cocked at the table's edge. When she was younger, she would hollow a door into her scoop of mashed potatoes, push her peas inside, and seal them up with a spoonful of potato she'd left at the side of her plate. No one would notice but Katia, and Katia had been different then; she'd looked up to Laura.

Sonia waits for a moment, as if trying to hold on to her patience, to achieve consistency between words and actions. She knows what she should do: she should gather up the younger children and take them off to Venus Variety for ice cream—she should leave Laura sulking at the table over a stupid little pile of peas. She should laugh at her, laugh at herself. But even as she waits, Sonia knows that she will not, cannot do what she should. Her voice goes hard, precise; she hammers out each word: "I've had enough of your sulking, Laura. Finish your supper this instant."

Laura doesn't miss a beat. "I'll be sick if I have to eat those peas. If you make me eat them, I'll throw up."

"You'll sit at this table—you will all, every last one of you, sit at this table till Laura's plate is clean."

Mother and daughter haven't taken their eyes off each other as they've spoken these words. The room is silent; even Darka stops tapping her fork against the oilcloth. Laura stares at her mother, at the pale blue lakes of her eyes. If Baba Laryssa were here, this wouldn't be happening; Baba would stretch out her hand and say, "Leave her be, leave her be, *donyu*." But Baba's dead, and there's no one to help her. Bonnie's too young, and Darka doesn't care. Besides, Sonia doesn't give a damn what Darka thinks, *a good goddamn*. Slowly, grimly, Laura lifts a forkful of peas to her mouth and pushes them in.

"Swallow!"

She swallows. And then another forkful, and another.

"What an actress," Sonia exclaims, brushing imaginary crumbs off her skirt. "Get the Jell-O, Darka. It's on the counter."

But before the glass bowl of ruby-colored Jell-O lands on the table, Laura lurches forward, Katia and Baby Alix staring at her throat as though it were a boa constrictor working in reverse, grayish-green paste spilling from her mouth onto her clean, clean plate.

KATIA AND TANIA meet Yuri by the abandoned car, its rusted hood pushed up by the weeds thrusting through it. No one knows whose car it is or how it got here, in the middle of the woods. Yuri says it was abandoned by a criminal, and when Tania asks what kind of criminal, he says, off the top of his head, a baby killer, a kidnapper. Katia rolls her eyes, but Tania shivers, which irritates Katia. All of a sudden she suspects her friend of playing up to her cousin, of going girly.

"So what are we going to do?" Yuri asks, standing as straight as he can—that way he's a quarter of an inch taller than Katia and level with Tania.

"Spy," Katia hisses.

"Where?"

"The Durkowskis," Katia snaps back.

Pan Durkowski works as a janitor at the cathedral downtown and at the hall next door; his wife helps him clean the buildings and works part-time at the Arka store on Queen West, selling stamps and weighing parcels to be shipped to Ukraine. They spend two weeks every summer at Kalyna Beach: Mr.

Senchenko gives them the use of a cottage, more like a shack, off Tunnel Road. He drives them up to the lake and then takes them back to their apartment in the basement of the Cathedral Hall. People say that Pan Durkowski was an architect in Ukraine before the war but that he hasn't got the right qualifications for Canada, qualifications meaning things like diplomas, contacts, language. Besides, he's old; it would take him too long to retrain.

"Not the Durkowskis," Tania complains. "They don't have any secrets—we'd be wasting our time."

"No, no," Yuri says, putting his arms around the girls, drawing them close, as if into a football huddle. Pan Durkowski, Yuri whispers, fought for the Germans during the war; he was on Hitler's side.

Katia's about to pull herself away, to say, in her most scathing tone, *That's crazy, Yuri—you don't know what you're talking about.* She's about to start singing a playground song she learned when she was Bonnie's age—*Whistle while you work, Hitler is a jerk*—when once again, she notices something funny about her friend. Usually Tania never believes a word Yuri says, but this time, for some reason, she is leaning into Yuri, widening her eyes, practically saying *oooooh.*

Katia reaches forward and snaps the elastic on the waistband of Yuri's trousers. Before he can slap her hand, she runs off, calling back: "I'm going off to spy; you two can stay behind and play kissy-face."

Yuri sprints after her; Tania waits for a moment, uncertain

whether to punish Katia by turning around and going home. Doesn't Katia understand that she's making fun of Yuri—what's her mother's word for it?—playing up to him so that she can knock him down all the harder? It's not like Katia to be so dumb. And then Tania has a flash of understanding, or suspicion, or both; she scrambles through the lush weeds back to the road, catching up with Katia and her cousin, keeping their silence, and watching them both on the sly.

The children tiptoe along the side of the Durkowskis' cottage, where the grass is sparse and pine needles fall into rusty pools. Pan Durkowski spends most of his summer holiday mowing what's left of the lawn, building paths lined with pebbles brought up from the beach, doing calisthenics. He tried to teach them to the boys, but they ended up laughing and running away, so he performs his exercises alone, wearing a white undershirt tucked into his bathing trunks and a handkerchief knotted over his head. They expect to see him doing exercises in the kitchen now, or else, Yuri hopes, polishing his Luger and looking over his military badges—swastikas, lightning stripes of the SS, all the paraphernalia Yuri has seen in the war movies he watches late at night, when his parents are asleep and he's sneaked down to the family room, where they keep the TV.

A little square of light glows from the cabin, soft, buttery light from a high window. Yuri gives Katia a leg up, and she stares through the screen, memorizing all the details that she can. It's the kitchen, not the bedroom: there's a ten-pound sack of potatoes on the counter beside a large aluminum pot. In the middle of the table jewelweed and chicory flowers are crammed into a jam jar—the kind of ditch flower that kids Bonnie's age pick for their mothers. The Durkowskis sit with heads bowed, peeling potatoes at a scarred, enamel-topped table and grating a huge block of Velveeta cheese. They are preparing to make *varenyky*, that dish for which there's no English equivalent, not dumpling, not pasty, not boiled dough-ball either. Pan Durkowski is in his undershirt and his gray city trousers; his wife is wearing only her slip and a scarf over her head—pale blue chiffon, pin curls showing underneath like metal snails. The white of the slip cuts into her chest, and pink flesh sags over the nylon, like curtains too big for their window. Katia's about to whisper something down to Tania about Pani Durkowska's breasts but changes her mind.

"Let's go," Tania says to Yuri. "Nothing's happening here." She's angry at Katia, and she's nervous too. For after the Ladies left the veranda that afternoon, after Sonia had gone into and then come out of the log cabin for her heart-to-heart with Sasha, nothing had happened. Tania had expected her mother to lecture her—though Sasha is the most easygoing of mothers, there have been times when she has been known to act no differently than any other of the Mean Mothers. She might have forbidden Tania to go to the store anymore or kept her from seeing Katia—but she hadn't said or done anything like that at all. Whatever she and Mrs. Martyn were talking about together must be bad enough that they're waiting for the fathers to deal

with it. Right now, the mothers think their daughters are reading in their rooms: *Little Women* and *Five Little Peppers*. They
think the girls are reading in their rooms in the pajamas they
slipped over their shorts before brushing their teeth and kissing
their mothers good night. "Let's go," Tania repeats.

But Katia's still watching through the bowed-out screen of the
kitchen window, as if waiting for something to happen—something she can make happen just by watching. What, she doesn't
know. Maybe Pani Durkowska will grab the paring knife from
her husband and stab him through the heart the way Katia saw
once in a horror film. Or Pan Durkowski just might pull out that
Luger Yuri's always going on about, might put it to his head and
squeeze the trigger. It's not that Katia wants violence; it's just that
the plots available to her are limited, even more so with people as
old as these, people who don't belong to anyone and who spend
their time telling other people what to do with their children.

But now something does happen, something more startling
than anything Katia can invent. Pani Durkowska puts down the
potato peeler and moves her hands not to the paring knife but to
the jam jar of flowers. She pulls out a stalk of chicory and holds
it against her face, just by her ear. And for a moment, just one
fraction of a moment, Katia sees what Pani Durkowska must
have looked like when she was young, when she was Darka's
age. The old man puts down his grater, reaches for his wife's
hand, the one holding the flower, and holds it against his cheek.
What startles Katia is the gentleness of the gesture and the way

these two worn-down people are joined by something so tender and yet so strong that she is suddenly ashamed. Ashamed not of them but of herself; to be witnessing what, she later realizes, is a gesture of love.

"What's going on?" Yuri hisses. His back aches; Katia is having all the fun while he does all the work. It's always the way. Yet for some reason he can't shrug it off, as he usually does, but takes it to heart. Katia lording it over him, digging her sandaled feet into him as if he were a horse or a camel.

"Nothing," Katia answers, in the clear, bright voice she uses when she's fibbing. "They're not doing anything—just peeling potatoes."

Abruptly, Yuri leans forward, so that Katia tumbles from his shoulders, giving a shriek as she falls. The girls start running as fast as they can toward the road, but Yuri stops to collect a fistful of gravel from one of the paths Pan Durkowski has built. He sprays the kitchen screen. He's starting to make a run for it when a hand seizes the back of his collar, the same hand that had been held up to an old woman's cheek moments before.

"Trrrr-ubble makers," Pan Durkowski cries out in English, the sound of the words bent out of shape by his accent. "Khood-looms."

By now the girls have disappeared; Yuri is alone. But as he's hauled into the Durkowskis' cottage, he hears the sound of chanting:

Old man Nicky
had a twelve-foot dicky.
He showed it to the lady next door.
She thought it was a snake
so she hit it with a rake
and now it's only two foot four.

The girls should be laughing, they should be holding their stomachs and rolling in the grass, but instead they stand there, listening to the echo of Tania's song. For Katia hasn't joined in. Though they've sworn a pact to share equally in the thrill of and the punishment for disobedience, for the first time ever, Katia's refused to join in. It can't be explained, Tania thinks, by Yuri getting caught by Pan Durkowski: Yuri asked for it, and besides, he could have run away if he'd really wanted to. He could have shaken free as easily as if it were Baby Alix who'd snatched hold of his collar. Tania chews on her lip and rubs the toe of her running shoe into the loose, pale dirt beside the road.

As for Katia, there's a taste in her mouth of something that shouldn't be there, like grass or earth. When she does speak, it's an excuse, not an explanation: she has to get home before her father arrives; her mother's in such a bitchy mood that she'll go berserk if she finds that Katia's sneaked out. Tania nods, and the two walk on in silence.

When they reach the Martyns' driveway, Tania spits into her hand, waiting for Katia to follow suit; the girls join hands as if nothing's gone wrong or awry, then pull away from each other. Tania whispers something about spying on Darka, just the two of them, without any boy along to spoil things. Katia nods, and her friend runs off down the road.

She stays put, rocking on her heels, her eyes fixed on her father's car, stranded in the gravel. The engine's still warm when she finally steps forward and puts out her hands to it. Warm as her father's face when he bends down to kiss her, as his chest when he holds her in a bear hug. Through the open window, Katia can see her father sitting at the kitchen table with his head in his hands; her mother stands beside him, her arms loose but her shoulders stiff as fire irons. Somewhere in the kitchen Chucha Marta is rummaging among the pots and pans, putting them away and muttering to herself in the voice that always makes Katia think of someone crushing shiny, crackly beetle shells under a shoe.

She waits for a moment, though she knows she could easily be found out; her mother might turn, her father look up and see her. It's Chucha Marta who gives her away: she's stepped out the kitchen door onto the little porch, starts shouting at Katia for being out of doors when she's supposed to be in bed, fast asleep, keeping out of trouble.

But still, Katia stands there, waiting. As if she could will them to turn to each other, not even to kiss, just to turn to each other gently.

Gently.

THE DOOR SWINGS shut behind him, and the cottage disappears, the cottage and everyone inside it: his bitter wife; his crazy, awful sister; the three sleeping children he doesn't want to wake and the one who's been caught sneaking out of her room at night, the one he will be expected to punish in the morning. If he were to turn and look back, he knows he'd see his wife at the picture window, her face a moon swallowed up by clouds. And he is the man in the moon, the man of the house, *paterfamilias*, but with no more power, really, than a moonbeam. Spank Katia? He didn't drive all this way to beat his children, Sonia should know that by now. But what Sonia knows—and doesn't, won't allow herself to know . . .

Max shoves his hands in his pockets and walks down the zigzag path to the beach, the yellow square of light on his back, the impress of his wife's face getting smaller, weaker with every step. No moon at all, tonight, but not because of clouds—stars salt the blackness overhead, as many stars, he thinks, as there are hairs on his body: a carpet, a pelt like an animal's. He tightens his lips, thinking of the dog Sonia won't let Laura have, no matter how hard, how relentlessly she begs. He should just go out and buy Laura the dog, any dog, and have done with it. It would do her good, his poor, clumsy Laura, who should have been a boy; she isn't quick-witted like Katia, or pretty and pleasing like Bonnie, but the awkward, stubborn kind who'll always know too much for her own good.

Down at the shore it's so quiet he can hear each wave as it licks, then kicks back against the sand. The dark—it's the thing he loves most about this place: you can actually see the dark. In the city there are always too many lights or the hum from power lines overhead; everyone, everything's on the move, rushing and racketing about, but here— He takes a trim, silver case from his shirt pocket and pulls out a cigar; holding it under his nose like a pretend mustache, he breathes the scent in so deeply he might be calling up the coconuts and sugar cane from the island where the tobacco grows. For some reason Marta had been going on and on in the car about last year's Cuban missile crisis. How the Americans had lost their nerve; how they should have stood up to the Russians and that ex-Ukrainian party-boss who is no more Ukrainian than the shoe he thumped on the table at the UN. In spite of himself, Max had let her get to him; he'd actually turned around for a second, asking her whether she'd have preferred Khrushchev—or Kennedy—to have pushed the button. "Button—ha!" she'd exclaimed, using the Ukrainian word, *gudzyk*, making it sound like something out of a children's game. And then, to top it off, she'd screeched, "Keep your eyes on the road—do you want to kill us both?"

Max allows himself the first rich puff of his cigar; expels a fragrant plume of smoke into the air, a plume that gathers, then wavers, slowly pushing itself apart. It's the only sign of anything that's stirring here, beside the barely beating waves and the stars overhead, the stars that move so slowly they might as well be nails hammered into a board. The same stars the president in Washington could be staring at this very moment, the rich-boy president with his rugged good looks and his cool millions; his beautiful wife and perfect children: a girl, a boy. A man no older, and perhaps no smarter, all in all, than Max Metelsky, but with his finger on the life-or-death of the very planet.

He's glad, suddenly, that his children are in bed, safe and sleeping peacefully. If the bomb were to hit (he always thinks of it as one single, silver missile, some gigantic bullet), they would never know. But this is morbid, outrageous—this kind of think-ing is worthy of Marta. He draws intently on his cigar. Three hours of Marta in the car, and then Sonia, shouting loud and clear as always with that stiff silence of hers, and what the *hell* did he do wrong, just what was she punishing him for *this* time? For not leaving Marta to asphyxiate herself—he says the word over again, it soothes and supports him, a word Sonia wouldn't know, never mind use—*asphyxiate* herself in that oven of a house they should have got rid of long ago?

But then where would Marta have gone; would Sonia prefer Marta to be living with them—would she prefer to have Marta to put up with, instead of a dog? It's not as though Sonia didn't have family of her own to hang around his neck. Of course it was a terrible shame, her mother dying so suddenly, but she should be able to cope with that by now—it's been four months already.

Look at Peter, he isn't exactly wailing and beating his breast. This show she puts on—not that she's pretending to grieve, but it's the performance that gets him: crying all the time, or else silent; wearing sunglasses to hide her wept-out eyes. It's bad for the children to see their mother affected this way. His mother had never cried once, he had never seen her weep, and God knows, the life she'd had—or Marta, for that matter. *She* had a tongue all right, but he'd rather that than Sonia's dagger silence and red-jelly eyes.

"Hail Caesar, back from the wars!"

Stealing up on him, as usual: how is it he never hears Peter coming? He's carrying his shoes in one hand and his jacket in the other. It looks like he hasn't even gone inside to toss his jacket on a chair, kiss his wife hello.

"So. Peter."

"Come on, Max, you can do better. Why not 'Hail, fellow, well met' or *'morituri te salutant'*? And come to think of it, a cigar would go down a treat right now."

They say you can choose your friends but not your family, but what is Peter to Max? Neither one nor the other. His wife's brother, no-account, devil-may-care—what was it in the commercial?—*debonair*, that was the word for Peter. Rogue, idler, jack of all trades, master mimic—he'd been taking off Rex Harrison with that cigar remark, and to the life. In spite of himself, Max holds out the cigar case as if he had a hundred more Havanas back at the cottage. Sonia hates the smell of them, they give her headaches, she is famous for her headaches; but look at Peter, his life shot all to hell, yet smiling like he hasn't got a care in the world. Peter, who never gives a thought to the power-monger men in Moscow or Washington.

They sit side by side on a boulder by the shore, as if they were the closest, the easiest of friends: two men gliding into middle age, whose hair is starting to thin. Peter's is carelessly tinged with gray, as if he'd been painting a ceiling and had forgotten, as usual, to put on a protective cap. But Peter is lean, still has an athlete's body. He played what at university? Soccer, baseball, various amatory sports—he got in on a serviceman's scholarship but let his grades drop like a pair of pants around his ankles. Had Peter ever had so much as a scrap of ambition—was there anything he'd ever meant to become before good looks, and easy charm, and native laziness got in the way? A teacher, a doctor, a plumber, for God's sake? No, nothing so exalted, so practical, but an actor—an actor!

Max throws his cigar as far as he can toward the lake, waiting for the hiss of fire on water. He's remembering the ass Peter made of himself acting up last weekend, at the Plotskys' party. Remembering, too, some shred of gossip—and Max is, most often, immune to gossip, so he can't be sure he isn't making it up—about Peter having fallen for someone in his youth, fallen hopelessly, as you'd expect a man like Peter to do: no sense of proportion or judgment. A miracle, that he'd ended up with Zirka Senchenko and, through Zirka, her millionaire brother.

Better luck than he deserved, although God knows that woman would drive you to worse than drink. He coughs to cover his thoughts—as if Peter had *that* trick in his bag, mind-reading, of all things.

"Christ, the traffic's awful—I swear it gets worse each time I come up—and I thought leaving after supper there'd be no one on the roads."

"It was okay when I drove up," Peter says, flicking ash into the remains of a fortress the kids have been building, a moat lined with small, white pebbles. "But I started out at two o'clock. I decided to take the afternoon off, things are always slow on a Friday."

"Funny, it's the busiest time of the week for me." Max can't keep a flick of disapproval from his voice, and Peter can't help catching it, wearing it like a rose in his buttonhole.

"Man's got to live a little before that big old spitfire pilot in the sky trains his guns on him. Haven't you ever cut a workday short, Max?"

"No."

"Not even when you were courting my sweet sister?"

"If I were the type to play hooky from the office, there's no way your sweet sister would have let me look at her, never mind court her." Max hasn't meant to say this much, he'd meant to ignore the question or change the subject. Peter's capable of taking his answer as a sign that he wants to talk, not about the things men usually talk about, the way they talk—stock market, sports, politics—but things better left private, things you don't even want to think about, never mind confess to someone like Peter Metelsky.

"Things aren't going so well between the two of you these days, Max?"

"I don't discuss my private affairs. Besides, you're one to talk."

"I thought as much. Sonia's funny like that, always has been. Goes off the deep end. About our mother, I mean, all this griev-ing—"

"Sonia's a wonderful woman."

"Of course she is, Max, of course she is. So are they all— wonderful women."

He's waiting for Max to ask him something about Zirka, about the desert of their marriage. Max knows that if he gives even the slightest sign—a shrug, a grunt—Peter will tell him everything. As if Max wanted to hear, as if he doesn't have enough on his hands with Sonia, Marta, Laura—a houseful of women at war. Peter at least has sons. If only, Max thinks, the next one could be a boy, everything would be all right again. There is still time for a boy. It wouldn't weigh on her so much, then, her mother's death, and she'd stop worrying so much about Alix, thinking it's her fault the child won't speak, is so cold, so closed off to them all. Saying she hadn't wanted her, and the child knows it, is punishing her. Crazy talk: the child is going to be fine, she's a late bloomer, that's all; it's only if they keep worrying, carrying on about her that there'll be a problem. Hasn't the doctor said so? Always having to hug some guilt to her chest, is Sonia, some thorn or spike of glass. He has never known a woman with so small a gift for happiness.

And yet she was beautiful, is still so beautiful he can be stunned, winded, just by looking at her. Seeing her when she thinks she is alone, or the rare times when she doesn't give a damn how she looks, how decently she is dressed. That afternoon she'd stormed into his office, crying out—her father had been rushed to a hospital, Max had to come with her now, right now, this very moment. He'd almost forgotten about the client sitting there, had almost gone to her and taken her in his arms to comfort her, tell her all would be well, he was with her, he'd make sure that nothing bad would happen. But by the time he'd made his excuses to his client and spoken to his secretary to cancel the remaining appointments, Sonia had already left. And she'd refused to greet him when he showed up at the hospital, ten minutes after she'd arrived. Fifteen minutes at the most, he'd swear to it.

"Better be getting back," Peter says, throwing his cigar butt, like Max's, into the water. No hiss this time: it's drowned in the soaked sand at the very rim of the lake. Peter shrugs, jams his hands in his pockets. But he makes no move to rise. "They'll be wondering where we are," he says at last. "They'll be thinking us drowned at the very least. We should be so lucky."

Max isn't taking any bait. Though he knows what Peter is saying, knows what he, Max, would like to be able to ask, if not of Peter then of someone who'd value the question, even if he had no answer. Not a priest, not a teacher or doctor, not even the huge blue eye painted on the cathedral dome, but just someone he doesn't know and will never meet again. Some perfect stranger who happens to walk by and see him, sitting here by the water:

Is this what my life, and hers, have come to—just this, and no more? If those men in high places, with their oh-so-powerful fingers, decide to push that button, will it all have been for nothing but this? And my daughters asleep in their beds—if they're spared to grow up—will there be nothing more for them than this? A man like Peter, a man like me? A man whose life will add up, at the end of each week, to five days slogging at the office, two days at the cottage fixing a few of the hundred things that have gone wrong or need replacing, six hours' driving here and back in bad traffic?

Peter stretches out his arms and yawns so lazily, so voluptuously that it has to be an act. "Two whole days I've got free, forty-eight fine and blessed hours, and I'm not going to spend even one of them fixing a single thing, no matter how many fits Zirka throws."

"Lucky you. Enjoy yourself."

"You taking any time off this summer?"

"I have to make up for the time I took off when your mother died."

It sounds like a reproach. It is. Sonia collapsed, and Peter was no goddamn help—you'd think a brother would be able to support a sister, talk to her, make her see sense the way a husband couldn't. Useless, Peter—utterly useless.

"Good night, then, Max." Peter is starting to walk away, not in the direction of his cottage but farther up the shore.

"Good night. And Peter—"

Max waits for a moment, until he assures himself that Peter has stopped walking, has turned to face him.

"Don't act the fool in front of everyone again. Once a summer's more than enough."

If Peter's angered by Max's warning, he doesn't show it. "Good night, sweet prince," he calls out. "Flights of angels, and all that." He resumes his stroll down the beach, in the direction of the highest bluff, the one the kids have named Gibraltar.

Max, climbing heavily up the steps to the cottage, doesn't answer. The porch light's out, the window looks like a socket without an eye. He knows that Sonia will be sleeping or pretending.

HE'S LYING WITH his back to her, snoring, the sheets and covers rolled around him, turning him into a thick white spool of thread. For a while Sonia stays in bed, beside him, knowing she won't sleep but that it's far too complicated to get up and that while he sleeps so soundly, she is safe. Once again she goes through the list of things that have to be done in the next two days: get Max to buy the lumber to fix the porch steps; stand over him to make sure he actually does the carpentry; handle Marta's interference, her snorts of criticism. Then, when he's finished the steps, when he's in a thoroughly bad mood, about to head back to the city along with all the thousands of other husbands in their lonely cars, hand him the letter to give to Olya, whom he has never really cared for and who lives far enough away from them for it to be an imposition. Hand Olya the letter and reassurances about Darka, lies about what a willing helper Darka's been.

And last of all, Peter. Talk to Peter, though how can she begin to say anything to him about so painful a subject? If Sasha thinks he'll listen to her because he's her brother—but what business is it of Sasha's, anyway? Why doesn't she talk to Nadia instead; butter wouldn't melt in that one's mouth: *I'd rather read Shakespeare.* Peter's never taken advice, that's why he's always in one kind of a mess or another. She told him all those years ago it would be a mistake, marrying Zirka; he had only smiled at her in that careless way he had, smiled and never really trusted her again. Thinking of Peter makes Sonia's legs and arms cramp up; her heart performs its somersaults the way it always does when she forces herself to be still, to lie back and relax. Surely it must be getting on to morning?

At last she rises silently, cautiously, without letting the bedsprings creak even once, groping her way to the kitchen for a drink of water. The stove clock with its cracked face tells her it's only two. Not a sound from the room where Marta's sleeping— Darka's room. Darka's been packed off to the sleep-house, and Sonia doesn't like the arrangement at all, it makes her nervous not to have the girl under her roof. Though what good would that do—how could you keep the worst from happening, when what was supposed to have been the best has turned out as it has?

Carefully, as gently as if she were touching the face of one of her sleeping children, Sonia opens the side door and looks out across the lawn to the sleep-house. Still as the grave, she thinks, pulling the lapels of her pajamas closer. She doesn't want to think about graves, she can't stop herself hearing her mother, in her hospital bed, in pain so fierce you'd think it was skinning her, saying, "I would grab at a straw floating in the river just to try to keep on living."

The kitchen clock says 2:14, as if to spite her: it seems to her hours since she left her husband's bed, opening the door onto a skyful of stars. Sonia makes her way once more to the children's rooms, going into them, covering the children if the blankets have been tossed to the floor, sometimes bending to stroke their hair. By Laura's bed she stops for the longest time, afraid to touch her—she's no longer a child, she has lost that ferociousness, that fever-sleep the little ones are still consumed by. And here, sleeping spoons beside her, Sonia's golden one, her sweet, sunny Bonnie, whom she always has to keep herself from kissing, from throwing her arms around and holding, lest the others see that she's Sonia's favorite, the only one she loves without reserve.

Across the hall, Katia lies with her arms flung back, as if she is dancing wildly in her dreams. But when Sonia bends over the baby, the one who will only let herself be kissed when she is sleeping, she gives a little cry that makes Katia stir in her sleep, stir but not wake. Alix's round black eyes are wide-open, staring up at her mother like pools into which the whole night has fallen. "Go to sleep," Sonia whispers, using the old language, the one in which her mother sang lullabies to her in the Old Place. But Alix keeps staring up at her, her eyes accusing, as always. Until it seems to Sonia that the only way she can close them is by lifting the baby into her arms, pressing her head against her breast, and carrying her outside.

Out onto the veranda and the stairs that so badly need fixing. So warm, still, though it's the middle of the night, a dark fragrant with pine and cedar, not the chocolate smell of summer nights at her mother's house downtown. Not her mother's house anymore: it was sold weeks after her death. They'd had to scramble to clear it out, lugging boxes and boxes of what Max called junk to the basement of their house in the suburbs. Lamps and blankets and cooking pots; an envelope of yellowed paper on which, in pale purple ink, were marked the fields that had never been sold, that now lay under the jaws of some giant tractor on a collective farm. *Moyee polya*—my fields: words like a tongue dipped in chocolate, as soft as the most expensive velvet. Or the angora muff Mr. Streatfield had once given her as a present, and that she hadn't dared to show her mother, keeping it always in her drawer, taking it out sometimes to hold its impossible softness to her face.

Settling herself on the top step, holding Alix against her, feeling the child's open eyes against her breast, Sonia tilts her head to look up at stars scratched upon the sky, endless and unreachable. She remembers waking up from the anesthetic after Alix was born, a belt of stinging blisters below her breasts, around her back, cinching her tight, so tight the skin felt rubbed entirely away. Shingles, it was called; it had been too painful for Sonia to nurse the baby, and so her mother had looked after the child, feeding her from a bottle every few hours. If it hadn't been for Baba Laryssa, Alix would never have thrived, and now her *baba* is lying in a place dark as a night without moon or stars, without the smell or feel or even the memory of milk, or skin, or angora.

Sonia gathers Alix to her, the child's body no longer stiff in her arms, no longer holding out against her but soft, collapsed into sleep. So that the mother can drop her mouth to her baby's head and kiss the thick, dark hair, not demanding anything back, just feeling the soft warmth of the small body next to her own. "She's dead, baby, and I will die, and you will die, too, and there's nothing any of us can do about it." The boat out from Gdynia, the *Marshal Pilsudski*, with the brass band and the sailors more like machines than men in their uniforms so spanking new, trouser creases you could cut yourself on. Holding Peter's hand, pushing through a forest of trousered legs and thick wool skirts, lisle stockings. Till they got to the railings and held on for dear life, breathing in the salt sting of the sea so far below. No river that could drown her, filling her nose and mouth with dark; no river but a blue-black road that would take her away, forever. From the village where she couldn't face anyone, could hardly breathe anymore; from the best part of her life, the child she'd once been in that village: at home, at one, complete.

The stars are sailing wherever it is they are meant to go, or not meant, it is all the same, thinks the woman sitting on the rotting steps of a summer cottage, holding a sleeping child against her breast. Throwing her head back and staring up at that starry, inky double of the sea, that road that she will never travel now, no matter how urgent, how huge her longing. The child's mouth lies open at her breast as if she were about to nurse, drinking the milk her mother no longer has and never wants to have again. Sonia recites, very softly, the words of the rhyme her children have taught her, words that have no meaning for her, or a meaning that is faint, unreadable, like the print on a dress that has been washed too many times:

> *Ladybug, ladybug,*
> *fly away home.*
> *Your house is on fire,*
> *your children are gone.*

All save the little one,
whose name is Ann,
and she's hiding under
the frying pan.

PART TWO

KEEPERS OF SECRETS

SUNDAY AFTERNOON, WHEN it's still too early to think of to-night's traffic and tomorrow's appointments, Max goes down to the beach. He's finished whatever jobs could be compassed in a forty-eight-hour stay: putting a patch on the leaky roof; fix-ing the latch on the kitchen door. The steps on the front porch will have to wait till next summer. These two hot, empty hours in the afternoon are his gift to himself: he's going to bake in the sun for a while and then play with the children. Sonia's up at the cottage with Marta, who refuses to come down to the beach: she will get sunstroke, the arthritis in her legs is so bad she can barely move, she needs to take her medicine at three. It has already begun, the two-step Marta and Sonia will perform for the next six days of Marta's stay; Marta piling up objections, Sonia attempting to knock them down: you will not get sun-stroke, thanks to the beach umbrella bought at the hardware in Midland, just for your visit; the hot sand will be good for your arthritic legs, much better than a heat lamp; you can take your medicine with some lemonade I'll have ready in the cooler I'll carry down to the beach. But as in any dance, only one person can lead: already Sonia has bowed to her partner, spending the best part of the day keeping her company in the stifling cottage, while the rest of them enjoy the breeze rustling the grasses in the dunes or send beach balls spinning across the sand. Marta frowning over her crochet work that she holds up to her eyes as if each stitch were a prisoner itching for jailbreak. While if Sonia were to dare to sit down on the sofa across from Marta, sit down with something as useless, as silly, as a book, Marta would light into her about all the work that needed doing in the cottage, the dusting and sweeping, the washing of windows and floors. Just as she'd done with him when he was studying law, as if he'd been reading Ripley's *Believe It or Not* instead of a textbook on torts.

"Tatu," Katia yells, rushing up to where Max lies spread-eagled on his blanket. "Tatu," she cries, "*please* let us bury you!"

At first he pretends not to hear, but then, as the other children dance around, even Laura, who's been in one of her moods all weekend, he flaps his hands on the beach blanket, a signal for the kids to jump on him and tickle him till he begs for mercy. Until he finally rolls over and off the blanket, landing on his back on a platter of pale, dry sand.

It takes them a good twenty minutes. At first the sand is hot; it stings as it sprays across his face, over the lips and eyelids he's trying to shut tight. Of course you're not supposed to bury anyone's face, that's against the rules, but sand meant for your shoulders always ends up in your eyebrows and salting your mustache. Soon, however, the children reach the excavating stage, when the sand they heap over their father's legs and chest and arms turns heavy, damp, like cold brown sugar. He imagines his body rising up like some mountain range—the Rockies or the Himalayas. He thinks of his head islanded in all this sand, taking in the sounds of his children, their frantic pleasure, the gravity of Laura's directives—"Not like that, Katia, you'll cause a cave-in at his elbows"—and Katia's blithe disregard—"Hey, his kneecaps keep showing through, they look like volcanoes!" A scrabbling pressure on his chest—"Somebody get the baby, she's ruining everything!"—and then a crescendo of yells as Darka carries off Baby Alix.

At last, when the children have stomped the sand down with their feet and then heaped on another few pails for good measure, comes the chief delight. Their father, shaking his head and yawning as if roused from a hundred-year sleep, flexes first one arm and then the other, tries and fails to shake a leg free, wriggles his toes and sets off the first of the avalanches. Until, with the roar of a lion, he heaves his whole body up in one great rush, throwing fans of sand into the air as he plunges into the lake, the children screaming as they run in after him.

Once they've splashed him clean, and he's dived down to grab their ankles, once they've all lined up to wriggle through his outstretched legs, he tells them it's Tato's time now, which means he swims out, with his powerful, steady crawl stroke, far away from the group of small, tanned bodies. Bonnie, standing on a rock so the water reaches only to her waist, watches him with her fingers in her mouth, sucking anxiously each time his head disappears, praying, *Pleasepleaseplease let him come up again.* But at last, after he's swum sixty, seventy, eighty strokes, so that his handsome head is only a dark dot, he turns, waves— and comes back to them. How they love it when he stands up on the first sandbar, ten feet tall, the water streaming down his arms and chest, and how they love the way he cleans the water from his eyes with the flat of his hands, then combs his thick hair straight back with his fingers. He is the best-looking father at the whole beach, the best swimmer, and the only grown-up, besides Uncle Peter, they will ever include in their play.

Now it's leapfrog on the sand, Max pretending to trip and making spectacular, somersaulting falls. "Horsing around" is what Sonia calls it, standing at the lookout post on the edge of the lawn while Marta's still in the washroom. Horsing around. Her father had never played with her or her brother like that— and yet he'd been a good man, decent and hardworking even after his accident, managing the pain with sips of what he called "medicine," from a shot glass. But never to excess—he was always dignified, her father. Unlike Peter. Unlike Max, making a fool of himself now in front of everyone. She bites at her lip, pushes her hair out of her eyes. He makes a fool of himself and they love him for it—when they are grown and think back to their summers at the beach, they will remember playing leapfrog with their father, burying him in sand, and never spare a thought for the days and days she's spent washing and cooking and cleaning, rubbing calamine lotion on sunburns, cutting up endless watermelons, making hundreds of jugs of lemonade.

"Soniu! *Shcho tam?*" Marta's voice, flapping from the porch off the kitchen.

"Nothing," Sonia shouts back, knowing how it annoys Marta when they speak to her in English. What would happen, she asks herself, if instead of turning back to the cottage, where Marta will be sitting with a heap of darning (she has found a plastic bag of the children's socks with great holes rubbed through the heels, socks Sonia was going to use for cleaning rags), if instead of turning back, she were to run down to the beach and join them, laugh and tumble with them on the sand? *Go if you want to.* She hears a voice, her mother's voice, like a flower tucked behind her ear. But something huge and smothering settles on her shoulders, pushing her back to where her sister-in-law is waiting for her, holding the door open, letting in the mosquitoes they'll be swatting all through the slow August night.

IT'S BONNIE HE catches in his arms, swinging her high, high in the air and down to his shoulders, wading with her into the water. It's the last treat of the afternoon, one of them getting to ride on their father's back to the rock they've christened Australia, to lie down in the sun beside him, having him all to herself for a whole half hour.

His daughters are all dear to him—Laura because she's his firstborn, the details of her infancy and childhood etched on his memory, so that with each subsequent baby he's relived Laura's first tooth or word or step. Katia because of her flair for mischief, the way she dances her way through life without caring what anyone will think or say, knowing she can outwit them all. And Alix because she's still a baby, and he has no idea yet of what she will become. But Bonnie is the gentlest, and with her red-gold hair, her brown, gold-speckled eyes, the most beautiful by far. No one in his family or Sonia's has that coloring. None of the children looks like her mother—is that why, in spite of nursing them through fevers and all the childhood diseases, dressing them so smartly and making sure they get their vitamin this and that, and brush their teeth at night, she's held herself apart from them? As if her heart's a small room into which she's locked herself, with no place for anyone but her parents' ghosts and whatever she thinks she might have made of herself if she'd never married or, at least, never married him.

"Bonnie," he says, sitting her down on the rock, heaving himself up to its broad, blank face, the water sluicing off his back, trickling through the brown thicket of his chest. "Bonnie, I want you to be a help to your mother this week. It's hard for her with Chucha Marta here."

"Yes, Tatu," Bonnie says, shifting closer, leaning her small, damp body in its frilled suit toward him.

"You know your mother's still sad about Baba Laryssa. It takes a long, long time to get over . . ." His voice trails off; he is reluctant to say the word *death* in front of his daughter, just as he wouldn't be able to tell an off-color joke or swear in the presence of any of his children.

"Tell me again about Chucha Marta," Bonnie asks, "and why we have to be nice to her."

He sighs and stretches out his legs so they lift slowly from the water, then splash back.

"You know that when Baba Motria and Dyeedo Martyniuk came to Canada—"

"There was a war on."

"Clever Bonnie. Can you tell me which war?"

"Worldwarwon."

"Exactly. And at that time, the part of Ukraine where Baba and Dyeedo were living was under Austria."

Bonnie pictures her grandparents in a pool of murky water; someone is trying to hold their heads under, the way Pavlo Vesiuk tried to do with her last week, though she never told on him.

"If Baba and Dyeedo hadn't escaped, secretly, in the middle of the night, Dyeedo would have been taken into the Austrian army. He would have ended up in the trenches, he would probably have been killed. A friend came to warn him: they had to flee."

Bonnie bites her lip at the word *flee*: it's a sign that something terrible is coming, the part in the story she can never understand.

"You know that Baba and Dyeedo had two little girls back

in the Old Country. They were very sick; they had diphtheria. The name doesn't matter—what you have to remember is this: there were no doctors and no medicine. No one knew if those little girls would live or die—they were far too sick to be moved. And so . . ."

He doesn't say *they got left behind*. He doesn't say it was eight years before the sister who survived got off the train at Union Station, a sign around her neck, so that the parents who couldn't recognize her anymore, and the brother she didn't know existed, would be able to greet her. He doesn't say that Marta did not laugh or cry or spit or smile all the way from Union Station to the dark, narrow house on Dupont Street, where she finally fell asleep clutching the carpet bag that had been her only luggage and sucking her knuckle. He doesn't want his daughter to know what he knows.

"You have to be kind to Chucha Marta because of what a hard life she's had. She doesn't mean to be scolding and complaining all the time—it's just the way she is, like someone with a handicap, with a blind eye or a wooden leg. A week isn't such a long time, Bonnie. Be as nice to her as you can, it'll make things easier for your mother. I'm trusting you—you're the only one I can trust to help me out like this."

Bonnie puts her arms around her father and leans into his chest. The thick hair tickles her, the ooze of suntan oil that hasn't yet washed off in the water. She is thinking not about Chucha Marta or about Baba Motria and Dyeedo Martyniuk, long in their graves. She is wondering whether Chucha Marta's sister is with Baba Laryssa, looking down at them all from the edge of God's eye in heaven.

"Okay, *rybochko*? We'd better go back." *Little fish*: it's his own name for her, though he's long been reconciled to "Bonnie." Funny, how after his father's thunderings and his mother's head-shakings, he'd finally come to realize that Bonnie is the perfect name for this daughter, the only name that could ever do her justice. *Rybochka* is a pet name, a private name, but Bonnie is the name under which she will sail out into the world, a flag spelling HAPPILY EVER AFTER. Funny, too, how after all these years and all these second thoughts, he has never been able to confess as much to Sonia: *You were right and I was wrong.* What if he were to tell her tonight, when they get into the sagging bed together, the bed with the antique mattress he's been meaning for years to replace? With something new, untouched and unstained, far too good for the cottage. Far too good, but never good enough, and yet exactly what is needed now.

Bonnie clambers onto her father's back, hugging his neck just tight enough that she won't fly off when he dives. It always terrifies her; her stomach is a knot like a tangled skipping rope as they plunge. Holding tighter as they hit the water, she swallows a mouthful, coughing and spluttering, as her father calls out, "*Dobreh, rybochko?*" and she can barely answer back, "*Dobreh*, Tatu." And it's true; everything is fine as they swim back to shore. As long as they're together like this, everything will always be fine.

HUNGRY OR NOT, the whole family sits down to what Sonia calls "a proper supper" at six o'clock each Sunday, while everyone else, Katia keeps pointing out, eats sandwiches on the beach or does a lazy barbecue—hot dogs, hamburgers, relish for a vegetable—on the lawn. "We are not," her mother answers, "everyone else. Decent families sit down to a proper Sunday meal together." *You are a decent family,* sings the ham that's been roasting for the past three hours, sing the potato salad and runner beans and glazed baby carrots on plates Laura thinks of as planets stuck in low gear or seats on a Ferris wheel with a stalled motor. Plates her mother heaps with food, then hands to Max to pass around, the first one traveling from Darka to Laura to Katia to Bonnie to the guest, Chucha Marta.

"Is anything wrong, Marta?" Sonia calls out to the woman sitting with lips pursed, fork poised to stab the ham as though it were going to rise from the plate and attack her. Marta's shrug is the only answer Sonia gets: *Things can't help but be wrong in a household run by such a featherbrain, so what's the use of asking?* Immediately, the ham on Sonia's plate starts to look raw and slippery, the potato salad becomes a pile of furred, white pebbles, as Max says *"Smachnoho,"* and the eating begins.

What little talk there is takes place in Ukrainian, the children reduced to "Please pass the milk" or "May I have the butter?" "I suppose the traffic will be bad tonight," Sonia says to no one in particular, to ease the strain. Max just shakes his head, and Marta, making a comment on the stupidity, the waste of buying summer cottages, might just as well be spitting out a caterpillar.

Sonia sits back from her plate on which the food's been cut up into pieces small enough to fit the baby's mouth. She is studying some screen inside her head, on which is projected the intricate ballet of bringing Marta to the cottage in the first place. Max driving through a brown haze of traffic down Queen Street, going under the railway bridge, past the sweet stench from Canada Packers to the mausoleum of a duplex in which Marta's been waiting since nine that morning. There's no need for him to stop off at home, since his cottage gear is stored at Kalyna Beach—his new swimsuit, his golfing pants, his windbreaker and short-sleeved shirts, which he hardly ever wears. For the most part, he spends the weekend in droopy trousers, smeared all over with oil stains, or a faded swimsuit in place of shorts, with an even more faded appliqué of a woman in a black swimsuit doing a jackknife from an invisible diving board.

Chucha Marta's house is the last of the dozen or so houses Max grew up in. Against all common sense, he gave it outright to Marta when their mother died, though she'd willed everything to him: house, furniture, books (all the Ukrainian classics, plus Ukrainian translations of Tolstoy and Dostoevsky, none of which Marta will ever read but whose spines she lemon-oils religiously). Marta makes him wait at the door, forcing him to ring the bell and pound where the knocker should be, till she feels paid back for the endless hours he's kept her waiting. When she finally opens the door, she doesn't kiss him or even say his name in greeting, just points to her suitcase at the top of a steep flight of stairs (she's refused Max's offers of free renovations: moving her bedroom downstairs, putting in a bathroom on the main floor so she could rent out the top floor if she wants or simply board it up).

Staring down at her untouched plate, Sonia allows her imagination to add scrolls and flourishes to the script she's devised. She watches Max struggle with Marta's case to the car—there must be bricks in it or gallon jugs filled with powdery dirt from the doll-sized yard. She sees her husband opening the back door for his sister, who refuses to sit beside him in the front—*That is the wife's place,* Marta's saying. *Thank God I am no man's wife.* Two blocks on, she makes him turn back; she has to check to see the stove's turned off, the upstairs windows are closed, the door to the summer kitchen is locked. When she gets back into the car at last, she makes him swear, yet again, that when he returns to the city late on Sunday night, he'll stop by—then and every other night that she's away—to make sure no one's broken in.

By the time they reach the highway, it will be rush hour and will continue to be so for another three hours. Marta, thank God, will have nodded off to sleep, though she'll wake up every time traffic slows to a standstill; wake up to give Max assorted pieces of her mind on whatever subject occurs to her—the small investments he's made on her behalf (she suspects him of trying to steal her life savings), the bills he sorts out and pays for her, the weather (those Russians are putting chemicals in the clouds, preventing any rain from falling—didn't he know that? She heard it from the bishop, the same one who addressed the congregation when the Russians sent up Sputnik, assuring them that they'd find green cheese up there and nothing more). Sonia lifts her napkin to her mouth, to smother her laughter. Max doesn't notice, but Marta stares at her, those flinty eyes that seem to nick the surface of everything they touch.

"I'll get the dessert," Sonia says, scooping up her plate before anyone notices how little she's eaten.

"Chucha Marta," one of the children calls out. Sonia clutches the bowl of Jell-O she's rescued from the overcrowded fridge. It must be Katia speaking—who else would dare to provoke her aunt's attention? Calling her Chucha, too, when the child's been told again and again that the proper title for their aunt is "Teetka," that "Chucha" was Laura's invention, baby talk they all should have outgrown by now. But Chucha Marta she remains and always will to her nieces, especially Bonnie. She, not Katia, is the brave one calling on her aunt.

"What!" Marta barks.

Bonnie waits as if there's something in her mouth that she

needs to finish chewing. And then she blurts out: "What was her name? The sister who got left behind."

Silence thick and quivery as the lumps of Jell-O Sonia's dishing into the mismatched bowls. "Shh," Laura hisses; Katia kicks Bonnie under the table, and even her father stares down at her as if she's said something so terrible she will have to be punished. But she hasn't been able to stop thinking about the dead sister all that afternoon. Suddenly the table and the faces turned to her with such ferocious disapproval go murky, as if they've been plunged into dirty water. Bonnie stuffs a finger into the corner of each eye, to stop the tears.

"Sonia, are you going to stand all night over that bowl? Can't you see your husband needs to get on the road? It will be midnight before he gets home. Give us the rest of our dinner!"

"Here you go, Marta," Sonia says, making a point of serving her first. Isn't it just like Marta to go for two birds with one stone, accusing her of being a bad wife as well as a heartless sister-in-law?

Max takes out his handkerchief and mops his forehead. Thank God Marta didn't hear. What an idiot he was, talking to Bonnie this afternoon—now he'll have to unsay it all, warn her not to bother Marta again, to keep out of her way. Sonia will be after him, urging him to stand up to Marta, have it out with her at last. If only he could get her to talk about that time in the war, what had happened to her after she'd been left behind; if only she would come out and accuse him—he hadn't even been born when it happened—then maybe she wouldn't have this power over him, making him bow to her every wish, and making Sonia rail at him.

She's risen from the table, Sonia; she's clapped her hands. "We'll have to hurry now. Come on, girls—*pospeeshymo*! Max, you can have your coffee later." Sonia holds out his jacket in one hand, the car keys in the other.

He's supposed to drive them out to Painter's Point to see the sunset, the way he always does on Sunday nights. Marta knows perfectly well that Max prefers to wait till dark before leaving for the city—he says there's less traffic, or, at least, you don't get so frustrated when you can't see how slowly the landscape's going by.

Marta folds her arms across her narrow chest. "I'm not going anywhere."

"But, Marta, it's so beautiful, and besides . . ."

Besides, if she doesn't come, then Sonia can't go, because someone other than Darka will have to stay behind with Marta, as if Marta were more helpless than Baby Alix. Marta, who lives every day and night of her life alone in the dark, twisty, narrow house on Dupont Street. Marta, who rushes to shut the curtains on every window as soon as the sun goes down. Marta, who takes pleasure, Sonia's sure of it, in crossing her at every step.

"How can I come along? Use your head, Sonia, there's no room in that car of yours."

"Laura will hold Bonnie, and Katia can easily squeeze in beside you. I'll have the baby on my lap—"

"You want to squeeze me in till I can't breathe? Do you know what that will do to my heart?"

"I never said—"

For Christ's sake, let's just go before I pick up the axe and split someone's head open. Of course Max hasn't said this out loud, he's simply grabbed his jacket and slammed the screen door behind him. The children rush after him. Sonia scoops up Alix in one arm and shoves the other arm through Marta's, walking her sternly to the car.

As for the sitter without a baby, she stands on the porch, her hands on her hips, the roots of her bleached-out hair shining darkly in the bold evening light.

PAINTER'S POINT IS a fifteen-minute drive from Kalyna Beach: it's in a provincial park, and the view of the lake from the hills is especially lovely at sunset. They've watched the sky turn from gold to rose; now the sun is caught in a narrow band of cloud and looks like Saturn in Bonnie's *Wonder Book of the Stars and Planets.*

The girls are sitting cross-legged near the edge of the bluff, apart from their parents, who are stationed at a picnic table farther back, with Alix and Chucha Marta. The grown-ups could be in three different rooms: one in a Toronto office, one at the North Pole with a baby on her lap, one in an Old Country that has the dim gleam of a black-and-white photograph. The parents are angry; what's worse, they can't even have their argument and be done with it because of Chucha Marta. Yet while Marta pushes Sonia and Max apart, she brings Katia and Laura together, as close as shared hostility permits.

"I hate her," Laura says. "I wish she'd fall into the lake and drown."

"We should feed her salad made from rhubarb leaves," Katia suggests.

"What if we took her for a walk down Tunnel Road and through the poison ivy patch?"

"She hates walking," Bonnie reminds Laura. "She's got arthritis." She was going to tell her sisters about her plan for Chucha Marta but decides that it has to stay a secret. And so she sits with her chin in her hands, her fingers caging her ears as Laura and Katia rhyme off all the reasons Chucha Marta is so awful.

Because she's jealous of their father, who is handsome and successful.

Because she's jealous of their mother, who used to be a fashion model and is beautiful and married to their father.

Because she was made to polish their father's shoes up to the day he got married.

Because she never got married.

Because her house is small and dark, and the only chair with upholstery is still in its plastic wrapper that's gone all cracked and yellow.

Because she has a mole like a piece of chewed-out gum on her forehead.

Because there's always a funny smell in the bathroom after she's used it.

Because all she can cook is beans and wieners.

Because she's never learned to speak proper English.

Because she's got fallen arches and has to wear men's shoes.

Because she was born a girl. If she'd been a boy, they would never have left her for dead in the Old Country.

Sonia is watching the water that refuses to catch fire from a crimson sun. The weather's turning, and they'll be stuck in the house together the whole week long. If only she'd listened to Mr. Streatfield all those years ago, become the signature model for Sunny Sportswear . . . But where would she be now, at her age? There was no work, no paying work, for models getting on to forty. If only she were clever like Sasha or solid, practical like Annie; if she could have done something other than stand before a camera showing off clothes she didn't own, and a smile that wasn't hers, she might have been able to be happy. Being happy, she's decided, is like being beautiful: no matter how good your skin or bones, you have to work at it. She counts on her fingers the women she knows who could be called happy. Men she leaves out of it. They don't need happiness—they have their jobs, their factories and offices and professions. But if happiness is something you've got to struggle for, what about misery—

the kind of pure misery, powerful as ammonia that Marta's
drenched in?

Marta was a child once—children are born neither happy
nor sad, they get slapped at birth but it's to make them breathe,
not cry. Sonia's mother had once said something about a woman
she knew having drunk sourness in with her mother's milk.
Maybe that's what happened to Marta. Of *course* she'd had a
hard start in life, they must never forget what happened to her.
Sonia's mother would never have left a child of hers alone somewhere for eight hours, never mind eight years. Sonia swallows
hard and puts her arm around Marta's shoulder, wanting to say
something welcoming, comforting. Marta shakes her off, glar-
ing at her as if she is allergic to or even terrified of tenderness.
All Sonia can think of now is how she'd like to grab the kerchief
off Marta's head and tie it around her face instead, like a gag.

"Girls!" They can tell from the sound of their mother's voice
that she's just as angry as when they started out.

"Come on, kids, I've got a long drive ahead of me." Even their
father sounds cross.

They know better than to point out that there's still a blob of
sun that hasn't dropped into the lake. They brush off their shorts
and walk back to the car, following their father and mother and
Chucha Marta, who carries her big black handbag on her arm
as if it were the coffin she'd spent her life savings on.

•　•　•

MAX EMERGES FROM the bathroom with his hair brushed, his face damp and fragrant from the soapy water he's splashed across it. One by one, he picks up the girls and kisses them; even Laura he holds high, and Laura weighs almost as much as her mother. Sonia puts out her face for him to kiss. His lips touch her cheek, and then he's nodding good-bye to Marta, who's never been known to kiss anyone or to suffer being kissed. He waves to Darka, who lifts her hand distractedly.

As the car pulls away, Marta turns to Sonia. On her face is a look that could be mistaken for a smile. "He should have gone earlier."

"He likes driving at night."

"You should have made him leave at six, like the other men."

"He leaves when he wants to, Marta."

"He was angry—it's bad to get into a car when you've been quarreling."

"We were not quarreling."

"If something happens to him on the road tonight, you'll have to live with it for the rest of your days."

Sonia turns on her heel. She goes off to the children, making sure they're washed up and in bed; she turns off all the lights in the kitchen and living room. Out on the front steps the air is little cooler than the soup they have to breathe indoors, and yet she shivers, thinking of Max and the icy fist inside her, in the place where her heart should be. She closes her eyes, remembering that first year of their marriage, how they'd had to live with their in-laws, saving money so they could buy their own home outright: no debt, no being beholden. Laura had been born from the Martyn house; not until Katia was well on the way had they been able to move into a home of their own. She will tell all her daughters when the time comes for them to marry: live in a broom closet if you must, but live with your husband on your own.

Such freedom she'd felt on her honeymoon, the reckless joy at being alone with someone, intimately together. Not the sex so much as something tentative and trusting forming inside her. How it had shown itself in the way she'd been able to join in with Max, keeping it secret from everyone else, this new life starting between them. The teasing, the jokes, the codes they'd worked out to use in front of the waiters and the other guests at the hotel. She'd been stupid enough to take it all for granted, never giving a moment's thought to whether or for how long it would last. So that when they came back—back to Motria's endless sighs and Marta's sharp, narrow glances, all that buoyant joy had vanished. Locked into the bathroom that first night at her in-laws' house, they'd splashed and giggled in the tub together, until Max's father had started banging on the door, bawling them out for wasting hot water. She had frozen, right then and there, as if the bathtub had become a snowfield, and her nakedness were something raw, skinned over with ice.

Last night, when Max had leaned over her, stroking her bare

arm shyly, as if they'd never lain together before, that was how cold she'd been. She'd tried to open her arms to him, but they'd felt like laundry frozen to the line. All the words she'd practiced saying, all the endearments, every attempt at gentleness in her voice had come out as anger and reproach. About Marta, how he let her bully him, scare his children, and wipe the floor with his wife. And Max had sworn under his breath—how could she blame him?—and fallen back to the lumpy mattress; he'd turned his back against her, abandoning her to the stew of her misery, her helplessness, everything she couldn't show him, share with him, any more than the drowning can share the air in the lungs of their would-be rescuers.

Sonia's seen how fast Max drives when he's angry; she knows how tired he is. Already she hears the knock on the door, sees herself at the hospital, and then the funeral parlor, the white, bewildered faces of the children, Marta in her customary black, croaking *ya tobee skazala*, I told you so. How the loving widow, her lips quivering, will long to throw herself on his body, and how the embittered wife will hold herself back, all the words she could never say to him stuck in her throat, words she'd been made to feel afraid of, ashamed for him to hear, even in the dark. If she could call him back, if it were somehow in her power to make the car turn around and bring him back, she would cover his face with kisses, let him make love to her again and again, and let there be another five or ten or twenty children born, it wouldn't matter, if only she could bring him safely home.

It is not her imagination, it really is the car, wheels churning up gravel, the door slamming. Max, safe and well, walking up to her. It's like watching a film in slow motion; there's all the time in the world for her to see and know what is happening; how the fist of her heart, instead of letting go, clenches even colder and tighter. So she doesn't throw herself into his arms as she longed to only a moment before, when the drive was empty and the car had vanished. She simply sits on the step, looking up at him as he says, "Forgot my briefcase" and goes inside to pick it up from the coffee table where he left it. And then he's back again, so quickly the children haven't had a chance to register his presence; he's at the car and she forces, has to force herself, to rise and go to him.

"Max," she calls out. He turns to her, impatient. He's already in the city, thinking about tomorrow's cases, that world of his with which she has nothing to do. Instead of *sorry*, or even just *drive safely*, she says, "Don't speed."

He gets into the car, slams the door shut. But then she stands by the window until he finally rolls it down.

"What is it now, Sonia?" That weary inflection of his voice. He's as bad in his way as Marta—why had she ever married him, the both of them?

"I don't want you dead, that's all."

"No such luck." He starts the car and then remembers: that is Peter's line. He isn't Peter; he refuses to be. And so Max stretches out his hand and puts it on his wife's cool, slender arm. "It's only a week and then she'll be gone. You won't have to see her here for another year."

She looks at his hand on her skin: she touches it, lightly, so quickly that he can't be sure she has made the gesture at all. Her voice when she speaks at last is muffled, as if she's talking in her sleep.

"It's okay. You'd better go now."

This time he drives off for good.

WHEREVER CHUCHA MARTA goes, even if she's only moving from her bedroom to the kitchen or from the kitchen to the living room, she always takes her handbag with her. It belongs to her, Bonnie decides, like the scarf she wears on her head or her underclothes. The handbag is black; it fastens with a shiny, gold-colored clasp attached to a spring; if you were foolish enough to try to open it, your hand would be snapped off clean. This is what Chucha Marta has told each one of them, even Baby Alix, who has shown no signs of wanting to snoop and pry. The clasp on Chucha Marta's handbag is first cousin to her only other treasured possession: a mink collar made of one long pelt, with small, sorry paws dangling from it and a fiercely pointed head with brilliant, beady eyes. The mouth of the mink opens like a clothespin to snap shut on its tail: from the start of November straight through to the end of April, Chucha Marta wears the mink collar on her plain black coat, to church and funerals and family gatherings at her brother's house.

No one can remember a time when she didn't wear black. Bonnie imagines a small, skinny Chucha Marta—no smaller and skinnier than Marta is now, but aged fifteen instead of fifty-three—getting off the train at Union Station. She's wearing scratchy black woolen stockings, a black skirt and blouse, and in place of the head scarf, a straw hat with roses around the brim. Young as she is, Bonnie knows a straw hat would never have survived the journeys in farm wagons and crowded trains and steerage berths that her aunt would have suffered through. Yet she has to give her one article of dress less ugly than her standard gear, something as fragile yet detailed as the clothes worn by Bonnie's paper dolls.

What's in Chucha Marta's handbag? Secrets, Bonnie thinks. She's seen her aunt pull all kinds of objects out of the great black bag. Balled-up Kleenexes, a cracked change purse made out of some bashed brown material that tries to look like leather, keys on heavy metal rings. Small, flat boxes of aspirin for Chucha Marta's arthritis; tubes of Rolaids (taken copiously and conspicuously after dinners prepared by Bonnie's mother). Bobby pins and paper clips; small combs with half the teeth missing; even a candle stub and a box of matches. But there are vast numbers of other things in Chucha Marta's handbag, secret things that make a rich rattle whenever the bag's lifted up or shoved down. The bottom of her aunt's handbag is, as Bonnie imagines, the seabed to be: littered with treasure from ocean liners like the *Titanic* and the *Andrea Doria*, about the sinking of which Laura's read to her, from a magazine.

Bonnie is sitting on the sofa in the living room; it is Monday morning, and she's still in her pajamas, wrapped up in a cotton blanket. Complaining of a headache, she's asked her mother if she could stay up at the cottage rather than go down to the beach—stay with Chucha Marta. Her mother's face, already creased with the day's impending complications, tenses.

"Are you sure? Really sure?" She puts her hand on Bonnie's forehead, checking for fever, calculating the odds of this being scarlatina, since all four of her daughters have already had chicken pox and measles. At last she gives a small sigh and says yes, Bonnie can stay in the living room, as long as she doesn't make any trouble for Marta, as long as she keeps herself wrapped up and quiet on the sofa. But to Sonia's astonishment, Marta insists on her sister-in-law going down to the beach with the others. She's no invalid or idiot child, Marta declares—she doesn't need to be spied on, kept under observation. No, she will not have that fool of a Darka foisted on her. And yes, she is perfectly capable of keeping an eye on the child.

Heading for the beach, Sonia wonders what kind of game Marta's playing: halfway down the stairs she's about to turn back, run inside, and rescue Bonnie, when she tells herself that she's overreacting. She'll go up to check on them both in an hour's time.

• • •

MARTA AND BONNIE are alone together, or at least they occupy the same room. For Marta seems oblivious of her niece's presence. Her eyes are fastened on the piece of crochet work in her hands, work that puzzles Sonia's daughters—why does Chucha Marta spend so much time making holes out of thread? What do her tablecloths do but show what's underneath them, what they can't hope to cover up? Dozens and dozens of tablecloths that Marta makes obsessively and that Sonia stores unused in a trunk in the basement.

"Chucha Marta?" Bonnie calls from the sofa.

There's no reply but the tug of thread through the crochet hook. Bonnie tries again, going over to the chair by the window where her aunt is working.

"What was she called?"

"Who?"

"You know."

"Why should I tell you? It's a secret."

"Please tell me. I promise I won't let anyone know."

Chucha Marta puts down her crochet hook and draws her handbag onto her lap. She frowns at Bonnie, and the mole on her forehead doesn't look like chewing gum anymore but wet and purple, the way you might imagine a bullet hole to be.

"Why do you want to know?" There is no softening of Marta's voice, no lessening of suspicion. It's almost as though she's been expecting the question, inviting it, for the sheer pleasure of denying her niece what she most wants to hear.

"Because I'm sorry that I never knew her," Bonnie says. "If I know her name, then maybe I can make her up in a story, the way I do our-brother-who-died-before-he-was-born."

"You're crazy. You can't make people up out of nothing. The dead are dead, and they'll stay dead no matter how much you call them to come back."

"My brother's five now. He's got hair just like Tato's, and he's so smart he can read the newspaper already—" Bonnie stops speaking, not because she's run out of things to say but because Marta has slapped her face, hard enough to make the skin burn and then go numb. Bonnie has never been hit before.

"Never talk like that to anyone again. That baby's a secret— he's not your secret, he's your mother's. You keep him in here—" Marta may be pointing to her heart, but she's holding up her handbag against her chest and thumping it as if it were her breastbone.

Bonnie doesn't cry out, and she doesn't cry, though her face stings and the whole room is shuddering from the force of that slap—the curtains shake on their rods, even the glass in the picture window shivers. She sits there watching Chucha Marta clutch her scarred black handbag to her chest, and then, summoning all her courage, she puts her hand out to the bag and touches it.

"Your sister isn't a secret, Chucha Marta. Tell me her name."

For a moment, Bonnie's afraid that Marta is going to hit her again, but Marta only pulls the handbag out from under her niece's hand and drops it to her lap. And then she opens the clasp and plunges into the jumble of things that swim in that dark, sealed sea. She pulls up an ancient peppermint, closes her hand around it, then reluctantly offers it to Bonnie. But the child won't touch it; she just stands there, waiting. Till Chucha Marta snaps her handbag shut and answers her.

"Lyalka," she says at last.

Bonnie nods—she knows that word; it means *doll*. A nickname. Her dead aunt was Chucha Marta's baby sister, the way Alix is hers. Bonnie's about to press Chucha Marta about her sister's real name, her proper name, when Marta speaks again.

"She had your eyes. Brown, with little gold fish swimming in them. And your hair—just that golden-red."

Bonnie nods, trying to keep her mouth from falling open. For Chucha Marta's voice, as she has spoken these words, is the voice of an utter stranger. It isn't harsh and shrill anymore: it's hoarse, as if the tenderness in it has grown a rough coat of rust.

"You are too trusting, little one," Marta whispers in the same hoarse voice. "Someone has to teach you not to trust anyone— not your parents and not God either."

When Sonia comes up from the beach to check on them, she finds Marta crocheting, her back turned to the window overlooking the lake, and Bonnie asleep on the sofa, clutching her blanket high against her face.

• • •

THICK AS THIEVES, Sonia moans to Sasha. Her daughter, her beautiful little Bonnie, who has never made trouble for anybody, the one even Laura loves without reservation, is thick as thieves with Chucha Marta.

Sasha pours Sonia a glass of ginger ale with a dollop of gin in it. Sonia is too upset to know how strong her drink is; in fact, Sasha observes, Sonia is as upset as she's ever seen her. It must have to do, she thinks, with the death of Sonia's mother: Laryssa was the only one who could handle "the harpy," as Sasha calls Marta, giving the word a Ukrainian flavor, rolling the *r* in a way that usually sets Sonia laughing. But not today.

"She says she pities me for being married—she goes on and on about how stupid I was to ever give myself away! She says I've turned Max into a spoiled child. And the girls—she makes it crystal-clear what a rotten mother I've been—"

"Send her over here, Sonechko, and I'll set her straight. Can you imagine what she'd say if she saw this house and my kids? Come on, cheer up: you've only got her for a week. Thank your stars you're not Annie. Can you imagine what it's been like for her, having her mother-in-law move in with them even before they got back from their honeymoon?"

But Sonia derives no consolation from the comparison of her lot with Annie Vesiuk's. She drinks up her gin and ginger ale and walks foggily back to the cottage, where Darka's been left in charge while Marta naps (though according to Marta, the Whore of Babylon would have made a better babysitter). At the steps leading up to the screened porch—the rotting steps Max has been promising all summer to fix—she stops, listens for any noise of battle inside, and sits down to puzzle out what's happening. It's not that Marta's showing any sign of affection toward Bonnie, it's just a sense Sonia has of a thickening of the air between them, of something holding them together, like the loops of thread in Marta's crochet work, the webs she spins like the spider she is. And that's what makes Sonia so uneasy—not the thought of Bonnie as a fly caught in Marta's web, but of Marta turning the child into another, smaller spider, infected with Marta's own bitterness and spite.

She sits with her head in her hands, resisting as long as she can, and then resigning herself, at last, to Bonnie's defection. If it were Laura instead of Bonnie, she would put a stop to it, even if it meant bloodshed—and Marta is the kind of person who makes you think blood. Laura, Sonia's often thought in her dark, dark moods, is really Marta's child—she can see in Laura the same foul temper, the will to sour and spoil things. How can it work that way—that a child could be born not just with her aunt's shade of hair or shape of foot but also with her anger? And how can Bonnie seek out Marta's company, how could she not run screaming from that harpy hooking a hangman's noose disguised as a tablecloth?

On Tuesday, Bonnie had spent all morning with her aunt.

She'd been ordered down to the beach in the afternoon but had raced back to the cottage before any of the others, supposedly to help Sonia make supper. She'd spent too much time looking into the sitting room, where Marta was jabbing at her crochet work, to be of much help. The third morning, no excuse was offered; Bonnie got dressed with the others, but instead of trooping down to the lake with them, she settled onto the sofa across from Marta, with some old *National Geographic*s and the piece of cross-stitch she'd been torturing for as long as Sonia could remember. "It's okay, Mama," she called out. "I'll stay up here with Chucha Marta while you go down to the beach." It was then that Sonia had proved weak—she should have ended it then and there, but the thought of being down at the beach with all the other women and their children, instead of spending the day with Marta in the confinement of the cottage, was too tempting.

On Wednesday, she put her guilty foot down. Bonnie was looking pale; she needed to be out in the sun, that's what they'd bought the cottage for in the first place, to keep the children strong and healthy, soaking up vitamin D. Her sisters missed her company; Darka needed Bonnie's help with the baby. So Bonnie went sadly down to the lake, and Sonia punished herself with cleaning out the big sideboard where the battered games and incomplete puzzles were kept, the odd socks and broken things she could never bring herself to throw away, in case their mates could be found or their innards fixed—and that she hated herself for hanging on to, out of some reflex of early poverty. *Keep a thing and its use will come—you never know when you'll be worse off than you are now.* Her father's words, spoken with the gravity of experience.

But within an hour, Bonnie had sneaked back to the cottage, back to Marta, who betrayed neither pleasure nor irritation at the small girl with scuffed sandals, the child-skin smelling of lake water and suntan oil. After lunch, Marta had gone off to her room as usual, taken off her dress, and lain down on the bed in her slip, with her lisle stockings rolled to her knees. She'd slept for exactly two hours, emerging disgruntled, as if sleep and dreams had lost any power to refresh her. Bonnie had taken her nap in her own room, as always, and Baby Alix in hers, while Katia and Laura visited their friends. Darka had held the fort while Sonia fled to Sasha's in despair.

By Thursday, there was nothing left for Sonia to tidy or sort through in the cottage. She'd sent Bonnie down to the beach with the others, giving Darka strict instructions to keep her there, but Bonnie had crept back up—to use the washroom, she explained later on—how could anyone scold her for that? But what had been stranger, and far more disturbing to Sonia, was this: how, while she was off making lunch, leaving Marta crocheting by the picture window, the woman had vanished. Sonia had come out of the kitchen to ask whether Marta would prefer boiled or deviled eggs and had found an empty chair. She'd made a fool of herself, calling Marta's name, searching every room, even the bathroom, frightened half to death her sister-in-law might have had a stroke or a heart attack there and be lying in a heap by the toilet. Sonia had found no trace of Marta until she'd rushed out to the lawn: from the lookout point under the empty flagpole, she saw the two of them, side by side. They were standing at the very edge of the lake, where the water rolled in clear and intricate, like some ruffled fabric far more delicate than glass. The two of them, Bonnie and Marta, standing side by side on the smooth, packed sand, Bonnie in her flip-flops and Marta in her men's shoes, her stockings rolled down to the ankles, water splashing over the toes.

Side by side, not touching but seeming to be holding hands, though what Bonnie was clutching was one of the straps of Marta's handbag, while her aunt held the other, the bag suspended between them like a sad, dark fish.

SONIA KNOWS, OF course, that it's not going to last, this collusion between Bonnie and Marta. Not only that it won't last, but that when the rupture comes, it will be painful. But she hasn't expected it to be brutal.

It happens on Saturday morning—just after Max has finished his coffee. In spite of the traffic having been so awful last night that the car didn't roll into the driveway till eleven and Sonia was on the verge of calling the police; in spite of how late it was before he finally was able to fall asleep, his nerves keyed up, his neck muscles aching, Max doesn't allow himself to sleep in. Sonia is reading the letter he's brought her from Olya. Marta has emerged, at last, from her room and is standing by the table, looking over Sonia's shoulder in a way that would have infuriated Sonia if she hadn't known that Max's sister had never learned to read in any language. Marta doesn't wait for Sonia to finish with her letter, or for Max to drain his coffee cup, before she drops the bomb:

"She's been stealing money from my purse. I caught her red-handed!"

Sonia, clutching Olya's letter, is about to leap to Darka's defense when Marta cuts her short.

"Bonnie—what kind of a name is that for a child! And what kind of a child would steal from a poor old woman who has nothing, nothing in all the world!"

Sonia is speechless. Max, on the other hand, falls straight into Marta's trap. When he protests Bonnie's innocence, Marta cries out in triumph.

"My own brother is calling me a liar. The only family I have left in the world, and he accuses me of lying—which is even worse than stealing. Why don't you just take that knife"—she is pointing to the bread knife, its handle loose, its teeth dulled—"and stab me to the heart. To the heart!"

There is more in this vein, and before he knows it, Max is apologizing to Marta and promising that he will speak with Bonnie; he will punish her. As for Sonia, she has stormed out of the kitchen and over to Sasha's house—she doesn't trust herself to go down to the beach, she would explode in front of the children. Liars, the two of them, Max and Marta—for Max's promise to punish Bonnie is so much hot air; he is groveling in front of his witch of a sister. Though if he dares say a single word to Bonnie, if he so much as frowns at her, she will pack up the children, all of them, then and there, and— Max has gone out to the porch and yelled for Darka, who finally comes up, flustered, from the laundry room in the cellar and agrees to sit with Marta while Max goes down to the lake to have a word with his daughter.

Sasha pours out a glass of gin spiked with tonic water and forces Sonia to take a sip of it. "Relax, Sonechko—don't let Marta get at you—that's exactly what she wants. Just smile sweetly and imagine one of those crochet hooks going straight into her heart. Like in 'The Snow Queen,' when Kai gets a sliver of the mirror in his—"

"Snow queen? It's summer, Sasha, what on earth are you talking about?"

"My God, Sonia, here I've been giving you *Fanny Hill* to read when I should have been starting you out on fairy tales!"

"Fairy tales," Sonia says bitterly. "You haven't even been listening to me! Marta's trying to—"

"Marta's straight out of a fairy tale, Sonia—maybe not 'The Snow Queen,' but 'Snow White' for sure. Now, drink up and calm down. And save your anger for something that really matters. I mean your brother, and whether he's going to behave at the Senchenkos' party, and how we're going to stop Nadia from jumping into the lake. I'm only joking, Soniu, don't look like that!"

Sonia's face is white as soap. "What a"—and here she pauses, startling Sasha with a bitter little smile—"what a *Sarah Bernhardt* Nadia is." She's still as angry as when she first ran into the Plotskys' cabin. "Joke all you want," she exclaims, banging her half-empty glass on the table. "Because I still haven't talked to Peter. And I'll bet anything you haven't said a word to Mrs. Senchenko!"

Slamming the door behind her, Sonia rushes out, as Sasha drains what's left of the gin and rubs her eyes with the heels of her hands.

IT ROLLS ON wheels, it's all like a perfect piece of theater. Even Sonia, who's in no mood to forgive anyone, acknowledges the cleverness of Katia's plan. Max is as grateful and astonished as he would be if Katia had shown him the solution to a legal problem that had stumped him.

The word Max had with Bonnie was, of course, a confession of helplessness and not an accusation. If Bonnie didn't apologize publicly to Chucha Marta for what she hadn't done, there would be outright war. And if she did pretend to have stolen coins from Marta's handbag, there would also be war, if not murder—Sonia was in a state, he confided—he didn't have to say what kind of a state. Though the last thing he'd ever wanted for his daughter—any of his daughters—would be to have her mixed up in a lie.

At which point Katia, who'd been hovering on the sidelines, spelled out her strategy: their father was to give Bonnie fifty cents and send her to Mrs. Maximoynko's store. There she would buy a slab of Macintosh's toffee, for which Chucha Marta is known to have a weakness. Bonnie would take the toffee to the cottage and present it to Chucha Marta, saying she'd borrowed the money from her aunt to make her a going-away present. Not having any money of her own, what other way did she have to spoil Chucha Marta? For everyone knew that Chucha Marta would never buy treats for herself.

"Is that okay with you, Bonnie?" her father asked. Bonnie nodded her head quickly. There were some things you shouldn't think about too hard or too long, and the surrender—the weakness—of a beloved parent was one of them. So she duly went off to Venus Variety with two quarters in her hand and returned with the toffee, which she now presents to Marta, in front of everyone. She isn't able to say a word, though; it's her father who has to explain that borrowing isn't stealing, how a surprise is nothing like a theft.

Chucha Marta stands there, her handbag clutched in her arms, her lips tight, her small eyes glittering. She, too, refuses to speak, except by finally taking the toffee from Bonnie's hands and throwing it to the floor. Whereupon Katia nimbly jumps in, picking up the package, extracting the toffee, now shattered into bite-sized pieces, and handing them around to everyone. Only Bonnie and Chucha Marta refuse to eat. Not a word more is said on the subject.

Sonia makes and dishes out lunch, after which the younger girls go off for their nap, and Laura and Katia sit on opposite sofas, reading, or pretending to read, battered copies of *Nancy Drew* and *Cherry Ames*. Chucha Marta has her customary rest and makes her customary fuss at the supper table, though everyone smiles politely, as if she has been praising the food and the company's manners to the skies. For tomorrow Chucha Marta is going home; their father will head back to the city earlier than usual, so that this will be the Last Supper—until Christmastime, at least.

Everyone goes to bed early tonight. Katia's been allowed to sleep over at Tania's house, as a reward for her cleverness, but the rest of the family is apprehensive lest Marta break the shaky truce they've all agreed to. Bed seems by far the safest place, even to Bonnie. Tonight, Laura isn't asked to let her sister into her bed, to tell her stories. Listening to Laura's steady breathing, Bonnie lies awake, thinking of the trick Chucha Marta has played on her; paying back, in some small way, the trick her own parents had played on her, leaving her behind with a dying sister as they ran away to Canada.

But is it a trick Chucha Marta's played, or has she given Bonnie a lesson? And what should she take from what her aunt has tried to teach her? The curtains let in a stab of moonlight.

Bonnie closes her eyes tight, until she's able to see a house un-like the dark, dank, narrow one on Dupont Street, or her own split-level suburban home, or even the cottage, with its thin, white-painted walls. In the dark in her head, lanterns are moving through a wooden house with chicken legs, like Baba Yaga's hut in the book of fairy tales. People are throwing clothes into chests, gathering up pillows and bedding. Except for one room, in which two little girls are tossing and turning, their bodies simmering with fever. An old woman is sitting beside them, rubbing their faces and arms and legs with a cloth dipped in well water, squeezing water from the cloth onto their gummed lips. The old woman looks just like Chucha Marta, with her black clothes and her old black scarf like a beetle's shell. But one of the children lying on the bed is also Chucha Marta, and the other is her sister. *Lyalka: Dolly.*

And now the dark wooden house, filled with lanterns and people with huge, soft bundles in their arms, gives way to a scene of broken trees and drifting smoke. Guns are firing, and people run in all directions, searching for shelter. A girl in a black dress trails after them, clutching someone's skirt or trouser leg, so as not to get lost in all the smoke and ash raining down on the road. Sometimes she hears Russian being spoken around her, and sometimes Polish or German; some of the time—the only time she may be safe—she hears Ukrainian. She spends four years running like this, never settling, never having time or means to go to school or learn to do anything but survive. Until finally the war stops, like a watch that's run down, and she's taken back to the village where she was born, to relatives who take her in, because her own house has been burned and there is no place else for her.

And just as she's beginning to forget her life before the war, just as she's given up hope that anyone will remember her, send for her, a letter arrives in the village, a letter from a strange city in a foreign country. In the letter is money and instructions for Chucha Marta, who is now older than Laura, to take the farm cart, and then a train, and finally a ship and then another train to the place her parents will be waiting for her. One of the relatives, or maybe only a neighbor, comes with her all the way to the boat. Who takes care of Marta on the boat? Bonnie can't picture this, or what it would be like to find yourself so utterly alone, even when she remembers how she got lost, one time, on a boat to Centre Island. How she sat on the steps leading to the upper deck, people nearly crushing her with their feet, until she heard her father's voice calling out her name. She just sat there, her throat parched, with no voice to answer him, and yet she wasn't afraid, for she knew he would keep on looking and calling till he found her.

What must it have been like stepping off the train from Halifax, which to Bonnie is as remote a place as Austria? People speaking nothing but babble all around you, none of the words you know in Ukrainian or Polish or Russian. Around her neck, Marta has a signboard spelling out MARTA MARTYNIUK in the Cyrillic letters Bonnie has just learned to write at Ukrainian school. And here, at last, are the parents Marta last saw ten years ago, greeting the daughter who looks nothing like the dying child under the lantern's light. Here is the brother who has taken her place and the place of her dead sister. What do they say to each other on the platform at Union Station—do they just go home, have supper, wash the dishes, and go to bed?

It is late by now, late enough for all the lights to have been switched off, and all the grown-ups to be asleep. Bonnie lies listening to her sister's breathing in the bed across from her, looks at the moonlight cutting through the windows. Against the white-painted walls she makes out shapes and stains projected like images from the home movies her father takes every Christmas. And suddenly it comes to her, one of those truths that startle and convince at the same instant. If Laura were awake, she would call out to her, crawl into her bed to whisper the truth of the secret Chucha Marta has been hiding from them all this time.

But Laura is sleeping, and besides, Bonnie has learned that secrets—someone else's secrets—are something you are bound to keep. And so she lies back in her bed, with her hands clasped tight, as if to keep her from letting go of it. Not the real name of Marta's sister but the fact that her aunt has forgotten that name.

This is the only secret Chucha Marta keeps.

WHILE BONNIE LIES awake in the moonlight, Katia is wishing she hadn't gone to sleep over at the Plotskys', after all. For the something that has surfaced between her and Tania has put both girls on their guard.

They are standing before the spotted mirror in Tania's bedroom, under a lamp filled with the bodies of fried flies.

"*What* did you call them?"

"Teddies."

"Are you sure?"

"Of course I'm sure," Katia says crossly, elbowing Tania away from the mirror. If someone were to ask her why she's so irritable, she would answer, *on account of Yuri*. For in some way that Katia doesn't fully understand, but that she knows in her bones, it is because of Yuri (whom neither girl mentions by name, or even as "he") that they are jostling for space in front of the mirror in Tania's bedroom, their pajama tops rolled up, the startlingly white skin of their chests exposed.

Katia touches the reflection in the glass: two small, dark circles, like tarnished pennies.

"Whatever you call them, yours aren't any bigger than mine," Tania declares.

"They're not doing anything much for either of us," Katia says sourly.

Now it's Tania's turn to push Katia out of the way and to mo-
nopolize the mirror. The poor showing of their teddies is partly
the mirror's fault, she decides. It's old and the silver backing is
worn away in splotches; it looks as though it has some disease,
like the one that kills off her grandmother's roses.

Tania frowns, pushing her elbows together, making a *V* of
her arms. A faint line forms at her breastbone.

"Look, Katia, do you see that? It's a *cleavice.*"

"No it's not—it's just your skin wrinkling up. You can't have a
cleavice without breasts, and all you've got are teddies. All *we've*
got," she adds, trying to be fair; pulling her pajama top back
down. They have both asked their mothers, in vain, for training bras. Sonia rejected the idea with a flat no, refusing even to
discuss the issue. Sasha laughed, saying she'd never thought of
breasts being like puppies or horses, needing to be broken in.

After Laura had turned thirteen, Katia had had a chance to
read the *You're a Young Lady Now* pamphlet that their mother
had left on Laura's bed one day. The pamphlet was tinted a soft
pink, and the paper looked as if it were made of marshmallow.
There were roses in soft focus on the cover, and the text was all
in italics. Before Laura had come home from school, Katia had
read it from cover to cover, but the purpose of the booklet had
baffled her. It made no mention of the body parts whose names
she'd learned years ago from the older kids at school and whose
proper names she'd seen on a mimeographed sheet handed out
by Laura's health-and-gym teacher. The pamphlet was as bewil-

dering as the "Modess because . . ." ads in their mother's *Vogue* magazines, which always featured a woman with prominent collarbones in an evening gown, standing alone on a terrace at sunset. "Because what?" she'd ask her mother, whose invariable reply was, "You'll understand when you're older."

Tania, however, had proved the best detective of them all; snooping in her mother's dresser back home, she found, under the chiffon scarves and never-used embroidered handkerchiefs, *The Woman's Lifelong Guide to Health and Happiness* by Dr. Reginald Thwaites, a thin volume containing a detailed description of puberty, pregnancy, and menopause. She locked herself into the bathroom—the only room in the house to possess a lock—and wolfed down the first two sections, passing on the information in chunky parcels to Katia, and thereby supplying most of the information that *You're a Young Lady Now* had omitted from its rose-colored pages.

It had been a considerable shock to them both, this news that every twenty-eight days their bodies would start to bleed and that they'd have to wear something like giant bandages between their legs. And curl up with hot-water bottles and take aspirin for cramps that the book described as an early form of the pain a woman experiences in childbirth. The idea that they will have to go through all this just so they can have babies is completely unacceptable to them: babies shriek in the middle of the night and throw up on your shoulder or soak your lap when you're asked to hold them. Babies generate mountains of wash so that, from the time of their birth till they hit three, their mothers disappear behind a wall of white-flagged laundry. What is even more appalling is the fact that they will be expected to feed these babies from their own bodies, from breasts they imagine will turn as long and hard and narrow as the bottles dropped off in the milk box each morning.

"We don't have to feed babies—we don't have to *have* babies—because you can't have one without a husband, and we're never getting married," Tania had pointed out.

"Won't we end up like Chucha Marta, then?" Katia had asked, imagining a fate even worse than being mummified in diapers: that of wearing a head scarf and old black cardigan all of your life, sitting in a house that smells sour as chopped onions, and glorying in your own misery, as she's heard her mother say of Chucha Marta.

"Of course we're not going to become like her," Tania had scolded. "We're going to China, remember?"

Katia did remember, but now, as she lies back in the top bunk bed, with Tania fidgeting below her, she's not so sure. Whether geography is stronger than biology. How far Tania is to be trusted.

The one part of puberty that does not seem to be painful, gross, or imprisoning, the girls have decided, is the actual growing of breasts. In fact, Tania's mother's book specifies that the pain and mess of menstruation are more than compensated for by the shy pride a young girl may take in the development of her bosom. If Tania had read further in the book, in a section called "Some Problems You May Need to Know About," she would have learned that many women develop painful lumps called cysts, and that any changes in the breast, painful or not, should be checked out immediately by a doctor. But she reads only the puberty section, from which she memorizes the various names for the parts of the breast (*nipple, aureole, ducts*) and agrees with Dr. Thwaites that breasts are not only desirable but downright prestigious. Unless, of course, you happen to have been born to a flat-chested woman.

It's one more thing, one supreme grudge, to hold against their mothers. The girls understand what the term *heredity* means, and they're unconvinced when Sonia and Sasha reassure them that of course they'll develop one day—that every girl does. These speeches always end with remarks about how they should just enjoy being children; how these, after all, are the best years of their lives. Listening to such advice, the girls don't groan, or shrug, or roll their eyes. Instead, they look down or away, embarrassed at the pity they feel for their mothers, who don't understand how different their daughters' lives will be from their own, and how the very shape of their future is tied up, somehow, in that most conspicuous of secrets, the growing of breasts.

Katia has no memory at all of Baba Motria, who died when she was the age Baby Alix is now, but what she'd loved best about Baba Laryssa, besides all the baking she did for them and the preserving of strawberries and raspberries in thick glass jars, was her bosom. Lying with her head against it, falling asleep in her *baba*'s lap on winter afternoons, when she and Laura had been left at the big house on Dovercourt Road so their parents could attend what they called a "function." In the summer Baba Laryssa wore cotton shifts in bright colors, with V-necks; the skin of her bosom always felt cool and moist, reminding Katia of the times when she'd helped her *baba* with the kneading and punching of dough.

What Katia is thinking, as Tania's fidgets finally give way to long, steady breaths, and Mr. Plotsky's snoring rattles the partition, is that her mother had been some kind of exception to the rule; that had she worn a training bra, Sonia's breasts would have attained the same bountiful size as Baba Laryssa's, and as Katia's own could do. Not once does she turn her thoughts to Chucha Marta's hard and skinny chest: as far as Katia can see, her aunt can only doubtfully be called a woman and had certainly never been a young lady. Lying back with her arms crossed tight, trying to shore up the muscles of what Dr. Thwaites calls the "chest wall," Katia concentrates her thoughts instead on Mrs. Maximoynko.

Of all the women at Kalyna Beach that summer, with the possible exception of Darka, there is no woman whose body so fascinates the girls as that of the owner of Venus Variety. Tania had once shown Katia a picture of the Venus de Milo, with her arms cut off just below the shoulders, which only made her breasts the more noticeable. And there was nothing wrong with them as breasts, the girls agreed, until they saw Mrs. Maximoynko's—really saw and appreciated them—that summer. After which they felt a generous pity for the Venus de Milo, who might indeed have given both her arms for the shopkeeper's breasts.

Mrs. Maximoynko is barely five foot, stocky, strong, and sporting that mysterious attribute called a widow's peak, which no one has ever been able to explain to the girls' satisfaction: Why does she have one if her husband is still alive? Why doesn't Mrs. Baziuk have one? Though very short, Mrs. Maximoynko never wears high heels because she thinks them an invention of what she calls "that devil known as the common man"—a phrase she pronounces as though what she has in mind is the common housefly. Mr. Maximoynko, she makes it known, is thoroughly uncommon: an excellent businessman, he runs Superior Fruits and Vegetables on Augusta and knows enough, as she puts it to Pani Durkowska, not to bother her. The Maximoynkos had met in one of the displaced persons camps in Germany, after the war; they have no children. Such a shame, the women sigh; such a waste, say the men, raising cupped hands to their chests and making jokes about evaporated milk.

She is short, Mrs. Maximoynko, but she has enormous presence that makes you think she should be five foot ten at the very least. Partly on account of her voice, which is both deep and loud—if she stands at the door of her shop and yells after you as you're running down to the beach with a Fudgsicle you've pinched from the cooler, you can be sure your mother will hear her half a mile away. She has never yet told on Katia and Tania, though she might have done so a hundred times over: for spoiling merchandise (the cakes with their pushed-in maraschino cherries), minor shoplifting (not only Fudgsicles but also Jell-O powder to be poured from the waxy package straight onto the tongue, turning it purple, yellow, green, and rotting the teeth, as Mrs. Maximoynko has observed to herself with grim content). Plus general disturbances, of course: bursting into fits of giggles at the sight of certain brand names: Skwee-Gee, Betty Brite.

The other source of Mrs. Maximoynko's overwhelming presence is, of course, her breasts. She is not a fat woman, and this makes the architecture of her bosom all the more imposing. There is no nonsense about her dress or appearance: habitually, she wears flip-flops, navy blue shorts, and washed-out sleeveless blouses. But under the blouses, she wears a bra that, Sasha Plotsky swears, must have been designed by a structural engineer. She doesn't care that the bra straps—broad slabs of dingy white cotton—are plainly visible on her shoulders or that when she bends down to fish some disobedient sack of ice cubes from the freezer you can see right down her blouse to her brassiere and the flesh that erupts from the cups, no matter how many wires and ridges and bones there might be underpinning them. For they aren't made of fat or anything jiggly or jelly-like, Mrs.

Maximoynko's breasts, but a substance that makes the girls think of a cross between the marble from which the Venus de Milo is carved, and the resistless, overpowering flow of lava, as they've seen it in a documentary film at the museum. No one could push you around, they think, with those defenses: you could cut your way through the most difficult life like an ice-breaker cleaving vast northern seas.

"What do you think they look like when she isn't wearing her bra?"

"Do you think she ever takes it off?"

"Of course she does—to sleep and to put it through the wash."

"I just can't picture her without it. It's like the queen—she must take her clothes off to have baths and change into her pajamas, but I can't think of her without her crown and those ball gowns she wears and the elbow gloves."

Some days later, the girls have come up with a plan to spy on Mrs. Maximoynko, to create a situation in which she will expose herself without her bra on. They have been driven to this expedient on account of Darka, who has proven far less amenable to being spied upon than they'd hoped. The only window into Darka's room is at the back of the cottage, located in a place where anyone could catch them lurking. Besides, they'd need a ladder—there are no trees under the window offering footholds and no shrubs behind which they could conceal themselves. The bathroom's worse than useless: its sole window is equally high up and smaller than a porthole. At last they decide that the only thing to do is to reverse their intention: they will attempt to catch a glimpse not of Darka's breasts but rather of her bra, from which they can hypothesize what the reality of her breasts might be. Of course, they've had plenty of chances to watch Darka's breasts wiggle and jiggle as she picks up Baby Alix on the beach: the top of her two-piece is as revealing as any bra could be. But there is something about an intensely intimate object of dress that is meant to be hidden from view: a brassiere—any brassiere—has an aura of power about it that no bathing suit could match.

Darka is unexpectedly modest, or at least wary, as far as her laundry is concerned. Where the washing line strung from the Martyns' kitchen porch to the flagpole across the lawn is dotted, among the bathing suits, shorts, and tops, sheets and socks and towels, with several pairs of white cotton panties as large as platters and the inevitable ribbony flag of a brassiere, more foam-rubber padding than anything else, Darka's undergarments are absent. She was not, she'd decided early on in her stay with the Martyns, going to give those kids any ammunition. She'd anticipated the practical jokes—bras and panties being snitched off the line, waving from shrubs at the edge of the lawn or decorating the sand dunes. She'd mounted a laundry line in her room, from the curtain rod to the antlers of the one-eyed moose over her bed; she would swish her bra and panties through her bathwater in the evenings, then carry them rolled

up in her towel to her room, where she could personally super-
intend their drying.

There is no lock on any of the bedroom doors at the cottage: it is one of Sonia's rules that doors should be left open; on
more than one occasion she's found an opportunity to express
the belief to Laura that a demand for privacy is tantamount
to a confession of guilt. "If it's not something you can do out
in the open—other than changing your clothes or using the
bathroom—then it's something you shouldn't be doing at all.
Especially a girl of your age." This rule was even more flagrantly
enforced for Darka, who, being that much older and more developed than Laura, gave all the more cause for alarm.

Tania had thought of involving Laura in their project, rea-
soning that three heads would be better than two, in planning
strategy, but Katia had threatened to throw the whole thing over
if Laura was included. "She'll tell on us—or trick us into giving
it away. Besides, all she cares about is that stupid Cleopatra."
The extent of Laura's involvement has been Katia's borrowing,
unbeknown to her sister, the dog-eared souvenir booklet, over
the photographs of which, in the cool privacy of the crawl space
under the Plotskys' veranda, the girls have pored. They have
appraised the depth of Elizabeth Taylor's *cleavice*, noting the
beauty spot on her left breast, exposed by the décolletage of her
Queen of Egypt dresses; they've attempted to discern, through
the cloudy blue waters of her bath, the shape of the bosom that
the water just covers, while dismissing the nineteenth-century

engraving of a small-breasted Cleopatra kneeling before Julius Caesar. In the engraving, she is wearing what looks like the reverse of a brassiere: a contraption of broad leather straps under and around her breasts and over her shoulders, leaving totally bare a surface bland as the frosting on the cakes in Venus Variety, with nipples as ridiculous as maraschino cherries.

One afternoon, when they are supposed to be resting and when Tania has come over to eat lunch with the Martyns, the girls get their chance. Bonnie and Baby Alix are sound asleep, Laura is off at the Shkurkas' cottage, Sonia is paying a visit to Auntie Zirka, who has hinted that Sonia's been neglecting her, and Darka has asked them to keep an eye on things, as she's got to go to the store for emergency supplies—by which they know she means the sanitary pads that Mrs. Maximoynko keeps behind the counter, dispensing them in brown paper bags to the needy.

They watch Darka disappear down Tunnel Road; they listen at the door where Katia's little sisters are sleeping, then check from both the kitchen and the front porch to make sure no visitors are coming by, from any direction. And then they turn the handle to the door of Darka's room, feeling a pleasurable guilt as they tiptoe inside, closing the door softly but firmly behind them.

It's hot and close, though the window's open behind the yellow curtain. Sun pours through fabric the color of raw egg yolk: it bathes the girls, their hands, and the objects through which they're rifling in Darka's chest of drawers. It doesn't take long to find what they're looking for: Darka keeps her bras (she has two, one of which she's wearing) where you'd expect her to, in the top drawer, next to a pile of underpants shoved in any old how. The only other thing of interest is a photograph lying at the bottom of the drawer, a color photo of a boy sitting in a fire-red convertible, with a black-and-white dog in the passenger seat. The boy has a University of Toronto pennant in his hand, and he's waving at whoever is taking the photograph. On the back is written *Jamie, March 12, 1963, Toronto, Ont.* in Darka's stubby handwriting. The boy, Katia decides, is of little interest; it's the red car and the spotted dog that draw her attention, so that she nearly forgets why they've come into Darka's room in the first place.

"Quick, Katia—come *on*," Tania hisses, forking out the bra. Together they examine the label. GOTHIC, it says. 38C. It doesn't have foam padding the way their mothers' bras do; it isn't soft or clingy at all but fashioned from harsh, stiff cotton. Even dangling from Tania's hands like a pair of eyeglasses, the cups jut out into severe triangular points, like miniature pyramids.

"You first," Katia says.

Tania pulls off her shirt, holding out her arms as if she were a knight donning armor for battle. Impatiently, Katia fastens the hooks, and Tania turns to look at herself in the mirror, both from the back (she bunches up the cups of the bra so that it looks to be a perfect fit) and from the front. This latter view is far less successful: Katia hands her some of Darka's socks, rolled into tight little balls, and Tania stuffs them into the cups that droop so disconsolately from her chest. It helps but only moderately so—what Tania sees in the mirror is nothing more than a mutant and unconvincing breed of falsies.

"Here," Katia says, "put on your shirt—see if that helps."

Tania buttons the shirt to just above where the bra cups start, then steps back from the mirror and examines herself, in front view and in profile. She puts her hands on her hips and points one toe; she adjusts one of the cups, in which a sock is starting to come loose from its ball.

"Do you want to have a go?" she asks Katia, who shakes her head. In the yolky light in the small, stuffy room, things have taken on a confusing quality, as if time has suddenly jumped forward. It's like her father's home movie projector when a splice comes undone, and the film starts pouring out from the reel, with a stink of burning. What she's seen in the spotty light of the mirror is not Tania's reflection but an image of what Tania will be like when she's grown up, when she stuffs foam rubber instead of socks into her bra. And what she'll be is nothing more than a version of her mother, full-view and profile. They have imagined it so differently: they were going to have adventures, take ocean liners to Shanghai, dig for gold in Siberia; the last thing they would ever do is become their mothers.

"Katia? Are you okay? Then help me get out of this thing."

They think they hear the screen door slam on the front

porch: Katia nearly tears the hooks off the bra trying to undo it. The brassiere is shoved back in the drawer, over the photograph, but the socks lie scattered on the floor where they fell when Tania finally tugged herself free. The girls haven't noticed: they run wildly out of the room. If they hadn't imagined the slam, if someone really had been coming home, they would have been caught red-handed. But all is well: the little ones are still sleeping, Darka and Laura and Sonia are still off on their errands and visits. White-faced, hearts pounding, they dash from the cottage. Minutes later, hunkered down behind the sleep-house, they decide that if they're going to run the kind of risks they just have, they'll need to get something out of the ordinary at the end of it all. And so they spend the rest of the afternoon and well into the evening devising a strategy for seeing Mrs. Maximoynko's breasts.

THE DAY AFTER the raid on Darka's room, the girls abandon the sand dunes behind which they've been sunbathing and set off for Venus Variety. Though it's nearly noon, no one calls after them or is sent to bring them back lest they spoil their appetites; nearly everything happens as easily, as flawlessly as they'd imagined. Having confirmed Mrs. Maximoynko's presence behind the cash register and having, to avert suspicion, trailed down the aisles on which all maraschino-cherry-dotted cakes have been replaced by sponge rolls, the girls do not return to the beach when they leave the store with their licorice ropes but sneak to the back, to the apartment Mrs. Maximoynko has made for herself out of an addition. Tania has a bobby pin at the ready to pick the lock, but the door swings open easily. The girls have an excuse ready if they're caught: they will say they noticed a smell of burning and rushed in to investigate. After the tar-paper fire, they will say, everyone has to act on even the slightest suspicion.

No excuse is necessary, except, perhaps, on the part of the apartment itself. For it's such a tiny, dingy space, crammed as it is with an Arborite table and chairs, a fridge and stove and sink, as well as a shower rigged up in a windowless alcove, and a toilet in plain view. The whole place is so small that they can't imagine how Mrs. Maximoynko maneuvers in and out; they can't imagine anyone spending even an hour here. There are a few hooks in the wall, from which hang a dressing gown and a nightie; you might have expected a calendar at least or an icon, but there's nothing, just a coat of paint, that robin's-egg blue that Katia always associates with the classrooms in which she's disgraced herself when asked to recite the tributaries of the Dnipro.

No silks and jewels, no marble bath—none of the trappings of a Cleopatra. Had they really been expecting them? But what good are breasts like Mrs. Maximoynko's if all they get you at the end is a shack stuck on to a variety store and a husband who wholesales fruit on Augusta? And how were they going to get a look at those breasts if there aren't any hiding places in Mrs.

Maximoynko's apartment? Their plan had called for them to conceal themselves behind a sofa or anything from which they'd have a vantage point for spying when Mrs. Maximoynko closed the shop, as she always did at noon, and lay down for an hour on her bed. They had seen with their own eyes the tightly closed curtains, lots of times; the real reason to shut those curtains, they had figured, was not to shut out the light but because Mrs. Maximoynko took off her clothes for her noontime nap. Certainly they are sweating, now, in their shorts and halter tops; the shack's tin roof might as well be a burner turned up all the way to high. Surely she'd at least take off her top, unhook her sweat-soaked bra, towel herself dry?

The girls look at one another, shrug. How Mrs. Maximoynko prepares herself for her hour-long siesta, they are in no position to discover. But now that they're here, it would be a waste to just walk out the door—it would be weak. Tania nods at Katia, who steps up to the bureau and prepares to pull open the top drawer, in which, they know, they'll find a heap of brassieres with cups so big you could fit your whole head into each one. But before the drawer can be opened and a bra pulled out, they have registered what's standing on top of the bureau, exposed for anyone to see.

If God is looking down at them with His big blue eye from the dome of the summer sky, He has decided to be good to them, this once. Mrs. Maximoynko doesn't come upon them in the act of trespass because she's taking longer than she expected talking with Mrs. Senchenko about the supplies needed for Saturday's party. The women are in the store, by the cash register; everyone else is home eating lunch; there's no one to hear the girls slip out of the shack or catch them stealing away to Tunnel Road and hiding themselves in the undergrowth on the side farthest from the beach. They have forgotten all their mothers' warnings about poison ivy and nonexistent bears; they have plunked themselves down, catching their breath, unable to meet each other's eyes.

"Could it have happened in the camp?" Tania asks, her voice streaked with bewilderment. She can imagine no other kind of camp but summer camp.

Katia shakes her head, furious. "That's not the *point.*" Tania waits for her to explain, but there's nothing more, just the echo of anger that Katia knows to be unfair but cannot apologize for.

She is more than angry; she is terrified at what she's suddenly been made to learn. For the secret displayed on Mrs. Maximoynko's bureau isn't in the order of a boy with a spotted dog and a university banner, or even a Luger, as Yuri would have liked to find. It is something far more potent, having to do with how cruelly the body can change its shape, and why. For anyone who cares to look, there it is: a card in a frame, a card containing a black-and-white photo of a young woman with a heart-shaped face and widow's peak; a small woman, needle-thin, hollow-cheeked, her chest caved in. She is standing beside a baby lying on a table, a baby decorated with embroidered cloths and paper flowers, holding a cross in its tiny hands. A dead baby whose skeleton shape no amount of embroidery and flowers can disguise. At the side of the photo is an embossed cross and words written in Cyrillic, simple words that you could easily spell out: *My Baby Marusia, died January 12, 1946, Germania.*

When the girls finally get to their feet, they brush themselves off, though nothing of the woods is caught in their clothes or hair. They don't even shake hands as they turn in different directions to walk home, to the cottages where their mothers are waiting lunch for them. Neither girl will be able to eat, whereupon their mothers will scold them for ruining their appetites, as well as for running off from the beach, coming home so late, worrying them half to death. (Unlike Sonia, Sasha will say this in what she calls her Sarah Bernhardt voice; unlike Sasha, Sonia will be as distraught at her daughter's misbehavior as she is relieved to see her safe and sound.) Of their own free will, the girls will go to their rooms to lie down, without any fuss or complaining. So that Laura scarcely feels any pleasure at being free, for once, to come and go while Katia's condemned to her room. And condemned as she is, it is Laura, not Katia, who must face the interrogation squad of Darka and Sonia, who confront her after lunch with the news that someone's been sneaking into Darka's room, going through her drawers, rearranging things.

"I don't want to hear it," Sonia says, when Laura starts to

protest her innocence. "I don't care who it was, but it's going to stop right now, and you are going to apologize to Darka."

Laura's about to protest that it's Katia's doing (for since it wasn't her, who else could it be?) when she decides this battle is not worth fighting. So she turns to Darka and says, in the sweetest singsong she can muster, "I'm so terribly sorry, Darka, for not going into your room and not messing around with your things—as if I'd want to handle them anyway!" And turns and runs, slamming the screen door of the front porch behind her.

DARKA IS SITTING on the steps off the small porch by the kitchen, thinking over the situation. She has no reason to believe that Sonia would go so far as to actually rummage through her room; besides, Sonia's too neat and tidy to leave sock balls lying under the bed. It has to have been one of the girls. Judging from the performance that's just taken place, it hadn't been Laura snooping in her room, so it must have been Katia, conveniently in bed with a tummy ache. Darka hadn't wanted to get either of them into trouble—though God knows they deserve to be smacked, with all that they get up to. But she has to scare them off. So far she's been lucky: they haven't thought to look in the back of the wardrobe, or else they haven't had time to, yet.

Darka sighs, scratching the place in the small of her back that is always so difficult to reach; suddenly she hears a small rip. *Kholyera yasna*—she will have to mend her blouse again; it ripped in the same place just two weeks ago. The same night that Mr. Martyn drove back to the city, after bringing that bitch of a sister to stay. They'd all gone off to look at the sunset—the Martyns, Marta, the children; she hadn't minded being left out, like some Cinderella with dishpan hands and a *khustka* on her head. Of all the things worth looking at, for God's sake, who would waste time on a sunset? She'd decided to race through her chores, then settle down with her stash of movie magazines: it was the best she could do in the entertainment line, stuck up at this *nudniy* beach. She had started laughing then, knowing what Jamie would do if he could hear her, thinking she'd said not *nudniy*, or "boring," but *nudie*. She'd laughed so hard she'd hugged herself to stop her belly from hurting, and that was when the shirt had ripped, just as it's done now, under the arm.

That was the reason she hadn't gone to the door when he knocked, asking through the screen if Max was in. She'd just yelled from the sink, "They're out at Painter's Point. They'll be back when it's dark."

He hadn't said anything about waiting, but she'd heard no footsteps going back down the porch steps. She wondered just how long he'd stand there. The latch wasn't fastened—he could have come in if he'd really had a mind to. But he'd waited—he'd outwaited her—and she'd finally put down the sour-smelling dishcloth, wiped her hands on the sides of her shorts, and braved the screen door.

It was Frank Kozak, Lesia Baziuk's "special friend." Darka knew what that meant—she wasn't the fool everyone took her for. From behind the screen, his pale-pink skin didn't stand out so much, nor did the sandy-colored lashes around his eyes. It had been a nice enough evening, and the kitchen was steamy with dishwashing, so she'd decided to open the door and step out onto the landing. She can't remember now whether she nodded at him or ignored him as she made her way down the stairs to the lookout point across the lawn. She does know that she had to brush against him to go down: he took up room, he was like one of those plastic containers filled with gravel or water in which you plant a table umbrella so it doesn't blow away. She grazed his belly with her arm; she smelled whisky—a not-unpleasant smell, golden, not sour like wine—and felt his breath on her face, her neck, the way you feel the sun on your skin the very moment you realize you're getting a burn. And then she ran down the steps and leaned over the railing at the lookout, staring through a screen of leaves at the water below.

After a while it occurred to her that he might tell the Martyns she'd been rude to him—disrespectful—so she turned around to where she thought he was standing but saw no trace of him. Then she guessed he might have gone inside to wait for the Martyns in their living room, reading an old issue of *Look* or *National Geographic* as the sunset blazed across the picture window. She thought they might not like her leaving somebody alone in the house like that, even a neighbor, so she ran back to the cottage, tramping up the steps and slamming the screen door behind her as loud as she could, to give him notice of her intentions. But there was no one on the sofa; no one's feet were up on the coffee table. And then she remembered that she'd left a pot to soak, and that Sonia would get after her about it. It was when she went to finish her chores that she found it on the windowsill, as if it had been waiting for her there all day.

Sphinx Pink. Its metal cap looked like gold; when she pulled it off and swiveled the lipstick up, she saw that it had never been used. It wasn't Sonia's, left out by mistake. It was hers.

The very next evening, he'd come by again. This time Sonia had been inside with Marta, and Katia and Laura had been sent to their rooms in disgrace, for fighting at the dinner table. She'd been on the little porch off the kitchen, throwing soapy water onto the parched bed of dill and parsley below: Sonia can't stand anything to be wasted, even dirty dishwater. She paused for a moment, with her elbows on the railing, as if waiting for something—and sure enough, it had come. A movement first, in the bushes beside the sleep-house, and then a soft whistle. She left the basin on the porch and made her way down the steps toward the sleep-house. If Sonia were to see her, she'd tell her the truth: that she was investigating something fishy in the bushes. But Sonia hadn't been looking; no one was there to witness how he beckoned to her from the side of the sleep-house, and she followed him, walking carefully because of the poison ivy. It hadn't occurred to her to ask him why he was doing this.

She does wonder whether she was just being stupid, or whether she wanted not to know.

Her *special friend*. He didn't offer her a drink from the silver flask that he carried with him and that she could see in outline beneath his sports jacket. He said he didn't like to see young women drink—or had it been young ladies, was that what he'd said? He had an air about him, that's for sure; he was always nicely turned out, smelling of Old Spice as well as the whisky. They stood behind the sleep-house where no one could see them from the cottage. There was a small moon, low in the sky, and it painted rough silver on the leaves of the bushes around them. He didn't say anything for a long while; then he pulled from his pocket a compact—not plastic, but that same shiny metal as the lipstick tube, and put it in her open hand like a giant coin from some pirate's hoard.

"They work you hard here?" he asked. With concern, she thought, not just out of curiosity. She started talking a little, telling him what her chores were and how boring it was, each day the same. When she told him about how she was made to do the laundry each morning, how her knuckles were rubbed raw by the washboard, he asked her where; she'd been about to show him her hands when she understood he was asking where she did the wash. She told him about the cellar, how cool and quiet it was with the pack of them gone down to the beach each morning. And sure enough, when she went off to do the wash right after breakfast the next day, she found, propped up on the scrubbing board, a small, prettily shaped bottle of cologne, the glass ribbed and twisty, the cap shaped like a heart.

Later that day, down at the beach, she heard the women talking about him—how he was up for his week of holiday, more's the pity for Lesia Baziuk. "I guess we women are gluttons for punishment," somebody said, and Darka remembers hugging her knees and smiling, liking the sound of the word *glutton*, liking even better the secret that none of the women knew she was keeping.

The next day, when she went to the cellar, she nearly jumped out of her skin, opening the door and seeing him there. He was leaning against the wall, his pale skin and sandy hair making him look like a giant mushroom in the cool dark. She'd been about to say something when he put his finger to his lips, pointing upward: sounds of children running, doors slamming. The family was getting ready to go to the beach, though it would be another ten minutes or so before they'd make their way down.

"I have to get on with this wash," she whispered, feeling she owed him an explanation. He said that was fine; he'd just sit there and enjoy the coolness, if that was okay with her. She shrugged and continued with her work, though she couldn't help darting glances here and there to see if he'd brought her anything. She realized, suddenly, that she'd never thanked him, and then decided he didn't want her to—he'd be embarrassed, or he'd think her no better than a little kid. Liz Taylor—you wouldn't hear *her* saying *please* and *thank you very much*, not for a measly tube of lipstick!

How strange it had been, going about the washing, her back turned to him, feeling his eyes on her as she wiped a hand across her forehead to catch the sweat or wrung out the clothes, then stood with her hands on either side of the sink, watching the dirty water swirl away. She had her two-piece on under her shorts but no shirt, so her back was exposed, the straps criss-crossed so they wouldn't keep sliding off her shoulders. She was aware of the smell of her skin—the moist, slightly sour smell in her armpits that she couldn't disguise no matter how much deodorant she put on, and the ripe smell of her hair, which she hadn't had time to wash that morning. At last she'd turned to him, a basket of rinsed and wrung-out clothes weighing down her arms. He made no move to help her, he just said, "Come back when you're finished—come back when they've left," reaching into his pocket and pulling out a small, thin, silvery cylinder.

"Mascara," she'd said, by way of an answer.

LAURA'S THE ONE who named it Tunnel Road, because of the way the trees reach across the asphalt, joining overhead as you walk or drive below. So the road really belongs to her, she thinks, walking quickly along, tripping over a stone or fallen branch or sometimes her own feet, trying to pull her head up from her shoulders as her mother's always telling her to do. Though it's not because of her mother's nagging, this attention to her posture; it's because she needs to learn to walk like a queen, an empress of the Nile.

On one side of the road are cottages, and on the other, woods dense with spruce and cedar saplings and slender, gray-barked trees. Through the dark leaves, light boils like bubbles in ginger ale; if you walk as far as you can through the undergrowth, you find places where coolness rushes up, the way it does when you pass the opened door of a cellar on a scorching day. They are always warned not to go into the woods because of poison ivy and because of bears, but the children pooh-pooh this; Katia glimpsed a skunk once, making its way through the brush, and several porcupines have been sighted. Her cousin Yuri says he heard wolves howl at night, but no one believes him: wolves belong in fairy tales, not at Kalyna Beach.

At the end of Tunnel Road is the Shkurkas' cottage. Next to the Plotskys', it's the oldest building at the beach, and it's certainly the smallest. It needs fixing—the floors sag and the roof is nothing but patches, but Nettie Shkurka says she can't afford to have a man in to do repairs. She says this at the store or stopping in front of various cottages when she takes her morning walks along Tunnel Road, her daughter at her side, pale and plain as a pot of porridge. Nastia, who never looks anyone straight in the face and has a sleepwalker's abstracted gait. When the Shkurkas pass by, the women on their verandas wave and remind themselves to tell their husbands to stop by at the small, decrepit cottage to see if they can't give Nettie a hand with things. Though they know their husbands will never carry through with these good intentions. There's something so self-satisfied in Nettie's misfortune, Sasha says—something so righteous in her feeling herself to be poor and neglected and eternally shining up that crown in heaven she's buying on the installment plan. And then Sasha laughs and says she never could understand how Nettie ever let a man near enough to father that poor, scared rabbit of a daughter.

Laura has seen a picture of Mr. Shkurka that Nastia keeps folded in her prayer book: it's not a photograph but a blurred reproduction of one, printed in a magazine called *Glory to Ukraine!* There was an article on the displaced persons camps after the war, the educational and cultural events the inmates had organized there. Ostap Shkurka had been part of a musical ensemble including singers from Kyiv Opera and Ballet Theater; they had staged parts of *Taras Bulba* with improvised costumes and minimal props. The picture showed Mr. Shkurka in a sheepskin hat and wide-skirted coat that were far too big, making him look like a small boy dressed up in his father's clothes. He had played the part of the son who betrays his father by falling madly in love with a Polish countess. "He had a wonderful voice," Nastia had whispered, holding out her hand for the magazine clipping, as if terrified her mother would walk into the room and find them. Laura had nodded, wondering if Nastia really could remember her father's voice—she'd been younger than Alix when he ran out on them. And what if this Ostap Shkurka in the magazine had nothing to do with the man who was Nastia's father? What if he was someone who just happened to share with him a name as common in Ukraine as Joe Smith is here?

Now Laura is on her way to the Shkurkas' cottage, having waited and waited for her mother to settle down in her bedroom with the book hidden in her night-table drawer. It's not that her mother would forbid Laura to spend time at the Shkurkas' but that she'd go on at her about how Laura should be making friends with other girls as well, girls less delicate and, though Sonia never says the word, *peculiar*. Laura never responds to her mother's criticisms and suggestions but just stands staring past her, shoulders slumped like a drooping shawl. Her mother doesn't know anything; doesn't know how Mrs. Shkurka keeps Nastia under her thumb, as if she were a prisoner so important she has to be guarded day and night. If Laura wants to see Nastia, she has to see her at the Shkurkas' or not at all.

Always, when Laura knocks on the Shkurkas' door, she's met by Nastia's mother. For such a snip of a woman, she has an unusually powerful voice. Sometimes she refuses to undo the latch of the screen door: Anastasia's asthma is acting up again, she might say, or Anastasia's got a sick headache, or else a rash. Whatever the plot of Nastia's "bad days," the story always ends the same way: Anastasia has to lie down; she doesn't want to be disturbed. Laura knows it's useless, on such occasions, to ask if she could just call to Nastia through the screen door, just as she knows, but cannot actually say to herself, that Mrs. Shkurka's lying when she talks about Nastia not wanting to see her. Cannot say it to herself or to any of the mothers, for they'll never take her word for anything, and everyone knows that Mrs. Shkurka is a Mother in a Million. And so, on bad days, Laura leaves the Shkurkas' cottage, with its worn, gray walls and sagging shutters, and makes her way back up Tunnel Road, running the last few yards, till she reaches the birch tree with the sign bearing the letters *M A R T Y N* burned into the wood.

This afternoon, she knocks at the door not hesitantly or defiantly but with a certain cunning. She is not going to ask for Nastia when Mrs. Shkurka appears; she is going to ask if she can come in to borrow a book on the kingdom of ancient Rus´, which, as Mrs. Shkurka has so often told her, is the Glorious Cradle of Today's Ukraine.

Laura's plan works—or perhaps she didn't even need to try it, for when Mrs. Shkurka allows her inside, Nastia is waiting for her at the kitchen table. Nastia's mother is a skinny woman with unnaturally pale skin and features thin as the teeth of a comb. If she were Nastia, Laura thinks, she'd have run away a long time ago from such a flimsy jailer. But then, who in the world is like Nastia? Pale, quiet, good as gold and far more pliable, Nastia seems to know what her mother wants from her before Mrs. Shkurka says a word or even gestures to her. In fact, Nastia is closer to her mother than Laura has ever thought

it possible for any daughter to be. But then, Nastia has no father—or, at least, he's as good as dead and gone, and that would
make a difference.

Nastia is sitting at the kitchen table, her long, long hair pouring down her back and over her shoulders like some dark, silent
waterfall. Laura tightens her lips as Mrs. Shkurka tells her to
sit down and wait while she does Nastia's hair. She watches as
the brush comes down, hard, on her friend's scalp; she notices
the way Nastia nearly doesn't flinch as her mother explains to
Laura the importance of stimulating the oils in the scalp. Laura
prefers not to look at Nastia's face as Mrs. Shkurka proceeds to
braid her daughter's hair, pulling the strands so tight that the
two long ropes hanging down her daughter's back will look far
more tense and indestructible than chain mail.

Nastia's mother teaches school from September to the end
of June; she drives up to Kalyna Beach on the first of July with
boxes full of workbooks titled *Grammar Without Toil* and *More
Fun with Figures*. Nastia's shown them to Laura, and Laura
can't believe how they're all filled in with Nastia's perfectly neat
handwriting and pasted with golden stars that Mrs. Shkurka
keeps in a small glass jar that used to hold horseradish. She
also lugs up a gross of embroidery thread and coarse-grained
linen, from which she fashions cross-stitched bookmarks to be
sold at church bazaars and Easter teas over the coming year.
She is a tireless supporter of worthy projects in the Ukrainian
community, Laura knows, for Mrs. Shkurka has made no se-

cret of what she calls her "causes" and has even tried, so far in vain, to recruit Laura to help her out with them, as Nastia will, once they return to the city. Laura has seen with her own eyes how ardently Mrs. Shkurka kisses the cross and the gold-plated cover of the Gospels at the cathedral each Sunday. She knows by heart how many A+s Nastia has racked up on her report cards over the years, for Mrs. Shkurka has never failed to tell her. So why, then, has Laura come back to the Shkurkas' cottage over and over again this summer? Why does she befriend a girl like Nastia, the kind of prim, proper, perfect daughter that her own mother wishes she had?

Perhaps it's because Sonia, for all the faults she constantly finds with Laura, has never warmed to Nastia. Down at the beach Laura once heard Mrs. Vesiuk telling her mother what a shame it was, the way Nettie had pinned her daughter down, like linen in an embroidery frame. And Sonia had nodded, said something about how overprotective Nettie was, making Nastia wear those long-sleeved blouses and ankle-length trousers. She's making a hermit out of that girl, Sonia had said—it's all very well to say she has sensitive skin and needs to keep out of the sun but to keep her locked away from all the other girls, as if she thought nobody was good enough for her, when anyone could see that— And then Mrs. Vesiuk had nodded, and they'd switched to some other topic, and Laura had been left trying to puzzle out her mother's disapproval, not just of Nettie Shkurka but of Nastia as well. For in spite of what she'd just told Mrs. Vesiuk, Sonia had never tried to invite Nastia over to their cottage; she had even hinted to Laura that it wasn't a good idea, putting all her eggs in one basket where friends were concerned.

LAURA AND NASTIA'S friendship has nothing to do with chickens, as far as Laura can see. They know each other from Saturday Ukrainian school, at which Nastia's distinguished herself for her ability to memorize vast chunks of Shevchenko, Franko, and Ukrainka, while Laura stubbornly refuses to answer anything she's asked and comes last in everything, from dictation to dancing, where her lack of balance and her inability to tell her left foot from her right make her sadly conspicuous. Yet it's only this summer that the girls have really taken to each other, becoming as inseparable as their mothers will permit; that is to say, they spend the odd afternoon together, from one till three, the universal quiet time. On this particular afternoon, they are sitting out at the back, on rickety lawn chairs. The trees have grown up to block the view of the lake, and the path down to the shore is overgrown, though they can easily hear the waves crashing below.

Mrs. Shkurka sits close by in a rocking chair, doing embroidery while the girls talk, and listening in on their conversation with a clear conscience. She frequently chastises or upbraids them—most often because of Laura's ruling passion for the history of ancient Egypt, which, Mrs. Shkurka constantly reminds her, is far less improving and important than the history of ancient Rus´. That depraved woman Cleopatra wasn't to be mentioned in the same breath as the saintly Knyahynya Olha—does Laryssa know that Olha sought conversion to Christianity and tricked the sultan of Constantinople into being her godfather instead of the husband he had so wickedly plotted to become? And does Laryssa also know that Her Majesty Queen Elizabeth the Second, queen of Canada, is descended in the thirty-first generation from a prince of Ukraine? For King Harold the Second of England, killed at the Battle of Hastings by an arrow through the eye, had married his daughter Gytha to Grand Prince Volodymyr Monomakh.

Whenever Mrs. Shkurka lectures her like this, Laura turns her face away, making savage scowls or sticking out her tongue, shocking Nastia with her bravado. If Laura has to look Mrs. Shkurka in the eye, she bites the insides of her cheeks to stop herself from saying something rude. Such forbearance is only possible because sooner or later Nastia's mother always falls asleep—she sleeps poorly at night and is ruining her eyes with her embroidery, Nastia says. Whenever she talks of her mother, she sounds as though she's quoting her—not Mrs. Shkurka's exact words, uttered in the heat or damp of the moment, but what that lady would like people to believe she's said. Laura isn't interested in Mrs. Shkurka, and, truth be told, her attachment to Nastia isn't entirely disinterested. For Nastia has provided Laura with a rapt audience for her obsession with Cleopatra, queen of Egypt—and her alter ego, Elizabeth Taylor. Nastia can be counted on to listen, mouth agape, as Laura reads aloud whole paragraphs from the souvenir booklet she's smuggled into the Shkurkas' cottage:

She is a beauty beloved of photographers, for in the professional world of photographers it is axiomatic that it is next to impossible to take a bad picture of her.

She is the foremost star of the screen, because she is beautiful, and because she is an actress of enormous talent.

When she was not yet thirty, she fought and won a battle for her life.

The costliest film production in the history of the cinema, the finest accumulation of talents, surrounds her appearance as Cleopatra, Queen of Egypt. . . .

"What do you suppose she was sick with—asthma?" offers Nastia.

"Of course not. She would have had some kind of terrible fever. They would have had to watch at her bedside night and day, feeling her fluttering pulse for vital signs."

"Maybe it was TB."

"Maybe," Laura answers cautiously.

"Lesia Ukrainka had TB. She spent her winters in Egypt;

she would have died of cold if she'd stayed in Ukraine." Nastia brightens; it pleases her to be able to share this knowledge. It's like a gift she's making Laura, and she has so few things to offer. Emboldened, she ventures a little more. "I had a positive reaction to a TB test once. My whole arm swelled up and went bright red."

"Then it wasn't TB Elizabeth Taylor had, *that's* for sure!" Laura knows she's being unkind, but she has the actress's glamour to protect, and there is nothing, absolutely nothing that Elizabeth Taylor and Nastia Shkurka could ever have in common. She decides to change the subject, repeating another passage from the souvenir booklet, one that sends shivers down her crooked spine. (Her mother is always at her to stop slouching, warning her she'll be a cripple by the time she's twenty.)

Burton is five feet, nine inches tall, is as wide-shouldered and rugged as a fullback, can blaze into righteous anger on occasion, and will calm down just as quickly. Splendidly educated, he will in conversation range over a host of subjects with keen, piercing intelligence.

If there's anything that Laura longs for, other than being Elizabeth Taylor, it is the chance to have a keen, piercing conversation with Richard Burton. She imagines Richard and Elizabeth sitting by the pyramids or riding camels through the desert and ranging over a host of subjects: Shakespeare, and

Shevchenko, and Skin Tone. Of course they wouldn't discuss anything so trivial as the latter—but it so happens that Laura is preoccupied with skin tone right now, and she would dearly like to know what a splendidly educated man could say to her upon this subject.

If there's anything that Laura envies Nastia, it's her complexion. Not its color—sallow, like ancient ivory—but its porelessness. A tight weave, something Laura's heard her mother say about fabric: nothing can get in or out. Laura has terrible skin. Sonia's is flawless. Once, watching Laura finish a plate of French fries at a restaurant, she had said mournfully, "You had such beautiful skin when you were little." As if it were Laura's fault, Laura's decision that the pores of her skin should each become a pit filled with tar; as if she'd taken a darning needle heated to some unimaginable temperature and gouged her face, every half-inch, with its tip. Gross pore structure: this is how it's described in the beauty magazines Laura reads surreptitiously at drugstores and dentists' offices. It's a sign of ruggedness in a man, and hence desirable, or at least acceptable. Richard Burton, in his leopard-skin tunic, looking on at the banquet Cleopatra has conjured up for him, looking up, from under beetling brows, not at the Nubian dancing girls, or at the platters of jellied peacock, but at the flawless skin of Elizabeth Taylor.

Nastia, unsure of whether her friend has fallen asleep or gone into a trance, reaches for the souvenir booklet lying in

Laura's lap. Timidly, she takes it up, turning the pages until she finds a passage that she reads out in her whisper of a voice:

> *If a scene requires from her the enacting of virtual hysteria, she seems to lose herself, as though unaware of the glare of the lights, the crew standing around. The moment the director has said, "That's it!" she is back to herself again. Her hand reaches out for a lit cigarette (there is always someone there to supply it) and she waits quietly for the director's appraisal.*

> *"I have no acting technique," she has insisted. "The only thing I know how to do is be." Unfortunately, talent and schooling alone don't guarantee a fine actress. Miss Taylor learned acting through acting, and was lucky enough, also, to be born with inherent talent.*

For once, Laura isn't angry or upset at having her thunder stolen from her. She makes no move to grab the souvenir booklet back from Nastia but merely hugs her knees, repeating, "The only thing I know how to do is be," her eyes gazing out at where the lake would be, if you could see through the screen of oak and poplar trees.

"What do you think she means when she says that?"

Occasionally, Nastia surprises her with a question that triggers the deepest pleasure Laura has yet experienced: that of thinking something through for yourself, thinking past what you've been told or taken for the truth.

"Well, she has servants, of course—to do her laundry, and look after her children, and cook the meals."

"Like Mrs. Senchenko," Nastia suggests shyly, and Laura doesn't dismiss the comparison. Of all the grown women she knows, Nadia Senchenko is the only one you could speak of in the same breath as Elizabeth Taylor. They both have a regal, distant quality, and nothing they do, no amount of mixing with ordinary people, could ever tarnish them.

"I suppose it means," Laura continues, "that she doesn't ever need to think, that everything falls into place for her."

"That everything makes sense," Nastia adds, "and nothing happens that isn't supposed to. Or else that you can't help being the way you are—it's nobody's fault what you look like, or who your father is, or why you can never do what you're told."

Mrs. Shkurka is snoring—a fact to which Laura makes no allusion whatsoever, knowing that Nastia would be deeply ashamed, and that as long as neither of them says a word about it, they can pretend the short, snuffling breaths, the almost animal sound, isn't coming from Nastia's mother's mouth. Instead, they listen to the sound of the waves, Laura dreamily, remembering Cleopatra's barge and the oarsmen beating time to a great bronze drum; Nastia shivering.

"I hate the sound of the lake," she confides. "I hate hearing the waves pounding and pounding at the sand."

They sit for a long while in silence together, until Nastia gestures for Laura to follow her to the bathroom. By now Laura is bored and hungry: she feels like going to Venus Variety for a Freezie or having a swim and then baking in the sand, none of which Nastia would ever be allowed to do. So there's a frown on her face as she follows Nastia to the room where hangs the cottage's only mirror, a large rectangle of silvered glass screwed into the wall: a pond for the fish on the wallpaper to swim around or toward but never inside. The girls are out of earshot of Nettie, but still Nastia doesn't speak. Nor does she stare at her perfect, poreless skin in the mirror or point out the flaws in Laura's own.

What the mirror shows is how the frown on Laura's face turns from resentment into astonishment and then to something almost like envy, as Nastia takes a nail file from a drawer, holds its point against the wallpaper beside the mirror, a place where tropical fish hide behind long, wavy reeds. With great neatness and control, she incises four words: *I hate Nettie S.* And then she puts her finger to her lips, miming the word *secret* and smiling, as Laura nods once, twice, three times, the way you do when you're swearing a sacred oath.

THE GAME, WHATEVER it is—hide and go seek, fox and geese— is getting out of hand, Sonia decides. She leaves the picture window, from which she's been watching her brother and his sons running helter-skelter over the grass, with Katia, Bonnie, Tania racing just as wildly after them. By the time she gets to the flagpole, where they've ended up, Yuri and Katia are sitting on Peter's chest, Tania and Andriy have imprisoned his arms, and Bonnie is tickling her uncle's nose with a long blade of grass. Sonia sits down on her haunches, looking at her brother's face while he blows at the grass blade Bonnie's waving. He's still so handsome, she thinks. Having grown up with Peter, she's always taken his good looks for granted or registered them through the scrim of her mother's warnings: how he was trading on his face instead of his brains; how he'd fall on that handsome face of his one day, and then where would he be?

"That's enough, now," she tells the children. "Leave him be—come on, up you get! There's lemonade and cookies on the kitchen table."

Peter makes a show of wiping his brow and bowing down to her for having rescued him "from a fate worse than lemonade." Does Sonia have a bottle of beer anywhere in the house? Cold beer, warm beer?

She shakes her head. "Max is out getting some right now. If you don't want lemonade, I can make you some tea or iced coffee."

"Ah, Sonia, the answer to a brother's prayers!"

Peter sighs, standing up, brushing himself off, combing his hair with his fingers, hair blacker than a raven's wing, she'd heard it described—by whom? Probably Sasha, with her literary bent. Black hair and brows and eyes; the kind of dark skin that laps up the sun and never burns. Just like a gypsy, their mother had always said—a gypsy's child. He'd been treated so harshly, poor Petro. Boys have to be tough, their mother had said again and again. It does them no good to be fussed over. And when they'd come to Canada, their father had been just as severe in his own way, lecturing his son on the need to be serious, to have dignity, to pay attention to things that matter, things that won't always go his way.

Peter helps her up; he offers her his arm as if they were strolling on some boulevard in their Sunday best, though she's in shorts and a halter top, and his shirt is covered with grass stains. "Zirka won't be happy—" Sonia begins, fingering a long green smear down Peter's back.

"No, if there's one thing Zirka's bound not to be, it's happy," Peter agrees. But he throws the ball right back to his sister. "No more than you, *sestrychko.*"

"Never mind me," Sonia says, trying to find some way to turn the conversation in the direction Sasha has requested. She hasn't got her brother's gift with words—what their mother had reproved as "tomflowery." What if Sasha's right, what if Peter is on some wild-goose chase to do with Nadia Senchenko, laying himself wide open to being talked about, shown up as an aging fool, no longer a lovably young one? What if she were to ask him point-blank what he's up to? As always, Peter disarms her, stopping to pick a stem of devil's paintbrush, with which he traces two circles on her cheeks and the curve of a smile over her mouth.

"That's better," he says. "Now, my dear, you look like a woman on holiday, enjoying a run of splendid weather at the beach." He even looks like Cary Grant as he speaks the words, in a voice so like Cary Grant's that if Sonia had been blindfolded, she could have believed herself to be arm in arm with the movie star.

"Please, Peter," she says, pulling away, looking him straight in the eyes. He's her own brother, she grew up with him, crossed an ocean with him, learned a new language, a new way of understanding the world, in his company, and yet she knows nothing about him now: what he wants, what he needs, what he's up to, if he's up to anything at all.

"Yes, oh lovely one, Pearl of the Andes, Flower of the Sea of Azov, Goddess Incarnate of Kalyna Beach. Your wish is my command, although if you did have that bottle of beer or, better still, a shot of Max's single malt, wherever he keeps it stashed away, I would kiss your little snow-white feet."

Sonia sighs. She walks over to the washing line, where a few beach towels wait to be unpinned. Would he ever grow up? But then, why bother? Nothing he did could ever be good enough, he'd learned this lesson long ago, in the Old Place. A too-tall, too-skinny boy who was always getting into trouble: at school, around the house, with the neighbors. Who should have been a help to his mother, alone as she was, burdened with the running of a farm, the raising of two children, the absence of the man she'd married for love not land, the disapproval of both sets of family, neither of whom would lift a finger to help, even when Sonia had come down with scarlatina and the doctor had been called in from town, wiping out a whole year's savings. And for every smack or scolding Peter received, she, Sonia, had been caressed, made much of, protected.

Even when he'd signed up to go to war, had come home to say good-bye, all kitted out in his uniform, all their mother had found to say was, "You—a soldier?" And, true to form, Peter had belted out, *"I hate to get up, I hate to get up, I hate to get up in the morning,"* doubling up his fists in front of his mouth, blowing a slapstick trumpet. He'd made Sonia laugh, when she'd been biting her lip to keep her eyes from flooding. She should have shouted it out to her parents, right then and there: "He's going off to fight, don't you understand—he's risking his life for us. Why can't you be proud of him, just this once?" But her throat had seized up, her fear had choked her, fear of weakening their love, their support, fear of seeming to criticize the two people who'd given up everything they had to offer her this new, strange world she was supposed to call home.

Peter should hate her, by rights. Spoiled, adored, indulged as she'd been while he'd gone begging. The fact that he doesn't resent her, that however much he jokes with her, he's always been protective toward her—doesn't that prove his goodness, deep down? How could he be capable of what Sasha thinks? Surely everyone must see that Peter hasn't the pride, or the strength, or the blindness to make an approach to another man's wife, especially if that man is rich and successful, so rich and successful that he can afford to bail out his brother-in-law time and again. And no one in their right mind could believe that Nadia Senchenko would give Peter Metelsky the encouragement of a mosquito! So what is the point of Sonia's speaking to Peter about his intentions? It would only cause pain and confusion; it would only make everything a hundred times worse.

"Here," Sonia says. She piles the beach towels into his arms, stuffing the clothes pegs into her pockets. "I'll take a look in the sideboard for that bottle of single malt—"

But before she can finish, Peter has dropped the towels piled into his arms; has reached out to her, placing a hand on each of her shoulders.

"Sonia, tell me," he begins, but what he goes on to say is so entirely unexpected that his sister can give him no answer.

"What would you do if, suddenly, out of the blue, you were granted your heart's desire?"

PART THREE

WATER WINGS

THE LADIES HAVE put down their books and turned to a meatier source of gossip. And all because Jack Senchenko has bought himself a new motorboat, a zillion-horsepower Speed King, snapped up on sale at the end of the summer. For all his wealth, Jack is not averse to finding a bargain; he's almost as fond of revealing the fortunes he saves as he is of boasting of those he spends on what the Ladies and their husbands would all regard as hopeless extravagance, outrageous luxuries.

Who, for heaven's sake, was Nadia Moroz to have caught a Jack Senchenko? Nadia Moroz, a scholar's daughter, an only child. Sometimes you wonder how she ever got born at all, her father so unworldly, a small man with a dreamer's face and a voice so soft that when he talked to you, each word felt like a little pillow. He was a saint: he would, and often did, give you the shirt off his back; his wife spent all her time getting back enough of what he'd given away that there'd be bread on the table and shoes on their feet. She was a broomstick of a woman, a good six inches taller and five years older than her husband, with eyes like whips—this is what the kids at Sunday school said. Pani Professor Moroz was the only one who terrified them, so that never did any whispering or giggling occur when she marched them up from the cathedral basement to join the congregation above. More nun than woman was Sofia Moroz; you couldn't imagine her scraping off even one layer of the clothes she wore, summer and winter, geometric prints on murky backgrounds, and all that elasticated armor underneath. She should have been born a man, people reasoned: she could have been a general or at least a bishop.

The Morozes had come to Canada after the war but not like all the other DPs in Toronto. For one thing, they arrived speaking fluent English: they all sounded foreign, but though her parents' Ukrainian came through rich and heavy in their speech, Nadia's accent was just like what you heard on the radio when they played a broadcast from the BBC. She was born in a part of Ukraine that was then the east of Poland; she had moved to England with her parents when she was ten years old. Her father had been a student and then a lecturer in philosophy at the University of London. When the war broke out, Sofia Moroz thanked God for their escape from Poland; when peace finally limped in, she left God out of it and made preparations for the family's removal to Canada. Nadia and her father had no say in the matter: their happiness, their ties to England, and their settled life in London counted for nothing in Sofia's calculations. She was sick of war and a peace that made no difference to the meager amount of butter or eggs or meat or wool you could buy each week; she was sick of the ruins and rubble all around them (they had returned one morning from the shelter where they'd spent a miserable night to find that their home had been destroyed, along with all of Professor Moroz's books and papers). They were British subjects, and Sofia had a cousin in Oshawa, so the immigration people hadn't raised a hair, in spite of the Morozes' strong accents (they had let Nadia do most of the talking).

Why Nadia had accompanied her parents to Canada is a question debated endlessly, not only by the Ladies but by Peter Metelsky as well—Peter, who had once made a point of finding out every scrap of information he could about the daughter of Professor Nestor Moroz. Why Nadia had ever come to Canada was a far greater mystery than why, for example, she had married Jack Senchenko. She had been twenty-three when the Morozes had embraced Sofia's cousin and her family in the great hall of Union Station; she had been old enough to have stayed behind, to have been engaged if not to an Englishman, then in a course of study. Rumors had circulated that Nadia had, in fact, been a student, and of a subject as useless as religious studies: fine art. She had given it all up, Peter had mused: art school (about which he knew less than nothing), London (which he did know a little, from his army days), the country where she'd spent most of her life up till then.

She'd been a good daughter, the apple of her father's eye, but not necessarily a "good girl"—which was to say, Peter reasoned, that she wouldn't have been fazed by the prospect of living on her own in London. It couldn't have had much to do with a desire for security: her father had found a position at the University of Toronto, but his salary was modest, as opposed to the expenses of moving three people across an ocean and renting as well as furnishing an apartment (and Sofia Moroz had made it clear she wanted everything new, everything their own, after having lost everything they possessed in the bombing). You could even argue that the family would have been better off, economically, had Nadia stayed behind; they could have saved her fare, taken a smaller apartment, bought less furniture, but they'd come, all three—though Nadia, far more than her parents, had about her the air of a permanent refugee.

Peter Metelsky had first noticed Nadia walking along Queen Street one Saturday afternoon in late December, two years after the end of the war. Peter was dating, in a desultory way, Zirka Senchenko, an armful of a girl, a real butterball. Peter could have had his pick of any of the girls, but he was friends with Zirka's brother Jack: they were both on the Beaver Bread volleyball team, and they were going to set up a business together someday. It made sense, everyone agreed, for Peter to settle on Zirka, for Peter's family was even worse off than Nadia's. In other words, it made sense for Peter to settle on Jack, who may not have been much to look at—short, stocky, balding already at twenty-nine—but who had an eye for things no one else had his kind of luck at: buying and selling, wheeling and dealing, and, most of all, sweet-talking old Lady Luck. He had managed to spend the whole of the war in Saskatchewan; he was financing his business deals on his proceeds from the betting track. He had Ambition, whereas Peter had Style and the kind of amiable weakness that makes a handsome man friends instead of enemies.

Yet when Peter had walked down Queen Street that December afternoon, had run into Jack Senchenko with Nadia Moroz on his arm, he'd stopped dead in his tracks and been barely able to answer Jack's hello. Which came first, who can tell: Peter's alarm that his plans for Jack to marry Sonia had been shot all to hell or his shock at seeing, in Jack's possession, the girl—the only woman in the world—whom he, Peter Metelsky, Don Juan of the Dnipro, could ever desire? Right there and then, a double date was arranged: Jack and Nadia along with Peter and Zirka would attend the *Malanka* at the Cathedral Hall, see the New Year in together. As for Nadia, all this time she was looking off into the distance, towering over Jack and, after a first absent hello, failing to so much as glance at Peter. Nadia, awkward and aloof—though perhaps she was only dismally shy. Nadia, who held herself so straight she *loomed*—that's exactly the word for it—and who, what with looming and the silence she brought like a cold wind into a room, made most people uneasy, as if her eyes in their dark-rimmed spectacles could see through to your bones.

The night of the *Malanka*, Peter had walked into the hall with Zirka dressed up to the nines, all crinoline and bright, bouffant hair. And there was Nadia Moroz in a cheap, dark print, more like a spent umbrella than a ball gown. Next to her Zirka looked like a plump little bird of paradise, but the first thing Peter did was to release his date into her brother's care. Before anyone could say a word, he'd seized Nadia by the hand and led her onto the dance floor. It was the usual amateur band, heavy on accordion, all the old favorites like "The Anniversary Waltz" and "The Beer Barrel Polka"—none of the bee-bop and jive you'd have found at more glamorous dances on a Saturday night in Toronto. But never mind the music—what mattered was that Nadia Moroz, even in that awful dress, was held like something rare and fine and infinitely precious in Peter Metelsky's arms. Who would have suspected what a good dancer she could be, moving effortlessly across a floor packed with couples all ages from eighteen to eighty-three? Who would have imagined what a perfect pair they'd make—Peter a few inches taller than Nadia, as spare as she and extravagantly handsome? The perfect foil to the austerity of Nadia's jutting cheekbones and high, pure forehead; the severe, black frames of her glasses, which made her look like a swan plunged into mourning.

He was a magician with words, that Peter Metelsky. He could recite poetry by the yard, in Ukrainian and in English. He had *presence*—that's how everyone put it—"sex appeal," and something more. He was a natural for the lead in the play that the Cultural Society was putting on that spring. And of course they cast Nadia Moroz as his opposite number, Nadia about whom no one could invent or imagine anything that wasn't proper, *chemna*: Nadia, offspring of a Saint and a Broomstick. This was important; the Cultural Society had commissioned a dramatic adaptation of *Kateryna* from Pan Mudry, who'd been a theater director in Kyiv before the war. The audience would be made up of respectable people who loved and knew their Shevchenko. Only Nadia could play a girl seduced by a Russian soldier, a girl who bears a child out of wedlock and who then, expelled from her village, wanders off, babe in arms, in search of the lying Muscovite who'd seduced her. In short, only Nadia could play such a role without giving the audience *ideas*. And only Peter could carry off the role of the heartless hussar, making almost every woman in the audience fall shamelessly in love with him.

Whether Nadia fell for him or not, nothing stopped her from accepting Jack Senchenko's proposal. Jack was an up-and-comer, a man who would go places, who had only to look at a dollar bill for it to multiply and spin off in a dozen different directions. She married him because of her father's illness and the medical fees that had plunged the Morozes into the kind of debt that made their former finances appear as solid as the Rock of Gibraltar. But it's Peter Metelsky's belief that Nadia married Jack Senchenko because she was afraid of her own feelings, because she didn't love Jack and would therefore be perfectly safe with him, at no risk of losing herself. For it had been Peter's obsession, all through the rehearsals for *Kateryna*, to convince Nadia Moroz that she should have no fear of losing herself, if he was the one to find her.

Jack and Nadia married three months after the closing night of the play, Peter and Zirka a year later, by which time Nadia had given birth to her only child, a son, Jack Jr. She'd carried her child the way she always carried herself: so that nobody noticed, so that nothing showed outside the lines of what was expected, acceptable. She was a master at pulling herself in, vanishing into herself, so that her thoughts could be off in some other space while with her body she was shaking someone's hand, lifting a fork to her mouth, pressing her face against Peter's and Zirka's in the receiving line at their wedding. Where did she go when she performed her vanishing act? Maybe nowhere very far away but straight overhead, like the dove hovering over Christ's head at the Baptism. When Peter kissed her a moment longer than he should have, when Zirka hugged her so tight she seemed to be trying to crack her ribs, maybe Nadia could see it all as if it were a film projected in an empty cinema instead of a church hall dense with wedding guests and streamers and whisky-laden tables. As for when she went home and lay down in her husband's bed, who could tell where she was then, what she was or wasn't watching?

So that's how it went: Nadia keeping her distance, making Peter keep his; their dancing, their acting together nothing more than a joke remembered, it being understood by all that anything between them could only be a joke. After some years of trying, Peter and Zirka had had two sons. The business the two men had set up together fell apart, as Jack went into real estate, and Peter—who had a genius for bad investments—joined company after company, each time at a lower salary, with less and less responsibility. Gradually, the family gatherings tapered off and finally stopped happening, the Senchenkos and Metelskys having moved to very different sides of the social tracks. Until, if it weren't for Kalyna Beach, Peter and Nadia would hardly see one another at all, in or out of the water.

WHAT DOES IT look like to Sonia, or Sasha, or to any of the other Ladies at Kalyna Beach—a pure accident or a game of chicken? Especially after what happened not so long ago at the Plotskys' party. Does Jack even care? He's such an easygoing man, so bluff and large and generous that he seems to be above anything as small as suspicion.

Isn't it just like Jack, showing off, taking his wife and sister and brother-in-law for a spin on his new speedboat, *Svoboda—Freedom* painted on its side in heavy, gilt-edged letters? True, Peter and Zirka are here as replacements for the business associates from the city, who've canceled their visit at the last minute; they are stand-ins, invited to *ooh* and *aah* over the speed and power of Jack's latest toy. What's surprising is that Nadia has come along, too, a scarf tied around her head, dark glasses on—the expensive, prescription ones that make her look like Jackie Kennedy at Hyannis Port, only this is Kalyna Beach, and her husband is president of no superpower but of Senchenko Enterprises Ltd. Zirka's as excited as a child, so delighted with Jack's urging her to sit up front, where she can have a turn at the wheel, that she neglects to consider the implications of Peter settling himself in the back seat beside Nadia. They say not one word to one another, Nadia and Peter, there's too much noise for that, for Jack's intent on showing off, zooming across the lake like some maniac horsefly.

It's Nadia who leans forward, at last, calling out, "Slow down, for heaven's sake. There's no need to go this fast, you could cause an accident. There are swimmers in the water, can't you see?"

Jack just keeps grinning and gunning it, as if his wife and their guests and all the people at the beach have asked to be given the show of their lives. Peter is about to stand up, stand over Jack and physically force him to slow down, when Nadia rises from her seat, clutching the side rail, the wind whipping the scarf from her head. And before Peter can begin to comprehend what's happening, she climbs up on the seat and tumbles overboard, into the wake they've torn up behind them. Even before Jack kills the engine, Peter is jumping in after her, Zirka screaming at him to stay put, to think of the children.

That rough, sudden silence as he hits the water, the breath nearly knocked out of him. Somehow he is swimming out to her, strong, swift strokes, though each wave is a glass door to be crashed through, over and over. The look on Nadia's face as she flails her arms in the water: not terrified but pitiless, that is what amazes him. As if, instead of reaching out to grab hold of him, she is inviting him to come drown with her. Somehow he gets a hold of her, somehow he manages to swim back with her to where the boat is waiting, its lack of noise as jolting as its stink of gasoline. His arms around her waist, her thighs, hoisting her up to Jack, who hauls her in, one eye on the shore—who is watching, what has been seen? An accident, of course: disobeying the rules, standing up in a speeding boat. Who wouldn't have fallen in entirely, irresponsibly, by accident?

ANYONE WHO THINKS otherwise, Sonia had protested, has been reading too much Harold Robbins and Jacqueline Suzanne. Or watching films like *Cleopatra*, reading the movie magazines Darka's addicted to and that Sonia confiscates, which she only manages to do when Darka leaves them lying about like empty banana peels. Sonia doesn't want her daughters coming across such trash, she tells herself: she doesn't, however, throw the magazines out but takes them down the road to her sister-in-law, as a guilt offering. For Sonia has failed in her sisterly role, failed wholeheartedly. She doesn't invite Zirka over for coffee or dinner, not when Max and Peter are here for the weekends and certainly not when they're off in the city. She does her best to ignore Zirka both on the beach and on Sasha's veranda. And she isn't nearly as attentive to her nephews as she might be. Her excuse is that she knows nothing about boys, which, as Zirka points out to her, is nonsense: didn't she grow up with a brother?

There's much that Sonia could say by way of reply to this question, should she so choose. The fact is that she's reserved, or, as Zirka likes to put it, cold, proud, and holier-than-thou. Very much like Nadia, as a matter of fact, but without the inestimable advantage, as Zirka sees it, of being married to Jack Senchenko. Still, Sonia brings her sister-in-law the movie magazines with which Darka had filled her suitcase on coming up to the cottage. Zirka, of course, would rather die than be seen actually buying a *Hollywood Stars* or *Movie Times*; she has her reputation to think of, after all. Movie magazines are for ignorant sixteen-year-olds like Darka and not for sophisticated married women, the mothers of sons. Still, she's not averse to thumbing through the copies Sonia hands over without a kiss or a hug, since, as everyone knows, it's the worst kind of luck to embrace across a threshold.

On this evening, as on all the others, Sonia refuses Zirka's invitation to come in for tea and honey cake; she has to get back to the children, she says. As usual, Zirka warns her sister-in-law that she'll wear herself down to nothing if she doesn't eat. The *medivnyk* Sonia's just refused is one of the specialties Zirka is famous for; pepper and rum are the secret ingredients—not that Sonia would care to find out, she is the only person Zirka's ever met who seems to be allergic to the very thought of food. She's not skinny, exactly; Nadia Senchenko's skinny, but Sonia has a perfect figure—if you like small-breasted women, that is. She seems immune to age, childbirth, and the bad habits induced by motherhood. Zirka has just finished her own dinner and the half that Yuri left on his plate before running out the door to meet the Vesiuk boys, who are waiting for him on the porch.

So it's with Andriy, her youngest, her favorite, that Zirka sits down to tea and slightly boozy honey cake. He leafs through the old *Macleans* that have piled up on the end tables, while she goes for one of the magazines Sonia's brought her, the one with SYBIL'S ANGUISH in letters two inches high on the cover. She's a terribly impatient reader, Zirka: she can't follow any kind of plot or argument but looks through each article for what she calls "items" she can lift and plunk into whatever context pleases her. What she's gleaned from the cover story reassures her. Mrs. Richard Burton, it would seem, has been through this kind of emotional tornado before. Her husband may be notorious for "forming attachments" with his leading ladies, but—and Zirka straightens her spine as she reads this—he always comes home to his wife and two kids and "the life he has made with them"—that "made" sounding to Zirka's ears like the making of bread or borshch, something serious, beneficial, nourishing for all concerned.

But it's the feature on the current cause of Sybil's Anguish that Zirka saves for the moment she's alone at last, once Andriy has had his bath and been tucked into bed and Yuri's come home from his visit with his friends. The visit has made him impossible: slamming doors, refusing to answer when spoken to, sticking out his tongue. "Your father will hear about your behavior when he comes up on Friday, don't think I—" But Yuri's slammed yet another door, cutting off his mother in mid-sentence. "And don't wake your brother," she yells, as if Andriy were a cranky newborn instead of an eleven-year-old known for the soundness of his sleep and the mildness of his disposition. Zirka shakes her head, cuts herself another big piece of *medivnyk*, stirs two spoons of sugar into her tea, and curls up in her nightie on the sagging sofa.

"Elizabeth Taylor: Starlight All the Way!" reads the title of the longest story in the magazine, stretching far beyond the center page, with plenty of the glamour shots that Zirka loves. There's something so glossy, creamy, sweet, and sumptuous about the photographs—they make her think of pale-pink-and-green meringues or the sugar roses on a birthday cake. She devours the pictures: from teenage starlet to teenage bride, from wife to divorcée to widow to wife; from El Mocambo to Egypt and the set of *Cleopatra*. Of course she knows what some gossip columnist once wrote: *"There isn't a woman alive who doesn't want to look like Elizabeth Taylor, or a man who doesn't want to sleep with her."* Zirka brings the magazine closer to her face; stares at the beautifully arched brows and the dripping, violet eyes. Well, she's the one in a zillion, she tells herself. She wouldn't want to look like Elizabeth Taylor; not for anything would she want to look like that temptress, seductress, man-eater.

It's not, she decides, letting the magazine fall from her hands and picking cake crumbs from the nylon of her nightie, the *looks* she's after. It's the life—the life! For, as she has just learned, never, ever has Elizabeth Taylor had to wash a dish, iron a dress, slice an onion, take out the garbage, or rinse a stinky diaper— though it's true, she has a zoo of pets who run in and out of the house, leaving God knows what kind of a mess behind. The point is, Liz Taylor never has to pick up after anyone, even her- self. It can take her three hours to put on her makeup and get dressed for a party; as for her jewelry, she's got diamonds bigger than her boobs, from what the story says.

Zirka doesn't bother looking down to the ring digging into her finger: Peter had to borrow the money for the diamond from Jack, and even so, it's no bigger than a baby tooth. Grace Kelly got a friendship ring of diamonds and rubies just for posing for a maga- zine cover with Prince Rainier. He was no looker, that's for sure, but then what do a man's good looks do for the wife in the pic- ture? What had they done for Sybil Burton—or, more important, for Zirka Metelsky? It's just as Father Myron has told her, over and over again: marriage is a cross to be carried the way you carry home loads of groceries or baskets of laundry from the basement to the yard. Unless you're Elizabeth Taylor, that is, and can simply let go of what you're lugging, let it crash to the ground and walk away as if the law of gravity applied to everyone and everything but you.

If you're a Hollywood star, you can do exactly what you want, whenever you want, with anyone who takes your fancy. If you're Zirka Metelsky, née Senchenko, you're stuck with the bed you've made, the stew you've cooked—there's no getting rid of the mistakes ringing your neck, higher and higher. Zirka Senchenko, she'd been once: *senchenko*, another word for "millionaire," *zirka*, meaning "star." Some starlight she'd stumbled on, marrying a man with pockets like sieves and an allergy to an honest day's work—or a dishonest day's, at that! *Liz and Dick: The Romance of the Century.* If Jack hadn't been there to take care of things, if Jack hadn't stepped in, again and again, to make sure the Metelskys didn't end up on the rubbish heap—

Two boys, she'd produced; two bouncing boys, unlike that tribe of girls with which Sonia's stuck Max Martyn. Four girls to marry off! Forever giving herself airs, Sonia, with her delicate this and her fragile that, and the headaches—not common garden-variety headaches but *migraines*—she brings on herself. Elizabeth Taylor—now *she's* a delicate one, what with the meningitis and the pneumonia, the crushed disks in her back, the tracheotomy. You could see the scar on her neck, the article said, when she limped up to get her Academy Award, limped up on crutches—although, Zirka recalls, the cleavage was completely unassisted, no doubt about that. Well, who is she to fault a pair of knockers—isn't that her own strong suit? Zirka of the over-the-shoulder boulder-holder. If Peter had fallen for some

Daisy Mae type, if he'd even tried to feel up Darka—and the way that girl flaunts herself she wouldn't be surprised if all the husbands up for the weekends have got the hots for her—well, she could handle that. But to carry the torch for Nadia Moroz, that holy-holy titless wonder of a Mrs. Magoo!

Tears are rolling down Zirka's plump, flushed cheeks; tears are soaking into the faded pink of her nightie and onto the crumpled pages of *Hollywood Stars*. She lies back on the scratchy sofa, remembering the time she first met Peter, when Jack had brought him home for supper and he'd fallen on the food she'd prepared like a famished man, lavish not just with appetite but with compliments. Remembering but rearranging those memories so that she appears thinner, prettier, and Peter attentive, if not downright smitten, calling her *Zirochko moya*. She hugs herself, and mops her face, and falls asleep with the lamp still burning, only to wake an hour later in the thick of a dream.

She is standing naked, on the corner of Bloor and Yonge, naked except for a stack of wide golden rings around her neck, forcing her chin up from her goggling breasts, higher and higher until she can't see the ground at her feet anymore, or the people passing by, gawking and laughing at her. She can't see her husband's dark, handsome head walking straight past her, walking away from her, whistling as he always does. Not walking but running, running away from her, she knows this, knows exactly how far he will get from her, though all she can see, all the rings around her neck force her to keep seeing is the bright blue sky overhead—not clear, not cloudless, but like her head now that the dream has flashed through it: aching and empty.

ALL FAMILIES HAVE hierarchies of the heart: from the moment Andriy was born, he was Zirka's joy. In Zirka's defense, you had to admit that there never was and never could be any sweeter baby, boy or girl. Andriy's huge blue eyes and the blond buttercup curl on top of his head enchanted everyone; instead of turning to dirty blond as he grew up, his hair stayed flaxen and curly, so that his mother hadn't had the heart to cut it short. Alone of all the boys at Kalyna Beach this summer, Andriy sports no crew cut but wears his hair long—almost as long as Darka's pageboy.

Andriy has spent much of his time in Zirka's company: he happily helps her do housework, vacuuming being his specialty. He can be counted on, his mother claims, never to vacuum up the littlest Lego pieces, or the buttons, safety pins, and paper clips that somehow always find their way to the floor. He is a careful boy who likes to please, whereas Yuri has been a troublemaker from the time he was born. When Sonia considers her nephews, she tells herself to be glad she's only had girls: Yuri is so wild and rough and always getting into mischief, a hundred times worse than Katia. And Andriy, though he's so milky-mild—oh, she doesn't know, but she would have found it shameful to have turned any son of hers into a mother's help.

There is nothing to vacuum at the cottage. The floors are swept of sand every night, but that is Zirka's job, when the boys have gone to bed for the night. She insists that both boys go down with her to the beach every morning and afternoon, in spite of Andriy's protests that he'd really be happier reading comics at the kitchen table; she wants to make sure that her sons remember this summer at Kalyna Beach as the happiest, most carefree time of their lives. Andriy tries very hard to give nothing away, putting on a brave face when his mother shoos him away to go play with the other boys. He hides, as best he can, the terror he feels in the company of boys who are always pushing and shoving and pinching, daring him to hit back.

Which he will never do, for Andriy hates fighting: it sickens him. At home, watching cartoons on Saturday mornings, he feels like throwing up when Popeye and Bluto go at it, shoving their fists in each other's faces, tearing apart Olive Oyl's house plank by plank. He would look up from the screen and see light pouring from the ground-level windows into the dark well in which the television flickered. And then he'd feel queasy at how they were making themselves prisoners while the whole world was waiting for them, outdoors. The daylight they hadn't yet felt on their faces, the garden, the grass, the praying mantis hiding among the daisies or the skin of ice on the puddles—all of it unnoticed, eclipsed, as good as dead to them. It made his breathing go shallow and his chest ache. It wasn't that the world didn't exist when he wasn't outside in it but that he didn't exist when he wasn't face to face with things, real things and not crude drawings of them flashing on a television screen.

The great rock on which the boys are gathered this afternoon—the Seech—is hopelessly real. Andriy sits at the very end, while Yuri stands defiantly next to the throne. For Pavlo has demanded he announce his plan, describe, at long last, the strategy of the raid the *Zaporozhtsi* are to carry out, or else to relinquish his role as hetman. Yuri's eyes are painfully bright; he keeps blowing out air from his bottom lip, which he makes protrude until his upper lip has vanished. It's to keep himself still, Andriy understands, to keep himself from shouting at Pavlo, from bursting into tears at the way in which he, Yuri Metelsky, is about to be disgraced, like the great Hetman Mazepa, beaten and tied to his horse, wandering the steppes till he dies of exposure.

"So you have no clue?" Pavlo's question is purely rhetorical.

"We could always kidnap Darka," Teyko pipes up.

"For the last time, shut up," Pavlo warns his brother. He's not having Darka's name mentioned by anyone but himself. It was only yesterday morning that she made a fool of him in front of everyone, and all because he'd been trying to peer down the top of her two-piece while she was reading a movie magazine by the lake. "Go away," she'd grumbled. "Go away and don't come back till you've grown up!" She hadn't taken him seriously enough to be angry.

Ignoring Yuri, Pavlo walks right up to the throne, sitting down on the jut of rock as magisterially as he can. "While Yuri's scratching his head to come up with something better than burning another roll of tar paper, I'll tell you my plan. It's very simple, and it gives us a chance to carry out an operation that will prove just how cunning we are, how—" He is about to say *brave* but instead the word *diabolical* comes out.

"Meaning?" Olek asks dryly.

"Shut up, you. Look—who is the only guy in all of Kalyna Beach who's so tied to his mama's apron strings that he can't even go for a pee on his own?"

Andriy braces himself, but to his astonishment the name that rings out isn't his.

"Billy Baziuk!" Nick calls, sticking out his tongue, popping his eyes, and wagging his head from side to side. Everyone laughs, even Andriy, who still can't believe his good luck.

"So let's do old Billy a favor. Let's give him the chance to have a bit of fun, away from his mama and her makeup kits. Let's get Billy a date—a date with Darka!"

There is a hush: the boys are struck dumb by the audacity of Pavlo's plan. As he explains it, they will have all the fun of a prank, without any chance of getting caught. And even if they do, what's the big deal? No one gets sent to reform school for a practical joke. Pavlo is acclaimed not just as hetman but as resident genius as well.

Then Yuri speaks up. "She won't even let you get a peek at

her boobs—so how're you going to get her to go on a date with Billy?"

According to the code, Pavlo should be taking a swing at Yuri for what he's just said, but all Pavlo does is smile, a broad, deeply unpleasant smile, as he calls Andriy's name.

Andriy waddles over as quickly as he can. When everyone's eyes are on him, as they are now, he feels even fatter and clumsier: his walk becomes exaggerated, the wobble of his chest more pronounced. But for once there are no calls of Titty or Pampu, no wolf whistles, no feet stuck out to trip him. For some reason, Pavlo has singled out Andriy, and the rest of the boys are stumped, wondering why Pavlo's bestowing his favor on Yuri's kid brother. For Pavlo's voice isn't scornful, as it usually is when he addresses Andriy or deigns to notice his existence. Pavlo is speaking to Andriy as if he were a trusted lieutenant, almost an equal, while Yuri is pushed to the edge of the group.

And so the New Hetman of Kalyna Beach unveils to them all the exploit he's imagined, and the means by which it is to be arranged and carried out. When he has finished, he swears everyone to secrecy. Even Yuri, to his brother's great surprise, agrees to swear—what's more, he volunteers to get Katia on their side.

BOY-CRAZY IS THE expression all the Ladies are using, not just about Darka Marchuk but about what they call "the whole younger generation." Perhaps they pick the expression up from the books they're reading, or perhaps the words materialize from whatever's in the air that summer, and not just at Kalyna Beach. Girls today are boy-crazy, and it's simply a disgrace. The fact that there are no boys anywhere near enough for Darka to chase doesn't deter the Ladies: it's not the act so much, they say, as the state of mind.

They would never have been allowed to run after boys, calling them on the phone, hanging about at corner stores or soda fountains and making eyes at anything in a pair of pants. Not that they didn't have boyfriends when they were Darka's age, but that's all they were—friends who happened to be boys. They did everything in groups: picnics at Centre Island or Niagara Falls, dances at the Ukrainian Hall, or just walking home after school or church. And if a boy tried to get fresh, put his hand where he shouldn't or started to say things that you even suspected were wrong, you didn't, for heaven's sake, encourage him. Of course there were always accidents, but in most cases the boy lived up to what was expected of him: marriage followed, the baby was born, and the couple settled down to a respectable life like everyone else. It's this crazy idea these girls have today that they can get away with it all, that they don't have to pay for what they do, that they can slip into dark alleyways with every sweet-talker who comes their way and then prance down the aisle in pure white, with a boy from a good family, a boy with a future—that's what gets the Ladies' goat, as they gather on their faded blankets down at the beach on yet another perfect summer afternoon.

Not, Sonia ventures, that it's always the parents' fault. Olya's a wonderful mother, and Walter's always been a hard worker, if not the best provider. Darka's their only child, and if that's made them spoil her, who would have done otherwise in their situation? Darka's a good girl at heart, this is just a temporary wildness, but what's so hard is that she doesn't know, won't listen to how dangerous things are getting for her now. One slip and she could be ruined for life. You couldn't be too careful, especially if you had Darka's natural advantages.

"Thirty-eight–twenty-two–thirty-eight," Sasha quips, but Sonia continues, in a passion. "It's not just your measurements, it's the way you carry yourself—what you say about yourself by the way you walk, and sit down, and even drink from a bottle of pop. A man can always tell when he's dealing with a lady. I modeled for five years, and I can tell you, there were times when things could have got out of hand in the worst way, but people always knew I wouldn't stand for any of that, that I was a lady."

"*Nasha* Grace Kelly—our own Snow Queen of the runway."

"You can laugh all you like, Sasha," Sonia retorts, "but I know what I'm talking about—"

Zirka jumps in, on Sonia's side for once. "Just you wait another couple of years till Tania's Darka's age. You'll be laughing out of the other side of your mouth, just see if you won't."

But Sasha isn't about to be provoked. "Oh, I'll just pack them off to Samoa," she laughs. "They have a much healthier attitude toward life over there."

Zirka's never heard of Samoa; she's dying to ask Sasha to explain, but Sonia leaves her no room.

"It doesn't matter what's healthy, Sasha. What matters is that you have to pay for everything you want, and that it's better not to find yourself paying a whole lifetime for something you decide wasn't worth even five minutes of your time. That's what women do, what we've always done and always will—we pay, and we pay, and we pay."

It's safer, after this onslaught, the Ladies decide, to keep mum. Sonia has some bee in her bonnet, her whole body exudes tension like a halo made of a fire so keen that though it's invisible, it spits and crackles. They lie down on their blankets while Annie Vesiuk goes off to check on the kids, and Sasha keeps turning the pages of the copy of Margaret Mead that she's brought along, wrapped up in a towel.

THE COUSINS ARE walking into the undergrowth on the other side of Tunnel Road, dodging saplings and low branches and twigs that seem to grow for no other purpose than to gouge out an unwary eye. When they reach the place where a broad, high slab of granite sticks up from the tangle of sumac and goldenrod and wintergreen, they sit down with their backs against the rock. Katia sees no point in delaying: she asks Yuri straight out what happened the night that Pan Durkowski caught him spying.

"Did he have his gun? His Lager—his Luger, I mean."

"What do you think?"

"Well, did he interrogate you, did he slap you around under klieg lights, did he—?"

For a brief moment, Yuri considers telling his cousin the truth: how, when old man Durkowski collared him, he decided to go along instead of breaking loose. So he could be one up on Katia, who was always off plotting with Tania; so he could have an adventure and a secret of his own to keep. His ruse had worked only too well. He recalls each shameful moment inside the Durkowskis' cabin: the old man commanding his wife to empty a sack of dried peas on the kitchen floor, then ordering Yuri to kneel on the peas until he was man enough to apologize.

And himself, refusing, easily resisting the hands that are trying to force him to his knees, daring to provoke the old man: "Not until you show me your Luger!" Pan Durkowski staring at him as if he were crazy or senile. "The one you used when you fought with the Germans. Your Luger and your SS badge."

And how, out of nowhere, he'd felt against his neck the press of a cold, hard, narrow tube: the barrel of a gun. And a voice, a stranger's voice, neither a man's nor a woman's, shouting harshly, *"Hände hoch!"*

How he'd had no choice but to raise both arms and hold them up until they hurt. How he'd been ordered to apologize to Pan Durkowski and asked what they teach in the schools these days, that a boy of his age could believe it was something to be proud of—a Luger, the SS. How, as the gun had shoved into the nape of his neck, there'd been the click of a trigger, and a trickle of pee had run down his leg. How tears had welled in his eyes, tears of shame and confusion. And how, when he'd made his apology, and the gun had pulled back, a hand had been put on his shoulder, a hand that turned him around to face no enemy but Pani Durkowska and the length of cold copper pipe she held as she made with her mouth a clicking noise that anyone could tell was nothing like a trigger.

"Come on, Yuri, tell me," Katia pleads. "Unless all that happened was Pan Durkowski taking off his belt and smacking you. Bad boy, such a bad, bad, boy!"

She makes her voice as teasing as she can, to show Yuri that of course she doesn't mean it. But her cousin turns on her, shouting so loudly that his face looks as if it's about to break apart.

"Why should I tell you?" And then, pausing for effect, he fires the best shot he has: "You're just a girl."

Katia pulls back her arm and socks him in the gut. Yuri stares up at her, dazed and winded, before grabbing her shoulders and pulling her down against the boulder. They wrestle, two wiry kids, the boy with the advantage of strength, the girl with some fund of fury that lets her hold her own against him, until they both sink exhausted, side by side, their backs against the earth, their eyes staring up at a whirl of leaves and sky.

IN HER NARROW room, at the back of her wardrobe, in a cardboard box that once held a pair of too-tight, barely worn shoes, lies Darka's whole stash of treasure: mascara and half a dozen lipsticks, a compact, three different kinds of cologne, eye shadow in plum and turquoise and pearly white, two pots of rouge, foundation, pancake makeup with a little sponge to apply it, and, best of all, a set of false eyelashes. She hasn't yet had a chance to try on the eyelashes—she's afraid they'll stick for good and she'll have to cut them off, so that no one will discover what she's been up to. If they weren't so blind they'd have guessed already: it's not like she could have walked out of Venus Variety with all this loot. But they were born blind, or else they don't think she's worth a second glance, for all they're after her to watch this, stop that, and stay within the lines.

She hadn't had to tell Frank, he'd known by instinct—or maybe she had said something to egg him on, a complaint about how they were shifting her around like a piece of furniture. The sleep-house wasn't such a bad place: there was a three-quarter-size bed, plus a table and chair; there was even a shower and a toilet, so that it was a little like having your own apartment. They should have let her stay there from the beginning; it would have meant she was up here not as the hired help but as a guest who would naturally do her share in making the household run, looking after the kids, doing the occasional load of laundry. But she'd been offered the sleep-house only when Marta had come up for a week of what no one could describe as holidays.

They couldn't have made it easier for him if they'd tried. There's a back door to the sleep-house, so he never risked being seen from the main house. They didn't need to worry about being heard, either: the mattress was soft and saggy, the springs so shot they barely creaked.

When he'd come to her first, in the cellar, it had been like one more set of chores to cross off her list. And he had asked so politely; he had kept his distance. *If you please, Darka, pull down the straps of your bathing suit; would you be so kind, Darka, as to show me your breasts?* He hadn't touched her at all, just leaned against the wall, sipping from his silver flask, watching her step out of her bathing suit and back into it. As if she were on stage and he were in the back row of the audience, as if she were modeling for him, not a swimsuit but her skin, or as if her body were nothing more than a swimsuit. It got so she was hardly aware of him being there at all, in the dim, cool cellar: it was as if she were in her own room, standing in front of the mirror, looking her body over, checking it against the list in *How to Have a Perfect Body*. Breasts should be pert, not floppy: the perfect breast is one that fits into a champagne glass. Hips: full but not pudgy. Buttocks: nicely rounded and, above all, firm. When you stand with your legs together, there should be three diamond-shaped spaces: between your calves, just under your knees, and between your thighs.

What he'd done to her in the sleep-house, what she'd let him do to her . . . Because she was scared he'd tell on her, tell about the gifts he'd given her—accuse her of stealing them. Because he'd say she asked for it, she never stopped him. Because if she didn't let him do it to her there, then, no one else ever would: she'd be stuck up at the cottage with a bunch of old women and their brats for the rest of her life. Because she was curious about how it happens, from start to finish, and with Jamie it'd always been a little bit of this, a little bit of that, and never all the way. Because when she poured him a glass of the whisky she'd stolen from the main house, he drank it down like a glass of milk. Because he'd wanted it so badly, wanted her, Darka, and not that stale crust of a Lesia Baziuk, who always looked at her as if she were so much dust on the road. Because for once she, Darka Marchuk, has the power to give someone what he wants, what he says he's dying for. Because he calls her honey-baby and says he'll help her, he'll do anything she wants, give her anything she needs, take her away from here, far away and forever.

Because when they do it, it's as if there are two of her, one sitting on the edge of the bed, leaning forward, watching, and the other one lying back, as he parts her legs and shoves into her, pounding again and again and again. And then it stops, and he rolls back as she stares at the ceiling, the way she'd stared at the ceiling of her dark, narrow room in the main house, wondering if anything would ever happen to her, if her life would ever begin.

The first time, he'd left right after, putting his finger over her lips, not saying a word. She'd counted to a hundred after she heard the door close behind him; she got up, reached for the bottle of whisky, and, remembering an ad she'd read in one of her movie magazines, set about douching. The whisky hurt, and she was glad: it was like pouring hydrogen peroxide into a cut; if it foamed and stung, you knew it was working. She had felt very grown-up, very sensible, very calm, as she rinsed the sheet and took her shower, letting the water run a long, long time, washing her blood and the smell of him out of her skin.

DARKA HASN'T BEEN stupid enough to give up thoughts of Jamie Ashford just because of her gentleman caller. Where does she get that expression from? Not the movie magazines, which her mother so disapproves of—and yet the expression is something Darka associates with her mother's world, her mother's time. She is wondering about this while the Ladies gather on Sasha Plotsky's veranda for an impromptu meeting of the Lending Library, a Wednesday pick-me-up to break the back of what always seems the longest week of the summer, the last week before the End, as interminable and impossible as the last week of a pregnancy. Darka's still working at the riddle even as she's sitting Katia down at Sonia's dressing table. *Gentleman caller.* She undoes Katia's ponytail and starts teasing her hair, from tips to scalp, so it sticks out like a dark dandelion clock all around her.

"You're lucky," Darka tells her. "You have good, thick hair— not coarse but with a lot of body."

Darka is going to become a beauty consultant when she

leaves school this year. She doesn't want to be any old Avon lady, though. She wants to have a shop of her own; she wants to do a hairdressing course; she already has a diploma from the charm school her parents finally agreed to send her to, after she'd begged and pleaded and threatened not to eat or drink until they gave in. She'll even be helping to pay the fees with money she's earned from babysitting and stacking cans at Stenko's grocery.

"What did you learn at charm school?" Katia asks, eyes on the mirror that shows Darka spraying and shaping the puffball of hair into a rigid helmet. With enormous satisfaction, Katia decides that the hairdo adds ten years to her face.

"How to put on makeup," Darka answers. "We sat at this long, white counter, with white smocks on—everything was so clean, like at a hospital. Each of us had a mirror with a ring of light bulbs—they were so hot, they were always melting the makeup. We always started with the concealer." *Gentleman*. She shakes out the shoebox she's brought along, till a mass of makeup litters the tabletop. Then she picks up a fat stick like a pale orange crayon. "You don't have anything to cover up yet, but let's pretend we want to hide that beauty spot over there. See? It's vanished. Magic."

Katia touches the place where the beauty mark was. She can see the ghost of it under the orange blob, but she would rather die than say so.

"Now for the foundation." Darka opens a jar of something

beige and slippery that she strokes over Katia's face. "Then pow-der—that's to set the look—you know, like after you mix up a cake and put it in the oven. Close your eyes."

Rouge is seared on Katia's cheeks from a small, greasy pot; from a little palette of colors for her eyelids, Darka chooses Dusky Dreams. Eyeliner. Mascara. She's talking all the time, Katia responding with *yes*es and *uhm*s and *really*s, her eyes shut tight while Darka tells her how she was taught to do a gliding walk, as if every bone in her body were made of Jell-O. How to pull on gloves, both wrist-length and elbow. The correct way of getting up and sitting down, and how to cross your legs. *Gentle man.*

"Now open your mouth—just a little. Good, now smack your lips, just to spread the color—just a little, I said—do you want to end up like Bozo the Clown? Okay, all done—take a look."

Darka snatches the scratchy towel from around Katia's shoulders as the girl stares into the glass. From chin to waist the mirror shows the skinny body of a twelve-year-old wearing a halter top over a chest flat as an ironing board. But there's a line drawn, like the borders that divide countries in her school atlas, countries tinted different colors to show they're meant to be separate. The line appears at her chin, where her tan turns into something peachy-orange. Her lips have a completely different shape, and her cheekbones jut out angrily, as though she'd held them against something hot. And her eyes—they are long and slanting and smoky, somehow.

"Wait!" Darka takes her comb, wets a few strands of Katia's hair with spit, and sculpts a kiss curl hanging down from the middle of her forehead.

"Gorgeous."

"Gorgeous," Katia whispers back.

She looks at herself in the mirror, turning her head this way and that, pursing up her lips, frowning, smiling dopily, like Marilyn Monroe. She leans forward, tugs the straps of her halter top down over her shoulders, and pushes up her nonexistent breasts with her hands. "Look, Darka," she cries in her best imitation of a grown woman's voice, "I'm a sex kitten! I'm a slut!"

But there's no response from Darka, neither laughter nor impatience. Katia wheels around, looks up at the older girl and gives a little cry. Darka looks as if she's been turned into wood; her shoulders slope, and suddenly her eyes are the eyes of an old, old woman.

"You okay?" Katia asks. There's no answer, so she tugs at Darka's blouse. "Why don't you make yourself up like Cleopatra, Darka? I bet you'd look a million times better than that old Liz Taylor. I bet if you did your hair and put those long black lines on your eyes and went out to Midland and sat in the diner, they'd be rushing up to sign you on."

Suddenly, angrily, Darka comes to. "Who, Katia? Who's going to rush up to me?"

"Producers—you know."

"In Midland, Ontario?"

"Maybe they're on vacation—maybe they've just stepped off their powerboats and they're hungry and they want to grab a bite to eat, and they walk into the diner and see—"

"Darka Marchuk? Sure."

Now comes Katia's moment of inspiration. She jumps up and grabs the older girl's arms. "Come on, Darka. Let me do your face."

To Katia's amazement, Darka slumps down at the vanity table, keeping her eyes fixed on the laundry-reddened hands in her lap. *Caller. Call her. Collar.* First Katia takes out the rollers and the pins that skewer them in place. She brushes Darka's hair so that it makes a golden cloud around her face, with the inky roots barely visible. She puts no foundation on Darka's skin, which is beautifully tanned, but slaps on the rouge and lipstick as thick as she can. Finally, she takes the eyeliner, and then, when it proves too delicate, the eyebrow pencil, drawing a thick line all around Darka's eyes and from the corners almost to her hairline. *Bedroom eyes*, Katia once heard someone say, and now she knows exactly what such eyes must look like, though not why. While this transformation is taking place, Darka remains still as a stone, the way an actress would keep perfectly calm and still, having her makeup applied before she steps onto the stage.

"Hail, Great Enchantress of the East, Cleopatra, whose name means 'Glory of Her Race.'"

Katia's imitation of Laura at her most pompous and self-absorbed is dead-on; Darka can't help but laugh. But when she looks up at the mirror to see what's been done to her, her mouth falls open. Apart from her hair, which is dyed anyway, she could be—she *is* Cleopatra. If he could see her now, if he could see her like this—

"Wait," Katia says, running to the closet, pulling wildly at the clothes hanging there, till she finds, at the very back, the perfect thing. A gold, clingy dress, as out of place among the shorts and shirts and pedal-pushers as a chocolate on a plate of pork and beans. "Lamé," whispers Katia. It's a word she pulls out of the air, part of the magic that's turning Darka from a drudge into a movie star—into an Egyptian queen.

Darka hesitates, afraid that Sonia might come home early from the Plotskys' or that Laura will burst in, cross at being left out, threatening to tell on them. "All right," she says at last. "I'll be careful."

She orders Katia to close her eyes, then tugs off her shorts, stepping into the web of shimmering gold, sucking in her belly as she zips up the back.

"Now you can look."

Darka is reclining on the bed as if it were a barge. She could have been poured from a bottle of syrup. "Come here, O Antony, and do the bidding of the empress of thy heart," cries Cleopatra.

Katia can't help herself. She makes a low, sweeping bow and struts to the bed, where she's enfolded in a pair of queenly arms, just like in the photo in the souvenir booklet. The lamé scratches worse than the rollers; Katia can hardly breathe, and Darka's breasts suddenly seem to her enormous, deformed, with pointy nipples jutting out, instead of being perfectly round and smooth as foam. There are holes in the dress, just below the bust—she puts out her hand to touch one, and Darka slaps it away, then bursts into giggles. Suddenly, they are jumping on the bed, Darka holding the gown up in both her hands, the bedsprings squeaking and thudding, the two of them breathless with laughter, till they collapse, at last, in a heap. Katia's face is pressed against Darka's breast; when she pulls away at last, two black, eye-shaped streaks appear on the gold lamé.

"*Bozhe*—she'll have kittens—quick, we've got to hide it."

"Fix your face first," Darka hisses. She shoves Katia toward the bathroom, wriggles out of the golden gown, and leaps into her clothes.

Katia scrubs at her face as hard as she can; when she returns, the dress has been shoved back to the farthest reaches of the closet. Now it's Darka's turn to scour her face with the washcloth Katia's brought her, swearing when the mascara gets into her eyes. Katia doesn't hear her: she is scrabbling to sweep the tubes and pots littering the dressing table back into Darka's shoebox. When she finishes, she goes at her hair, yanking the brush through till her scalp aches, while Darka smooths the bedclothes, saying words Katia's never heard before: fat, ugly words made uglier by panic.

When the door bursts open at last, they scream as if they're expecting a posse, but it's only Baby Alix, her face pale, her eyes bright and black as ever. She stands there with her arms at her sides and no expression on her face. If she'd looked angry or amazed, it would have been all right; it's the blankness that spooks them, so that Darka scoops her up and carries her out. It's up to Katia to collect the washcloth and shoebox; to make sure the room looks just as it did before they came in, as though nothing out of the ordinary has happened here, no makeup, no dress-up, no magic. Softly, Katia closes the door behind her, then dumps the shoebox in Darka's room, and stalks off to the porch.

There are at least six dead flies on the floor, but she makes no move to sweep them up. That is Darka's job, she tells herself. She jumps into the hammock, setting it swinging wildly. It helps her to get over her distress and then her fury at herself for having talked Darka into making her up in the first place; at Darka for having frightened her so by the way she'd seemed to burn out, just like a light bulb, with no warning; and at the Cleopatra dress for having been hanging there in the cupboard at all. Her mother will kill her! It's all Tania's fault; if she and Tania were still best friends, she would never have spent the afternoon with Darka, never gone near the shoebox full of makeup. Best friends, worst friends: what are they now, she and Tania? They haven't had a fight; there have been no scenes, no heated words. There have been no words at all, and that's the trouble.

Suddenly, Katia finds herself saying her grandmother's name, softly, sadly, then coaxingly, as if she could make Baba Laryssa appear beside her, just by the force of her wanting. Her *baba* would have been able to help her, would have taught her what to do. She would have started by asking Katia a few questions, not trick ones, not angry ones that supplied their own wrong answers, but questions that made you think about what mattered most, and what didn't count. She wouldn't have lectured, and she wouldn't have shouted; she'd just have asked questions and made Katia think, until everything became—not easy, but clear.

Katia sets the hammock rocking again with a fierce shove of her foot. She wants to tear the hammock from its hooks, rip it into pieces; she wants to hurt something as badly as she herself is hurting now with missing her *baba*. *Missing*—as if Baba Laryssa were a shoe or an umbrella, something you could find at a lost and found. Katia pounds her fist into the palm of her hand. She will not cry—what good would that do? She will not call out her grandmother's name anymore: she doesn't believe in ghosts. And she won't pray to God, either, the way the priest said they must do at the *panakhyda*, pray that Laryssa Metelsky be forgiven her sins, voluntary and involuntary, as her soul stood before her God. It was God who ought to be asking forgiveness of Baba Laryssa—of Katia, for having taken her *baba* away from her.

When the hammock stops rocking, a phrase comes into Katia's head, a line from a movie she's seen on TV. *What's eating at you?* Was that it? *She's eating her heart out*—maybe that was how it went. She bites at her lips, bites down hard, till she reaches the salt and rust taste of blood. She curls herself into a ball and, raising her hand to her face, starts biting at a hangnail on her thumb. Before she knows it, she is sucking her thumb, her eyes shut tight, and the hole in her heart as small as she can make it.

She falls asleep like this; she turns in her sleep and the thumb, thank God, drops out of her mouth, so that when Yuri creeps up to the hammock and starts tickling her with a leaf he's plucked from a sumac tree, she's not doing anything to give herself away. It's as though she knows he's there even before the leaf touches the tip of her nose: she opens her eyes and stares right into his face, startling him by not crying out, by showing no sign of surprise at all.

Slowly, Katia pulls herself out of the hammock and walks down the porch steps to Tunnel Road, Yuri at her heels. She walks deliberately, keeping her eyes from straying to the clambering weeds that only last year had been her grandmother's carefully tended rows of beans and carrots and onions. When she reaches the road, Yuri puts out his hand to her shoulder, stopping her. He nods in the direction of the sleep-house, and after a moment, Katia shrugs and makes for the little track to that building's back door.

Abandoned, the hammock swings gently to and fro, until it

finally comes to rest. Flies keep crawling up the screens, clinging to the mesh, waiting to join the others on the floor.

"SO?" SHE HAS her hands on what will be her hips one day;
there's a band of bare skin between the place where her halter
top ends and her shorts start.

"So—let's see," he says, scuffing his feet against the floor,
sitting on the sagging bed in the sleep-house across from the
Martyns' cottage.

"Only if you do," Katia insists. "At the same time."

Yuri shrugs, then drags himself off the bed so that he's standing opposite his cousin. They are the same height, their bodies
lean and muscular. With their dark eyes and hair, their olive
skin, they could be brother and sister.

Anyone spying through the window would swear that what
happens next has been carefully rehearsed: Yuri unbuttoning
his faded cotton shirt as Katia crosses her arms to pull up her
crinkled top; Katia pulling at her shorts as Yuri unzips his. Their
clothing falling to the floor, pooling at their ankles as if it were
something foreign to them, a puddle of brackish water they must
wade through to get to some cleaner, drier destination.

Watching at the window, glasses pressed against the glass,
she notes the moment's hesitation before boy and girl, thumbs
hooked into the elastic of their underpants, tug the white cotton down, and then, in the first awkward moment of this mu-
tual disrobing, wriggle free, balancing first on one leg, then the

other, for all the world like fledgling storks. She notices how solemn they look, and how, instead of giggling or pulling faces, they seem to recognize the gravity of this first moment of nakedness not just between them but for each. For no matter how many times in the past they have stripped for baths or changed from wet bathing suits, their bodies have been as weightless, as careless as the clothes they discarded. Only now, in this protracted moment on a hot summer day, in a sleep-house smelling of pine resin and sun, do they seem to register the shock of nakedness. The air prickles their skins, drawing a sharp, indelible line around their bodies.

This moment is so full and so charged, so intensely private, that the watcher at the window closes her eyes, withdrawing her face from the glass, sinking onto the earth on which, straining, on tiptoe, she's been planted.

THE LADIES ARE cradling their glasses of gin. They have been talking of *Lady Chatterley's Lover,* or at least deluging Sasha with questions, until Halya, thinking ahead to Labor Day weekend, calls out to Sonia.

"Come on, tell us what you're going to wear. You always look like a million dollars, even up here, and I've never seen you in the same thing twice at the Senchenkos' party."

"It's going to be a surprise," Sonia answers, hugging to herself the image of the golden Cleopatra dress hanging in her closet like a rare, caged bird. All during this last meeting of the Library, she's been avoiding Sasha's eyes. Sasha's been expecting her to confide the results of the talk with Peter: the promise she was supposed to extract from him about being mature and putting others first; about respecting the difference between the plots of books and movies and the plod of real and ordinary life.

"Where's Nadia?" Zirka interrupts, as if on cue. "Does she think she's too important to meet with us, all of a sudden?"

"Maybe she still hasn't got over what happened out on the lake," Stefka suggests, a little too eagerly.

"Nothing happened out on the lake," Sasha jumps in, before Zirka can. "Don't you remember that scene in *Lady Chatterley*, when Clifford insists on working his wheelchair himself, and it rolls down the hill, and Mellors has to run after it?"

"Why did he?" Stefka pipes up. "I mean, it would have been so much better for everyone if he'd just let it smash—and the book would have been a lot shorter, too."

"That's just the way it goes in books, and movies too," Halia sighs. "Look at Cleopatra—if she'd just stayed home at the end and let Marc Antony go off to war—"

"Stayed home to look after the kids and do the laundry? Oh sure," Zirka gloats, knowing she's stolen Sasha's lines. But Sasha doesn't seem to notice; she's busy replenishing glasses, doling out the last of the gin. No one refuses, not even Sonia. They are suddenly, passionately grateful to Sasha, the author of wisecracks and sallies, the dispenser of gin and books. Sasha who brings them all together and keeps them connected: devil-may-care, saintly Sasha.

The Ladies of the Lending Library pull their chairs into a tighter circle, raising their glasses to Sasha, who doesn't toss off a *"Dai Bozhe,"* as she usually does but actually gets to her feet, as if to make a speech.

"Ladies, whatever happens, let's promise that we'll meet right here next summer, drinking gin and gossiping and swapping books." And then, in a different voice, as if she were speaking lines in a play, Sasha declares, "Let's promise to stay together, one for all and all for one. And let there never be the shadow of a parting between us."

Abruptly, she drinks down her gin, as if disconcerted by her eloquence. As the ladies belt back their drinks and scrape back their chairs as they prepare to leave, Sasha is thinking that only Nadia, were she here, would know from what books her lines have been stolen.

"IT'S OKAY, ANDRIY," Katia croons, as if he were a baby to be sung to sleep. "It's just pretend, like dress-up. No one's going to know—right, Yuri?"

"Right. Hey, Andriy, remember *Fantasia*? Remember how Mickey wears a dress when he's working for that Sorcerer guy?"

Andriy just hangs his head and shuts his eyes. He doesn't need eyes to see himself tricked out in one of Darka's skirts and cotton blouses, under which he is wearing his swimming trunks, and her brassiere stuffed with socks. On his feet are Darka's flip-flops; his longish butter-blond hair has been wetted with spit and carefully waved by Katia.

"Good," Katia says, moving in with the shoebox where Darka keeps her makeup. "Now, don't move—just keep still. By the time I've finished, you are going to be *bee-yoo-tee-ful!*"

They are in the sleep-house; Pavlo is posted as lookout by the front door, in case any grown-up or that lemon of a Laura should come by. But there's no need for him to sound the warning: nobody shows any curiosity at what such quiet, out-of-the-way children could be up to. Once Katia is finished with the lipstick and rouge, the eye shadow and eyebrow pencil, she hands Andriy a mirror, exclaiming, "You're much prettier than Darka!" quite honestly, no cruelty intended. Andriy refuses to look at the face that's no longer his own; he stares at his feet as Katia undoes the bib around his neck and whispers, stagily, for she is boiling over with pride and excitement: "Quick—let's go. We can't afford to take any chances. We've got to hurry before they start missing us."

Pavlo gives the all-clear, and they sneak out the back door, the one facing Tunnel Road. They've chosen the time of day when the mothers are busy making supper and Darka's sweeping out the cottage, and Laura's telling stories to Bonnie and

Baby Alix. It's a Friday, and there's the extra work of tidying up to do, so that the cottages will look decent by the time the husbands arrive. Yuri is confident that at this particular moment, no one will have the leisure to come strolling by.

For Yuri, not Pavlo, has reclaimed the major role. When he thinks about it, his insides go cold. He doesn't need any grown-up to tell him that there's nothing heroic in taking advantage of someone weaker, less fortunate, than they: about tricking Billy Baziuk, using Andriy as bait. So Yuri doesn't think about it. He concentrates, instead, on undoing the damage. That trickle of pee down his leg at the Durkowskis—peeing his pants because some old *baba* pretended to hold a gun to his head. Losing authority that day at the Seech to Pavlo Vesiuk, of all people—Pavlo with his narrow eyes and sleek, flat head, more like a weasel than a lion. If he had taken the time to think things through, Yuri might have wondered why Pavlo hadn't insisted on grabbing the spotlight for himself. But Yuri has been too busy arranging things, building the trap, earning what Pavlo calls "credibility."

Every afternoon for the past week, Yuri Metelsky has been a model child, helping Mrs. Baziuk by watching Billy for her. It's a way of making amends for having been part of that gang of boys who'd nearly burned down the whole beach at the start of the summer, Lesia tells herself. Not that she wasn't suspicious at first, but the Metelsky boy's eagerness and sense of responsibility had quickly converted her. On Yuri's urging, Mrs. Baziuk has aired out the small, dark bunkhouse that has been waiting for guests to sleep over in it for years now, ever since Mr. Baziuk ran not into the deer he was stalking but into a bullet meant for that deer. She's set up a card table for Billy and Yuri to play on, a simple game, war, in which the deck is divided in two, and each player slaps down a card, the one with the higher number winning the trick. It is a mindless game of indescribable tedium, and the delight of children ages three to six, as well as sedated twenty-five-year-old men.

Every afternoon for the past week, Yuri has taken Billy by the hand and led him from the front porch of his mother's cottage, across the grass, and over to the spruced-up bunkhouse. Many times, that first afternoon, Lesia checked up on Yuri and her son, sneaking down to the bunkhouse, peering in at the edge of the window, making sure that everything was "just as it should be." On Tuesday afternoon, she made two duty calls; on Wednesday, one; and by the time Friday rolled around, she was confident enough to leave the boys to themselves. She was actually singing as she prepared Frank Kozak's favorite meal. He was getting fretful now that his week's holiday was drawing to an end; she would let him have a good, large rye and ginger, followed by cottage cheese topped with sour cream and chopped chives—and then peach shortcake for dessert, made from peaches brought in from Mr. Maximoynko's fruit store on Augusta, to grace the shelves of Venus Variety.

On this particular Friday afternoon, Yuri and Billy are down in the bunkhouse. They are laboring on yet another endless game of war in the dim light provided by a single small window, when there's a rustling in the grass and a triple knock at the door. Suddenly, Yuri sweeps up the cards, much to his companion's displeasure.

"It's okay, Billy," he whispers, as if Mrs. Baziuk were in the next room and not a hundred yards away. "Remember that treat I promised you, if you were good?" Billy nods, quiet and expectant.

He isn't, Yuri decides, that creepy-looking, after all: his eyes are green as leaves and his thick brown hair, combed strictly to the side by his mother, has got rumpled during the stress of the game. Billy's dressed in a neat, white, short-sleeved shirt and khaki pants: if it weren't for the way he has of breathing through his mouth and the foolish look in his eyes—foolish because it so openly conveys his hungriness and eagerness—you couldn't really tell, Yuri decides, that Billy Baziuk is a moron.

Why did the moron throw the clock out the window?

Because he wanted to see how time flies.

Now the door pushes open, and to Billy's and even Yuri's amazement, in comes an apparition as marvelous, as unfamiliar in Billy's experience as a winged dog or a talking tree. It is a girl, a girl as tall as Darka, and with Darka's prodigious bosom and flaxen hair. In the half-light, her huge, bright eyes and her scarlet mouth, her crimson cheeks and darkened brows seem to gleam and beckon. Yet this girl is shy, staring down at her feet in their flip-flops, twisting a fistful of skirt in her hand.

It is all going so well, Katia thinks, peering in at the window, while the boys behind her jostle for a view; it is successful beyond their wildest dreams. Except for the fact that Yuri's forgotten his lines. What is it that's supposed to happen next? she wonders—had that ever been explained? She's about to go inside, poke Yuri on the shoulder, when Pavlo takes charge. He steps into the bunkhouse, which is crowded by now, and gives Billy a little shove.

"Go on, Billy, say hello to the girl. She's come all this way to see you. She's in love with you, Billy—don't you want to kiss her? Haven't you ever kissed a girl, Billy, a grown-up guy like you?"

Now Katia has joined Pavlo in the bunkhouse, and the rest of the Cossack Brotherhood is crowding around the door. Yuri's been pushed back to a corner. Katia registers the tenseness of his presence, his silence as she watches Pavlo giving little shoves to the small of Billy's back, guiding him toward the person they all think of, now, as The Girl. Until suddenly Billy grabs the girl's shoulders and shakes her till her face tilts up to his; until Billy is kissing her, his tongue inside her mouth. Billy is kissing The Girl, and you could hear a pinecone drop, when out of nowhere comes a roar—no other word for it—a roar from Yuri.

Charging from his corner, he tears his brother out of Billy's arms, while Billy starts shouting and kicking. Now Katia and Pavlo are tugging Andriy out of the bunkhouse; they're tearing along the forested path from the bluff to the beach. Halfway down, they pause to tug off the boy's skirt and blouse and brassiere, to scoop up the socks. Pavlo runs off with the clothes, while Katia uses spit and dock leaves to clean the makeup from what has become, once more, Andriy's face. Meanwhile, Mrs. Baziuk has flown from her kitchen to the bunkhouse, where Billy's yelling as if someone's taken a cleaver to him. Blood is trickling from his mouth, where Yuri has punched him; Yuri is lying on the floor, where Billy has thrown him.

Yuri's hand is bloodied and his voice hoarse: "You leave him alone, all of you bastards, just leave him alone."

Mrs. Baziuk doesn't understand why Yuri, who has just attacked her Billy, is now demanding he be left alone. There are no assailants lurking nearby, no other culprits: it's clear as glass what's happened here. Zirka has to agree, though Peter, when he visits Lesia Baziuk later that night, isn't so sure. He apologizes to her on Yuri's behalf, assuring her that it was nothing premeditated but just what-boys-can-get-up-to. Lesia Baziuk makes no comment, stands with her arms folded, her teeth clenched behind her open lips. Yuri's a good boy, at heart, Peter pleads. A good boy who needs "a good licking," Lesia supplies. "Spoil the rod and spare the child, eh, Lesia?" Peter shoots back, so quickly that she doesn't catch him out. He walks purposefully back to his cottage, relaxing his stride when he's certain he's out of Lesia's view. If she weren't such a fool, she'd have realized that there'd been more going on in that bunkhouse than Yuri suddenly turning on a defenseless Billy. What, he doesn't know.

Yuri has refused to say anything in his own defense to either of his parents, and Andriy hasn't been able to throw any light on the mystery, either.

It's Katia who fills him in, Katia who's been waiting in her pajamas on the front steps of the Martyns' cottage, listening to the crickets and waiting for her uncle to make his way back from Mrs. Baziuk's. Even before she sees him, she hears his whistling; she runs up to him and takes him aside, into the trees beyond the edge of Tunnel Road. It's not Yuri's fault, she insists: Billy had got upset when he kept losing at cards. He'd taken a swing at Yuri, and Pavlo Vesiuk, who'd come in to watch, had egged them on, the both of them. When her uncle asks her how she knows all this, she confesses that she's as much to blame as anyone: she'd been spying on the boys, peering in at the bunkhouse window. She'd heard and seen everything; she should have tried to stop them, and she never should have run away.

He listens to her carefully, and when she's done, he puts his hands in his pockets.

"Uncle Peter?" she asks, in a voice she hardly recognizes as her own, a frightened voice. "What are you going to do?"

He reaches out his hand and, making a fist, touches her ever so gently on the chin. "I think enough's been done already, don't you, Katia? I think we should learn from our mistakes and get on with things."

Katia nods, then turns and sprints to the cottage. When she reaches the porch, she looks back over her shoulder, not really expecting to see him. But there he is, waiting at the end of their drive, waiting to make sure she gets safely back inside. She waves to him, and he lifts both hands in reply, the way the priest does when he's giving the blessing. And suddenly Katia is filled with compunction. Was she wrong not to have mentioned Andriy—has she lied to her uncle? Or has she just kept him from knowing what could only hurt him and hurt Yuri even more? She doesn't know, and so she turns her face away. She slips into the cottage, listening for her parents' voices in the living room and sliding into bed under Alix's black, wide-open eyes.

LYING FLAT ON his back—not down at the beach but up by the cottage, alone, under a fine old birch tree—Peter Metelsky stares at the blue overhead, both limitless and encompassing. When he tries to imagine the world he knew inside his mother's womb, it is exactly this blank and endless blue he conjures up; and when he thinks, as he does more and more these days, of what will meet his eyes the very last moment he has eyes to see, he envisions it not as black and lusterless, like a wiped chalkboard, but as this hard and glinting blue.

Peter has been lying here all afternoon, keeping company with Yuri, who is grounded for the rest of the weekend and spending his time indoors. When Zirka had gone down to the beach, Peter called the boy outside, and they sat together in a companionable kind of silence. Watching his son's bare chest move up and down, the delicate ribs and collarbone like splintered wood, Peter had been filled with tenderness; he'd started to ask Yuri about what Katia had told him, but the boy had shaken his head, refusing to talk about Billy Baziuk, saying he'd feel better going back inside. So Peter is alone, on the lawn, leaning his head back onto the triangle of his arms, an easy cradle that allows him to pursue his thoughts, which compose their own triangle, focusing as they do on a slap to the face, a jump from a boat, and the possibility of a jailbreak.

He'd been a fool, of course, to have approached her at the Plotskys' party all those weeks ago, but he saw her so seldom, how could he have ignored this chance? The very fact that she was there at all, that Jack had persuaded her to accompany him, that was miracle enough. But there'd been more to come. When he'd gone over to the corner where she was standing, alone as always, and asked if he could get her something to drink, she hadn't refused him, as she'd always done before, on any of the myriad occasions when he'd offered her some small service—the only kind within his power to perform. She'd looked at him with an expression on her face that had stunned him, so naked had she seemed in her unhappiness. But like the idiot he was—a thousand times worse than Jack—he'd been afraid to answer that look she'd given him, to answer it in kind. And so he'd fallen back on his party trick, playing the buffoon, dropping to one knee, addressing her as the Empress of the Nile, in case, just in case, he'd mistaken her expression, gotten it all wrong, as usual. Afraid he didn't have it in him to ever get it right. No wonder she had slapped him; Nadia who, for eighteen years, had been like ice whenever he'd so much as looked her way; who was given to no public gesture more compromising than taking off her glasses.

His heart's desire was nothing so grandiose as to possess Nadia but just to provoke from her some sign that his existence mattered to her—mattered enough to anger, if not to please her. She'd given him that sign, and like the coward he was, he turned it into a joke, something for which Jack could pat him on the back, and Zirka reproach him for making a fool of himself once again. She waited till they got home, till they were in their bedroom, undressing, before she lit into him. He hadn't listened to the words, the tone of her voice had been enough, and the sight of her, poor Zirka, the puffy flesh that reminded him of tomato soup boiling over; the skin untouched by the sun, so that, naked, she looked as though she were trussed up in lard. He lay on his side of the bed, his face turned to the wall, wondering if he'd only imagined that look of shameless unhappiness on Nadia's face, while Zirka accused him of every marital crime in the book. To quiet her—he could hear the boys mumbling in their sleep—he had to promise he would keep away from her brother's wife. And he had kept away, to his shame; but also, if he were being honest with himself, to his secret joy. For as long as he kept away from Nadia, he could believe that she cared for him, cared enough to be furious with him—to touch him, even with the sharp flat of her hand.

Oh, yes, he'd kept his promise to Zirka—until Jack made him break it. Jack with the flashy new toy he'd so badly wanted to show off, and his need of an audience. Nadia hadn't even said hello to him as he climbed in beside her at the back of the boat. Nadia had been ice and stone, plunging him into an agony of unknowing: Had he been utterly mistaken at the party, had her gesture been a mark of contempt for him, and nothing else? But then she stood up and begged Jack to slow down, and then calmly—as calmly as you could move in a speeding boat—jumped overboard. He knew that kind of senseless risk, also called courage. He knew it from the five years of his life gone down that blood-clogged drain called war.

Wasn't it that which had made such a mess of his life? So many meaningless deaths; his own survival so random, un-merited by anything other than sheer good luck. When he'd returned home to the shining future he'd been promised—an immigrant and the son of immigrants, off to university on a soldier's scholarship!—he hadn't known what to do with it. The easy lie of it, the happily-ever-after he had only to sign on to possess. What could he do but play the fool, lazy, careless Petro Metelsky. The trouble being, the trouble having always been, that he could never act in his own best interests, that he knew he didn't deserve any better than he got.

Look at him now: eighteen years in a trap sprung by his own

foolishness and, yes, weakness. Marrying Zirka—marrying her not, as everyone supposed, because of her brother's deep pockets but because it was the only way he could stay in touch, however rare, with Nadia, catch a few crumbs from her table. Nadia, the only woman who'd ever refused him. How he'd fallen for her—off a cliff, down a mountain, all at once, and forever. And how different his life—he himself—could have been, if only she'd accepted him. Closing his eyes against the green-fringed sky overhead, Peter allows himself the bittersweet pleasure of remembering the opening night of *Kateryna*.

He'd thought it the absurd magic of stagecraft, how, in the thick of wheezing machinery and cardboard sets of thatched cottages choked by sunflowers, he had known, not only that he was in love but that he had to marry Nadia Moroz. Without exchanging more than a few words with him and spending more than one dance in his arms, she had cut a hole in his heart that nothing has ever filled, certainly not Zirka, and not even his children, dear as they are to him. Standing next to Nadia in the dark closeness of the wings, that night of the first and only performance of *Kateryna*, he'd felt the warmth of her thin body through the curtains serving for her cloak, and all the layers of wool and starched cotton underneath. Her dark hair was so glossy he could have seen his face reflected in it if he'd had the courage to look. It had all been exactly like the folksongs he'd always whistled in public and laughed at in private: lovers meeting in cherry orchards or on a riverbank—stars, a slender moon bathing the sky.

Petro Metelsky, so good with words, such a smooth, sweet talker, panicking in the wings as the children finish their dance with flags and wheat sheaves made of stiff, yellow-painted cardboard. Just as they're given their cue to proceed onstage, maiden and evil Muscovite, he lurches into a declaration she must, he now believes, have taken for a joke. With no time for "There's been something I've been meaning to tell you," or even "I love you," he blurts out, "Marry me!" as he gropes for her hand to lead her onstage—she is blind without her glasses. A little pause, and then her words clear, colorless as window glass: "Jack proposed to me last night. I said yes."

This is the last of what he remembers of the evening: Nadia's words, and then a huge blank in which he somehow goes through the motions of his role, not a step wrong, not a line forgotten. Prolonged applause from the invisible faces in the black sea in front of them, applause he hears as laughter at his own expense. For even if he'd beaten Jack to the mark, how could she ever have accepted him? What could Peter Metelsky have offered her but the sum of his disillusionment and the uncertainty of his future? Whereas Jack, with his easy laugh, his get-up-and-go, his eye, as he was always boasting, for quality. He'd found it in spades in Nadia Moroz: educated, elegant, and lovely in a way that left even the prettiest girls—Sonia included—at the starting gate. When Jack reclaimed Nadia from his arms, that night of the *Malanka*, Peter stood on the sidelines, watching how the height and grace of his partner transformed Jack from a squat Saskatchewan farm boy into a perfect gentleman.

Which was exactly what he had tried to be, standing by as best man while Jack and Nadia went through the wedding ceremony and Zirka—the only bridesmaid—caught the bouquet with a delighted squeal. It hadn't taken much for Jack to maneuver him into doing "the right thing" by Zirka, whom he'd taken out perhaps a total of half a dozen times, always in company. Didn't Petro see how humiliating it was for Zirka to be left on the shelf? Hell, he'd lend Petro the money for a ring as big as an apple, if only he'd step up to the plate—take the plunge, face it like a man! Newlywed Jack, slapping him on the back, rolling his small eyes, as if life with Nadia were some bitter dose he had to swallow every morning, every night.

All the times he'd tried to end the travesty of his marriage to Zirka; all the times he'd been prevented. Not by cowardice, believe it or not—not by cowardice but something he wanted to call decency. Hiding his relief when, month after month, no sign of any baby had appeared; unable to take his leave of a woman railing at what she kept calling her fault, her failure. And then, after the trips to the specialist (paid for by Jack), after the operation, and the birth of the two boys, how could he have given the lie to his marriage? And for what? No sign of anything but indifference, cold and blind indifference from Nadia, whom he almost never saw once Jack moved her to the house he'd built on Hamilton Mountain, on Millionaires' Row. Indifference that crazily made him love her even more, scheming to find ways to catch a glimpse of her, sit next to her at the family dinners that became rarer and rarer, exchange a sentence with her on the cathedral steps each Sunday morning. Walking, every night that he's up at the cottage, walking along the shore to the point where the bluffs are highest, just to look at the lights in the windows of her cottage, warm, golden light, the color of perfect happiness, of heart's desire.

Sonia arrives so soundlessly that Peter doesn't hear her—is caught exposed, lying under the birch tree, the very picture of idleness. His sister imagines their mother folding her arms and saying something cutting: *What a fine* kozak *you'd make. Forget the fighting, you'd just swig* horilka *under some damned tree till you passed out.*

"*Brateh miy,*" she calls out, sitting down beside him, hugging her knees with her arms.

He smiles at her, though he'd give anything to be left alone, thinking of Nadia. "Sonechko," he says. "*Shcho novoho?*"

There's nothing new in Sonia's life, unless it's this new worry that's been heaped on her plate. After the scene on the boat last weekend, Sasha had gone after her, again: *Talk to him— make him promise to behave.* Sonia feels a prickle of irritation with Sasha: Why doesn't she go after Nadia? Nadia was the one who'd made this particular scene—unless people are accusing Peter of having pushed Nadia into the water! What business is it of anyone's, the mess Peter's making of his life? Leave him at least the dignity of going under in his own way; don't lecture him as if he were a child. If she is going to talk with Peter, let it be about something that matters more than the smug, small circle of Kalyna Beach. So Sonia asks her brother about work— whether his boss has eased up on the lectures, the demands for overtime to make up for the undertime Peter gives to his job.

It's a mistake, of course. For Peter replies with some fairy tale about how the boss is really a Russian spy, paid by the KGB to make life miserable for honest, hardworking Ukrainian immigrants. In spite of herself, Sonia's drawn in by the details Peter spins so effortlessly: how the boss, Mr. Anthony Horton, is really one Anton Hortinsky, b. Minsk, Order of Lenin, shoe-shine boy to Stalin himself before he graduated to spy school in Moscow. From which he'd managed to pass, a mere hundred-ruble note away from abject failure. The only job they could find to match his capacities, Peter is saying, was infiltrating a certain tool-and-die outfit in Willowdale, captained, of all patri-otic heroes, by one Peter Metelsky.

Peter is grinning at her now, for all the world like the ten-year-old he once was, shaking plums down from the neighbor's tree, filling his pockets with the ripe, red-juiced fruit as the neighbor shook his fist and yelled that Peter's mother would hear about it! Sharing the plums with her behind a row of grave-stones in the cemetery, where the tiger lilies grew thick and tall; feeding her plums till she nearly burst from the sweetness. And then, once they'd shuffled home at dusk, how Peter had taken the punishment their mother had prepared at the neighbor's urging, stealing smiles at Sonia while the switch came down and she'd huddled in the corner, knowing herself as guilty as he but spared all pain.

"Peter," she says, stretching out her hand to his mouth, stopping the words, the foolish, entertaining, cover of words. Her voice is careful, a whisper: "Peter, don't put on a show, not now. Tell me what's wrong."

He stares at her for a moment, then takes her hand, kisses, and releases it. Then he looks away, not up at the sky but at the grass on which they're sitting, the grass and the earth showing dry as powder between the blades. When he speaks, the words come quickly, as though he were afraid of running out of time to give her what she's asked him for.

"What's wrong, Sonia? I am. And that's the truth of it. No, listen, *sestrychko*. All my life, all my woefully misspent life, I've believed I could be somebody different than I was. Someone better, finer, the person everyone expected me to be. I thought I'd found a way to make the jump between who I was and what I could be when I went off to war. But I came back no different— worse, if anything. There was one more chance, which I lost before I knew it was there. I would have lost my belief in that better self, or what remained of it, except that I kept on wanting what I didn't—couldn't—have. Do you understand what I'm saying?"

Sonia shakes her head helplessly. Peter smiles at her, a wry, twisting smile.

"It doesn't matter. You know, Sonia, if I were to break my

neck in some accident on the highway, they wouldn't be any the worse for it, Zirka and the boys. There's my paltry insurance policy, but that doesn't begin to come into it. Jack is Zirka's insurance policy: there'd be much, much more for her and the boys if I were out of the way. Can't you just hear the talk in the community? '*What a guy, that Jack Senchenko, looking after his sister and her orphaned boys.*'"

"Don't, Peter, you mustn't even think that way," Sonia urges, but Peter keeps on.

"As far as Zirka and Jack are concerned, I'd be better off out of the picture. But the boys?" Peter's stomach tightens, as if his gut were a wire being tugged to breaking point.

This time Sonia rushes in before her brother can stop her. "Yuri and Andriy adore you, you know that."

"Two months of weekends spent building forts in the sand, swimming, wrestling. That's all I can give them—because once we're back in the city, well, you know how it is. Work and everything. But here—Sonia, I'm not a father to them, just some crazy older brother to horse around with. When I step into the Almighty Father shoes, they laugh at me—they're no fools, they can see those shoes don't fit, that they're a country mile from fitting.

"I'll tell you something, Sonechko. Every time I climb into that rusty old Chev to drive up here or back to the city, I'm wondering if this time it will be my car, bashed in and smoking at the guardrail; me being pried loose from the driver's seat. It doesn't even need to be my fault, or anyone else's—it might just be that little bunch of veins at the top of my head letting go: the ones that killed Tato, when he was about as old as I am now. The poor bastard never had much luck, did he, apart from marrying our mother."

"Peter," Sonia cries, *"Petro."*

The pain in her voice is absurdly poignant, like a blunt-edged knife; he is starting to reproach himself for having spoken so freely to her, having loaded his fears on her, vulnerable as she still is, when Sonia speaks with a fierceness that shocks him.

"Take your happiness, Peter. Don't just keep reaching out for it—take it."

His voice is angry now, a rough whisper. "And what if I do just that—what if I grab hold and discover that it isn't anything like I thought it was, all this time? And what if the person I catch hold of only wants me the way you want to hold on to a railing when you're climbing down a steep flight of stairs?"

"Don't give up on your life," Sonia pleads, her voice echoing against the leaves and the grass and the walls of the cottage, as if she doesn't care anymore who might hear her.

And then, as suddenly as she appeared, she's gone.

THAT EVENING, THE Metelskys sit down to a meal of salmon mousse and fresh corn and dilled potatoes, though as far as Peter's concerned, Zirka sighs, it might as well be Shake 'n Bake chicken and canned beets. Afterward, Peter plays a game of checkers with Andriy and chess with Yuri, allowing Andriy but not Yuri to defeat him. Once the boys have been packed off to bed, he flips through a junky novel while Zirka washes her hair at the kitchen sink and puts her rollers in, the sponge kind on which she sleeps. But after his wife's turned out the bedroom light and the boys are blanketed in dreams, Peter calls out, to the walls with their scabbed paint and kitten calendars, that he's going for a nighttime walk, as he always does, along the beach.

Like everyone else, Jack Senchenko has built his cottage overlooking the lake, but on a point of land far higher than the bluff on which the other cottages are built and at an appreciable distance from them. To get to the Senchenkos' on foot means a fifteen-minute walk along the shore, and then a hike up a steep trail through dunes and pine and undergrowth to the cottage and its twin flagpoles, flying the Red Ensign and the blue-and-yellow banner of Ukraine.

Light is spilling from the large screened-in porch. Peter makes his way slowly toward it. Looking past the moths clustered on the screen, he can see her in profile. She is alone, sitting at a small table; she is bent over a sheet of paper on which she is writing something. The dark wings of her glasses should make him feel, what? Pity for her short-sightedness, her solitariness? Pity instead of anger at the way she keeps her self to herself, the completeness of her presence at the table, the perfect geometry between her eye and the page and her hand. This desire of his, as sharp now as the first time he saw her—what proof does he have that she feels anything for him but pity, or contempt, or nothing at all?

A slap on the face, a leap into the lake, a leap to which he should have responded then and there by carrying her off, forever. From a husband so crude he leaves the price tags on the paintings he's plastered across his Hamilton mansion and buys a new, more expensive car every year: one in the garage, another parked in the driveway, just for show. From the boxed-in loneliness, the remote suffocation of Kalyna Beach. What must she have thought when he hoisted her back into the boat, handing her to Jack once more? What if she thought nothing at all—what if he mistook an accident for an incident? Yet isn't Sonia right? Isn't it time he risked finding out, once and for all?

Her feet are bare. The whiteness of her feet against the deep black of her trousers startles him. Seeing her like this, he is back in the cool deep waters of the bay, holding her up in his arms, his heart flapping like a flag in a gale. He's afraid that if he knocks at the screen door, she'll take him for an intruder, a prowler, and let out a scream, wake Jack, who is surely asleep in some far-off wing of this huge and horrible house, prison or castle or monster chalet. He is here to see Jack on a business matter, something urgent; she won't think any the worse of him for coming by. Or, better yet, he's here on a whim, having had one too many whisky and sodas: Peter the mimic, the clown, the spoiled actor. Star of church-basement stage and home-movie screen.

He forces himself to do nothing, say nothing but her name, "Nadia," which, as he reminds himself, means *hope*.

"Peter?" She hasn't yet turned to look at him.

From the sound of her voice, she isn't startled or displeased, yet there's an intensity he can hardly believe has to do with his presence, here and now. She shakes her head over the piece of paper. He sees that there's an old shirt lying crumpled on the table beside her—she must be mending it.

"Quiet, Peter," she says at last, though he hasn't shouted. "Be quiet and I'll unlatch the door." Nadia gets up from her chair, moving soundlessly toward him; he can feel the scent of her face, her hair, through the mesh of the screen.

"Hurry up, you'll let the mosquitoes in." Softly, she closes the door and they stand together just inside the threshold.

"Jack's not here," she says. "He's delayed in the city on business. He'll be back for the party tomorrow night."

"Oh, right, then. I'll try to bend his ear tomorrow—at the party."

"Is it something important?" Meaning, *Are you in trouble again?*

He shakes his head. And then, summoning all his courage, with as much difficulty as if he were only just learning to speak, he asks if that's coffee he smells.

"It will keep you up. Besides, it's bitter, it's been on for hours."

"I like it bitter."

She looks at him, then back at the table where she'd been sitting; she waits for a perceptible moment and then goes off to the kitchen. He stands there, unable to take a seat, and powerless to walk over to the table, to see what she's been writing. *Take your happiness, Peter—don't just keep reaching out for it—take it.* Though he's had the whole walk over to decide, he can't begin to think of what he'll say to her when she returns. The whole walk, and a whole life leading up to this walk, tonight. Hands in his pockets, he stares down at his feet in their shabby canvas shoes, as if they will help him. Her skin, under the white blouse, the black trousers—it must be bruised from that jump off the boat and the way Jack hauled her up the ladder. How could she have summoned the courage to jump, and how could he have gone along with the rest of them, pretending she'd fallen, lost her balance, when it was plain for anyone to see that she'd decided to jump. To stop Jack from killing some innocent swimmer or to remove herself, at once and for always, from the need to care?

Nadia is standing at the door, holding a tray and watching him—how long has she been standing there?

"You don't take sugar, do you? Or cream?" she asks, in that English voice that always makes him think of a tumbler of cool water. But she's brought them anyway, the sugar and cream, along with the percolator and a cup and saucer on a tray. As polite, as considerate as if he were a stranger who'd dropped by seeking directions or one of her husband's business associates, which in a way he is: Jack Senchenko's tame black sheep. Looking at her now, he can't imagine she is that woman on the speedboat; the girl he once saw shivering on Queen Street, danced with on New Year's Eve, stood next to, so close he could feel the heat burning from her body, in a basement theater.

He swallows hard, then walks toward her, taking the cup she offers him. "To Kalyna Beach," he proposes, lifting his cup.

Warily, she watches him take a sip of his coffee. Then there's silence: plain, simple, awkward.

"Have you ever tasted *kalyna*?" is the only thing he can think to say.

Nadia shakes her head.

"My mother used to brew up the berries in the Old Country—she'd make cough syrup out of it. Poor Sonia, the face she'd pull, drinking that stuff down. A cross between cranberries and rotting turnip, I always thought."

Watching her face reflected in the shiny metal of the percolator, black hair and white, white skin, he registers the fact that Nadia spends most of her time at Kalyna Beach indoors, much to Zirka's disapproval. *Why she comes up for the summer I can't understand. What does she do with herself all day long, with no kids to look after and her husband in the city? She doesn't sunbathe, she doesn't swim, she doesn't come down to the beach at all.*

"Sonia can't swim either," Peter blurts out. And then, blundering on, "She's deathly afraid of the water."

Nadia shows no surprise at the turn the conversation's taken. She puts the tray down on a low table between them. "I wondered about that" is all she says. She sits down in a chaise longue, and he pulls up a folding chair, facing her.

"When she was a kid—this is before we came to Canada—some boys chased her down to the river. They threw her in, thinking she could swim."

"And she couldn't?"

"Someone happened to be passing by and pulled her out."

"Have you always made a habit of rescuing people?"

It's the archness, the coolness in her voice that goads Peter into leaning forward in his chair. He notices how her hands are clenched so tight that the knuckles stick out, bone-white. "In the boat, last week—why did you jump?"

She says nothing, balancing on the chaise longue as if it, too, were a boat capable of capsizing.

"You were crazy to jump," he goes on, his voice both stern and tender. "You could have got hurt."

Now she leans back in her chair, her fingers still knitted together, but loosely. "It was like something out of a book."

"What?"

"People do risky, dangerous things all the time in books. It's only in real life we never seem to get the chance. Why do you think that is?"

"Nadia—"

She pulls herself forward, sits with her elbows balanced on her knees, her face leaning into his. "Peter, I need you to tell me something. What do you think of me? I don't mean do you think I'm bad or good, or ugly or attractive, but what were you thinking when you saw me sitting there, at the table, just before you called out to me?"

What does she want to hear? What can he say that will be the right words, the only answer, like in those fairy tales where the prince must choose just one casket or one gift to win his heart's desire? But he knows better; he knows nothing. He is lost for words, lost altogether. He can hear a branch tapping against the screen, in cruel imitation of the clock that is carving away his chances, second by second. So that it's Nadia who breaks a silence that seems to have lasted for hours: in her voice is something desperate, the pressure of anguish.

"Oh, Petro, Petro, what a coward you are."

Suddenly he is looming over her, shoving the little glass table so that their coffee cups rattle. His anger is a key thrust into a lock, turned violently. "Since I'm the coward, then you go instead of me, Nadia. Tell me what you think of me, Peter Metelsky, neighborhood dilettante, genial failure—"

Her voice now is merely sad. "Why are you always answering your own questions?"

She takes off her glasses to look up at him, as if she can see better half-blind. He can feel her eyes as if they're fingertips

tracing all the lines of his face, the tiredness that can't be undone by sleep, any more than the gray hair at his temples. Tracing what's inside his head, too, the chart with numbers crossed
off, his father dead at fifty-five, *twelve more years, only twelve to
go.* In the nakedness of her eyes he sees, all of a sudden, that
she, too, is counting. The days you can't pretend aren't passing
by, moment by moment, flakes of paper that jump up from the
fire only to fall back and bruise to ash.

If he sits down again, he is lost. He slams his fists into his
pockets as if to hold himself up and prepares to speak. What he
is about to say to her, the feelings he wills into speech, will be
the most important words he ever utters. Now is the time to tell
her what matters more than anything else. Now is the time to
stop clowning, stop dodging, to speak out at last, whatever the
consequences may be. But it all comes out differently from what
he means to say.

"You want to know what I thought of, Nadia, when I saw you
at that table, writing? I thought of when I was a kid of sixteen,
when I got a chance to spend a week at summer camp. How I
would run off by myself into the fields and lie down under a
tree, just lie there and watch the sky through the leaves."

He laughs, embarrassed; frowns, and goes on, not trusting
himself to look at her. "They would always come after me—
scold me for being lazy, making trouble for them. Once I was
angry enough to talk back to the woman sent to look for me;
she was one of the camp cooks, she knew my parents. I told her

that when I grew up, I was going to spend whole summers lying under the trees, looking up at the sky." He pauses, stealing a glance at Nadia; her face gives nothing away.

"In spite of everything I knew, in spite of the way it was in the Old Country, in spite of my parents' lives, I really believed that once you grew up, you could do whatever you wanted. That only people who were too dull or stupid or frightened to want anything better would end up working at a factory or office or in a hellhole of a kitchen all summer long."

Peter's staring at the floor again, as if his life depends on registering its strips of varnished wood. "She told me not to be a fool. Didn't I understand that things got worse instead of better when you grew up? That I would have no time to think of trees and sky and the rest of it, that nobody, nobody was free to do what he wanted. I swore at her, told her that she was the fool, that I'd prove it to her—she would see!"

He stops. There's nothing more to say, if he's been saying anything at all, that is. She must have heard his words as if they were being spoken in a language from outer space; she must despise or, worse, pity him. But when, at long last, he looks at her, he sees that she is smiling.

In all the time he has known Nadia, he has never once seen her smile. Not as she is doing now, here, for no reason at all, a smile that turns her face into a piece of paper that's caught rapid, joyous fire. Something shifts—something in the atmosphere, in the light of the screened-in porch, in Peter's own heart, which is no longer a soft balloon or a fist-size stone but a muscle, pumping out blood, keeping him awake, alive. So that he smiles back, a fine, open smile without a trace of mimicry or mockery, for once.

In some dream vestibule, Jack and Zirka are complaining, pouring out a job lot of disappointments and injuries to a God whose one blue eye is firmly shut, so that Peter can be alone here with Nadia. As if, eighteen years ago, she had held out her hand to him in that dark auditorium and said, *Yes, Peter, of course I'll marry you.* As though they were in their own, familiar home: a couple whose thoughts and hopes and imaginings are like books that they have read together—known, shared, puzzled through. He is alert now as he's never been before. He can't believe how keen his senses are, how much pleasure he's taking in the rasp of crickets in the bushes around the porch, in the look of black coffee pooled in a stark white cup. He wants to laugh, he wants to sing, he wants to blurt out, as he'd done all those years ago, "Marry me!"

But it's Nadia who speaks, holding out her hands to him, letting him pull her up from the chair where she is sitting. "Don't say anything more. Just look." She leads him over to the table, and he immediately sees his mistake. She wasn't writing, as he'd assumed, but drawing. There's a pile of sketches that she's been sorting; he goes through them, taking his time, amazed at how meticulous and yet moving they are. Small sketches of perfectly ordinary things—a pair of spectacles, a glass, a pine tree seen through the minute grid of a screen window. They are drawn expertly, beautifully, and so poignantly that he has to bite his lip. He pauses at an unfinished one of an old, crumpled shirt, with a button hanging by a thread.

"You know that Jack took me to New York to see *Cleopatra*? The world premiere, and we were there, along with the movie stars and producers and politicians: Mr. and Mrs. Jack Senchenko! We sat through the whole four hours—and all the way back to our hotel, Jack couldn't stop talking about that scene where Caesar and Cleopatra visit the tomb of Alexander the Great. Do you remember it?"

She doesn't wait for Peter's answer; she rushes on.

"There's this strange light playing over the tomb, so you can't tell whether it's a bas-relief of Alexander that you're seeing or the actual body—uncorrupted, like a saint's. But what Jack kept going on about was Cleopatra—not Elizabeth Taylor—Cleopatra. What a woman she was, and how a man backed by a woman like that could do anything. Could be not just anyone but Someone: a Conqueror of the Earth! That was when I finally understood how hopeless it was, our marriage, what I'd tried to make of it. After all those years—not that he didn't know who I was but that he still didn't want what I was, what I could give him. He thought that all I had to do was to make up my mind to do it: paint up my eyes, put beads in my hair, command his empire with him.

"Instead of which, I do this," she says, putting out her hand to the sheaf of drawings, just touching them. "They're nothing much," she says. And then, "They're what I am, Peter. They're all I am."

This time he doesn't hesitate or fumble. He draws her into his arms and holds her as close as if they were dancing. To the far-off beating of waves at the shore; to the clock ticking on the wall, to their very breathing. Dancing close, slow, holding tight to one another, as if to keep themselves from drowning.

FOR AS LONG as there has been a Kalyna Beach, there's been a *zabava* at the Senchenkos' cottage on Labor Day weekend. The party starts at eight on Sunday night, once the children have been fed and put to sleep, or been left reading comics in their pajamas in their bedrooms. The parents take turns checking in on them all, cottage by cottage; it's a regular patrol.

This evening party in cottage country is always as formal an affair as can be contrived. The men dress up in short-sleeved shirts and neatly ironed Bermuda shorts; the women all wear long, poolside dresses by Sea Queen, though no one's ever put a toe into the water of the Senchenkos' swimming pool. Sasha Plotsky usually shows up in something people agree to call "different"—a backless black dress, one year; Italian-designed palazzo pants, another. Sonia Martyn is always admired, no matter what she wears, though there are hints that this year, the year of *Cleopatra*, she'll dazzle them all with something spectacular.

As for the food, there are bowls of pretzels, chips, salted peanuts when you arrive, with wine, beer, and soft drinks to wash them down, as well as a bottle or two of Mrs. Maximoynko's home-brew that she sells to special customers only. The shelves of Venus Variety are well stocked with Eno and Alka-Seltzer, so she doesn't do too badly off the Senchenkos' hospitality, though Mrs. Maximoynko herself would never show up for the party. About midnight, Mrs. Matski, the Senchenkos' housekeeper, who's been brought up to the cottage for the occasion, appears with loaded roasters of *holubtsi* and *patychky*. There's always a sweet table, too, with cherries jubilee and platters of poppy-seed strudel baked by Jack's sister, Zirka, plus tea and coffee and more soft drinks. People start saying their good-byes well after one in the morning, and the very last hangers-on can be seen weaving over the dunes at three. Jack believes in showing people a good time, but Nadia usually says good night and goes off to bed just past midnight, after the food—none of which she's been seen to taste—is served.

The Senchenkos' cottage is a cross between a Swiss chalet and an apartment block. There are those who say Jack should have stuck to his own if he wanted the ethnic touch—a thatched cottage, whitewashed, surrounded by a wooden fence with glass jars upended on the staves to dry in the sun. Others cluck their tongues over the sheer showiness of a mansion that can sleep a dozen people at a pinch, that has window boxes filled with geraniums and fancy shutters, while other people make do with construction kits sold at Beaver Lumber. But that's the way Jack is; he has money and he sees no reason to hide the fact. It's good for business to show off what you've done for yourself, it inspires confidence. Money attracts money. Hence the *pièce de résistance*: the swimming pool, the most grandiose, utterly unnecessary item among the chalet's mod cons and luxury appointments.

People wonder what Nadia thinks of the whole business; they keep on wondering, since Nadia keeps her thoughts to herself. She never objects when, party after party, Jack takes people through the house, pointing out all the new additions, boasting about how much this or that appliance cost or the price of the baby grand by the picture window. There are some who are shocked by the fuss Jack makes about price tags, and others who denounce any objections to the show as worthy of the *Anhleetsi*, the Smiths and Jones with their paralyzing fear of being thought vulgar. Still others keep safely silent, visiting the Senchenkos' cottage and comparing it with their own houses in the city, hugging to their hearts the thought that you could lug a grand piano into the bush and turn a whole wall into a picture window but still behave like a farmer at a country fair showing off your prize pumpkins.

Everyone is preparing for the Senchenkos' party. Even the few who've not been invited, or who have refused their invitations, can think of nothing else. The children are as keyed up as their parents; with the disbanding of the *Zaporozhtsi* after the Billy Baziuk affair, all plans to spy on the grown-ups have been abandoned. The most the children can hope for is leftovers from the sweet table that will have been pressed on their parents by an affable Jack Senchenko as the party winds down. Leftover cake for breakfast; grumpy adults staggering around with small eyes and hands pressed to their heads and warnings not to make a peep, a single peep: warnings that, for once, will be heeded.

But that is all in the future: it's what's immediately at hand that presses on the Martyn girls—at least, the two oldest. Though, as their mother's said, they've declared war on one another, strenuously avoiding each other's company, behaving like armies pitched on opposite sides of a great plain, waiting for the right conditions to attack, they are, without knowing it, obsessed with exactly the same dilemma: what to do about their mother's dress. They can ask no one's advice on the matter; they come up with no inspired, or even desperate solutions. The dress is still hanging in their mother's closet, hanging like a murder victim, slashed and soiled and with their fingerprints all over it. The only wonder is that the corpse hasn't started to smell and give itself away.

They know, Katia and Laura, that this time it won't work: blaming another for their own misdeeds or protesting it had all been an accident. What do they fear when, this evening, their mother goes to her closet, reaching for the treasure she's buried in such perfect confidence of safety? Not that she will take her hairbrush or a wooden spoon to them; not that they'll be sent to their rooms, kept indoors, away from the beach, away from their friends. It is, after all, the last weekend of the summer. What the sisters are most afraid of, without being able to think it, to say it in words, is confirmation of the stomach-churning possibility that blood is thinner than water, that hate is stronger than love.

All the girls—except for Baby Alix and Nastia Shkurka, of course—are lying on their beach towels in the hollow behind the sand dunes. The towels are much the worse for a whole summer's wear. Some have rips in the eroded terry cloth, but it's far too late in the season to toss them out and ask for new ones: these will just have to keep on doing. For once, the mothers aren't encamped nearby. There's just Mrs. Vesiuk keeping an eye on everyone, a baby on one hip, a toddler pulling at her hand. The other mothers are up at the cottages, already immersed in the sweaty task of packing up. They calculate, Laura and Katia, that Sonia will be far too busy, even with Darka's help, to bother about the dress right now; they calculate they have another six or even eight hours before their mother discovers she has nothing to wear to the Senchenkos' party. Even so, they are miserable with worry—or, rather, with a sense of fatality they've never known before.

All the girls have reason enough to lie limp on their towels, as if they've just swum across the lake or finally dug that vanished tunnel to China. Tania, Vlada, Lenka, Rocky-short-for-Roksolana—they are all of them exhausted, as if a summer's worth of sun and sand and water, Popsicles bought at Venus Variety and hot dogs eaten out of doors, comic books read and stories listened to, bathing suits pulled carelessly on and struggled out of, had suddenly filled them to overflowing, filled them past moving even an eyelash. Tonight is the Senchenkos' party, and the last summer's day at Kalyna Beach. Tomorrow is Monday and might as well be winter. It's true that they won't actually have to cram themselves into their parents' cars, along with their duffle bags and suitcases and coolers packed with leftovers, until the afternoon. Yet they know that Monday morning will be drenched in the sorrow of leaving, shadowed by school, a whole year of bells and drills, homework and spot tests, exams, assemblies, gym class and those awful bloomers with their telltale names chain-stitched across the back. English school, at which, however much they excel in their studies, they'll be socially stranded, just different enough not to fit in. And Saturday school means yet another kind of failure, not social, this time, but a failure to do with something there's no word for in English: with *dukh*—a cross between "breath" and "spirit"—the *dukh* of Ukraine they're expected to breathe in and in, even though they're living in Canada.

One long drawn-out day lies between them and the bleak horizon of Monday. "Sufficient unto the day is the evil thereof," as Rocky's mother, who has a religious bent, is fond of quoting. And so the girls stretch out on their towels, pressing their bodies into the heat of the sand below and soaking up sun as if it were syrup you could never sicken of. Even Katia and Laura, lying as far apart from each other as they can, keeping Bonnie as a buffer between them, have let go of their separate bundles of fear, their minds replete with lake sounds and the rub of the wind in the tall, narrow grasses nearby.

The sun is hot, their stomachs are full. The girls in the dunes are on the verge of sleep when, whether out of malice or sheer ill luck, a voice breaks the calm. Perhaps it's to win back Katia's confidence, to regain her affection, that Tania drawls, "Anyone want to guess what Nastia Shkurka's up to right now? I'll bet she's putting Band-Aids on her pimples."

For a moment, there's silence. Then Laura sighs, taking off her glasses, rubbing them as clean as she can on the edge of her towel and putting them back on again. "I've already told you, she doesn't *get* pimples, you moron. She's got perfect skin."

"Purr-fect ski-in," Tania mocks. "How do you know that, Laura? Have you seen her bare naked or something?"

Laura sits up straight. "Shut up," she growls. "Shut your dirty trap!"

Tania pokes Katia; she's honor-bound to join in now. More from habit than from any desire to jump to Tania's aid or to rile her sister, Katia starts to chant, *"Nasty Nastia,"* at which Laura's face goes dark as thunder—purple thunder. *"Dupo,"*

Laura snaps. "You're one to talk. Don't think I haven't seen you—"

Something in Laura's tone, even more than her words, warns Katia, makes her try to drown out her sister. "Fatty and Nasty— what a pair! You two going steady?" And then she starts to sing: *"Laura and Nastia, sitting in a tree—"*

Laura staggers to her feet. Fists clenched, she leans over her sister, who doesn't even bother to look up at her as she completes the rhyme: *"Kay-eye-ess-ess-eye-en-gee."*

"Tell her, Katia," she hisses. "Tell Tania what you did with Yuri in the sleep-house, just the two of you. How you took off your clothes and rubbed yourselves together, bare naked. I've seen them, Tania, so don't go calling me a liar. I've seen them with my own eyes!"

And Katia, who should have laughed out loud at this ridiculous claim, who should have resumed the chant of "Fatty and Nasty," just sits there staring at the sand. She is not about to defend herself or betray her cousin telling them how, when she and Yuri had rubbed their bare bodies together on the sleep-house bed, they felt nothing at all—nothing except an embarrassment so deep it made them believe they must have committed the worst of sins. Tania won't believe her if she tells her—Tania standing there with her arms hanging and a sick expression on her face as she whispers, "Did you, Katia? With Yuri—did you? Did you?"

The other girls have gotten to their feet and are pulling their towels into their arms, their eyes round and staring. Something terrible is about to happen, they all know this. Something in them wants it to happen, wants there to be a scene like in the movies, with grand gestures and the scrub of violins; something earth-shattering, even if that earth is only the sand dunes on their little stretch of beach.

But all that happens is Bonnie, running up to Laura, grabbing the hand Laura's folded into a fist poised at Katia's head. Bonnie pulling and pulling Laura until, shaking her off, Laura staggers over the dunes, her feet sliding in their clumsy flip-flops so that she trips and falls and has to pick herself up again, in view of them all. As Katia throws herself back down on her towel, pressing her face as hard as she can into the sand.

IT NEVER RAINS but it pours, Sonia complains to Darka. There's Katia refusing to come in for lunch, Laura off sulking in her room, Bonnie sick to her stomach—thank God the baby's sleeping, at least. Sonia would prefer it, would be grateful, even, if Darka gave her a weary smile and said something like "No kidding" or "You bet"—something, anything that could be taken as assent, even approval of Sonia's having, this last day of summer, thrown in the sandy towel, given up on disciplining the children, keeping order. But Darka might as well be one of them, a fifth child for Sonia to keep in line, and the most difficult, the most frightening by far.

For Darka's changed in a way that Sonia can't pin down but

that worries her far more than the peroxide and baby dolls and movie magazines have done. All of a sudden, the girl has given up—given up on exasperating Sonia, flouting her wishes, rebelling. For the past few days, she hasn't worn a trace of the makeup she'd somehow smuggled up to the cottage—Sonia had pretended not to notice the smears of rouge, the gobs of mascara Darka thought she was being so careful in applying. Nor has the girl curled her hair or flounced about in her two-piece at the beach, when she should have been looking after Alix. Yes, Darka's given up—the way women of a certain age give up on looking or acting attractive.

Good as gold, Darka sits back on the kitchen chair, letting Sonia dye her hair back to its natural color. Fumes rise from the bottle, making Sonia frown and purse her lips as she applies the tint. Dark brown globs are staining the ragged towel around Darka's neck. They might as well fall on her face, for all she cares—he cares. His beach holiday's over; he's gone back early to town; she doesn't exist for him any longer. When he came down last weekend, he stayed put, smoking his cigarettes, reading the papers on Lesia Baziuk's veranda, drinking the glasses of rye and ginger she grudgingly doles out. As if he hadn't a care in the world, as if he'd made Darka vanish, not just from his view but from the whole wide world. She'd thought he was playing it safe, biding his time. But nothing had happened, nothing. Even when she walked past his cottage on her way to the store, he stared at his paper as if it were some ghost stopping before him, looking up at him, willing him to return her gaze. A ghost of a ghost, without the power to summon a single shiver from his pale, pink skin.

It's not the makeup she misses; to tell the truth, it isn't Frank Kozak she misses, either. It's the feeling he gave her of being the most important person in the world, the most precious thing he'd ever held. Far more important than his cigarettes or even the booze, she was his honey, his baby, his sugar-pie. Darka makes a choking, gagging sound.

Sonia's afraid that somehow she must have got some of the hair dye into the girl's eyes or even her mouth. "Darka?" she says, "are you all right? It won't take long, now—another five minutes. Darka?"

"I'm okay," the girl says at last. "It's the stink that's getting to me."

IN THE ONE room in her cottage with a lock on the door, Nettie Shkurka is washing her hair. Not that she has anything to hide: her hair really is her crowning glory—long as her arm and not a gray hair to disfigure the rich mahogany color that her daughter, alas, has failed to inherit. This is only one of many ways in which Nastia's been a disappointment to her mother, but Nettie has seen enough of the families at Kalyna Beach to know it's a universal law that daughters let their mothers down. She also recognizes that, as things go, she should feel relatively confident in the daughter department. Nastia would sooner throw herself under a bus than talk back to her; she's not going to run after boys; and she'll continue to do well at school, entering the teaching profession just as her mother and grandmother have done before her. In fact, Nettie's only worry about Nastia is how to keep her as good as she is now—if not as good as gold, then as copper: bright, serviceable, but needing to be shined up every so often.

If Nettie locks the bathroom door when she washes her long, thick, red-brown hair, it's more as a gesture against the evil eye than anything else. For she can't help feeling vulnerable when that hair is unpinned and splayed down her back; vulnerable when bending over the small sink, fearful lest the tap dig into her scalp, intent as she is on rinsing out each scintilla of soap. For Nettie's obsession is perfection. "People are always watching you," she has told her daughter from the moment the child could give signs of an independent will. "They're always watching and waiting for you to make a mistake, fall flat on your face. I never gave them that satisfaction, and neither will you."

The only way to achieve perfection, Nettie knows, is to have it beaten into you, beaten till you're black-and-blue. The way her mother beat her; the way Nettie beats her daughter at home in their cramped apartment and here in the equally constricted cottage. While the mothers of Kalyna Beach lie down on their blankets at the water's edge and their children make sand castles or sunbathe in the dunes, Nettie is taking a hairbrush or a wooden spoon to Nastia. Or else the peeled birch wand kept by the front door, that makes its whistling sound instead of the *thwack, thwack* of the hairbrush.

Nettie always makes sure the beatings start when Nastia's as far as possible from the bathroom with its lockable door—in the kitchen drying dishes or searching the bookshelves in the sitting room for something she actually wants to read. Always, they occur when the girl has let down her guard, can be taken by surprise by what, after all, she should have suspected was coming: the smack of something hard against a softer target, shins or arms or back. And the words, a rhythmic accompaniment to the blows: *"Ty dur-na kor-o-va."* Nastia never says anything in reply, for her mother's logic is unassailable: If she weren't a stupid cow, why would her mother be beating her? She knows she must save her energy for running, ducking, deking this way and that, so she can get to the bathroom without her mother realizing where she's heading.

Nastia is small for her age; there is scarcely room on her skin for all the bruises she wears. Were Laura ever to ask, Nastia would say the beatings hurt less than you'd imagine, that she carries her wounds as lightly as if they were the badges you get at Brownies or those fabric souvenirs of Pioneer Village or the CNE, meant to be stitched to your shirt or jacket. But Laura doesn't ask because, in spite of how smart Laura is, smart at things they never teach you at school, she doesn't guess what Nastia's secret is—not just Nastia's but Nettie's, too. Doesn't guess even though Nastia's given her all the clues she can, led her by the hand, shown her the writing on the wall.

As Nettie Shkurka lifts her long, damp strands of hair, sectioning them off with the end of the thin-handled, stainless-steel comb with its strong, small teeth, she gazes not in the mirror but at the wallpaper: she disapproves of mirrors, preferring the way she thinks she looks to what actually confronts her in the glass. Thus it happens that, scanning the pattern of tropical fish weaving in and out of ribboned weeds, she discovers a text as deliberate as a message in a bottle. Not some splotch of rising damp or dirt or grease but small, immaculate lettering scratched right into the paper, for anyone to find.

At first, Nettie can't believe her eyes. It can't be her name etched into the wallpaper; it can't be *I hate* in front of her name. Who would do such a thing? Who would wish her ill—who could say something so cruel? For a moment she feels as though she's going to faint; she wants to stagger off to her room and lie down, unpick the words from her memory as if they were a spoiled stretch of embroidery. But then she tightens her grip on the handle of the comb and pushes the tray of rollers away from her. Half her hair up, half down, her mouth taut, her eyes hard, she steals from the bathroom, down the corridor, to her daughter's room.

Nastia is sitting on her carefully made bed, reading a movie magazine Laura has pilfered from Darka's stash. She's feeling both guilty and bored: her mother says such magazines are garbage, and now Nastia's seen for herself that it's true. There's nothing in the words or pictures she can make sense of, no idea worth following, no story whose middle and end she can't see coming a mile away. So that when she looks up from the exposé on Eddie Fisher and sees her mother standing before her, her arm raised, she is almost willing to take the punishment she knows she deserves. Almost but not quite, for the woman by her bed isn't recognizable as her mother, this woman with wet hair swinging across her face and rippling over her shoulders, with half a helmet of rollers stabbed into her head. Even as the blows come down, Nastia's confused, unable to shield herself as she usually tries to do.

For this time, for some reason Nastia can't fathom, the beating isn't a matter of bruises but of jabs and cuts. She knows she must think harder, faster, must find some way she hasn't tried before to get away. Before the steel comb strikes not just at her arms and legs, which can be covered up with long sleeves, long trousers, but at her face as well.

DOWN AT THE beach, Lenka and Rocky are drinking cream soda behind the dunes, enjoying the absence of Katia and Tania who, they've come to realize, have lorded it over them far too long. Laura is helping Baby Alix build a complicated castle by the water's edge. Mrs. Bozhyk is on patrol; the boys are diving off the raft, the air is still, and the lake a bowl of blue cream. Sonia has come down with a pitcher of Kool-Aid for the children, accompanied by a listless Darka and a troubled Zirka; the women stand on the dry sand, absorbing the sun's heat into muscles strained from lifting and fetching. There is nothing to deflect the sound when it comes: a thick, dark, ugly sound, like the clots of blood at the bottom of the toilet bowl when it's *that time of the month* for those who are young ladies now.

The sound is coming out of an animal of some kind; it is tumbling down the bluff, at the far end of the beach, not falling off the edge but sliding and shoving through the undergrowth, holding on to the trunks of saplings, grabbing at bushes to keep its feet on the ground. Above it comes another sound, just as ugly but high-pitched, like a drill, shouting the same word over and over and over.

Laura clutches her shovel while her mother and Mrs. Vesiuk run toward the bleeding, shaking form that has come to rest on the sand. Zirka is struggling up the hill to where the shrieking has suddenly stopped. Now Mrs. Vesiuk lifts the thing in her arms and strides away with it as if she were carrying nothing heavier than a damp towel. If it's an animal, it's not the bear cub the mothers have always been warning them about; if it's a person, Laura doesn't want to know who it could be. Blood is pouring from the head, streaking the sugary sand below.

And then it's all over: Mrs. Vesiuk has disappeared with her bundle up the steps to her cottage, and Sonia seems to be apologizing to them all, mothers and children.

"Everything's all right," she keeps saying. "There's been a

little accident at the Shkurkas' cottage, that's all. Don't worry. Nastia will be just fine."

THE ONLY PEOPLE left on the beach now are Laura and her mother. They are standing apart, facing the lake, their arms wrapped around their waists. For once, an onlooker would be struck not by the difference but by the sameness between them: the sag of the shoulders, the hang of the head, the arms like bandages or a wide belt holding in what must not be let out.

Overhead, the sky is a pale, stainless blue; the water below it is still perfectly calm, unruffled by even a cat's paw of wind. Water slaps, slaps, slaps at the shore, and from nowhere a pair of dragonflies dart across the lip of wet, packed sand and over the water. For a long moment, Sonia cannot say where she is or even what time of day it is, and which day at that. It's not just the end-of-summer collapse, the weak but grateful giving-up, for just one day of the year, of all rules and order. It's the feeling that she's fought against all summer, struggling to keep it from drowning her: fear of the worst, no hope for the best.

Sonia knows that she must go to her daughter, must open her arms to her, hold her close, try to undo what she has seen, as if the blood streaming from Nastia's face and scalp, the smear of her mouth, could be smoothed away. But her arms stay cinched about her waist; the most she can do is sink, slowly, to her knees and then to sit on the sand.

Laura remains on her feet; she knows what her mother is

thinking. She is blaming her for not looking out for her friend, her best, her only friend; for not knowing what was going on at the Shkurkas' cottage; for not knowing or caring what she knew. And whether or not she knew why Nastia kept to her room so much, and what the word *asthma* meant from Mrs. Shkurka's lips, Laura, of all the spectators at Kalyna Beach, knows why this particular drama has occurred. Knows that somehow, while fixing her hair or washing her face, Mrs. Shkurka has found the message inscribed so meticulously on the bathroom wall. And suddenly Laura can't keep from crying out; she sinks to her knees in front of her mother, sobbing, "I'm sorry, I'm sorry."

Alarmed, mystified, Sonia raises her arms to her daughter, pulls her into an embrace. "Shh, shh, *donyu*, don't cry, there's nothing for you to be sorry about. There's nothing you could have done to stop it—nobody knew, nobody guessed."

Stroking Laura's limp, fine hair, feeling her daughter shudder so helplessly in her arms, Sonia feels something unlock in her, something buried painfully deep. Her voice is soft, as if it were a lullaby she were crooning. "Nobody asks to be born, Laura. We think we are born out of love, we think we are born for happiness. But even if our parents loved each other, even if they wanted us more than anything else, it changes once we come into the world. Everything changes. What's happened to Nastia—there's no excuse for it, *donyu*, and there's no way anyone could have stopped it."

Laura holds on tight to Sonia. For the first time in as long as she can remember, she has her mother all to herself; her mother is holding her, stroking her hair, speaking to her as if her daughter were a friend and not an enemy. And because of the pressure of Laura's arms around her, Sonia forgets, for a moment about her other children, the ones whom Darka's shepherded up the hill; forgets that Max will be back with the rest of the men at any moment and that tonight will be the party for which she's been longing all summer. She sits on the sand, with her daughter in her arms, and tells her a story.

"Once, in our village, there was a girl who was very pretty and very spoiled. Her mother adored her, and her brother loved her, and the girl ended up by thinking she was better than anyone else, that nothing bad could ever touch her." Sonia breaks off, starts rubbing at her foot, the site of an old blister, a bright pink scar.

"And?" Laura prompts, needing to break the silence that's fallen on her mother; afraid to break the delicate spell that binds them together. For she knows that this story, which has begun like a fairy tale, like the *baiky* her *baba* used to tell her, will be different from them in some crucial way.

"And so they decided to teach her a lesson, the people in the village—the boys in the village." Sonia draws away, a little, from her daughter; as she speaks, her eyes are fixed on the lake. Her voice is different now, the kind of voice you use to talk to yourself instead of to the person beside you.

"One day they followed her when she went walking by the

river—it was spring and so beautiful with all the trees in bloom, and her mother had let her spend the afternoon doing just what she pleased when she should have been working, helping . . ."

Laura frowns: she was wrong, this isn't a new kind of story but the same one she's heard so many times before. How the proud, lazy girl gets punished for her sins; how it's better to be busy and obedient and meek. But as her mother continues, she leans in toward Sonia, afraid to lose even one word.

"So the girl walks down to the riverbank, where the apple trees are in bloom; she thinks of herself as one of those blossoms, pink and white and free to fly off in the wind, wherever she chooses. And all the time the boys are watching her, thinking how pleased she is with herself, without a care in the world, because she *is* the world, all of it that matters. And just at the moment when she's most lost in herself, most careless and free, the boys rush up to her and grab her and carry her into the river. First they make sure she gets covered with the muck from the bank, they smear it all over her dress and her legs and her hair, and then they dump her in water just deep enough to cover her, all except her face. They laugh at her and leave her to make her way back to shore."

"And?" Laura asks again, eagerly this time. She knows that her mother's story has its own momentum now, that it has taken its teller to a place that is neither Kalyna Beach nor the Old Place but someplace in between, where remembering happens.

"She couldn't swim—and she was too proud to tell them.

They ran off and she became frightened, too frightened to cry out for help or to move to free herself, in case she drowned. She knew she was going to die in that river, and that nothing could save her, and so when he came at last to rescue her, she'd given up caring."

"Who rescued her? Who was it, *mamo*?"

But Sonia doesn't hear the question. "He carried her out of the water, and he washed her and fetched a towel and dry clothes for her. He walked her back home and she made him swear that he would never tell anyone what happened, especially their mother. And he kept her secret, even though—" And here Sonia breaks off the story. "It doesn't matter," she says sadly. "We'd better go."

But it does matter to Laura. It matters to her as much as knowing why Nettie Shkurka has battered her daughter's face. But neither mother nor daughter can say a word; all they can do is take in the sound of the waves Nastia hates so much, pounding steadily, uselessly, against the shore. Sonia has got to her feet and is brushing the sand off her shorts; the voice she uses to tell Laura it's time to get dinner ready is no longer the voice of the woman who held her in her arms or who told the story of the girl who was rescued from drowning. It is the voice of Our Mother: tired, resigned, commanding, but with something else folded into it, something that is almost a plea.

"Come along, Laura, they'll be wondering what's happened to us. Come on, *donyu*—we've got work to do."

It startles Laura: this is not a command so much as an invitation never before extended. *We've got work to do.* Join us, become one of us, women who know what life is and what it can never be; who must hoard what little power we have, power not to save the beaten or to keep ourselves from drowning, just power over our children's lives, for as long as we can hold them, nothing more than that.

Sonia looks at her watch; her voice takes on a hint of impatience. "Look, Laura, I know you're upset about Nastia. It's terrible, what's happened. But that's the way life is. If you'd grown up where I did—if you knew what kind of things can happen to people, not just being thrown into a river but things you can't even imagine, in the war—"

Laura has jumped to her feet; she's remembering the mess she made of Sonia's dress, she's anticipating the scene her mother will make when she discovers it, the accusations of deliberate destructiveness, of malice. Her mother won't want her company then, she won't be calling her *donyu*, she will never hold her in her arms or stroke her face again. And now, her head pounding, a stone in her stomach, Laura starts shouting.

"I don't care about the war—I don't care about the Old Place and what happened there. We live here, I was born here—that's what Baba Laryssa always told us. You don't know anything, you don't even try. I hate you. I wish you were dead. I wish you'd died instead of Baba!"

Sonia keeps herself from staggering; digs her bare feet into the soft, pliant sand. She has imagined Laura saying this—she has thought it herself, even wished it. She looks into her daughter's face, sees the glasses perched on Laura's nose like a thick-winged butterfly, the puppy fat that's swallowed her bones, the frown of puzzlement, of stubborn inability to accept or understand. Suddenly, she is filled with anguish, and a desire stronger than any she has ever known to become for her daughter what she can never be: the perfect mother, all-wise and all-loving. A mother with both her eyes open—unlike the eye of God on the cathedral dome, both eyes looking not just out, but in, as well. Knowing her own flaws and failings, struggling to change the bitterness and fear inside her to love.

But before Sonia can reach out her arms, Laura has run off into the lake, her chunky body churning through the still and silky water.

THE DISTINCTIVE FEATURE, the theme, if you like, of this year's party at the Senchenkos' cottage, is unmistakable. Yes, there is the same food and drink, the same banter at the bar. There are the same long dresses and Bermuda shorts, the same tours of the cottage to show off whatever choice piece of decor Jack has had installed over the summer. But this year the sameness is shot through with the excitement everyone shares about the Burton-Taylor affair, which is far more of a blockbuster than *Cleopatra*.

Jack is rigged out in a toga with a purple stripe down the edge and a laurel crown made out of gilded cardboard. Nadia, he explains, won't be down for a while; she's still in her room, altering her costume. He had it made up as a surprise by a dressmaker in town—an exact replica of the blue-and-gold dress Cleopatra wears in the throne scene. Damn thing hadn't been ready till this very afternoon—he arrived only a few hours ago, to discover when Nadia tried on the dress that it didn't fit. "So she's taking it in here and there," he explains, pointing to his chest and hips. "She's not exactly built like Liz Taylor," he says, flashing a grin at the men.

Ivan Plotsky sits down at the baby grand and belts out the *Cleopatra* theme song, waggling his bristly eyebrows to the lyrics he improvises, in which "nail her" is made to rhyme with "Taylor," "hurtin'" with "Burton," "quibble" with "Sybil" and—something of a stretch—"*kyshka*" with "Fisher." Joe Bozhyk is looking everywhere for Peter Metelsky, who, as everyone knows, does phenomenal imitations of Rex Harrison and has been known to drop beach balls down his shirt and take off Liz Taylor to a T. Even after Ivan leaves the piano, the conversation continues to revolve around the movie of the century.

"Joseph Mankiewicz—his name sounds Polish, but he's really Ukrainian, you know."

"I still think *Taras Bulba* is a way better film—Yul Brynner, now *that* guy can act."

"What are you talking about, he doesn't have to act, all he does is shine up his scalp and he steals every scene!"

"Didn't Tony Curtis have a thing for that German actress who was playing the *Polachka*? Christine Something—Krautman, Kauffman, was that it? She was only a kid, too—not much older than your Laura, Max. Yep, old Toothsome Tony walked out on Janet Leigh the way Burton's left what's-her-face, Sybil. Christ, and they think *we* have funny names."

Mostly it's the men talking; the women are still nervous—exhausted, really—with the aftershock of what they're calling Nettie's Breakdown. None of the men know anything about it, except Al Vesiuk, who'd driven Nastia to some friends who have a cottage farther along the bay. Dave Lazar is a skin specialist, one of the best there is. To a small crowd of women trying to cool off by touching their iced drinks to their faces, Annie gives the details: "He had to put in a few stitches, but it's not too bad, Al says. There'll be a few scars but nothing she won't be able to hide with a stick of concealer. Thank God she missed the eyes." She tells them that Dr. Lazar and his wife will keep Nastia with them while Nettie's medication is kicking in.

At the word *medication* the women nod sagely. Not a few of them have had episodes that gave what their doctors call "cause for concern." On their bathroom shelves, high up where they think their children can't see and read the labels, are prescription vials of Valium and Librium and sleeping pills that they only take—they swear it—when they absolutely have to. And none of them has ever been one-tenth as crazy as Nettie, who is sleeping soundly with the help of some NightEez administered by Halia Bozhyk. Stefka Stechyshyn is with her now—they're taking turns, the way they do checking up on the children. And so far, none of the husbands has a clue. When Nettie had her attack, they'd been away, most of them, at the hardware store in Midland and then having lunch together at the Captain's Tavern. Al, thank God, had been home—and Al can be trusted, Al who'd sworn the Hippo-something oath.

It's not that the women want to deceive their husbands— they don't consider it a deception, keeping the news from them, but a kindness. Everyone understands the need for secrecy, for which another word is *loyalty*, not so much to Nettie as to what Annie calls "their own kind." Not just Ukrainians—and can you imagine the scandal it would cause if word got out to the *Anhleetsi*? Loyalty not just to Ukrainians but to women themselves. For a mother to harm her own child—it's unthinkable. Spanking, yes; discipline, a swipe with the wooden spoon, of course. But to lose control like that—to *let go*. It's something far more scandalous than anything they've encountered through the Lending Library; something far more frightening, too, for nearly all of them can confess to moments, with their children, when they have lashed out, in Old Country style, or only just kept themselves from doing so.

But it is not to discuss Nettie Shkurka's breakdown that Sonia Martyn is closeted with Sasha Plotsky in one of the two ground-floor bathrooms. Sasha is livid at what's happened to Nastia, but she's even more upset at what she feels in her bones is a whole series of disasters brewing.

"*Bozhe kokhaniy*, am I the only one with eyes in my head? Nadia's in hiding at her own party, and Peter, Mr. Life-of-the-

Party, is missing—doesn't that spell out anything suspicious to you? What did Peter say when you talked to him yesterday? You did talk to him? Sonia?"

But Sonia doesn't answer immediately. She is studying her reflection in the mirror, the hang of the gingham shirtwaist she's wearing. Sasha can't help herself; she cries out, "For heaven's sake, Sonia, can't you stop worrying what you look like and give just five minutes of your attention to helping me prevent a colossal balls-up? Do you have any idea of what will happen if those two are allowed to get away with it? And don't ask what; you know better than I do."

In her ridiculously girlish dress, her face pale and her eyes burning, Sonia turns to her friend. For Sasha is her friend—her best, most trusted friend, and she is about to ruin this friendship, the way her beautiful golden dress has been ruined, beyond any wearing.

"From what Peter told me, Sasha, he's in no condition to think of anything but saving his job and keeping himself from throwing in the towel. He isn't the fool he pretends to be, you know. My brother's in a bad way, Sasha. I've never been so worried about him—he's much more likely to drive into a transport truck on the way home from the cottage than to run off with Nadia Senchenko. Nadia's no fool, either—what could Peter offer her that she would want to take, that would make up for what she'd lose if she walked out on Jack?"

"Jack doesn't have anything to do with this anymore. Listen, Sonia, I've talked to Nadia—not that she's gone into True Confessions—as a matter of fact, it's what she's not saying that worries me. Sonia, Sonia, a lot of people could get hurt—a lot of things are at stake here. I know Zirka's a royal pain, but there are the boys, too—and all this on top of Nettie Shkurka. Dear God, what's happening to us all?"

Sonia hasn't time now to consider Nettie Shkurka or her nephews; she's too afraid for her brother, afraid that he'll miss this chance just as he's messed up every other. "Look, I'll bet you anything that he's still at our place, telling the boys one of his crazy stories. They're spending the night in the sleep-house, so Darka can keep an eye on them. I'll go over there now and see."

"Just don't say anything to Zirka—she's raddled enough already, like a grenade waiting to be thrown."

Sonia nods. She is about to go off when Sasha grabs her by the sleeve.

"Listen very carefully, Soniu. If Peter and Nadia are having an affair, that's their business, so long as no one else finds out, and Jack and Zirka don't have to do anything about it—in public, I mean. So you find your brother and hold on to him—don't let him out of your sight. I'll go after Nadia. I'll sit on her if I have to or drag her down to the party, where she belongs. She's the hostess, goddamn it! Tomorrow we all go back to the city and everything will blow over, and things will go on the way they always have."

Sonia removes Sasha's arm from her own—Sasha grabbed her so hard that a seam has split in her sleeve. And in a sudden blaze of anger, recalling the ruin of her dress, Sonia comes as close as she can to risking it all.

"What if they don't want things to go on as usual? What if they want everything to change? What if they don't care who gets hurt? What if it hurts them much, much more to stay apart than to go off together?"

Someone's pounding on the washroom door. Sasha yells out, "This house has six bathrooms and you have to use this one? *Hai shlyakh tebeh trafyt!*" Then she addresses Sonia, slowly and sternly. "You listen to me. Peter and Nadia aren't movie stars; they're only people, like you and me. They're a part of us, they belong here, they can't be allowed to do something they'll regret the morning after—something that will rip this whole community into shreds. Now promise me you'll fetch Peter while I look for Nadia. If we can all just get through this evening, everything will be okay."

Sonia nods and Sasha puts her hands on her shoulders, affectionately. "Dab on a bit of lipstick, Sonia—you look like a ghost."

The two women emerge from the bathroom, Sonia going off in the direction of the sleep-house while Sasha searches the den, the kitchen, the dining room, the bedrooms and washrooms upstairs, even the huge veranda with its boxes of moonstruck geraniums. Nadia is nowhere to be found. Sasha returns to the party, joking with everyone, being outrageous in her usual way and keeping her eyes peeled for the delinquent lovers. Shortly after ten, a half-drunken Zirka comes raging toward her, mascara running and huge half-moons of sweat showing under her arms. She, too, has been going from room to room, looking for her husband, looking for Nadia; now she is gunning for Jack. She'll tell him everything, she swears, the whole dirty secret.

Somehow, Sasha manages to lead her off to one of the guest bedrooms, grabbing a bottle of vodka from a table as she goes. She pours Zirka a huge dose of what she calls medicine, and Zirka gulps it down with the resignation of a sick child. Sasha holds her hand and waits for her to fall asleep, murmuring, *"There there, there there."* What she feels for the woman beside her, face streaked with makeup, hands clutching the edge of the covers, is exasperation mixed with sorrow. For Zirka, after all, has played her part in the community of Kalyna Beach: she had gone to take care of Nettie that afternoon, and she'd gone on the warpath after Peter this evening. He is her husband, after all—she has a perfect right to light into him, keep him from—Sasha lights a cigarette, which she holds in the hand with which she's cupping her forehead, her elbow on her knee. It is her posture of defeat, of resignation. She knows by now that Sonia's betrayed her: all she can do now is to delay the public discovery, try to stem the damage. For there will be damage, she has no doubt about that. In her mind's eye, she can see a string of divorces, small at first, like a scrap of thread, and then longer and thicker, till it extends so far there's no way of telling where it will end.

Zirka sighs in her sleep. She's out all right—she might as well spend the night here, since the boys are sleeping at Sonia's. Sasha takes a long drag on her dwindled cigarette, then stubs it and leaves the room, turning out all the lamps but a night-light shaped like a seahorse with eyelashes.

CLOSE TO MIDNIGHT, Laura gets out of bed. She reaches between the mattress and the box springs and pulls out the long, thin package she's hidden there. Bonnie and Katia and Alix are fast asleep, and there's no light coming from the sleep-house. Darka has gone to her room, having spent most of the evening in front of the cracked mirror in the bathroom, teasing and brushing out and teasing again her dyed-back hair. Laura knows that her parents will return before long: if she's going to go through with her plan, it has to be now. She has spent the whole evening working out a way to set things right, so that even the terrible blue eye painted on the dome of the cathedral back home will see that she's tried to make up for what's happened, for the fact that it's been all her fault.

When, after supper—when no one but their father and Alix had eaten anything of the meal set down on their plates—Sonia had gone to her bedroom to dress for the Senchenkos' party, Laura had risen from the table to follow her. She had waited outside the door, imagining Sonia reaching into the very back of the closet, pulling out the dress, and then— But nothing like what Laura had imagined had happened: there had been one sharp cry, and then silence. Laura had waited for what seemed like forever and then fled to the sitting room, where Katia was reading the same page of *The Mystery of Larkspur Lane* that she'd been working on since supper. Tato was complaining, in a joking way, about how long it always took for their mother to get ready for a party, making his daughters promise never to torture their husbands like this. And then, at last, Sonia had come out of the bedroom, in the dress she wore to go on family outings to Santa's Village or to visit the Martyr's Shrine at Midland. Her old, pink gingham dress with the dirndl skirt and the three-quarter-length sleeves.

All of them had stared at her, unable to say a word, even Tato. And she had stared back but in a way that made it clear she didn't really see them. Her face was white and pinched, and her eyes like lightning: not the way they usually were, wet with tears she only just kept from falling, but dry and terribly, terribly bright. No one said anything about her dress or her face; everyone was waiting for some explanation. But all she told them was not to give Darka any trouble, and then she walked out the door, with their father shrugging at them and following close after her. It had been worse, a thousand times worse, than what Laura had foreseen down at the beach.

A light burns in the main room, but there's no one here.

No one to witness Laura reaching up to the brass jar on the mantelpiece, taking out a box of matches, and bending down to the hearth with the package she's locked under her arm. The wrapper is one of the brown paper bags in which she'd carried groceries home from Venus Variety; before she opens it, she smooths the paper with her palm. And then she draws out what's inside, slowly, carefully, as if it were alive.

But it's not, of course. It doesn't breathe or speak or smile or weep. It's just a pile of paper, stapled and printed, filled with paragraphs and photographs and, on the cover, a painting of two men standing on opposite sides of a woman with beaded, braided hair, sitting on a throne. The men are peering down at the woman with expressions of awe and adoration on their faces. The woman looks straight ahead, the beautiful woman in her magnificent blue-and-gold gown, staring blankly into the distance, holding a golden crook and scepter in her arms.

It takes forever to burn. As usual, Laura admits to herself, she's made a mess of things. The first two matches flare and die away without so much as scorching the paper. She has to reach into the cinders and bits of charred log on the grate and tear up the book; to do it all at once proves impossible; she must work page by glossy page. She must ignite the scraps with one lit match and a dozen others that she scatters nearby. Her hands are grimy now; there's a nasty smell from the photographs. Laura had thought they would burn as vividly as the colors they contain, but the pictures vanish in the same sour flame as the white paper, the black words. She sits for a long time, stirring the chunks of charred paper with the poker, making even more of a mess of herself and the hearth in the process.

She is not just burning Cleopatra and her lovers. She is burning Nettie Shkurka's steel-toothed comb and the boys who threw a frightened girl into a muddy river and left her to drown. She is burning the way she betrayed Katia's and Yuri's secret, and the way she'd pushed Bonnie away that morning at the beach. But even when the souvenir booklet has turned to ash, nothing has really been destroyed. Nor has anything been saved. Laura feels neither relief from guilt nor any lessening of pain. The sacrifice has all been for nothing. But that, she realizes, is why it's a sacrifice and not a bargain.

There's a small, shuffling sound behind her; Laura wheels around to find Bonnie, in her nightie with Snow White and the Seven Dwarfs printed over it, for once not a hand-me-down from her older sisters but a Christmas gift that's still as good as new. Bonnie doesn't say a word: she comes to where Laura is kneeling and sits down beside her, staring into the hearth. Making out the telltale flakes of the souvenir booklet, she still says nothing but waits awhile and then offers her own small sacrifice.

"I'm sorry I pulled at you down at the beach this morning. I'm sorry, Laura."

Laura takes the poker and hits at the ash, so that no fragments of faces or words remain to give her away. "Go back to sleep, Bonnie," she says. "You get into my bed—I'll be there in a minute."

And as Bonnie shuffles back to bed, tears start rolling down Laura's cheeks. She pulls off her glasses and shoves her palms into her eyes; she keeps her mouth shut, for fear of Bonnie coming back to her. What is she weeping for? Not just for Nastia and for the child that Sonia was. Not only for Bonnie, burdened with the need to keep peace between her sisters, with the need to love them all. But also for herself and for what she'll turn out to be. For she knows, now, who and what she is: her own self, however ugly and awful and stubborn she may be. And she knows how close she'd come that afternoon, folded in Sonia's arms, in the warmth of her lap, to giving herself up, to joining the World of the Mothers.

SONIA WATCHES THE car drive away from the Metelskys' cottage, bumping and rattling over the patchy asphalt of Tunnel Road. She hugs herself, as if it were an autumn night and she'd come out to look at the moon without a sweater. There is a moon, three-quarters full, gleaming through rags of cloud that seem to hang in the air instead of drifting by, as if something had happened to the mechanism of the universe and the earth had stopped turning, the winds forgotten to blow. And then Sonia shakes herself. "Don't be such a fool," she says out loud. Words that Sasha had told her to say to Peter, words of warning, pleading, and reproach, waiting to pour themselves out, words surging up from an overactive imagination, the imagination of disaster.

What is it but the unexpectedness, the mystery of any life, that makes it possible to go on at all? The chances that perch like birds singing on a branch or that whirl up like dust in your eyes: that a stranger might see your photo in a newspaper ad and declare to himself that he will marry you; that a child will fall so ill on the eve of a life-changing journey that she will be abandoned by her parents; that a spider-shaped cluster of veins will burst in your brain just as you are about to enjoy some small share of happiness, after so many years away from your wife and children and country? A mystery, yes, but not like the detective novel she's finally finished reading, with its suddenly simple answers to appallingly complicated puzzles. It's more like a fog that appears just when you think things are fixed and certain, a fog that shakes and blurs, gently or harshly, all the firm, dark edges.

She doesn't know where Peter and Nadia will go, what they will do, how they will live with all they'll have lost, and what they will make, together. If they fail, she tells herself, it will be worse, far worse than if the car they are driving out of Kalyna Beach should crash on the highway. And then she stops herself, steps back, examines, like a colt upon shaky legs, the field of possibilities in front of them. Would it really be worse, failure? Must it be so? Isn't there a chance of something emerging from this risky, haphazard escape that will be, if not better than what's gone before, then different? Different enough for an ending that, even if it isn't happy, could still be alive, could still be open?

All that Sonia knows is that she's had enough of living always in the purview of the Evil, or else the Ever-Watchful Eye. She wants something more, something far better from what's left of her life: she wants something like her mother's talent for hopefulness. Her mother, who had led no charmed life, who had made as many mistakes as anyone else, who had been as wary of showing love to her son as she'd been profligate in loving her daughter, and yet had done what she could, had given her children life, and kept them from knowing war and all the horrors that had poisoned Marta's life. Who had brought them safely here, to this new place where it was up to them to make good or bad but to make their own way, to live their lives, and not keep them locked up, frozen, like a dress in a closet, a statue on a mantelpiece.

Sonia is suddenly terribly, terribly tired. She wants nothing more than to go back to the cottage, and, without even changing into her pajamas, curl up in her bed and sleep. But she can't— not yet. She must return to the party and speak to Sasha, face Sasha, without excuses or consolations, or even confessions: just with the fact of what's happened, under their very eyes.

SASHA STEPS OUT onto the huge, empty veranda. Nobody's there, they are all inside, listening to Ivan playing "Moon River" on the piano. Max is standing beside the piano with Sonia, who came up to her not long ago; walked with her onto the balcony to tell her the news that Peter and Nadia are gone, and the rusty old Chev as well. And then there'd been nothing further to say. Sonia had returned to the warmth of the party, and Sasha had remained on the balcony, away from the lights and the laughter and singing, listening to the sleepy silence of the lake below.

It must be nearly midnight, Sasha thinks. Mrs. Matski must have finished loading the tables with cabbage rolls and meat-on-a-stick, the candied ham and the roast of beef, more fitting for December than August, but then, that's Jack's way—royal excess. The tables will be spread, and Jack will start bellowing for Nadia, who is supposed to serve her guests, like a queen putting on an apron at Christmas and filling the servants' plates with turkey. With any luck he'll think she's gone to bed. He won't be happy, but maybe he'll think it's just Nadia, who can't bear loud noise or too much of anyone's company. With all the luck in the world—

What will become of her? And Peter? Nadia can't be in love with Peter. That was kids' stuff, years ago—it wouldn't be half so bad if she was. Sasha leans out over the ledge of the railing, the way Nadia had leaned out the last time she'd come to a tea party, leaned out and looked at the waves, till Zirka had called her to account. Zirka and the children—it will be worst for Andriy; Yuri's a tough one, he'll survive anything. But it will be very hard for Andriy—Zirka will hang on to him, and hang on.

Nadia and Peter: Sasha wants to curse them both. The selfishness, the thoughtlessness—and yet a part of her looks out over the lake, as if they'd fled, not in Peter's car but in the speedboat tied up at the dock, as if they had just escaped some appalling catastrophe, an earthquake, a tidal wave, of which no one here has any inkling.

"The rest of our lives," she says aloud, not knowing why or what she means. She winces, thinking of the ugly explosion on the cliff edge that afternoon, the rage of a woman wild with pain and lost power. Then she hears something her mother used to say, one of the few things she remembers spoken in her mother's voice. *"You've made your bed, now you'll have to lie in it."* But not Peter and Nadia; they've broken the bed apart, they are cruel and selfish and for this one night, free, like characters in a book, escaping the covers.

It's so strange, Sasha thinks, that she should be the one to really mind about what's going to happen, that she should care so much for this fragile group of women and children and absentee husbands. She's always been the one to make fun of it; she's laughed behind her hands at all the Zirkas and Annies and Lesias who think it's the only place on the planet, this obliging little world of Kalyna Beach. But she knows it better than anyone else, and she loves it best. It's the kind of love that comes with understanding that life's a matter of meat and drink, a feast you sit down to together, making room for everyone at the same table—even a Zirka and, God help her, even a Nettie Shkurka and her battered daughter. For what would become of them if they were to be cast out? And what might have happened differently had they been drawn in, somehow, to the world of the Lending Library? Standing there, looking out over the lake, pressing her fists on the balustrade, she can feel it weighing her down: the loss of community, so carefully built and contained, nursed along, laughed at, yes, but never scorned.

Ivan is calling to her from the doorway: Al Vesiuk is playing a waltz on the piano, she must come and dance. The tried-and-true, the old-time favorite, "The Anniversary Waltz." But when Sasha goes to Ivan's side, taking his hand in hers, she doesn't move with him onto the floor. Instead, she watches, as everyone else in the room is watching, the couple dancing together as if they were the only people here.

Max and Sonia. Max in a white shirt and worn khaki trousers; Sonia in her gingham dress, more suitable for *Little Women* than *Cleopatra*. Yet they could be wearing a tux and a gown of gold lamé, the way they sweep across the floor, eyes locked, hands placed so lightly on each other's bodies. Sasha hasn't seen Max smile like that in years. And Sonia—the beauty of her face, not pale with grief or fear but fiery with the joy of the moment. She is looking straight into her husband's eyes; she is looking at him without reproach or apprehension; she is fierce, almost reckless in her happiness. Knowing that for once, even if only for the space of a waltz, the short space between anticipation and experience, she has been swept up, body, soul, and riddled heart, into a melody sweeter, stronger than the one Al Vesiuk is coaxing from the out-of-tune piano.

Now Max and Sonia are beckoning to the others in the room to join them, for all the world as if they were bride and groom claiming the first dance of the evening and finally acknowledging their wedding guests. Ivan steers Sasha by her elbow onto the dance floor: a little drunk, a little too satisfied with himself and the hit he's made tonight with his improvisations and his jokes, but still, her own, dear Ivan. Sasha shuts her eyes and surrenders to the dance, wishing the waltz to go on forever, for Max and Sonia to keep them all together, in this rare romance of the present moment. And yet what she sees is the two who are gone: no longer Peter and Nadia but simply two lovers, driving together in the dark somewhere, on the way to Thunder Bay or Fort Garry or Montreal—wherever they're headed to make this outrageous, impossible break with the way things are and have to be.

She wants to lash out at them, as Nettie's done with Nastia. And she wants to shower them with rose petals, to rush down to the dock to wave them off on their reckless, needy journey into possibility.

ACKNOWLEDGMENTS

Kalyna Beach is an imaginary place, although its geography bears some relation to Georgian Bay, where my aunt Vera and uncle Gus had a cottage that was the paradise of my childhood. The characters in this novel are as imaginary as the setting and bear no resemblance to the cottagers of that stretch of Georgian Bay where I was lucky enough to spend so many of my early summers.

Readers of Katherine Mansfield will recognize the debt that I owe to the author of "At the Bay."

I am grateful for the acumen, patience, and kindness of Dean Cooke, Iris Tupholme, and Claire Wachtel in reading and helping to shape so many versions of this book. My thanks to Irene Guilford and Donna McFarlane for their writerly responses to this work and to Taras Koznarsky and Olga Gardner Galvin for their help with my Ukrainian.

The
LADIES' LENDING
LIBRARY

a novel

JANICE KULYK KEEFER

A READER'S GUIDE

QUESTIONS FOR DISCUSSION

1. What does the reaction of the members of the Ladies' Lending Library to *Cleopatra* and the much-publicized extramarital affair between Elizabeth Taylor and Richard Burton reveal about the condition of their own marriages?

2. Why does Darka's presence at the Martyn cottage threaten so many of the wives of Kalyna Beach, and how does her presence affect the husbands?

3. How does Laura's obsession with the figure of Cleopatra relate to her own adolescent anxieties?

4. What does Chucha Marta's behavior toward Bonnie reveal about her strengths and weaknesses? To what extent is her portrayal by the author sympathetic?

5. Why does the summer idyll of Kalyna Beach serve as a domestic nightmare for the many spouses who spend their weeks apart and their weekends together?

6. Why do so many ghosts and memories from Ukraine, "the Old Place," pervade the community in *The Ladies' Lending Library*, and how do they affect your appreciation of the issues these characters face as first- and second-generation immigrants?

7. How does the discovery of Mrs. Shkurka's brutal treatment of her daughter, Anastasia, bring Laura and Sonia closer, and why is that closeness only temporary?

8. How is the seaside setting—with its implicit embrace of physicality and liberation— responsible for the overtly sexual nature of many of the incidents in which the inhabitants of Kalyna Beach find themselves?

9. To what extent does Sasha's fear that Peter Metelsky's relationship with Nadia Senchenko will cause the web of relationships of Kalyna Beach residents to unravel seem likely?

10. How are the themes of sexual desire and longing, wish-fulfillment, and self-denial significant to the plot of *The Ladies' Lending Library*?

AN INTERVIEW WITH JANICE KULYK KEEFER

Q: Why did you decide to use *Cleopatra* as the theatrical backdrop for so many of the events that transpire in the summer of 1963 at Kalyna Beach?

A: The last time I was moving house I happened to come across a box of papers that my mother had saved for me—school report cards and high school essays and, at the very bottom, the program for *Cleopatra*. I had completely forgotten about the role that this film and all the scandal and gossip in which it was enmeshed had played in my life: reading the program, looking at the photographs of the film's stars and minor players, brought back a host of memories and questions and launched a lot of fictive possibilities

Q: You are of Ukrainian heritage. To what extent do you feel a moral obligation as a writer to examine the lives and experiences of characters of Ukrainian descent in your fiction?

A: The history of Ukraine and the stories of its emigrants are extraordinarily rich and haunting. Any writer would be happy to delve into such fascinating material; for writers with a Ukrainian background there is also a desire, I think, to give voice to lives and experiences which have been largely submerged or disregarded vis à vis North American culture. I believe that any one who is the child or grandchild of immigrants feels an obligation, moral or imaginative, to understand as much as possible about the hopes and sacrifices, the struggles and the joys involved in their families' dislocation from all that was familiar and in their embrace of the staggeringly new and different world to which they journeyed.

Q: You acknowledge a debt to the author Katherine Mansfield in *The Ladies' Lending Library*. How influential has her work been for you as a writer?

A: Mansfield's short stories, and her writing on the art of fiction, the account she gives of the challenges and often horrendous difficulties of writing well and honestly, have been hugely important to me. My novel *Thieves* is an attempt to explore both the extraordinary dimensions of Mansfield's short, brilliant, poignant life, and the debt I owe to her as a writer.

Q: How did the decision to write a novel set at the beach inform the contours of your novel's plot?

A: The beach—or cottage country in general—is for me more than an attractive setting. I spent the best and most important times of my childhood at my aunt and uncle's summer cottage, as part of a community of children and adults whose experiences were heightened by the air of possibility exuded by the very idea of holidays, of being somewhere where the rules and conditions of ordinary life are altered so that you really do have a chance to learn those things about your self and others that, for better and worse, comprise your true education in being human. If we're all haunted by the idea of lost or misplaced paradises, then mine is Georgian Bay in the 60s, with its mix of pine trees and cedar-smelling cabins, driftwood and crashing waves and sun-struck sand!

Q: Why did you decide to devote as much attention to the teenage characters as to their adult counterparts in *The Ladies' Lending Library*?

A: Adolescence doesn't make sense as a lived experience unless it's seen in contrast to the certainties of childhood on the one hand and the mysterious country of adulthood on the other. One of the most memorable—and problematic—aspects of my adolescence had to do with my perception of the way in which my own mother, and the mothers of my friends, were shaping and grooming their daughters to become women just like them—in spite of the painful or frustrating limitations they had experienced in becoming ideal wives and mothers, according to the cultural norms of the 50s and 60s.